Band of Gold

Maggie Christensen

Dedication

For Jim, all my love always.

Acknowledgements

I wish to thank

Jim for listening to my plotlines without complaint, for his patience and insights as I discuss my characters with him, for confirming for me the male point of view, for being there when I need him.

John Hudspith, editor extraordinaire for his ideas, suggestions, encouragement and attention to detail.

Jane Dixon-Smith for my beautiful cover and formatting.

My writing group, the Inkstained Groupies for their continued support and encouragement and my critique partner, Helen, for her unstinting patience.

http://maggiechristensenauthor.com/
https://www.facebook.com/maggiechristensenauthor

One

'I don't want to be married anymore.'

The band of gold, symbol of our twenty-five years of marriage lies on the table between us. I am stupefied, unable to speak. Tears prick my eyes as my first coffee of the day grows cold beside me. The sun is shining brightly through the kitchen window. The turkey is sitting on the kitchen bench waiting to be cooked. My parents, daughter, brother and sister, along with her husband and children are due to arrive in five hours' time. The house is redolent with the scent of pine needles and Christmas pudding. It's Christmas morning and my world has collapsed.

'What do you mean?' I finally utter, thinking this must be Sean's idea of a bad joke. My mouth goes dry. My head begins to spin. The bottom has dropped out of my world. I look over at the man I have loved for over twenty-five years, his bushy greying blonde hair, his ruddy cleanshaven cheeks. He looks no different from any other morning. He's wearing the bright yellow tee shirt we bought on our holiday in Bali last year. His steely blue eyes meet mine. This isn't happening.

'I can't do this anymore, Anna.' His waving arms take in the kitchen including me, 'All this; family, house, job. I need to get away.' He pushes his chair back from the table and strides out of the kitchen. I sit there in a daze, my mind going round in circles. *Is it too late to call off Christmas lunch? How can I even think of such a thing? Does Sean mean he's going to leave right now? How will I explain his absence? God, this is really going to be the Christmas from Hell.* But mean it he does. 'I'll be in touch.' His head peers around the door. I see his small backpack hanging from one shoulder and a weekend bag in his left hand.

'What?' The sight of him standing there looking so calm goads me into action. 'What the hell… Are you joking?' My voice rises as I jump up from the table, my feet slipping on the tiled floor. 'You're not serious. You can't do this.' I grab Sean's arm, forcing him to drop his bag. I begin punching him, my blows ineffective on his rugged body. 'You bastard! You shit! It's Christmas!' I yell. 'Everyone's coming. You can't do this to me!' I take a deep breath. 'Sit down!' I demand. 'We can talk this through.' I try to sound sane, though it's the last thing I feel. My stomach is churning. 'Maybe we…' I'm not sure what I'm saying.

Sean's hands grip my upper arms, and he holds me away from him. 'Don't make this harder, Anna. It's over.'

My heart drops. This is real and it looks like it's no sudden impulse. He smiles grimly and picks up his bag. He's off, making for the front door with me flying behind him, still yelling. I follow him to the car, pulling on his arm in an attempt stop him. 'Sean…' I'm wailing now. I stand there in the driveway in my summer nightie. 'You can't do this. Come back inside. We can sort this out. Think of Lissa. What…?' But it's too late. He's in the car. The door slams shut and he engages the central locking. I rush to the car window and hammer on it making one last ditch attempt but it's useless. The window slides down.

'Just leave, it, Anna.' And he drives off.

I stand there, immobile, gazing after him. I hear a scream and realise it's coming out of my mouth. The tears begin to run down my face, but I don't have the energy to wipe them away. I taste their saltiness on my tongue as I lick my lips. I don't know how long I remain there unable to think clearly. It's as if all this is happening to someone else; that it's a dream and I'll eventually wake up, describe it to Sean and we'll both have a good laugh about it. But it's no dream. Eventually the warmth of the sun reaches me and my body comes alive.

From somewhere I find a tough determination. Christmas lunch must go ahead. The turkey has to be cooked with all the trimmings and I have to make it through family questions and joyful gift giving before I can curl up into a ball of misery.

*

'What a pity Sean couldn't be with us.' My mother sighs for the hundredth time. 'Fancy his aunt demanding his presence at this time of year, and with so little notice too. He's a good man.' She smiles in my direction and I manage to smile back. I'm only relieved they bought my lie: an urgent trip back to Scotland at the behest of his aged aunt. I've noted the worried look in Lissa's eyes and know that my daughter hasn't been fooled. Time enough for her questions later. The worst is almost over.

'It's been lovely, Anna!' My sister Jan gives me a hug and I'm enveloped in a fog of her favourite scent, expensive. 'Hope Sean makes it back for New Year. Remember you're coming to us this time.'

I mutter something as my stomach plummets. I've forgotten the next family get-together is only a week away. *How long can I keep up the pretence? If they would just all go, go and leave me alone.*

'Are you sure everything's all right, Mum?' Lissa's eyes seem to bore right into me, threatening to reveal my innermost thoughts. 'I mean, Dad's trip, it was awfully sudden, wasn't it?'

'I'm fine.' I manage a wide smile. 'You enjoy the rest of Christmas. A party tonight you said? Anyone special?'

As I expect, the question diverts her from my own situation.

'Will. We met last week. It's early days but I think you'll like him.' She spins out of my hug and stands in the doorway, an excited twenty-two year old with her life ahead of her. She tosses back her hair, thick and blonde, reminiscent of her father when we first met, and gives me a serious look. 'You would tell me. If anything was wrong, I mean.'

'I'm fine,' I repeat, and close the door before she can ask anything more. Alone at last, I turn and lean my back against the door, oblivious to the fact that, if she turns round, Lissa will see my slumped body against the frosted glass. I give a sigh of relief as I hear her car start up and drive off. I slide down to the floor, legs outstretched and arms hanging loose like a rag doll. I begin to sob uncontrollably.

Eventually I manage to push myself up and walk past the dining room where the table has been cleared of most of the remains of Christmas lunch. Only a few guttering candles and the remnants of hats and crackers lie abandoned on the white linen tablecloth. Peeking into the kitchen I note that, despite my protestations, the family have completed the washing up and piles of clean dishes and leftover food, tightly sealed in plastic wrap, are waiting for me to tidy away.

My hand reaches for the handrail on the stairs. My instinct is to call Gina, my best friend and yoga instructor, but she's told me she's spending Christmas with friends in Byron Bay. Otherwise I'd have invited her to join us despite Sean's derisive comments about aging hippies. But Sean isn't here. Another sob escapes me.

I push open the bedroom door seeing the empty space on Sean's side of the bed, usually cluttered with his current book, reading glasses, watch and other impedimenta waiting for his return. They are gone, like him.

Another sob wells up and I brush it away with the back of my hand. I catch sight of my running gear pushed to the side of the ensuite where I left it on Christmas Eve. *Was that only yesterday?* I debate calling Gina's mobile, and actually have my phone in my hand, but I think better of it and drop it back into my pocket. I'm not ready to talk to anyone yet.

*

I need fresh air. It's five o'clock on a glorious summer's afternoon. All over Australia everyone and his dog is celebrating Christmas, and I'm standing here relieved that my family has gone. I don my running gear and take out the car.

When I reach Manly beach I can see that most of the celebrating groups are winding up for the day. Parents are gathering up children, chairs and blankets. Fathers in shorts, their naked chests bronzed by the sun, are dumping the remains of Christmas lunch into the overflowing bins. Some are desultorily playing a game of beach cricket while others have succumbed to post prandial lethargy and are lying prone while squawking seagulls demolish the remains of their food.

I walk slowly to the edge of the water, my shoes making deep imprints in the packed wet sand. I look out at the vastness of the Pacific Ocean and stretch my arms up high. I wish I could sail away, away from having to explain to everyone and be the subject of their pity. I stand, oblivious to the waves lapping against my favourite running shoes, and gaze up at the buildings etched against the skyline on top of the cliff. Northern Beaches Girls Grammar School is where I spend every day during term time, teaching English to a combination of eager and reluctant young girls. It's going to become my lifeline now.

Turning, I begin to run. If I can run fast enough maybe I can forget, forget that my husband has abandoned me, that, at the ripe old age of forty-seven, I've become a statistic, an abandoned wife, a single mother.

By the time I stop, the beach has become deserted. It's too early for the evening parties and too late for the family gatherings. I gaze along the sand, deploring the debris my fellow humans have left behind and begin the run back. Halfway there, the memory of Sean's face at the breakfast table rears up again and I slow to a halt and drop to my knees in despair, tears once again streaming down my cheeks.

'Are you all right?' The voice comes from somewhere above my head. I look up into a pair of concerned brown eyes framed by black-rimmed spectacles. Floppy brown hair is falling over the lenses and, as I look, a hand pushes back an errant lock.

'Are you all right?' the voice repeats. 'Is there anything I can do?'

I rise slowly, gulping back the tears, embarrassed to have been caught in such a state. 'I'll be right, thanks.' I brush the sand from my knees and I wish I could brush away his presence as easily. 'Really,' I assure my prospective rescuer, and run on, feeling his eyes boring into my back as the distance between us lengthens.

Two

It's January second. Somehow I've made it through the New Year celebrations using a migraine as my excuse. It wasn't too far from the truth. In the week since Christmas I, who no one could consider to be a hard drinker, have managed to drain all the liquor in the house. We'd stocked up for the holidays so there was a good supply. It blurred the edges and I've spent many of the days and most of the nights trying to work out what has gone wrong; why Sean has left. Only a week before Christmas we spent an evening planning a trip to Adelaide for Easter. Sure, Sean hadn't been as keen as I had, but I'd put that down to his usual disinterest in going away anywhere. My Sean has always been a homebody, loving nothing more than time at home with me and Lissa when she was younger.

I'm guiltily aware that somewhere along the line I have called and texted my errant husband. I have no clear recollection of these actions but my mobile bears testament. It also shows me there has been no reply.

Gina is back today. I've decided to wait till she's home instead of calling her mobile and pick up the phone with anticipation. I need to talk to someone, someone outside the family who'll understand what I'm going through. I've kept Lissa at bay till now as I need to work out how to break the news to her. She's always been Daddy's girl and will take this hard. Not that I want to turn her against her father. I need to find a way of telling her that won't make her feel she's stuck in the middle of some family feud. I'm banking on Gina's advice on this one. Plus I know she'll understand how I feel.

'Gina? Thank God you're back!'

'Hey, Anna. What's up? You just caught me. I got in two minutes ago.'

'I need to talk with you. Can I pop round?'

'No, better not. As I said, I'm just back and the place is a tip. Remember I told you Tom and his mates stayed over Christmas? They've left the place like a pigsty. I wouldn't want anyone to see it like this. Tell you what, give me an hour and I'll meet you.'

We make arrangements and I hang up feeling confused. I'd forgotten that Gina's nephew was staying there. Tom is around the same age as Lissa and I know how messy kids can be. But her voice didn't ring true. Something is bothering me, but I can't put my finger on exactly what it is. I shrug it off and make myself a cup of herbal tea to pass the time; camomile, supposed to be calming. As if anything can calm me these days.

*

I arrive at the café first and choose a seat by the window. I rise as Gina breezes in; a flurry of colour in her usual gypsy-like garments and dangling earrings. I swear she's wearing more jewellery than I own. After the usual kiss and hug we subside onto the cane chairs and I take a good look at her.

'You're looking well. The air in Byron must agree with you. Good weather?' I'm bursting to yell out my news, but I'm somehow reticent about jumping in feet first. I swallow the words. They'll keep for later.

Gina spends the next thirty minutes regaling me with tales of her exploits over Christmas. If she's to be believed, she had a whale of a time. But then, she's always been prone to exaggeration. That's part and parcel of Gina. Finally, I can hold it in no longer.

'Sean has left me. Walked out. On Christmas morning, no less. Can you believe it?'

'What!'

I'd expected a stronger response than that from my best friend. My jaw must have dropped because her eyes widen and she adds, 'Without any warning?'

'None at all. He could have chosen a better time.' For the first time I hear a note of bitterness in my voice.

'How do you feel?'

'How do you think I feel?' *Is this the friend I've turned to for support? What's happened to her over Christmas?* 'Stunned, shattered, devastated, mortified, humiliated. You name it and I've been there in the past week. And, so far, I've managed to keep it to myself. You're the first person I've told.'

I stop. Saying it out loud makes it real. I realise that while no one else knew Sean had left, a small part of me has been able to pretend it hasn't really happened.

'Were you really all that close?'

'What do you mean? Of course we were. We…' I stop, considering her question. 'We've been married for over twenty years. Of course we're close. Why…' I stop again and remember something, something on the edge of my consciousness, pushing to be noticed.

Brushing the thought aside, I pick up the coffee I've ordered, then put it down again untasted. 'What am I going to do, Gina?' I wailed. 'I'm forty-seven, for God's sake. This isn't supposed to happen. What am I going to tell everyone?'

'Everyone?'

Gina seems particularly dense today. This is not what I expected. *What did I expect? Lots of sympathy. A big hug. A tirade against Sean for being a rat. Where is all this?*

'Lissa for one. I can't hold off any longer. She's already suspicious about Sean's supposed urgent trip to Scotland.'

'His…? Oh, that's what you told everyone on Christmas Day?'

'Well, I couldn't tell them the truth, could I? I could scarcely believe it myself. There was no sense in spoiling their day too.'

'So you soldiered on in typical Anna fashion. Played the perfect hostess as usual.' I ignore the hint of bitterness I detect in her voice. Best friends are allowed to say it like it is and I do have an inbuilt sense of pride, I admit.

'Lissa?' I repeat. 'How do I break it to her? It's her dad we're talking about. It'll kill her.'

'I doubt it.' Gina sounds more guarded than usual. 'Just tell her the truth. You've grown apart. It's not unheard of, you know. She'll come to accept it. She'll have to, won't she?'

'But we haven't… hadn't. Grown apart, I mean. Everything seemed fine.' As I say the words, that niggling thought edges into my mind again and again I thrust it aside.

'She's left home after all,' Gina continues, 'so it's not really as if he's abandoned her.'

'Just me.' I know I sound sorry for myself but I can't help it. *Where is the support I expected?* I shrug and pick up my bag. 'I guess I'll be off. Things to do,' I say, trying to sound bright.

'Will you be all right?' Finally Gina seems to be offering some concern.

'I'll be fine.' I seem to have been repeating that mantra to myself since Christmas.

We walk outside and stop at the door of her car. As she opens it, I spy a book lying on the passenger seat.

'Where did you get that? Didn't think you went for that sort of thing.' I point to the copy of *Rotten Gods*. 'More like Sean's taste. He was reading it…' Her choice surprises me as we share reading tastes and have often laughed together at Sean's passion for political thrillers.

'Oh that.' Do I imagine it or does Gina sound a tad flustered? 'Picked it up in Byron. Haven't started it yet. Thought I'd give it a try. See how the other half live.' She slides into the driver's seat and, with a wave, she's off leaving me wondering why I feel uncomfortable.

Gina and I go back a long way. We first met at uni, freshers together in the hallowed hall of Sydney University. We formed an immediate bond, me the north shore girl from the private girls' school and Gina who'd grown up in the western suburbs in a single parent family. We'd been inseparable for that first year but, whereas I loved the study, the environment, the whole excitement of being at university, Gina had rebelled and, in the November of that year, had dropped out. After bumming around all summer trying to 'find herself' she'd gone travelling, spent time in the UK and Europe, ending up in India where she'd lived for a time in an Ashram. I'd received the odd postcard and had consigned her to the outskirts of my consciousness. In the meantime, I'd formed a new group of friends, paramount among whom was Sean.

Sean never approved of our friendship. He always referred to her as 'your hippy dippy friend'. But, despite that, Gina and I have remained friends over the years, using each other as a sounding board and whinging platform. I've never left her feeling as ill at ease as I do now.

*

I wander around the house unable to settle. Everything is tidy, too tidy. I long for the trail of detritus that Sean always seemed to leave behind; the newspaper left open on the floor, the empty mugs beside the chair or computer, even the wet towels on the bedroom floor. These are the familiar irritations to which I have become accustomed, the signs that there is another human being in my life, even if he's not physically present. My musings are interrupted by the shrill ringing of the telephone.

'Hello, Anna Hollis speaking.' I remain standing at the kitchen counter, unwilling to be drawn in to a long conversation.

'Anna, Bill Smart here.' The familiar deep voice sounds awkward. The partner in Sean's accountancy firm has never found it easy to make telephone conversation. He is happiest with his numbers and spreadsheets. He clears his throat. 'It's Sean. I received this strange message. Something about taking time out. Is everything all right?'

I curse silently and, from some unknown quarter, find an inviolable core of resilience. I stiffen and pull myself up straighter. 'Your guess is as good as mine, Bill. He walked out on me on Christmas Day.' My words seem to drop into a deep pool and there is silence at the other end of the phone as I imagine his consternation. *Is he going to have to deal with a weepy woman too?*

Bill clears his throat again. 'Umm. Is there anything? Do you need…?' His voice peters away into silence.

'No, I'm fine.' There, I've said it again. Maybe one of these times I'll believe my own words. 'No, really.' I reassure him anxious to end the call, and, as I put down the phone, I hear the doorbell ringing insistently.

'Hang on,' I say to my impatient visitor as I hurry to the door. I open it just as my visitor is raising her hand to ring again.

'You're here!' Jan's strident tone pierces me as she bustles past me in her tailored pants and shirt, her neat blonde bob putting my own wild curls to shame. I've never known how our parents could have reared two such different children. I follow her into the kitchen, always the heart of our home. She sits at the table.

'A coffee would be nice.' Then, never known to be one for beating around the bush, my older sister gets right down to the purpose of her visit. 'What's up? Where's Sean? What's he really doing in Scotland? I didn't swallow that tale of a migraine at New Year. You've never suffered from them in your life so why start now?' The last is a rhetorical question. My sister knows me too well. 'Sean?' she prompts, as I pour coffee and sit down opposite.

I pick up my cup with both hands and take a long sip as I consider what to say, but this is my sister after all and she would know if I was trying to pull the wool over her eyes. I put down my cup carefully and spread my hands, palms down on the table. I raise my eyes to meet hers.

'He's gone. Left me.' I pick up my cup again, hands shaking, then put it down, coffee untouched. 'On Christmas morning, at this very table,' I say conversationally. 'He told me he didn't want to be married anymore.'

'What!' I've shocked her. This isn't what she'd expected. 'But you didn't. The trip to Scotland…'

'A figment of my imagination. Pretty good, huh?' I grin, a teary grin, but the first one I've managed in the past two weeks.

Jan puts down the cup she's been holding tightly since I first spoke. 'But where is he? Surely he's been in touch?'

'Not a word.' I get up and begin to wipe down the immaculate kitchen bench. Jan follows me and I'm enveloped in a warm hug. I feel myself start to crumple. She leads me back to the table.

'What are you going to do?'

I shrug and begin to pick at invisible crumbs on the table. I sweep them away with a wide swipe and meet her concerned gaze.

'Not much I *can* do. Soldier on, I expect. School starts at the end of the month and that'll get me back into a routine. As for the rest… I'll have to break it to Lissa. I've been avoiding that. And Mum and Dad.' I sigh. 'Then the whole family will know.'

'Bob?' Jan raised her eyebrows as she uttered our brother's name.

'Oh, he'll say he told me so. He and Sean never got on.'

'No, Sean wasn't a rugger bugger. Bob could never understand what you saw in him.'

We smile together in understanding. Our sports-mad sibling has no time for anyone who doesn't share his obsession. As girls we were tolerated, but he expects the men in the family to be up to date with all the various sporting events. Sean had opted out of these discussions early on in our relationship. That may have been one of his attractions for me. He was a pleasant relief from the continual talk of sport in our house.

'But really, what do you intend to do? Will you divorce?'

'Divorce? Jan, it's only been two weeks! Maybe...' As I speak, I realise that a small part of me has been hoping that it's not real, that Sean is going to come back, and that everything will carry on as before.

'Best to face facts. He may be gone for good. Is there anyone else?' When Jan gets the bit between her teeth she's like a terrier and won't let go.

'Someone else? You mean another woman?' This time I laughed out loud. 'Sean? You must be joking. He's been so engrossed in his bloody work he wouldn't see another woman if she stood naked in front of him. What makes you ask that?'

'It's the usual scene.' Jan bites her lip. 'Are you sure? I mean...' she pauses delicately, then continues. 'What's your sex life been like?' Only my sister could come out with such a blatant question but the look in her eyes is gentle.

I've had enough. 'Okay, that's it. You've had your say.' I rise. 'Have you finished your coffee? I'm sure you've lots to do. Thanks for dropping round.'

Jan picks up her bag and I see her to the door. Once there she turns to hug me once more. As she steps away she asks, 'Would you like me to tell Mum and Dad?'

'Would you?' I realise I've been hoping she'd offer. I can't imagine telling my parents that my marriage has failed, that I've not lived up to their expectations. And with this thought I realise that part of me is taking the blame for Sean's defection, that no matter how much anger I feel for him, in my heart I wonder what I've done to drive him away.

As if reading my mind Jan says, 'It's not your fault, you know.

Male menopause. Whatever. These things happen in the best ordered houses.' On this note she takes her leave and I watch her drive out of sight before I close the door and return to my thoughts.

I try to locate something that's been nagging at the back of my mind, but it eludes me. It'll surface in its own good time. In the meantime, work, I decide. It's always been my salvation. I drag out the class texts for the year and, before long, I'm lost in the trials and tribulations of the Bennet family, working out how to make their lives and customs relevant to teenagers, many of whom may already have an active sex life.

I'm lost in Jane Austen's world when the phone rings and I answer it with a sigh, expecting it to be Mum ready to castigate me on the loss of my husband, *that good man*, as she's always referred to him, as if amazed that he has been attracted to me in the first place.

To my relief the voice is that of Heather, my Headmistress and long-time mentor. We have worked together for ten years, and she is a woman who has gained my respect.

'Heather, great to hear from you,' I begin. 'I was just getting in some prep for the term. Thought I'd get a head start.' I'm about to go bubbling on when she interrupts.

'Oh, Anna. Some bad news. I won't be back this term. In fact, I won't be back again at all. My doctor has spoken and he's insisting I take extended leave. Since I'm due to retire anyway at the end of the year, it looks like that's it for me.'

I'm struck dumb. I can't imagine Northern Beaches Grammar without Heather's hand at the tiller. She has steered us through a number of difficult years and the school is soon to celebrate its diamond jubilee. This news is a disaster as far as I'm concerned.

'I'm calling from hospital.' I gasp at this. 'I was rushed in a couple of days ago,' she continues. 'It's not as bad as it sounds. I've still got a few good years left but only if I stop working now, or so I'm told.' Heather's hoarse laugh echoes over the line. 'The smoking has finally caught up with me and my lungs are shot to hell. Should have listened to the pundits and given up years ago.'

I find my voice.

'But…what…how…? It's almost the start of term.' I find myself wailing into the phone when I know I should be offering comfort.

'That's the good news. The Board has found a replacement, for this year, anyway, then they'll see, probably advertise. Seems one of them has a relative just back from the US. A PhD no less, who's been teaching in university over there and just happens to be looking for a stop gap. Should work out well. Comes from Queensland originally, University of Queensland trained and taught in Grammar there before hightailing it off to the States.'

I make the expected responses, all the while thinking this is the last thing I need. Probably some arrogant bitch full of herself and completely out of touch with current Australian thinking. I have agreed to visit Heather in hospital later in the week when she drops her final bombshell.

'By the way, did I mention? The new Head is a man, Dr Marcus King.'

Three

Lissa is coming to dinner. It isn't a big event. Although she's moved to share an inner city house with two friends, she drops back most weekends to catch up on laundry and stock up on meals. Only the round of festive season parties and the new boyfriend have kept her occupied this past couple of weeks and given me some breathing space.

I still find it hard to realise my baby girl has grown up. Little Melissa whose lisping voice shortened her name to Lissa – an abbreviation that stuck – is now grown up. How is she going to take the news that her dad and I are no longer together? I haven't heard from Sean. His clothes are still hanging in the wardrobe and taking up space in his side of the chest of drawers, and his absence populates the house like Banquo's ghost.

Despite the stifling humidity of the day I've cooked Lissa's favourite meal and the kitchen is redolent with the aroma of roast lamb and rosemary. As I put the final touches to my signature dish of potato salad with mustard dressing I hear my daughter's car in the driveway. I'm conscious that part of me hopes that by cooking her favourite food, I can somehow erase Sean's absence, pretend everything is as it should be. Another part of me knows better, and it's that part which quickly checks the hall mirror to ensure my face doesn't give me away. I could do with a facelift but, apart from that, my slightly wrinkled everyday face surrounded by fading blonde hair looks back at me. I push my fingers through the tangle of my shoulder length curls and open the door.

'Mum!' Lissa whirls in, an excited bubble of youthfulness. We hug and I hold her at arms' length, taking in the enormous grin and the sparkle in her eyes. My eyes begin to mist as I acknowledge that my daughter is now a beautiful woman with a life of her own.

'Do I smell lamb? Oh, you wonder, my fave! I've been having such a time. This summer is…. Will is… Oh, Mum!' She smiles, a wide smile that seems to reach right around her face and, extending her arms to take my hands in hers, she waltzes me around the hall. My daughter is in love! I remember when I felt that way about Sean, when he was in my every thought, when the very prospect of seeing him caused a flutter in the pit of my stomach. When had that changed? When had the minutiae of everyday life taken away the excitement of being in love?

'Is Dad back?' She looks around as if to conjure him up. 'He's not still over there in Scotland is he? Has he forgotten us? It *is* the festive season after all, a time for family and his place is here, not with some fuddy duddy old aunt on the other side of the world. Oh, Mum, the party last night! Will.' I let her babble on, taking in only a fraction of what she has to say. When she finally runs out of steam, I touch her on the back of her hand, the hand which is waving in the air to emphasise her final point.

'Come through.' I lead her into the kitchen. 'You'd better sit down.' I pick up the glass of wine I've been drinking to fortify myself for this conversation which I'd hoped to postpone till after dinner.

'What's wrong? It's Dad, isn't it? Something's happened to him.' She looks wildly around as if seeking an escape.

Placing the glass carefully on the table I take both of her hands in mine.

'Nothing's happened to him. But it *is* about Dad. He's not in Scotland.'

'Where is he then? When did he get back?'

Oh dear, this is going to be more difficult than I expected.

'He never went.'

Lissa's eyes widen. 'He never went,' she repeats woodenly. 'Then why? Where? What's going on?' She pulls her hands free and glares at me. 'Why have you been lying? Where is he?' she demands again.

I look down at my empty hands, now lying aimlessly on the table.

'I don't know.' Our eyes meet. 'Lissa, dear, your dad walked out on

Christmas morning and I haven't seen or heard from him since.'

'But he can't just… he can't do that to us.' She starts to stand up then subsides into the chair again. 'Poor Mum,' she says finally. 'You've kept this to yourself all this time. How're you coping?'

'I'm coping,' I reply drily. 'I've told Gina, and Aunt Jan knows too. She'll probably have told Gran and Gramps by now.'

'But how could he just walk out? Is he sick or something?'

'I think he's decided he wants something different.' I choose my words carefully. This is not the time to rant and rave about what a shit her father is. He *is* her father and has a right to her love and respect.

'Different?' she echoes. 'But he's still going to the office, right? I can see him there.'

'No. I had a call from Bill Smart and it seems he's decided to take time out from that too. But I'm sure he'll be in touch with you soon,' I try to reassure her. 'He loves you and it's me he's left, not you.'

'I need to go to the loo.' Lissa pushes her chair back and disappears upstairs, while I gulp down the remains of my glass of wine, pour another and continue preparing dinner.

When Lissa returns, I can see she's been crying. *What a shit Sean is. He could at least have been in touch with our daughter over Christmas. Hasn't he thought what his leaving would do to her, his baby girl?*

'Is dinner ready? I'm starving,' she says in a wobbly voice. 'Is there any wine left for me?'

'Help yourself.' I nod towards the bottle sitting on the bench. 'You know where the glasses are. Sit down when you're ready. Thought we'd eat here in the kitchen if that's okay with you.'

'Sure. I'll set.' Lissa proceeds to put out the cutlery and plates while I dish up the food into serving bowls and platters.

We've almost finished our meal when Lissa again broaches the subject of her father.

'I'd like…' She pokes with her fork at the food remaining on her plate. 'I'd like to talk to him. How can I…?'

'I know you would, honey. He's your dad and, no matter what happens between Sean and me he'll always be there for you. I'm sure of that. He'll be in touch with you, I know. When he's ready.' My voice tails off as I try to imagine where he might be and what he might be doing. I can't.

'Did he take much with him?' Lissa tries again. 'I mean, if his clothes and things are still here then maybe… At least he'll have to come back for them.' She puts down her fork and pushes her plate away.

'Maybe.' I don't want to give her false hope. I've spent the last two weeks wondering about that very matter. Surely, wherever he is, he's going to need more than the small bag of clothes he took with him. All his suits are still here. Wherever he is, he's going casual.

Lissa sits silently, elbows on the table, hands propping up her head.

'Can I stay here tonight? I can't face going back to Glebe right now. I need…'

'Of course you can. Your bed's always made up. Do you need an early start in the morning?'

'Yes – no. I'll just get up when I wake up. No need to worry about me in the morning.'

I recognise my daughter's hankering for the comfort of her childhood home and watch her climb the stairs heavily. This has hit her hard, but she's young and resilient and it'll all look better to her in the morning. I tidy away the dishes and follow her upstairs to another sleepless night of tossing and turning and wondering where we've gone wrong.

*

I awaken to the sound of a pair of kookaburras laughing in the trees outside my bedroom window and realise I must have fallen asleep after all. In fact I even feel refreshed. I rise and open the vertical drapes to see another sun-filled day with a heat haze already gleaming on the driveway. I'm startled for a moment to see a car parked there, then I remember that Lissa has slept over. I shower and dress quickly, pulling on an old sundress. It's going to be another hot one. I'm in the kitchen starting breakfast when Lissa makes her sleepy entrance.

'You didn't have to make pancakes for me, but it's good all the same.' She pushes back her thick mop of hair and yawns as she sits down. She's wearing an old tee shirt she's long outgrown and looks about sixteen. 'It's nice to come home and be spoiled.'

'What do you normally have for breakfast?'

'Oh, toast, fruit, whatever's there.' She stretches, arching her back like Simon, the Siamese cat we had when she was a child. He ran off somewhere along the line and we never replaced him.

'Mum…'There's a question in her voice and I'm not surprised when she continues, 'would it bother you if I called Dad, on his mobile I mean?'

I've been expecting this. 'No. It's up to you.'

'You haven't…?'

'No.' She's expecting me to elaborate, but there's no more to say. 'Are you working today?'

'I said I'd go in later. Seeing Will for lunch.' She yawns again and smiles, then seems to focus on me. 'Would you like me to stay, move back in? I can, you know. Must be a bit lonely for you with Dad gone.'

I stop what I'm doing, pancake batter dripping from the wooden spoon and gaze at her, speechless.

'Don't you think it'd be a good plan?' Lissa looks at me, her head on the side in a gesture I know well.

For a moment I toy with the idea. Lissa and her friends would fill up the emptiness of the house with their chatter and laughter. Then I give myself a mental shake. Who am I kidding? I'd end up cooking for and cleaning up after a retinue of young people. My home wouldn't be my own. It would turn into the sort of hovel she's living in, her share house in the inner city.

'Thanks for the offer, darling, but I don't think so. You need your independence and I have to learn how to cope on my own. I never have been on my own, you know. Straight from home to married life. I didn't stretch my wings in shared accommodation at uni like you've done.'

'You won't sit around and mope, will you? I don't want to think of you here on your own all the time.'

'Promise,' I say, turning back to find my pancakes beginning to burn. 'Term starts soon, anyway and I've lots to prepare. Heather's in hospital and I'm visiting her today,' I add.

'Hospital. Is it serious?'

'Well, she's been sick on and off for a long time. She has chronic obstructive lung disease. It's a mix of chronic bronchitis and emphysema. Her lungs are operating at around fifty percent capacity.

She's been managing to hold on, but it looks more serious this time. She's not going to be able to come back to school.'

'You mean this term?'

'I mean ever. Gosh that sounds terminal, but she was due to retire at the end of next year anyway. This has just brought it forward. I'll find out more when I see her.'

'Gosh! She's a smoker isn't she?'

'Since she was a teenager. Reason enough to keep away from tobacco yourself.' But I find myself preaching to the converted.

'Ugh! Can't stand the smell of cigarette smoke. Heather always stank of it, the few times I met her. Can't imagine how people can throw their money away on them for pleasure.' She shudders and I'm glad that's at least one vice my daughter has eschewed.

'You're not going to the hospital like that are you?' Lissa's eyes rake over me, taking in the sundress I've had since forever.

'What?' I carry the pancakes to the table and put the plate down carefully before I continue. 'What do you mean?' I look down at myself.

'Well,' Lissa picks up a couple of pancakes with her fork and dowses them in maple syrup. 'You're in danger of letting yourself go. Happens all the time to women of your age.' She waves her fork in the air to emphasise her point. 'What you need is…'

'Women my age? Wash out your mouth. I'm not decrepit yet.' I'm stunned to be having this conversation with my daughter. I've always thought of myself as keeping up with the times and not letting myself go, but curiosity gets the better of me. 'What do you mean exactly?'

'Exactly that sundress for one thing. I remember you wearing it when I was about twelve. That style went out so long ago it's about to come in again.'

'In that case maybe I'm ahead of fashion,' I try to joke.

'No, no. To visit the hospital you need something more…' She hesitates. 'More decorative – to cheer Heather up. And we need to do something about your hair too.'

'My hair?' I touch the curls which I've tied back in my usual band to keep the ends out of my face. 'What's wrong with my hair?' I'm beginning to wish we'd never started this conversation.

'Nothing really, but…' Lissa shovels a large piece of pancake into her mouth and is silent while she chews it. I take a small bite of mine, wash it down with a gulp of coffee and wait for her response.

'Why not go for a complete new look?' she suggests at last. 'Do you the world of good and be a fresh start to the year.'

I pull out the ends of my hair and consider her suggestion.

'Maybe,' I concede. 'But not today. Heather will have to take me like this.' We finish breakfast without any further discussion of my proposed makeover.

*

'Hello there!' I peer round the door of the private hospital room to see my friend and mentor sitting up in bed, her dark hair making a splash against the whiteness of the hospital linen. She's looking tired, but livelier than I expected. 'How are you?'

'Hanging in there. Come and sit down.' Heather's voice is breathy and hoarse and she coughs as she points to the chair by the bed.

'Can't speak too well,' she whispers, 'but I'm better than I was before the surgery.'

'Don't try to talk,' I caution, placing a bunch of flowers on the bedside locker.

Heather gives me one of the looks for which she is famous. 'You're not looking too hot yourself. What's been happening to you?'

'Sean has left.' I've become used to telling people by now and the words trip off my tongue. 'It's okay, really,' I reassure her. 'I didn't come here to pour out my troubles. What have they been doing to you? What's this about surgery?'

'Oh, it's my airways. They've become so narrow. Got all clogged up again. Could barely breathe. So the quacks got me in here and tried to extract the gunk from my lungs.' She coughs again and raises a handkerchief to her mouth. 'Didn't get it all out,' she tells me almost gleefully.

I must look shocked because she adds. 'They're doing some biopsies later in the week, so it looks like I'll be here for some time.'

'We're going to miss you.' The words seem to stick in my throat. 'Northern Beaches won't seem the same without you.'

'There'll be some glad to see the back of me.' She chuckles, an attempt that ends in a cough. Then she smiles, her incorrigible smile. 'And they'll have other fish to fry: Dr Marcus King. He'll set the cat among the pigeons for sure. Just what a lot of those old biddies need.'

'What do you know about him?' I'd relegated the news of the new Head to the back of my mind, but now I start to wonder about him. 'Why would he want to take on an all-girls school? Must be desperate,' I joke.

'I think he is.' Heather wriggles in her bed. 'Can you help me with this pillow?' She pushes herself up while I adjust the pillow to her liking.

'Word is he left the States in a hurry and needs something to tide him over. Friends in high places so it's a *fait accomplis*. It's a pity. I'd hoped…' She looks at me meaningfully.

'Oh no, not me, Heather. I'm a happy little vegemite as head of English. I'd hate the responsibility you've shouldered all these years.'

'Pity. Still, never mind. Back to Dr King. Think there's a wife somewhere – and a child.' She looks pensive. 'Bright boy it seems. Don't see him staying for long. The arrangement's a gap filler for both parties. Should set the girls' hearts aflutter too, having a cockerel among the hens.' She laughs her throaty laugh which ends in a cough again.

'I'd better go. I'm tiring you out.' At this moment an officious-looking woman in blue pants and a shirt patterned in blue and black diamonds opens the door.

'Time for your meds, Heather.' She gives me an indignant look and sweeps past me so close that I feel the air move against my face.

'See you next time.' I wave to Heather and leave.

As I drive home across Middle Harbour I turn on the radio to my favourite Radio National. The morning Book Program is interviewing the author of *Rotten Gods*. I remember the book in Gina's car. Her taste has certainly changed. I shake my head. Byron Bay has a lot to answer for.

Four

I look into the mirror aghast at the sight of the scissors snipping away at my hair. *Am I really ready for this?* I've taken Lissa's advice and told my usual girl I want a complete change but, as the locks fall to the floor, I wonder if she has taken me too literally. Sean has always loved my long tresses. He likes to wrap then around his fingers and… I stop myself in the midst of this reflection. *Sean is out of the picture. This is the new me!* Determinedly I close my eyes and keep them that way until I hear a laughing voice in my ear.

'All done, Anna. You can look now.' I do, and see a bedraggled version of myself. I lift my hand then let it fall. 'It'll look better when you're dry.' She plugs in the hairdryer and I sigh and close my eyes again, falling into a doze with the soporific sound of the hairdryer in my ears.

I realise the noise has stopped and feel the change in temperature in the air around my head. I'm lighter too. Cagily I open one eye, then the other. *Is that really me?* The mirror shows a youthful-looking woman with a curly cap of highlighted dark blonde hair. I turn from side to side, then look into the hand mirror held behind me to take in the back view.

'It's… it's certainly different,' I manage.

'Takes years off.' My hairdresser has never learned the meaning of tact. 'They won't recognise you up there at the Grammar.'

I preen. Maybe she's right. I certainly feel different. I'm having lunch with Lissa in the city so I'll see if it meets with her approval. After all, it was her idea in the first place.

I decide to take a cab into town. It's an extravagance, but the new me wants to splash out. I sail in like a celebrity.

Lissa is waiting for me at a corner table and I do a double-take. My view of her is partially obscured by the wide shoulders of the man sitting opposite her. She smiles, waves and says something to him and he rises. As he turns to face me I'm dazzled by a pair of deep blue eyes and a flash of white teeth. So this is her Will. Not quite the uni type I'd envisioned. His tailored appearance speaks loudly of the city. My baby has found herself a real man.

'You must be Lissa's mum. It's a pleasure to meet you.' He shakes my hand, a good firm handshake, I note. 'I'm just off. See you later, sweetie!' He gives Lissa a peck on the cheek and, before I can reply, strides off leaving me staring after him mouth agape.

'You didn't tell me…' I begin.

'I didn't know myself. He just appeared. His office is somewhere over there.' Lissa waves vaguely in the direction of George Street. 'Isn't he gorgeous?' She hugs herself in delight. 'I'm so glad you've met.'

'I'd hardly say I've met him. But, yes, quite gorgeous,' I agree.

'You look wonderful.' Lissa suddenly eyes me up and takes in the transformation. 'Turn round and let me see the back. Yes,' she murmurs, as I do her bidding, 'and you've added some colour too, and highlights.'

I finger my new short curls. 'Just a touch.'

'You look ten years younger.' She sits back with a self-satisfied look on her face. 'I knew it was a good idea.'

Wondering just how old I'd looked before this morning's efforts, I pick up the menu and we fall to discussing what we'll have for lunch.

We chatter inconsequentially through the main course.

'Dessert?'

Lissa frowns and shakes her head.

'Just coffee for me. I'll have a skinny cap.'

'Me too.'

The waitress delivers our order and Lissa spoons up the chocolate topping leaving a rim around her lips reminiscent of the little girl who is never too far away.

'Umm,' she begins.

I look up.

'I've seen Dad.'

It's my turn to busy myself with my coffee, stirring it furiously.

'How is he?' I manage at last.

'Good. We had lunch on Sunday. He wants to talk with you but he's not sure…' Lissa's voice tails off.

'Not sure,' I repeat faintly.

'He's not sure how you'll take it.'

'Take what?' I can't see where this is going. 'Where is he living anyway?' I ask.

'That's just it.' Lissa looks at me over the rim of her cup. 'He's with Gina.'

I remember Gina's evasiveness and the book lying on her car seat. *Why on earth has my best friend given sanctuary to my errant husband.*

'I mean he's *with* Gina.' My eyes meet hers in sudden understanding.

'What!' the word explodes from my mouth like a bullet. The couple at the next table look round then turn back to each other in embarrassment.

'I know, it's awful. But…' Lissa runs her fingers through her hair, 'he seems more… I don't know, relaxed maybe?'

'But he doesn't even like her!' I can't take it in. Sean and Gina, the woman he's always derided, mocked. The friendship I've had to defend over the years.

Lissa looks concerned as I try to remember any hints that there has been anything between them, but nothing comes to me.

'I can't believe it! Gina! How could she? How could he?' I don't know which of them arouses my greatest anger. I want to punch them both. Hard. But I sit there in a civilised fashion and pick up my now cold coffee.

'You're not going to do anything stupid, are you?' Lissa is beginning to look worried, making me wonder if my thoughts are reflected in my face. 'Maybe I shouldn't have told you. But I thought you should know.'

I take a deep breath.

'So. Your dad. Is he planning to call me?'

Lissa looks awkward and I realise the role she's been thrust into.

'He's asked you to sound me out, hasn't he?'

She nods, embarrassed at the admission.

'It's not fair of him to put you in this position, as a go-between.' My anger flares up again. 'He should be fighting his own bloody battles not hiding behind you.'

'He's not. Oh, Mum!' Lissa wails, tears beginning to trickle down her cheeks. 'I just wanted to help. I mentioned I was meeting you today and we thought... Oh, shit. I shouldn't have said anything. I should have left it to him to do his own dirty work.'

I draw myself up and take another deep breath.

'No, darling. It's not your fault. You love us both. It's not fair for either of us to use you as a go-between, I can see it puts you in an untenable position. Let's pretend it never happened, shall we?' I manage a tight smile and see an answering one appear on Lissa's face.

'We're good then?' she asks.

'Always.' I reach across the table to squeeze her hands. I pat them instead.

'Now, tell me more about this young man of yours. I thought he was a student like you but he's not, is he?'

Lissa glows, all upset forgotten. *The young recover so quickly.*

It seems he's the brother of one of her housemates and they met when he was helping move some furniture for them.

'He's twenty-six!' Lissa enthuses, as if his age makes him worldly-wise which I suppose it does in her eyes. 'He's an accountant like Dad. Well, not exactly like Dad,' she qualifies. 'He's with one of those big companies. They're called the big six or something. I don't understand it, but it sounds important.' She sits back smugly, as if basking in his reflected glory.

'Wow!' This seems to be the appropriate response as the glow deepens and she clasps her hands together.

'And you're still intent on enrolling in a Master's?' Lissa has revelled in her studies and, after graduating with an Honours Degree the previous year, has decided that, rather than seek a permanent position, she'll continue studying.

'Just did. Will likes the idea. Says he regrets not doing further study himself.' She preens herself in congratulation.

'It's another three years.' I try not to sound like the concerned mother. 'Years when you could be earning. Have you thought of studying part-time?'

'Mum! I love the ambiance of the University. I don't need much and

I can earn enough from my occasional waitressing. The tips are good. Plus…' and she smiles across the table, 'I might be able to pick up some tutoring. My supervisor is optimistic he can put in a good word for me. That would be wicked!'

'Well, if it's what you want.' But I can't help worrying. No point in reminding her of the huge student debt she's incurring. She's happy and that's the important thing.

'What are you up to this weekend? I hope you're planning an outing to show off the new look,' Lissa adroitly changes the subject.

'Yes, actually I am. I reach into my bag and take out an embossed card. As I hand it over for her perusal I add. 'Received this on Monday. An invitation from the Chairman of the Board, no less. They're holding a cocktail party for the staff to meet the new Head, and vice versa I suppose. Anyway it's tonight so I thought, since I'm in town…'

'You'll let me help you choose a new outfit!' Lissa fingers the embossed writing on the card as she speaks. 'They've pulled out all the stops on this, haven't they? Who is he, this Dr Marcus King?' She hands it back.

I tuck it back into my bag.

'Some guy who's just returned from the States. He's evidently a friend of one of the Board members. Should be a great evening. I can't wait!' I grimace.

'Well, I'll help you find a stunning outfit.' Lissa stands up and shrugs her bag over her shoulder. 'Let's go!'

*

I stand in front of the mirror looking at a stranger. The new dress Lissa has helped me choose is red. It's not a colour I'd ever have chosen for myself, but I have to admit that, teamed with the new hairdo and a pair of black patent sandals with killer heels – I hope my feet can survive the evening – I'm looking pretty good. I slide my hands down over my hips and reflect that I seem to have lost weight in the weeks since Christmas. This dress is one size down from what I was wearing last year. The vee neckline and the new hairstyle make my neck appear longer. I could even be called elegant. I grab a clutch bag and head off to the car. One taxi ride a day is enough for my bank balance, so I won't be drinking much tonight.

By the time I park my trusty beige Volkswagen and enter the Great Hall, the evening is well underway.

'Wow, Anna, look at you!' It's the school secretary, Betty, who greets me at the door and offers me a glass of champagne.

'Wow to you too. Really pushing out the boat tonight are we?' I counter, sherry being the usual tipple on such occasions.

'It was Dr King's idea,' she simpers, if a hefty fifty-something year old with a greying bob can be said to simper. 'He thinks it'll help break the ice.' She looks around as if seeking to conjure him up. 'He'll be here soon,' she assures me.

I sip my champers and begin to mingle, surprised by the complimentary comments I receive on my changed appearance. About half an hour has elapsed, and I'm discussing Year Eleven texts with one of the other English staff members when she nudges me and points with her elbow.

'That's him!'

I follow the direction she's indicating, but all I can see are a set of wide shoulders clothed in an ubiquitous pinstriped grey suit topped by a head of unremarkable brown hair cut in the requisite short back and sides. Looks pretty normal to me, so I can't see what the fuss is about, but notice the beginning of a wave of excitement ripple across the room.

I'm about to look away again, when he turns and… My God, it's the man from the beach! I try to duck out of his line of vision, but he catches my eye and, for a moment, looks puzzled. Then I see recognition flood into his eyes. He smiles and turns to speak to his companions. I mutter something and walk quickly out of the room, placing my half empty glass on a table as I leave.

I head for the toilet and hold onto the edge of the sink. *How can this be happening to me? The guy who caught me at the worst moment in my life turns up here as my new boss. What despicable trick of fate could have planned that?* I take three deep breaths – a trick I've learned to help me in stressful situations – and if this isn't stressful, what is? It doesn't help. I'm wishing I'd brought my drink with me when I hear the door open behind me.

'Oh, there you are!' Betty exclaims. 'We wondered where you had got to. Dr King wants to meet you.'

I pretend to touch up my hair, pushing my fingers into the curls as if to fluff them up, turn and respond brightly.

'Yes, I'm here! Just coming.'

I re-enter the hall quaking in my shoes. I feel as if I'm sixteen again about to have my first job interview. My throat is dry, my tongue sticking to the roof of my mouth. As I pass the table at the door I grab another glass of champagne and take a gulp, almost choking as the bubbles go up my nose. Shit! As if things aren't bad enough.

'Here she is, Dr King.' Betty is at her most subservient. 'Let me introduce Mrs Hollis, Head of our English Department.'

I look up. Even in my new heels, the new Headmaster stands head and shoulders above me. I meet his amused gaze.

'Anna. Pleased to meet you,' I say and look away, down to my feet, but not before I spy his outstretched hand. I offer mine.

'I'm Marcus to my friends and I hope we'll be friends. Heather has told me a lot about you and the wonderful contribution you make to the school.' His handshake is firm and there is a smile in his voice. I wonder just how much Heather has told him about me. Wait till I see her again! 'I understand you've taken on some school productions?'

'Oh that, yes.' God, I sound like a fool.

As if recognising my embarrassment, he drops my hand. 'We'll meet again next week,' he says, and moves off leaving me a trembling mess with my hand tingling from his touch. I begin to blush.

'Mrs Hollis?' I turn to find myself facing one of my Year Twelve students proffering a tray of mini bagels which appear to be filled with smoked salmon, capers and cream cheese.

'Thanks Amelia.' I hoist my bag further up my shoulder and take one.

'Gee, Mrs Hollis you look sick.' I blanche but Glenda, my deputy, is immediately at my side whispering.

'That's their way of issuing a compliment. Sick means grouse.'

'Must be the new hairdo,' I answer with a smile.

'And that dress,' Amelia adds. 'It's really great. Suits you. You should wear red more often.'

'Hmm. Trying to impress the new Head?' Glenda is still at my ear.

'Amelia's right. And she should know. Did you see the article about her mother in the latest Women's Chat? She's a real fashion plate.'

'I'm not trying to impress anyone. Just felt it was time for a change.'

'He's a hunk, isn't he? And I hear there's no wife in sight. So he's fair game for us singles. Pity about the seriously married like you, but them's the breaks.' She walks off leaving me diving into the depths of despair again. How could I really have imagined that a new hairdo and a new dress could change anything? I may look different on the outside, but inside I haven't changed. I'm still the insecure woman who's lost her husband to her best friend. And to cap it all, my new boss is the man who encountered me at my worst moment, on the beach, on my knees, in tears and with the sweat running down my face. What a start to the year!

Five

I dress carefully in a pair of white pants topped with my favourite sky blue silk blouse. I fasten my pearls around my neck to complete the look and check the mirror. The pearls may be a bit over the top, but they give me the courage I need. They belonged to Grandma Parker, Mum's mother, and have seen three generations though more difficult times than this.

I touch the round globes with trembling fingers hoping for reassurance. This will be the first time I've seen Sean since he walked out. His phone call last week came out of the blue. He wants to talk. I agree and decide to do it on home ground. I've packed the remainder of his clothes and they sit in boxes in the hallway. I bite my lip and peer out of the window. He's due soon. I hope I can keep my cool.

The doorbell rings and I walk downstairs, amazed at how outwardly calm I feel, though on the inside my heart is beating madly.

'Hello Sean,' I greet him coolly as if he is a casual friend. He steps forward to kiss my cheek and I evade his touch. 'Come in.' I lead him into the lounge where he stands awkwardly for a moment before taking a seat in what was his favourite armchair.

He sits silently, his hand stroking the arm of the chair where he has spent every night for the past twenty-five years. Until Christmas, that is. I sit opposite him, knees together, hands clasped on them. I am not going to make this easy for him.

I wait for him to speak. The house is quiet, the only sounds the ticking of the grandfather clock in the corner, another relic from my grandparents, and the cars passing on the Wakehurst Parkway in the distance. Nothing is said. Finally I can bear it no longer.

'Would you like a coffee?' I ask politely.

'Umm, yes.' I barely hear his response as I rise and go into the kitchen where I stand breathing deeply with my hands gripping the edge of the counter as if they'd never let go. I set about fixing coffee and soon the kitchen is full of the scent of my favourite hazelnut coffee and the sound of the percolator heating up. A sense of detachment descends on me as I perform the familiar actions.

'Can I join you?' The voice comes from behind me. I'm shaken out of my composure. I turn to see Sean standing by the kitchen doorway.

'Uh, sure.'

'How have you been?' Sean seems more comfortable here in the kitchen, while I'm conscious of my sanctuary having been invaded.

'Oh, you know, coping.' I silently castigate myself. I want to sound positive, as if I'm making a life without him, not a sad case who can't survive on my own.

He sits down comfortably at the kitchen table as if by right.

'I hope… I mean…' He stumbles over his words.

I pour the coffee and take it over to the table, placing his before him with such force that it slops over onto the table top.

'Okay, out with it.' I sit down and take my own mug in both hands as if to ward off what he has to say. 'What is it you want? Your clothes are in the hall. I'd be grateful if you take them with you when you leave.' It's as if I'm speaking to a stranger.

'Anna, don't be like this. Can't we be civilised about things?' I don't deign to reply.

Sean sighs wearily.

'I've come to ask for a divorce.' The words seem to sit on the table between us like some inanimate objects. They echo in my head drowning out all other sounds.

'Of course.' My response seems to shoot out unplanned. 'I expect you and Gina…' I stop as the image of my husband and my best friend rears up in my imagination. But he seems to take this as encouragement to continue.

'Yes,' he says eagerly. 'I knew you'd understand. We want to go back to Byron. Gina's buying a house there.' His eyes take on a glazed look. 'A house by the beach.'

'I understand only too well. How could you, Sean? With my best friend? How could she?' I shake my head to rid myself of the image of them together.

His eyes widen and he stretches his hands out palms up.

'These things happen.'

These things happen! He's shattered my life into pieces and that's all he can say in explanation.

'You mean shit happens?' I spit out the words.

'That's a bit strong.' He begins to look uncomfortable again.

'How long has it been going on?' I'm curious. 'How long have the two of you been carrying on behind my back and laughing at me?'

'We haven't been laughing at you, Anna. It hasn't been easy these past few months. It was… remember when you went on that excursion with the school, to New Zealand?'

'The ski trip? That was last July.' I think back.

'And you asked Gina to look in on me, make sure I was eating properly.' He looks sheepish.

'It started then?'

'We got talking. She began her usual diatribe about the environment. You know, all that Greenie stuff.'

'Yes, the stuff you've always denigrated and mocked her for.'

'Well, somehow.' He rubs his head. 'I don't know what happened, but it suddenly seemed to make sense, so I agreed to go along to one of her meetings and a yoga class.'

'You! At a yoga class?' This is beginning to sound seriously weird.

'I know,' Sean chuckles, suddenly more at ease as he acknowledges the ridiculousness of his actions. 'But you were gone and I was at a loose end. And, well, one thing led to another.' His voice peters away.

'And now you're planning to move to Byron Bay?' My voice reflects my amazement at the apparent transformation of the conservative man with whom I've spent the past twenty-five years.

'We are.' His eyes meet mine. 'You can't believe how liberated I feel. I want you to be happy for me, happy for us.' He reaches out his hand toward me. I ignore it.

'I think that's expecting a bit much.' I say stiffly. 'I am prepared to consider a divorce.' I get the word out with difficulty. I've been expecting it. 'So what happens now?'

'Well, I guess we see our lawyers. I'll use Gina's,' he says hurriedly as my brother Bob has been our lawyer since he qualified. 'And…' he coughs, 'there's the house.'

I get a sinking feeling in the pit of my stomach. This house is my home. I look across the table trying to appear calm.

'The house?'

'Well, it *is* in both our names.' He pauses. 'I need to contribute to the Byron house, pay my share, you know.' He coughs again. 'Maybe… maybe you could buy me out.'

There, it's said. The real purpose of his visit. A divorce isn't going to be enough for them. They want to turn me out of my house too. Forgetting how big and empty I'm finding it without his presence, I react angrily.

'So, not content with stealing my husband, my so called best friend wants to do me out of my home too! You know I can't afford to buy half of this place. Why the mortgage alone…' I slump in my seat conscious of the bills which have been piling up since Christmas. I've been meaning to do something about them, but it's all seemed too big an effort so I've been stuffing them in the drawer of the hall table intending to get round to them.

I rise to my feet.

'I think you'd better go.'

Sean gulps down the last of his coffee and stands up too.

'Think about this, Anna. Please?' He moves into the hallway and opens the door. 'I'll be in touch.'

I sit on the bottom step of the stairs and listen to the sound of his car backing out of the driveway. The boxes of clothes are still sitting there, a reminder of his visit. I walk back into the kitchen kicking one of the boxes as I go. It would serve him right if I put them outside at the mercy of the weather and the friendly fox who sometimes visits in the early hours of the morning.

My coffee is cold so I brew another cup and take it outside into the courtyard. I sit in my favourite chair and, holding my coffee mug in both hands, I survey the garden, my garden. Sean never evinced an interest in it but, over the years, I've planned and planted a garden in which I've taken pride. I'm saddened to realise I'm already thinking in the past. But how can I afford to keep it? I haven't allowed myself to think about moving, however Sean's visit has forced me to consider it. I sip my coffee and weigh up my options. I stand up slowly. I need to call my little brother for advice.

'Calm down, Bob.' I hold the phone away from my ear as my brother's angry voice shouts down the line. Never Bob's favourite person, Sean's demands have caught him on the raw. He may be my younger brother, but since we've grown up, he likes to think that he can look out for me in anything to do with legal matters.

'Look, I'm coming to terms with the fact that I'll have to move. I don't like it, but the bottom line is that I can't afford the mortgage by myself and a place like this takes a lot of maintenance.' I'm trying to sound calm and logical, all the while hurting like hell. My gut is twisting in knots as I look around the sunny living room which holds the memories of my life with Sean and of Lissa's growing years. *Shit, Lissa will go ape when she learns that her home won't be here for her. Telling her is going to be another hurdle.*

I finally hang up the phone, having agreed to meet Bob in his office the next week. It will be school holidays. I can't believe that Easter has come around already and that I've managed to survive a whole term since Christmas.

*

For the most part, I've avoided meeting the new Head – Marcus as everyone calls him – on my own. On the few occasions when it's been unavoidable, I've managed to remain businesslike and, to give him credit, he's never referred to our first encounter. I think I've caught an amused look in his eyes a couple of times, but it's probably a figment of my imagination.

Rumour about him is rife. The girls love him, and most of the staff are running around after him as if they've never seen a man before. I have to admit he's pretty dishy if you like that sort of thing, but I've had enough of men to last me a lifetime. I just want to sort out my life.

So it's a bit of a shock when, gathering up my books in preparation to leave for home, I hear a gentle knock and turn to see Marcus hovering in the doorway.

'Can I have a word?' He is looking a bit like a Greek God with the afternoon sun picking up the highlights in his hair. I'm wearing my workaday flats so he towers over me as he takes my silence for assent, and walks over to place a hand on the table next to my pile of Year Twelve homework books.

'I guess so.' I try to sound nonchalant, dropping my bag onto the floor and raising my eyes to meet his.

'I don't quite know how to put this,' he begins, and I wonder what major sin I've committed. My mind goes back over the term, but nothing glaringly obvious comes to mind. I wait expectantly, willing him to hurry. I'm having dinner with Lissa and Will and have to get home, shower, change and make my way into the city.

'It's the Board Easter dinner after the Passion Play on Thursday,' he explains. 'I'm expected to take a partner.' He has a bewildered look in his eyes and, with a lock of hair falling over his forehead – the short back and sides is growing out rapidly – he looks more like a small boy in trouble than the Headmaster of a prestigious girls' school.

'I don't suppose…?' He looks at me beseechingly. 'I don't know anyone in Sydney. It's best if I'm accompanied by a senior member of staff. Everyone probably has plans already and Betty suggested I ask you. But I'll understand…' The words seem to tumble over each other. I decide he's more like an anxious puppy than the little boy I'd earlier envisaged. *Damn Betty. Why can't she mind her own business?*

'Are you asking me to be your partner at the dinner,' I ask smiling. He looks so helpless that, for a moment, I forget this is the man who saw me in the depths of despair on Manly beach only three months ago.

'I am.' He seems greatly relieved that I understand and begins to smile. 'Purely professional.' He assures me. 'It's most appropriate really since the English Department has worked hard on the play and, if you don't have any other plans…' There's a question in his voice.

I answer without thinking.

'No. I'll be at the play anyway – it's expected – and I'd only be going home afterwards.'

'Your husband won't mind?'

I realise he's managed to stay immune from the school gossip mill which knows quite well that Sean and I are no longer together.

'No.' I say briefly.

'Good.' His sigh of relief is palpable. I'll get Betty to tee it all up with you. I believe it's a formal do at the…' I tune out of the remainder of his conversation, mentally kicking myself. *What have I let myself in for? Why couldn't I just have said 'No'?*

I pick up my belongings again and head off. I drive home bemused. What has possessed me to accept what is tantamount to a date with Marcus King? At least he thinks I'm still married, so there's no chance of his hitting on me. Who am I kidding? God's gift to Northern Beaches Girls Grammar isn't going to be interested in a forty-seven year old English teacher with faded hair, wrinkles and the beginning of a middle age spread. I'm way outside his range even if I were on the market which I most decidedly am not. I can't believe I'm even thinking this. I turn on the radio to drown my thoughts.

*

I enter the restaurant with a spring in my step and spy Lissa and Will immediately. They look so right together, their heads almost touching as they laugh at some private joke. They sense my arrival and look up.

'Mum!' Lissa jumps up and gives me a hug. 'We were just talking about you. Champagne?'

Will calls over the waiter and orders a bottle, while Lissa passes me a menu.

'Are we celebrating something?' I look from one to the other.

'Easter!' Lissa replies airily. 'We won't be around at the weekend so it's an early celebration.'

I'd guessed as much when she issued the invitation. I've kept up the family tradition of making a special breakfast on Easter Sunday over the years, but this year it will be different. Sean won't be there, so I've been wondering what to do. This settles it.

'I may go off somewhere too.' I surprise myself. It's not something I've even considered till now, but suddenly it seems like the right thing to do.

'You will?' Lissa sounds relieved and Will jumps in.

'Great idea. Where will you go?'

I have to think quickly and suddenly the words tumble out.

'I thought of the Southern Highlands. I saw a program about a Bed and Breakfast place that looked interesting. Be nice and cool down there at this time of year.' I'm amused at how genuine this sounds when I'm making it up as I go along.

'I'm glad you won't be on your own.' Lissa peers at me over the menu. 'I mean…'

'I know what you mean, but you don't need to worry about me. You're not responsible for your old mum. Where are you two off to?' I ask to change the subject. They look at each other in embarrassment, neither willing to be the first to speak.

'Umm…'

'Well…'

It dawns on me. 'You're going to see your dad, aren't you?'

'Yes. We're going up to Byron Bay. They're settled in up there now and… I haven't seen him for ages, Mum.' Lissa pleads.

'It's okay,' I assure her despite the twist in my gut at the thought of the young couple staying with Sean and Gina in what I imagine to be their romantic hideaway. 'He's your dad. Of course you must visit him. How long are you going for?'

'Just the long weekend. Will has to get back to work.' She gives him a shy smile. 'And I need to hit the library and get stuck into my literature review. I'm meeting with my supervisor at the end of the month and he expects to see some progress.' As I notice the pair holding hands under the table, I'm transported back over the years to when Sean and I were like them. It doesn't seem so long ago. Luckily the waiter arrives with the wine and, in the bustle of opening the bottle and pouring out the drinks, the moment is forgotten.

'Well, this has been lovely, but I have to work tomorrow. I'm not on holiday yet. There's still a lot to do before we finish and then on Thursday there's the Passion play and dinner…' I stop. I haven't intended to mention the dinner. Maybe they didn't notice but my daughter hones right in.

'Dinner? You haven't been invited to that before, have you? What's up?' A blush rises to my cheeks.

'Nothing. It's the new Head. He needs a partner. The Board…'

'The dishy one?' I regret having mentioned him to Lissa earlier in the term and now she's regarding me with wide eyes. 'You're dating your new Headmaster!' She sounds astonished and, although I'm quick to deny it, I'm somewhat chagrined that she doesn't consider me worthy of him.

'No, no. It's just a professional thing.'

'Why shouldn't your mum date this guy? Is there something wrong with him?' Will is quick to interrupt with raised eyebrows.

'Well, according to Mum, the staff and girls are all going gaga over him. You did say that, right?'

'I say a lot of things.' I try to brush it off. 'Anyway, as I said it's not a date. Subject closed.'

Six

I gaze around the room, glad I've chosen to wear a simple black dress. Its round neckline and cap sleeves make it a far cry from the flamboyant outfit I wore to the staff cocktail party. This promises to be a much more formal affair. Several of the women are wearing cocktail dresses which must have cost a bomb when they were new, but are now pretty dated, while the gentlemen are uniformly dressed in either pinstriped lounge suits or flannels and blue blazers with unidentifiable monograms on the pockets. It's a completely different world from the one which I customarily inhabit.

The gathering has divided the sexes, and Marcus has joined the men quaffing beer and whiskey at one end of the room, while the women stand in small cliques at the other. I accept a glass of white wine from a harried-looking waitress and stand alone, feeling a bit lost and twirling the stem of the glass while I work out which group I should join. I surreptitiously look at my watch. The Passion Play finished at six-thirty. It's now close to seven-fifteen. I hadn't expected the drinks and mingling thing, envisaging instead an immediate move to the sit-down meal. It's going to be a long night.

'Wonderful play wasn't it? I can't get over how it seems to get better each year. I haven't seen you at one of these dinners before, have I? And how's that friend of yours, Gina, isn't it? Lovely lady! I attended a few of her classes before everything became too hectic.' It's the wife of the Board Chairman who has pinholed me. I remember we've met on several previous occasions.

'I don't see much of her these days. She's moved up north.' The words come out more sharply than I intend, so I attempt a smile to dilute the tone.

'Oh.' As if realising I don't want to pursue that line of conversation, my companion changes the subject. 'What's the staff opinion of our new Head?' she asks with a gleam in her eye. 'I notice you're his partner for the evening.'

'Yes, well, purely on professional grounds,' I say hastily. 'As for the staff,' I laugh more naturally, 'they're bending over backwards to please him.'

'Not literally, I hope,' she flutters, and her lips form a moue at what she clearly considers to be a risqué comment. I look around wildly for support. It comes from an unexpected quarter as Joan, an old friend of my mother, appears, bearing down on us and sweeping me away. Joan has been part of my life for as long as I can remember, but I haven't seen her very often in recent years, and have forgotten she's a long-term member of the school board.

'You looked as if you needed saving.' Joan nods her head at my erstwhile companion. 'She can go too far when she's had a few. Now what's this I hear about you and Sean? Your mum told me last week. I can't believe it! How are you coping?' The questions run together, a habit of Joan's. My eyes take in the familiar figure in front of me, dressed this evening in a cream tunic outfit which flatters her fuller figure. Here is someone I can talk to, someone who can understand.

'I can empathise a bit,' she continues without waiting for a reply. 'Tom left me, you know, when I was much the same age as you are now. There's life on the other side. You need to know that. I don't suppose Susan took that tack with you. Dear friend though she is, she tends to have her blind spots.'

'No, you're right there.' I decide to ignore her earlier questions. 'I'm sure Mum thinks it's all my fault.' I take a sip from my glass, and the cold liquid is comforting as it slips down my throat.

'Don't let it get you down. Her heart's in the right place, you know, but she's always been a bit what we used to call jolly hockey sticks. I guess she's been hoping for a full family to celebrate her big day.'

'Big day?' I ask mystified.

'Your mum and dad, their fiftieth. It's coming up later this year. She's been full of it since Christmas.'

'Umm, yes.' How could I have forgotten? My parents' golden wedding anniversary in August. Mum has been talking about it for years. Despite Dad hoping for a quiet celebration at home, I seem to recall Mum planning to take the whole family off somewhere.

'Off to their honeymoon spot, isn't it?' Joan continues. 'I don't expect it'll be much fun for you. But you *will* try, won't you. She's really a rather special person.'

'Of course. It's her day, hers and Dad's.' I pull myself together. I must check in with Jan. I seem to have missed the family preparations. I make a mental note to call my sister next day.

'And Sean?' Joan returns to her earlier question. 'Has he really gone troppo?'

I have to smile at what I expect is Mum's interpretation of events.

'He's gone up to Byron Bay, if that's what you mean. With my best friend.' I take a gulp from my glass which is now almost empty.

'No! Your mum didn't add that piece of information. What a bummer, to lose the two of them in one fell swoop, like a double betrayal.' I let out a breath I don't even know I've been holding. At last, someone who understands the depth of my loss.

'Yes, don't know which hit me hardest.' As I speak, I realise it's close to the truth. Not only has Sean deserted me, but my long-time confidante has gone too.

'Well, despite it all, you're looking good. I'm glad to see you getting out and about. Who did you come with?' She looks around trying to locate a suitable escort.

'Dr King, the new Headmaster.'

'Oh!' The single word encompasses surprise and a touch of shock which she quickly overcomes. 'There's a sadness there, a troubled soul don't you think? He has a haunted look.'

'There is? He has?' I have to admit I haven't noticed it. I guess I've been too caught up in my own problems to even consider anyone else might be troubled. Before we can take the conversation further, the object of our discussion comes up behind us, and Marcus hands me another wine, adroitly removing the empty glass I've been holding.

'I don't believe we've met.' He looks enquiringly at my companion.

'Joan Wilson, board member for longer than I care to remember and you must be...'

'Marcus King…'

'The new Headmaster. We were just talking about you.'

I blush. What must he think? Fortunately we're interrupted by the deep sound of a gong and we're ushered into the dining room, where I find myself seated next to Marcus at a long table covered in crisp white linen, and with an elaborate centrepiece of cut flowers. I sit down with relief, close my eyes for a moment, and take a deep breath. I'm aware of Marcus' bulk seated beside me and open my eyes as he begins to speak.

'Sorry to leave you to the old biddies. Had to network. New boy on the block and all that. Hope it wasn't too tiresome for you.'

'It was fine.' I take a good look at the man sitting next to me. Joan's right. He does have a troubled look about him, frown lines between his eyes and deep indentations around his mouth signalling a deep sadness. But what would seem haggard on a woman, only serves to give him a vulnerable appearance, one which makes every woman want to take away his pain. That, I realise, is the essence of his attractiveness.

The first course is served and we are occupied with eating, each making inconsequential conversation with those on other sides of us. I find myself making polite conversation to Canon Brownlee's nephew, a recent addition to the school board. He's a tall, prim, axe-faced man with a high-pitched voice and glacial-blue eyes. He's wearing a religious cassock. I can't imagine him ever being untidy. He is ostentatiously drinking orange juice, having waved away all offers of alcoholic beverages.

It's only when the dessert appears, triple lines of crème brûlée decorated with tiny slivers of chocolate, that Marcus turns back to me. 'Sorry, I've been ignoring you again.' He brushes back an errant lock of hair and settles his glasses more firmly on his nose. 'I didn't expect it to be like this.'

'It's okay. I'm only your partner.' I wonder where the words came from and suddenly realise I've had more than my usual ration of wine with dinner. 'Sorry, I don't know why I said that. Of course you have to talk to them. It's your job. Ignore me, I'm afraid I've had a touch too much of this.' I hold up my empty glass to illustrate. We eat dessert in silence.

As the dinner comes to a conclusion with the usual round of speeches, thankfully kept reasonably short, Marcus stands up and helps me from my chair. I resist the temptation to tell him I can manage perfectly well on my own, recognising he is merely being polite. He sees me into the passenger seat of his car and we drive off.

'Where are we going?' I have been almost asleep, lulled by the motion of the vehicle, when I realise we are headed, not for my home where Marcus picked me up, but for the esplanade at Manly.

'Thought you might care to revisit our first meeting.' There's a chuckle in his voice, the dark timbre of which sends a thrill through my wine-laden body. 'No, seriously, I think we both need a breath of fresh air after the evening we've just suffered. It's a long time since I've been to one of those formal affairs and I'd forgotten how stultifying they can be.' I have to agree as I recall listening to a long diatribe on the education of girls from the ancient cleric seated across the table from me.

The car draws to a halt and we sit together in the silence before Marcus rouses himself and sighs.

'Looks beautiful in this light, doesn't it?'

I gaze out at the moonlight shimmering on the ocean and agree.

'We used to come down here a lot when I was younger,' I muse, remembering balmy summer evenings when Sean and I were courting, the secret times spent lying on the sands or entwined in the shallow waves. I shake my head. Those days are long gone. Maybe Sean is reliving them with Gina up there in Byron Bay, but it's not something I can bear thinking about.

Sensing my mood has changed, Marcus sits up.

'Let's take a stroll.'

Stroll? Who uses that term in this day and age? He's not the one who teaches English and is steeped in literary language. He takes my silence for assent and we both step out of the car to find a stiff breeze has sprung up.

'Wow, where did that come from?'

'There's always a breeze down here this time of year. Race you to the sea!' I take off my shoes and I'm off before Marcus has understood the challenge I've set. But he soon does, and I hear his feet thudding behind me. I'm like a child again as I run along the sand, the soft damp grains rising up behind me and hitting my calves. I feel carefree for the first time in weeks. I stop, turn my face up to the sky and stretch out my arms, oblivious of the man following me. The sea spray dampens my face and I taste the salt on my lips. It's as if I'm alone in the world.

*

Next morning it's a different story. I awaken to a headache of massive proportions and reach for some headache tablets before I swing my legs out of bed. I regret my liveliness of the previous night and hope I haven't made a fool of myself in front of my boss. I remember running barefoot along the beach and have vague recollections of strong arms supporting me, but the rest is a bit of a blur.

Once showered and dressed in shirt and jeans, I feel more human and, after a cup of my favourite hazelnut flavoured coffee, I decide I can face a slice of toast and marmalade for breakfast. The toast has just popped out when the phone rings. I check my watch and realise it's already half past nine, half past nine on the morning of Good Friday. Who can be calling me at this time? I pick up the phone gingerly.

'Hello?'

'Ah, you're awake then Anna. I wanted to check all was well with you this morning.' The voice is familiar, but it takes a few seconds for it to hit me.

'Marcus?' I can hear the surprise in my voice. *Did I really screw up last night?* 'Is everything all right? Thanks for last night by the way. It was kind of you to invite me.' Surely he'll say if anything untoward happened.

'The pleasure was all mine.' I hear a chuckle. 'Especially when you decided to go for a late night dip.'

'I didn't!' Shocked, I almost drop the phone.

'Not quite, but at one point you looked as if you were headed that way.'

'Oh, what must you think of me? I don't usually behave like that.' I bite my lip and pick the toast out of the toaster, wondering what else to say, and how quickly I can get him off the phone. 'Was there anything…'

'No, I'm sure you don't, but it was delightful to see another side of the controlled Mrs Hollis.' He pauses while I swallow hard. 'I just wanted to check all is well with you and to wish you a Happy Easter.'

'Thanks. You too.' I hang up the phone and proceed to spread my toast with butter and marmalade, but my headmaster is not far from my thoughts as I chew on my toast and drink my second cup of coffee. Breakfast over, I drop my dishes into the dishwasher, put him out of my mind and concentrate on what has to be done. First is a phone call to Jan to catch up with the parents' plans. I wait impatiently while her phone rings.

'Anna? I thought you were going away. Lissa said…'

Damn my family. I should have remembered telling something to one member tends to mean the grapevine goes to work.

'Haven't gone yet. There was the Passion Play last night then the Board dinner.'

'Mmm, Lissa did say you were going to the dinner. With the new Head, I hear. So what's he like, this new Headmaster of yours?'

I ponder then reply slowly. 'Think George Clooney,' I say. 'A bit younger, maybe a touch blonder, and with glasses.' I smile dreamily.

'But you've never been a fan!'

'I know.' I start to wipe the already spotless kitchen surface furiously. 'That's why I'm in no danger of falling under his spell.'

'But you have noticed him.'

'Impossible not to. He's standing there at assembly every morning, then there are the staff meetings and…'

'And you've had dinner with him, an actual date.' Her remark falls into a well of silence only broken by the sound of cutlery being slammed into the drawer as I multitask.

'Not a date as such. No.' I forbear to mention the episode on the beach, which I'm trying hard to forget.

I discern her unspoken questions and decide to ignore them.

'That's right. Well, I met Joan, you know, Mum's friend and she was talking about Mum and Dad's fiftieth. I've been so out of it these past few months. What have I missed? Anything I should be aware of?'

'You're spot on there. Glad to have you join the human race again.' Jan has never been one to mince words. She takes after Mum, whereas I've always felt closer to Dad. 'It was the big topic of conversation at Christmas. Where were you?'

'Not with it, obviously.' I don't try to hide my sharpness at her lack of tact. 'I had other things on my mind.'

Jan has the grace to apologise. 'Shit. I'm always putting my big foot in it. Anyway Mum has this idea of rekindling their romance by revisiting the scene of her and Dad's honeymoon. She wants the whole family to go for a long weekend, take a house, then go out for dinner on the day.'

'And where is this romantic location?'

'Didn't I say? North Stradbroke. It should be nice there at that time of year. It won't be too hot in August and it should be good to escape the Sydney winter for a few days.'

'True but… it's a bit isolated isn't it?' The thought of being stuck on an island with my family for four days doesn't thrill me, but I know there's no way I'm going to get out of it.

'It's only a short ferry ride from Brisbane and quite civilised, I assure you.' Jan sounds annoyed at my reaction. 'It's the least you can do. Just because your marriage is over…' She realises she may have said too much. 'Sorry, sis. I let my tongue run away with me again. But you really need to get over yourself.'

The mention of Brisbane has brought Marcus to mind again. I remember Heather saying he came from there, and wonder if he's off up north this morning. I picture him flying somewhere overhead as Jan and I are speaking. Automatically I look out of the kitchen window to the sky, where I can often see the planes flying north. Suddenly I realise Jan has been talking while I've been daydreaming, and that I've missed part of her conversation.

'What did you say?'

'Are you away with the fairies again? Anna, you need to take yourself in hand. Look, do you want to come over for lunch? It won't be much as we're off tonight for the rest of the weekend, but it would do you good, unless you're leaving early.'

I can just picture how Jan believes it would do me good to have her and Graham fuss over my future, and inquire into the ins and outs of my non-existent plans for the weekend.

'Thanks a heap but I've lots to do before I leave.' She accepts my excuses and, to my relief, ends the conversation with, 'Enjoy your weekend away. Put all this Sean and Gina business out of your mind and relax.'

Easier said than done, I think as I walk through the echoing house. What am I going to do with my weekend? It promises to be a fine day so I decide to spend it in the garden. Even though I may not be able to enjoy it for much longer, working there has always managed to relax me. I can tire myself out that way, then curl up with a good book. This is going to be my life from now on so I'd better get used to it.

Seven

'Is this all of it?' Bob looks up from examining the mess of paperwork in the folders I've handed him. It's taken me ages to put the material all together, and he's treating me like a naughty child.

'It's all I can find. What else should there be?'

'Maybe something about Sean's practice; his superannuation plan and so on.' Bob takes off his glasses and gives me a stern look. 'If I'm to do my best for you, I need to be apprised of all the facts.'

Oh dear. It's lawyer Bob talking and brother Bob has taken a back seat. I squirm in my chair.

'Sean may have picked it all up when he called round for his boxes of clothes. I know he spent some time in the office.' I say trying to be helpful.

'Mmm perhaps, or perhaps he kept it all in his workplace. Have you been in touch with Bill recently?'

'Bill? No, should I have been?' But there is no reply as Bob bends his head down again, and studies some of the documents. I twiddle my fingers and wonder what I'm doing here. Surely he can do this without my presence? But, just as I'm preparing to suggest I leave him to it and return another time, he looks up.

'You're right. You'll probably have to sell. The market's a bit depressed at the moment, but I've checked recent sales and the place should be worth around two million.' I gasp. We didn't pay anything like even one million for our home all these years ago. Well, that settles the matter. There's no way I can buy Sean out. It's not till now I realise the thought of doing exactly that has been lurking at the back of my mind.

'Somewhere smaller would be better, maybe an apartment now you're on your own. More secure, less upkeep and there would be other people around you.'

'I'm not decrepit,' I hurl back, unfairly taking my anger out on him, but the idea takes root. An apartment; somewhere overlooking the beach. I can see myself there, sitting in the twilight, sipping chilled white wine and watching the ocean. I float away on a cloud of fantasy as I picture the scene. I hear the waves pounding on the beach in the distance and feel the cool breeze on my face.

'Anna!' I realise I've been daydreaming while my officious brother is waiting for an answer.

'Yes,' I agree. 'Maybe looking out to the beach at Fairlight or Queenscliff?'

'Whew, you've got expensive taste, but you deserve it. We'll need to screw a decent settlement out of the bastard.'

'How expensive?' I enquire. I'm completely ignorant about real estate in the area. Well, I never thought I'd be moving, never intended to move. Seaforth is home, has been since we were first married.

'A lot!' Bob is tight-lipped. 'Look, leave everything to me. You should be able to get half of the house plus any savings, and half of Sean's super. I know he has a self-managed fund. I recommended he set one up when he and Bill went into partnership. What's happening with that, by the way? Sean has moved up to Byron Bay, you said. Is he selling out his share? You'd be entitled to half of his share of the business too.'

I'm hating all the talk of half of this and half of that. I just want it all to be over and done with.

'I don't know,' I reply, dragging my hand wearily through my hair. 'Should I call Bill or will you?'

'I will.' Bob rises, comes over and gives me a hug. 'It'll all be fine, you'll see. I'm going to take care of it all for you.'

I sigh with relief, not quite sure what 'all of it' is, but glad to drop it on someone else's shoulders.

'I can go now, then?'

'Sure. I'll get back to you when I've been in touch with Sean's lawyer.'

I leave and, since I'm close to Warringah Mall, I decide to browse around the shops and maybe stop in for a coffee. It's nice to be a lady of leisure. I'm flicking through a rail of winter clothes when my mobile rings. I don't recognise the number.

'Hello?'

'Anna?' I recognise the voice straight away, but can't imagine why Marcus King is ringing me in the holidays. It's still over a week till the staff meeting.

'Yes?' My voice holds a touch of reservation and not a little irritation to be reminded of work, just when I'm beginning to relax.

'It's such a lovely day. I thought… I wanted…' *Damn it, why does the man always seem to be so unsure of himself when he's talking to me? He's full of self-confidence at school.* He continues, 'Since we're both on our own, I wondered if you'd care to meet for lunch or something…' His voice tails off. I curse myself for having told him Sean and I have separated, but it slipped out after a few drinks at the dinner when he was confiding his own marital troubles.

'Oh, I don't know. I…'

He interrupts. 'I realise you're probably very busy, but I'm hoping you'll take pity on a stranger in town.' *Who is he kidding? He can't possibly be hard-up for company.* He continues, 'If lunch is out, maybe in the afternoon…?'

I'm a soft touch. Added to which he is the boss, and I can't afford to antagonise him. I need my job even more these days.

'Okay,' I hear myself saying. 'That will work.'

'Why don't we meet by the beach and take the hydrofoil into town?' he suggests, a smile in his voice, and I can envisage the amused look in his eyes as he remembers our two beach encounters.

'By the wharf,' I correct him.

'Two o'clock.' We hang up. What is it about this man that has me agreeing to things I really have no intention of doing? I shake my head in amazement and make my way into a nearby café for lunch.

*

I arrive at Manly wharf on the dot of two, and we run up the ramp in time to catch the hydrofoil.

'Made it!' I look up at a laughing Marcus. He looks different in the less formal setting; more like the person he was when I first saw him. His hair is tousled and hanging over the collar of his blue chambray shirt and, with his beige pants, he looks not unlike a younger version of David Attenborough. I begin to think this may not be such a bad idea.

The afternoon passes pleasantly as we take in the Sydney landmarks: the Opera House, Circular Quay, Lady Macquarie's Chair, the Rocks, ending up at the top of Australia Square around six o'clock. From this vantage point we look out on all of Sydney. I'm exhilarated. For the first time this year, I'm enjoying myself. Marcus really is good company and I find him easy to talk to.

'How about an early dinner? I understand there's a restaurant just below us.'

I realise I haven't eaten since lunch and then I only had a toasted sandwich, so I agree and allow myself to be led down in the elevator. Soon we're seated at a window table where Sydney is spread beneath us; a moving tableau as the restaurant takes its slow route around the building.

We've reached the dessert menu and have both decided to settle on cheese with coffee, when I catch Marcus looking bemused.

'Penny for them?' I offer.

'I was just thinking how Jon would love this.'

'Your son?' I ask, remembering his mention of Jonathon before Easter.

'Yes,' he sighs.

'Will he be visiting soon?' It seems like an obvious question to ask. He's told me he and his wife are divorced; that she has remained in California with Jonathon, so I assume he has some predetermined access arrangement, since I seem to recall the boy is ten years old.

'No.' The word comes out abruptly and, all of a sudden, my cheerful companion seems to close up. I say nothing and concentrate on cutting up my pieces of cheese and fitting them on to crackers. I sip my coffee, but there is still no comment from Marcus. I look across to see he is gazing into space, his eyes looking suspiciously misty.

'He's not my son.' I must look shocked as he immediately adds, 'At least that's what Lauren tells me.'

I find myself stretching out my hand to reach his over the table, but it doesn't quite make it before he lifts his cup and takes a long drink.

'Do you want to talk about it?' I ask cautiously.

'Why the hell not?' He puts down his cup and, taking off his glasses, rubs his eyes and, leaning his elbows on the table, begins his tale.

'Lauren and I met when I was a young lecturer in Brisbane. She was a journalist, was actually seeing one of my friends. Oh, I'm not proud of that.' He rubs his chin ruefully. 'But we had so much in common, or so it seemed. We met at a New Year's Eve party.' He looks up to the left reflectively and smiles in reminiscence. 'We were married the same year and had lots of plans to travel.'

'And did you?' I feel some input is required of me.

'We did. We agreed to put kids on hold, while we both built our careers and we had the most wonderful holidays. Lauren managed to get some travel assignments which meant we had free trips with fantastic accommodation.'

'Wow!' I'm not sure why this makes me a touch jealous. Sean and I have had several good trips over the years, but ones we had to save madly for.

'Yes,' he nods. 'We had a good life. Then I decided to do my doctorate, and all the advice I was given led to my applying to universities in the States.'

'Why so? Surely there are plenty of good places in Australia, if not in Brisbane itself?'

'Of course there are.' Marcus pushes back that errant lock of hair which likes to flop over his forehead. 'But everyone has a local PhD. Getting one from an overseas Uni, particularly one in the US gives a lot more cred.'

I nod as if I understand.

'We headed off to California in the winter of 2001. We wanted to do some sightseeing and get settled in before the University year started. Lauren didn't like the idea of giving up her job in Brisbane, but we were young, ambitious and sure she'd find something over there, once we'd sorted out the issue of a green card.'

'And did she?'

'Well, it wasn't as easy as she thought. She seemed pretty discontented for a time. I guess she felt lonely.' He rubs his chin and replaces his glasses. 'It was fine when we were travelling around, sightseeing and setting up house. But when semester started and I got stuck into my study, I guess it wasn't so much fun for her. She was trying to make connections, build networks, set up meetings, make friends. It was hard for her.' He sighs. 'Then we found out she was pregnant. That wasn't part of the plan.'

'So Jon… Jonathon was born in California?'

'Yes. On the fourth of July. Can you credit it? He's a true dinky-di American.'

'And…?'

'And I was besotted, right from the start. But it wasn't so easy for Lauren. She suffered badly from postnatal depression. She felt the distance from home keenly and missed her family and friends, who would normally have been around to help. There was just me!'

I begin to stretch out my hand again, then pull it back. I don't want to give him the wrong impression, but I sympathise for him alone, with his depressed wife and a newborn baby, in a strange country.

'Oh the guys at uni were great. There were other young married graduate students. Did I say we lived in student housing? A bit basic and noisy, but quite sufficient for our needs. She gradually came out of it. I was able do a lot of work at home, so I could spend time with Jon every day. He's a great kid!'

I smile at the obvious affection in his voice, and wonder how and when everything went wrong.

Marcus takes a few moments to sip his coffee and place a piece of blue cheese on top of a cracker.

'Where was I? Yes. Well, things improved a bit, and Lauren started helping out in the alumnae office, writing pieces for the magazine and stuff, pretty mild compared to what she'd been doing back home, but it took her out of herself and she got back to normal, or pretty close to it. Then, when the doctorate was done, I was offered a position on Faculty. It was a huge thing for me, an unhoped for opportunity. It gave me the chance to work with some of the big names; guys whose work I'd only read. I accepted it. We moved off campus. Lauren seemed happy too. They were good years. Jon was growing up and becoming a real boy. We managed a trip back to see the folks, but the uni scene in Australia wasn't looking good so we decided to give the States a bit longer. Then, just as it became time for Jon to start school, another position came up. I made some contacts at a conference and heard about this slot going in Portland, Oregon. It was a five year contract, a lot more promising than the one year ones I'd been getting there in LA, so I jumped at it.'

'Oregon, that's further north isn't it?' My grasp of US states is shaky, but I'm pretty sure I'm correct on this one.

'Right on. Not too much farther north, just far enough to be quite a bit cooler. It's not a bad place, in fact I rather liked it, but then, I was caught up in the university crowd. Lauren wasn't.' He bites his lip. 'That's when things started to go wrong. Jon was at school all day. I was at University, and Lauren was stuck at home. She found it more difficult to come by work up there and… well, she spent a lot of time on the Internet. She got back in touch with someone we'd known back in LA, one of my colleagues at University.' Marcus' face took on a grim look. 'He'd been married back then but his wife had left him. Seems Lauren and he started to correspond by email plus daytime calls, I expect. Anyway the fallout was, we'd only been in Oregon a few years when she decided to leave me and join him back in LA. Get a quickie US divorce.'

'But your son, Jonathon?'

'She insisted on taking him with her. I remonstrated of course and that's when she told me he wasn't my son,' he said bitterly.

I'm stunned. How can anyone be so cruel to a partner; someone they've loved?

'Did you…?' I venture.

'DNA? No, no point. She told me the father was my old mate down in LA. The dates worked. I'd been at a conference in Washington and, when I thought about it, the kid looks a bit like him. No, I left… and I ended up here in Sydney. Didn't want to show my face in Brisbane till I'd sorted myself out a bit.' He pauses to let it all sink in.

'So now you know,' he says, drawing lines in the tablecloth with the edge of his knife. 'The whole sordid story. It's the betrayal I can't stand,' he adds.

'The betrayal of trust,' I agree, then sit silently, unwilling to break the mood and wondering what on earth I can say. I can't believe he's sharing such personal things with me, a relative stranger. I'm so saddened for him and amazed at the depth of his trust in me. It's taken me right out of my own misery to see him sitting there in despair at having lost the son for whom he cares deeply. I don't know what to do.

Fortunately I'm spared by the arrival of the waiter.

'Everything all right, sir, madam?' The man hovers over us awaiting a response. Marcus seems to shake out of his trance.

'Yes, fine. Thank you.' He looks over at me. 'I guess we should go.'

I agree and pick up my things, while Marcus takes care of the bill. We leave without speaking. He lays his hand on the small of my back as we make our way to the elevator. Even when it's gone, I can feel the imprint of warm pressure through my cotton top as we return to the street.

Eight

My mobile rings as I dash to an after school staff meeting. A quick glance shows me the caller is Gina and I press *Decline*. I haven't spoken to her for close on four months now, not since I found out. I don't know why she keeps on calling though Lissa says she wants to apologise. Apologise! How can any apology absolve her from such a betrayal?

I slip into my seat just as Marcus opens the meeting, and earn a brief look of reproof.

'In the bad books!' whispers my neighbour, Kim, who is a stickler for protocol and heads up the Mathematics team.

'Have I missed anything?' I whisper back.

'If you two ladies have finished?' Standing at the front of the large classroom in his workaday blue suit, crisp white shirt and old school tie, Marcus makes an imposing figure whereas we, the senior staff, are squashed in seats behind student desks. I blush, embarrassed to be singled out, while Kim kicks me under the desk. I feel like I'm a teenager again.

The meeting progresses as always with the usual boring departmental reports, one of which I contribute myself. It's been a long day, and my eyes are drooping when I realise Marcus has mentioned my name and the entire room is awaiting my response.

'I'm sorry,' I say, my cheeks warming, embarrassed for the second time this afternoon. 'Could you please repeat that?'

'Daydreaming, Mrs Hollis?' Marcus' caustic remark is uncalled for. He knows I'm usually on top of things, but all the wrangling over the divorce settlement with Sean has got to me. It's been almost four months now and we seem to be no closer to an agreement. I must ring Bob again tonight I decide, as Marcus slowly repeats himself.

'We were discussing the Year Twelve ski trip. I understand you were a leading light last year. Can we count on your help again?'

'Oh, I don't think so!' The words are out before I can stop them. The very thought of taking part in this year's trip is anathema to me after what happened when I was away last year. I quickly take steps to ameliorate my bald statement. 'I think it should fall to someone else this year. I've had my turn.' I look around for support. No one meets my eye, everyone studiously looking in the other direction. Finally Glenda steps in.

'I don't mind,' she says. 'As long as Anna will clue me up.'

'No problem.' I sit back, relieved to have been spared.

'I understand the arrangements are all made and New Zealand is out this year. We're going local. Isn't that so?' Marcus looks across at the Head of PE who is quick to respond. Fay is a birdlike woman, whose fragile appearance hides an amazingly strong and well-toned body.

'Right on. Falls Creek, here we come. And we're going to need all the help we can get. Will you be coming yourself, Headmaster?'

'Umm,' Marcus demurs. 'I'll get back to you. It certainly sounds an attractive proposition - sharing the ski slopes with a bevy of beauties.' A titter echoes around the room. He hasn't lost his touch. Familiarity hasn't bred contempt as far as he is concerned. He's still the darling of the staffroom.

As we're leaving the meeting Marcus calls out, 'Mrs Hollis, Anna, a word.' I hang back reluctantly. I'm eager to get home, call Bob and put my feet up, maybe with a soothing glass of red wine.

I stand at the front of the room, clutching my folder of notes for the end of term reports, which I plan to complete this weekend, and hope Marcus will not take long. He farewells other staff members and waits till everyone else has left, then, gesturing to a chair, invites me to take a seat.

'I can't stay long,' I quibble, sitting down nevertheless, and place my folder on the floor at my feet. I catch sight of his approving eyes on my ankles and tuck them under the chair, regretting that today I have, unusually for me, worn a skirt. Despite being strangely drawn to the man, I'm not ready for any emotional entanglements at this stage. 'What is it you want?'

'Well, now.' His voice holds a playful note. 'That leaves it wide open don't you think?'

'I mean, what can I do for you?' Hell, that sounds even worse if double entendres are the order of the day.

'I wondered if you have some time this weekend?' He raises his eyebrows and gives me a quizzical look. Although we've seen each other a couple of times outside school since Easter, it's always been on school matters and his question flusters me. This business with Sean has been taking a lot of my energy, and the last thing I need in my life is another man, especially one like Marcus. I don't stop to consider why he has such an effect on me. I fold my arms tightly around my body as if to protect myself from the advance he is not making.

Instead of offering an immediate refusal. 'What had you in mind?' I ask tentatively.

'I've had a letter from my… from Jon.' He removes, then replaces, his glasses and drags his fingers through his hair destroying the immaculate image of the Headmaster. 'I need to talk it over with someone and I thought…' He gives me his little boy lost look again. 'I know it's an imposition but I'd really appreciate it.'

I think of all the things I've planned for the weekend, none of which is really important. As long as I can finish my reports.

'How about Sunday afternoon?' I ask after a long pause. 'Come round to my place. We won't be disturbed, and I'll make you some of my famous hot chocolate.'

'It's a date!' he says then, as if realising the implications adds, 'I mean…'

'I know what you mean. It's in your diary. I'm with you.'

We walk out to the car park together.

'Well, till Sunday.' He looks as if he is about to say more then, with a fleeting touch of his hand on my shoulder, turns on his heel and leaves.

'Till Sunday,' I repeat to his retreating back with a sense of disappointment. I give myself a mental shake and open my car door.

*

It's good to get home and, dinner over, I make the promised call to my brother. I don't welcome his news.

'It's going to take some time yet, Anna. Sean is being bloody obdurate and I can't seem to get through to his lawyer.'

'What do you mean?' I ask wearily, sipping my second glass of wine for the evening.

'I want to arrange a settlement which will give you enough to buy something in Fairlight. The sort of apartment you deserve, after putting up with that rat for so long and then being treated like shit.' Bob rants on, and I half listen and continue to drink my wine. I just want to know when everything will be settled and I can get on with my life.

I'm brought back to full attention when I hear the words 'another six months'.

'You mean it could go on for so long?' I put my wine down so suddenly the red liquid splashes onto my cream rug. 'Shit! No, I'm not talking to you, Bob. I just spilt some wine. But did you really say this could drag on till nearly Christmas?'

'I'm looking at the worst case scenario. Trying to get information on Sean's finances is like trying to get blood out of a stone. Then his side want similar information about yours.'

'Well, that's easy. I don't have any. This house is putting me further and further in debt by the day. Is Sean working up there?' I ask, curious as to what he and Gina are up to.

'Well, from what I can gather, Gina has started up another yoga school. It's doing quite well actually. And Sean, he seems to be doing her books and offering a similar service to some other small businesses. But I've been talking to Lissa and she seems to think her dad is doing some sort of teaching too.'

'Teaching? I can't imagine Sean doing that. He doesn't have the right training for teaching.'

'Anyway, the bottom line is that matters are not going to be settled in a hurry. So you'll have to be patient.'

I hang up the phone with a frown. Patience is not my strong suite. I've been trying to avoid thinking of the pair up there in Byron Bay, but it now seems that the man with Gina is not the Sean I knew and loved. He's changed. I finish my wine thoughtfully and press Lissa's number.

'Mum! What's up?'

'Did I catch you at a bad time?'

'No, we're vegging out with an Indian takeaway and some red wine. Will's had a heavy week so we decided to stay in.'

I picture the two of them, cuddled up on the sofa in Lissa's house, and anticipate it won't be long before they break the news they're moving in together.

'A quick question, darling. I was talking to Uncle Bob… about Dad.' I hesitate knowing that, despite her affection for me, she can be touchy about her dad. 'He seems to remember your mentioning something about his doing some teaching. Did you, or is Bob mistaken?' I wait for her reply, fiddling with the collar of my shirt.

'Dad? Teaching? Yes, I think he did say that. It's at TAFE or some private college. I think he had to do one of these certificate things first. Is there anything else?' I can tell she's anxious to get back to whatever I've interrupted.

'No, that's all, honey. Thanks. Talk again soon.'

So, I conjecture, Sean is teaching a Certificate IV course in Accounting. He certainly is a changed man. He's always derided these qualifications saying if a person isn't bright enough to get a degree, he has no business pretending to understand finance. Well, times change and people change with them. Clearly Gina has had some sort of influence. Whether for good or bad remains to be seen, but I won't see it. At least he hasn't turned his back on Lissa. And she seems okay with his new persona.

*

Sunday afternoon comes round all too soon. I've made an effort, cleaning the house thoroughly and ensuring there are fresh flowers around. I prepare a plate of *biscotti* to serve with the promised hot chocolate. Why am I going to so much trouble? It's only a work colleague. He's only coming around to talk things through. Nothing to fuss about. But I still want to make a good impression, though I'm not sure why. I suppress my doubts by trying to believe I'd do this for anyone, but I know it's not strictly true. I wouldn't go to all this trouble for Glenda, would I? I decide not to answer and to stop having this pointless conversation with myself.

The doorbell rings. He's here! I take a quick peek in the hall mirror as I pass through and pat my already immaculate hair. I've become accustomed to the new short style and wonder why I kept my hair long for so many years to please Sean. Now I can please myself. I smooth down the pink and grey tunic top I've chosen to wear with wide-legged black pants. No chance of ankles being on display today. I open the door to be greeted by a pot of vivid pink cyclamen.

'How did you know?' I exclaim. 'It's my favourite!'

'Matches you too,' Marcus points to my outfit. 'Good choice.' He looks pleased with himself.

I busy myself finding a spot for the plant on the coffee table, while he makes himself comfortable on the sofa.

'I'll just fix the hot chocolate I promised you.' I need some time out to collect myself.

'Do you want any help?' Marcus starts to rise.

'No! You stay there.' I slip out and put both hands up to my face in an attempt to cool it down. Perhaps inviting him here hasn't been such a good idea after all. Somewhere neutral might have been better. Well, too late now. I fix the chocolate, pick up the tray and return to find Marcus examining the family photos on the piano. Today he's wearing a pair of well pressed jeans with an open-necked pale blue shirt. A dark blue sweater is tied around his shoulders. Very casual and very fetching. He immediately moves across and takes the tray from me.

'Is this where you want it?' He places the tray carefully on the coffee table. 'That your daughter?' He nods in the direction of Lissa's graduation photo. 'She has a look of you.'

'Thanks. She actually resembles her father more than me.' There's an awkward silence. 'Have some *biscotti*.' I pass him the plate to change the subject. 'And help yourself to the chocolate.' I nod to the mug. 'Now, what was it you wanted to discuss? You said you'd heard from Jonathon?'

'Yes.' He's sitting down again by now, and I sit in the armchair across from him. He reaches into his pocket and draws out a folded sheet of paper. 'This arrived in the mail at the beginning of last week. I've been carrying it around since.' He pushes back his hair. 'I've read and re-read it, I don't know how many times. Lauren hasn't told him. Heck, what can I do? I love the kid. It's not his fault he's caught in the middle of all this mess. I'm the only dad he's known. Even though Rick's his natural father, they haven't told Jon.' He passes me the letter.

'Are you sure?' I take the piece of paper from him with my fingertips, uncertain if he really wants me to read it.

'Go on!' He leans his elbows on his knees and covers his face with his hands as I carefully open out the paper and read it silently.

Dear Dad,

Mom doesn't know I'm writing you. She said not to. But I miss you. Mom says your busy and since your divorsed you donet want to see me. It's quiet fun here in LA and schools good. Henrys my new friend. He has playstation and sum good games. We go swimming a lot and I want to get a puppy like Henrys but mom says there too much work and Rick dosent liek dogs. Mom says I'm to call him Dad but yore my Dad so I can't. Pleese can I come and visit you? I no your in a place called Sydney. I looked it up on the map and it's a long way away. I guess that's why your not writing me. I found your address in moms drawer and Henrys big sister is going to mail this for me. Pleese, pleese write me dad. I miss you a heap.

Love Jon xx

My eyes mist up as I read the childish words. I look across at Marcus, but his head is bowed, his face still buried in his hands. I place the letter down on the coffee table.

'It's a lovely letter,' I say, lost for words. What can I say to this man, who's being denied access to his most precious possession? He looks up.

'Isn't it? What in God's name am I to do?'

'Why don't you tell me a little bit about Jon?' I say gently, picking up my mug of chocolate.

'He's just a regular kid,' Marcus begins, picking up the letter, folding it lovingly and returning it to his pocket which he then pats. 'Loves sport, computers, animals. Not so great on reading and writing. You probably noticed the spelling, or lack of it. We were working on that.' He takes his glasses off, cleans them and pushes his hair back.

'He was just getting to the stage when we could do things together, you know, go to the ball game, hang out, make baskets together.'

This is all gobbledygook to me, but I do recognise American sport is a bit different to what I'm used to. Marcus continues, 'We were going to go rowing this summer. I planned to teach him. We...' His voice breaks and he rubs his fingers over his eyes.

'Rowing? You row?' I don't know why this surprises me given his lean build and broad shoulders. He perks up.

'First eight at Brisbane Grammar, then the University eight. Jon would be good too.' He sighs and replaces his glasses. For a moment, I forget about the boy we're discussing and recognise the man sitting opposite me would have a lot in common with my brother, more than Sean ever had. They must even be the same age. This gives me an unexpected glow. I've been thinking of Marcus as years younger than me and definitely off limits. But four years isn't so bad. I give myself a shake. What on earth am I thinking?

'I'm sure he was looking forward to that,' I say. 'But what are you going to do? Are you going to reply? Will his mother...?'

'I don't know.' Marcus leans forward, hands clasped. 'I want to, God knows I do. But Lauren will go spare if she learns I've been in touch, and she may take it out on Jon. Is it fair for me to do that to him?'

I consider his options and begin to speak slowly, thinking aloud.

'Well, seems to me you can do nothing, which leaves Jon wondering if you've received his letter and may encourage him to do something stupid. You can reply and risk Lauren's wrath falling on Jon, or...' I look across at him, unsure how he's going to take this, but continue regardless, 'or you can go over to see for yourself. But that could cause more trouble.'

Marcus seizes on my suggestion like a drowning man.

'Go there? Really? Do you think I should?'

'Well, it's either that or the school ski trip,' I say in an attempt to lighten the atmosphere.

'Hah! It's not so simple.' He rubs his chin.

'Look, drink your chocolate. It's getting cold'

He obeys automatically, then speaks in a low voice. 'I like the idea, but I can't just turn up at the door. Lauren wouldn't let me near Jon, for one thing. She'd probably call the cops,' he says ruefully. 'I need a good reason to be there.' He looks around the room as if seeking an answer hiding somewhere among the furniture.

'Let's think, then. What could be a good reason for being there? We're probably looking at July.' I'm amazed at how my mind is grappling with this. I really want to help Marcus come up with a solution. 'What's happening in California that you could be going to? Something which would give you the opportunity to call Lauren and suggest you drop by? Some sort of event?'

'Event?' Marcus looks at me as if I'm mad, then something seems to occur to him. He opens his mouth to speak when my phone rings.

'Damn!' I look at the caller. Gina! Again! I decline to answer.

'Don't you want to get that?'

'No, it's my former best friend, the one who's now with my ex. She keeps calling, though this is a bit soon after the last one. She only called the other day. Her usual pattern is about once every two weeks. She can't seem to get it into her head I don't want to talk to her. Ever again. Now, you were about to say?'

'I just remembered a flier I received about a conference, not in LA; it's in Vegas, but close enough.'

'What sort of conference?'

'It's about online learning.' Marcus' voice becomes eager. 'You remember. What we've been talking about at some of the staff meetings. I didn't consider actually attending but it could be a way to…'

'Kill two birds with one stone, as it were?' I suggest.

'Right!' He leans back into the sofa.

'Another hot chocolate?'

'That'd be great. This one's a bit cold like you said.' He helps himself to *biscotti*. 'Gosh these are good. Do you make them yourself?'

'No fear.' I pick up both mugs and go to the kitchen where I make fresh drinks. When I return, I can see Marcus is looking a lot more relaxed.

'I'll check out the flier as soon as I get back,' he says. 'Great idea of yours. I wonder if I can get Jon set up on an email account when I'm over. Then we could communicate regularly. He may even have a laptop or an iPad. Hey, I could get him one for his birthday… Sorry, I'm getting carried away. Lauren may put the kybosh on all of this. She doesn't want me to see Jon, or communicate with him. She indicated as much when she left. But it's something to go on.' He gulps down the hot beverage, leaving a rim of chocolate around his mouth. I want to reach over and wipe it off, but I restrain myself. 'I owe you for this. How about dinner? I need to be off now. Want to check on the conference and see what I can book. It's going to be pretty short notice. Maybe later in the week?' He stands up just as my phone rings again.

I take a quick glance and give Marcus an apologetic look. 'It's Lissa. I'll have to take it but I'll call her back.'

'Hi, honey. Look, can I ring you back I've someone…' I begin only to be interrupted by Lissa's tearful voice.

'Mum, I've just heard from Gina. She's been trying to reach you. It's Dad. He's dead!'

Nine

'What?' I gasp and sink into a chair. 'When? How?' I hear a commotion at the other end, then Will's voice comes on the line.

'Hi Anna. Lissa's pretty upset. She had this call from Gina. Seems Sean's had a heart attack. It was very sudden. Gina's beside herself. We're going up there. There's no one else,' he adds almost apologetically. 'We'll keep you in the loop, shall we?' This last asked tentatively.

'Yee…s,' I answer, not really sure if I want to be kept in this loop. I can't take it in. I put down the phone and Marcus, seeming to sense something is wrong, drops down to one knee on the floor in front of me.

'What's the matter? Bad news?'

'It's Sean. He's…' I can't seem to say the word.

'Has there been an accident?' Marcus takes my hands in his.

'He's had a heart attack,' I manage to get out.

'No!' Marcus moves closer and suddenly I'm aware of his arms around me and my face being pressed to his firm body. I lean into his shoulder and feel the pressure of his lips on my hair. It's a comforting sensation, safe, with just a hint of something more. Through my distress, I'm conscious of the smooth texture of his shirt against my face. 'How bad is it?'

I find my words. 'He's gone. Sean is gone.' It finally sinks in and I burst into tears. Sean may have behaved like a bastard, but he's been my husband for twenty-five years, the father of my daughter, and I still have *some* feelings for him. I can't believe his life has been snuffed out, just like that.

Marcus continues to hold me and pats my back ineffectually. We remain like this for a time then, as my tears begin to slow, he takes me by the shoulders and eases me back.

'Better now?' he asks. 'Where do you keep the brandy?'

'Oh, I don't think…' I start to object.

'You've had a shock. You're going to need something. Is there anyone I can call for you?'

'I don't know. Jan… Bob… maybe Mum and Dad. I'll do it myself in a bit.' I struggle to sit upright and sip the brandy he's managed to find and pour for me. He stands awkwardly in front of me. We're both slightly embarrassed about the embrace.

'I'd better be off…. If you're sure you'll be all right?'

'I'll be fine.' I struggle up. We stand awkwardly in silence for a few moments, while I gather my thoughts and he slides his hands up and down his thighs as if unsure what to do next. 'I'll see you out.'

'I meant it. About dinner, I mean. I'll see you at work and we can arrange something.' He looks at me as if I'm sick, and I realise the colour has probably gone from my face. He's may be worried I'm going to keel over on him.

'I'll be fine,' I repeat. 'And yes, dinner. We'll talk.' I want him to go. I want to be left alone to digest the awful fact of Sean's death, before I need to tell everyone about it.

He gives me a final squeeze of the shoulder. 'Soon then,' he says, and I nod as he turns and walks away

I pick up the two empty mugs and carry them into the kitchen. I open the dishwasher, close it again, turn on the tap to rinse the mugs, then turn it off. I look around the kitchen, amazed it still looks the same. Nothing has changed. Sean is dead and the house is still in its pristine Sunday best. Everything is quiet. I'm tempted to throw something and eye the mugs, but common sense prevails. I know I should call Mum or Jan or even Bob, but I can't do that just yet.

I struggle upstairs and fall on the bed, the one I shared with Sean. I give way to tears again, clutching a pillow to me. When I finally stop, I go into the ensuite. I turn on the tap and examine my face in the mirror. Puffy red eyes stare back at me. It's turning dark outside. I undress and get into bed properly, hoping for the oblivion of sleep. I toss and turn, everything going round in circles in my mind. Sean is dead. He's barely reached his fiftieth birthday, but he won't see another one. It takes some getting used to. Finally I rise and go to the bathroom cabinet. Somewhere, I know, are some sleeping tablets leftover from God knows when. I find them, toss down a couple with a glass of water and curl up again.

*

I'm awakened by the ringing of the phone, surprised that I've slept right through the night. It's six o'clock.

'Darling, how are you? Why didn't you call? We've just heard the news from Lissa.'

I try to pull myself awake. 'I… last night I didn't feel like talking. I took a sleeping tablet and…'

She interrupts me. 'So you slept? Good. Would you like Dad and me to come over?'

I sit up. 'No, don't do that. It's a school day. I need to go to work.'

'Not today. Surely they'd understand. Mr … what's his name? Your new Headmaster?'

'Marcus King. And yes, he would. But I'll be better off in my usual routine.'

No sense in my telling Mum Marcus is already well aware of the news. It would just start her thinking along lines which I don't want to pursue.

'Well, Dad and I'll come round tonight. I'll bring dinner so you don't need to worry about making a meal. How does five o'clock sound?'

I agree wearily. There's no arguing with Mum when she's in rescuer mode. It might even be good to be mothered a bit after the sort of day I'm likely to have. I slide down the bed again tempted to go back to sleep, but my system has checked in and I'm in my morning routine before I know it. As I shower I reconcile myself to Mum's arrival this evening. *She may not exactly welcome disasters or encourage them, but she does thrive on them and, in her mind, this will be a disaster of major proportions. Her favourite son-in-law has not only abandoned her daughter, but has had the bad grace to die. Thank goodness Dad will be with her. He'll protect me from her worst ministrations.*

I arrive at school as assembly is about to commence, earning a worried look from Marcus who is standing at the dais. As I slip in I hear a whisper from Glenda.

'Didn't expect to see you today.' I glare at her. Surely Marcus hasn't spread my private business all through the school. 'Heard you were sick.'

'Better now,' I whisper back, turning to focus on the weekly report which Marcus is reading in the deep accented voice so unique to him; an American twang overlaying his basic educated Australian tones.

*

The front door opens and Mum breezes in with a gust of fresh air. Dad, following behind, is carrying a dish covered by a tea towel. I'm engulfed in a warm hug. As the tears threaten to come to the fore again, I brush them aside.

'Hey, Mum, Dad, thanks for coming.'

'Couldn't keep her away,' Dad mutters under his breath, then in a louder voice asks. 'Where will I put this?' He lifts the tea towel to reveal Mum's favourite comfort dish. She's not a crash-hot cook, but she does do a great lasagne. It always appears at times of stress: after exams, when Jan or I were dumped by a boyfriend, when Bob failed to make the first fifteen in rugby, now, when my husband has died. I manage a weak smile.

'Just put it in the kitchen, Dad. I thought we'd eat there.'

'Righto.' Dad is glad to have something to do, while Mum fusses around me like a mother hen.

Finally we're all sitting at the table. I can no longer evade the conversation which I know is to come.

'And will you be calling Gina?' Mum asks, as she forks up her meal.

This is not what I expected. 'Gina?' I ask stupefied. 'Why on earth would I want to do that?' I glare across the table.

'Your mother only means…' begins Dad.

'I can say what I mean, myself.' Mum rears up and points at me with her fork. 'It's no use looking at me like that. It's in times like this you need friends around you, and who's been a better friend to you for all these years but Gina. I know I didn't always approve of her.' She pauses.

That's putting it mildly. When Gina came back from India with her hippie clothes, incense, and talk of meditation and yoga, Mum acted as if she was the Devil incarnate. She continues, 'But now you have something in common.' She takes a mouthful and chews it carefully. 'You're both grieving for the same man.'

Dad chokes quietly. This is rich, even coming from Mum.

'I don't think so.' I know this isn't going to satisfy her, so I add, 'We knew different men, or different versions of the same man. Sean had changed. Gina and I have nothing in common these days. Nothing at all. Not anymore. So, no I won't be getting in touch.' I can't make it any clearer.

We continue to eat in silence, then Dad decides to put his oar in.

'What'll you do now?' he asks. 'I mean, Sean's death changes things, doesn't it.'

'Well it means I'm a widow,' I state bluntly, the word sounding strange on my tongue. 'But I can't see what else is different.' I sigh. 'I'm still on my own with this house I can't afford.'

'Maybe Bob...'

'I'll talk to Bob tomorrow. He won't have to worry about the divorce now.' I continue eating, hoping the conversation is at an end.

I'm glad when Mum and Dad finally leave. It's good of them to have come, but their presence has been a strain. I can cope best when I'm left to myself. I take another of the sleeping pills and fall into a second night of dreamless sleep.

*

Thursday evening, Marcus greets me with a kiss on the cheek and I put my hand up to the spot. It appears there's been a shift in our friendship, as a result of the moments and confidences we shared on Sunday. We've moved into being more than just two colleagues offering support to each other in a family crisis. I'm not sure about moving so quickly. Marcus seems to sense this as he immediately asks,

'How are you coping? It must be difficult...' He notes my reticence.

'How about pizza?'

'Sounds good.' Hopefully we can get through the evening without him pussyfooting around me. It's been one of those weeks. Somehow most of the staff has found out about Sean's death, their reactions ranging from cloying sympathy to embarrassed avoidance. The holidays start tomorrow. They can't come soon enough.

We step into a small pizzeria, redolent with the aroma of tomato and garlic.

'Is this new? I haven't seen it before.'

'Opened last week,' Marcus observes, as he guides me to a corner booth. 'I think you'll like it.' I sit helplessly as he takes charge, ordering red wine and pizzas to share, without any input from me. My eyes drop to take in the black and white mosaic of floor tiles spotless from the recent application of a mop. For once I don't object to this high-handed behaviour. It prevents me thinking and that's good. There's an awkward silence, then we both begin to speak at once.

'Holidays tomorrow…'

'Did you manage…?'

We laugh, and the ice is broken.

'The holidays start tomorrow and I'm off to the conference. The one in Vegas.'

'Oh, you're going ahead with the trip, then?' I'm glad to have the focus taken off me for a change. 'Have you been in touch with your ex, Lauren isn't it?'

'Lauren, yes and no, I haven't been in touch. I'll call her when I get over there. No sense in giving her any more warning than I need to.'

By this time our pizzas have been served. I bite into a piece hungrily.

'Wow, this is good.' I wipe my mouth with a serviette, take a sip of wine then look across at my companion. 'This is the first food I've enjoyed all week. Everything's tasted like sawdust. So,' I continue with the previous conversation, 'do you think Lauren will agree to you seeing Jonathon?' I glance over at Marcus, who is taking a large bite of pizza.

He chews on it silently, then replies, 'I can't say. She was pretty shook up last time we spoke, but I'm relying on the element of surprise and the fact she and Rick have been together for almost a year now. With a bit of luck, some of her anger might have dissipated. Fingers crossed, eh?'

I smile at his optimism, hoping it's justified.

'I hope for your sake you're right. And for Jonathon's sake too. The poor little boy. How long will you be there?'

'Two weeks in all. I know it's not long, not long enough.' Marcus pushes back that errant lock of hair, and nudges his glasses up his nose with his forefinger. 'But the conference only lasts three days, so I'll have plenty of time left to see Jon before I need to return for start of term.'

'Time to do a bit of re-bonding?'

'Maybe. I don't know exactly what Lauren has told him about me. The kid's clearly dying to see me, but the reality mightn't live up to his expectations.' Marcus leans across the table towards me. 'What if… Oh, hell, you've got enough troubles of your own, and here am I saddling you with mine.'

'It's actually a relief,' I tell him. 'I'm tired of being ignored or treated with kid gloves. It's a relief to be faced with someone else's worries.' And I realise it's true. This is the first time all week I've been taken out of myself, when I've been forced to think of someone else besides myself. It's a sweet breath of fresh air.

'So tell me about the conference,' I encourage him.

Marcus raises his eyebrows and nods to the last piece of pizza. I shake my head. He picks it up, takes a bite and chews it reflectively then wipes his hands and begins to speak.

'It actually sounds pretty good. Should give me some ideas for how we can move ahead with the online stuff. It's about time we dragged the school further into the technology age. Oh,' he recollects, seeing my amused expression, 'not that the school is stuck in the dark ages, far from it but…'

'It's okay,' I reassure him. 'There were plans to do more, particularly with the slower maths classes, but when Heather was there, everything else seemed to be more of a priority. Everything moves so fast. And the only one pushing it was Rhonda.' I mention the ICT specialist with some reservation as I'm aware she and Marcus have had some run-ins. 'She…' I begin, but Marcus interrupts me before I can say more.

'Yes. I probably haven't been completely fair to her. She has some good ideas, but is a bit behind in her thinking. I might send her on a course to update her on current views. What do you think? She's a friend of yours, isn't she? Would she like to go? It's about time all the students had laptops too. I've been meaning to talk with the board about that. Yes,' he metaphorically rubbed his hands together. 'This conference has popped up at just the right time.'

I forbear to mention he has only decided to attend in order to see Jonathon, but he's fully aware of the direction of my thoughts as he immediately adds.

'I know I didn't intend to go in the first place, but I'm going now, and I can see I should have been going all along. Enough about me.' He fills up our wineglasses. 'How're you doing? Do you have any plans for the holiday? Will you be spending time with your daughter?'

'Well, I don't know. She and her fellow went up to Byron Bay when Sean… and I haven't heard… As far as I know she's still up there.'

There must be something in my tone of voice because Marcus counters with, 'And it bothers you?'

'Yes,' I say sharply. Admitting it aloud makes me realise that, yes, it is bothering me. I want my daughter down here, with me, sharing my grief. She's the one person who can understand exactly how I feel. And yes, it bothers me more than a little that she's spending her time in Byron with Gina, my nemesis.

'I expect she'll be back soon.' Marcus tries to reassure me, but thinking of Lissa and Gina together has spoilt my mood.

'I'm ready to go now.' I begin to gather myself together, preparatory to leaving. Marcus picks up the bill and settles it while I slide out from behind the table. By the time I reach the door, he's there to hold it open for me.

As we walk slowly to his car, I realise the holiday does stretch in front of me. Two empty weeks in which I'll be devoid of routine. I must make plans, plans are my lifesaver. I have a meeting with my brother on Monday. Hopefully that will provide me with some direction. Then, maybe I can bring myself to start packing up the house. Somehow, now Sean has really gone, the house and its memories have become less important to me.

I bid Marcus a distracted farewell, accepting his warm hug without comment or response and I'm conscious of him staring after me as I turn for home.

Ten

'I heard the news. This may change things.' Bob taps on his desk with a pencil as he speaks.

'Mum told you, then.'

'Can't keep a secret in our family.' He clears his throat. 'I suppose you'll be going up there, to Byron I mean.'

'I will not. What is it about this family? First Mum, now you. I have no intention of setting foot in that place, where he and Gina…'

'Okay, keep your hair on. I just thought, you know, you'd want to say goodbye.' He looks across at me, eyebrows raised, pencil in the air.

'I've said my goodbyes. I said them when Sean walked out on me. He's been dead to me since then.' I say the words, but I know they're not completely true. The news of Sean's death has affected me more deeply than I care for. But I won't give Gina the satisfaction of lording it over me at his funeral. 'Lissa and Will have gone up,' I add inconsequentially.

'Yes, well…' Bob pauses and taps his desk again. 'Has Sean… did he have a will, do you know?'

I stare at him open-mouthed. 'A will? Shouldn't think so. At least not while he was with me. We never thought we needed one. Don't know what he's done this year, of course. Why? What difference does it make? We're still married, aren't we?'

'Well, you can't divorce a dead man, that's for sure.' Bob's attempt at levity falls flat. 'I did advise both of you to make a will when you bought the house in Seaforth and that was…'

'I know, I know. It was ages ago, years. We kept meaning to get round to it. Even bought some forms. I think they're in the hall drawer… with all the other half-finished stuff.' My voice tails away. 'No need to finish them now,' I say with renewed energy. 'But surely… I'm still his wife. Doesn't that mean I can go ahead and sell the house?' I look at him expectantly. 'You said I couldn't do anything till the divorce was finalised, but now… surely it doesn't matter now? I was thinking of starting to pack up these holidays. Maybe look around for something smaller, just like you suggested.'

'Sis, your idea of smaller isn't any cheaper. You've got expensive tastes. Have you any idea what an apartment in Fairlight or Queenscliff costs? One with water views?'

'Well, if you're going to act all superior…' I pretend to get up to leave. 'Come on, Bob. I know that's what I said I'd like, but I'm not so stupid as to believe I can actually afford one of those apartments. Can I assume I own the house outright now? Apart from what the bank owns that is.'

'Perhaps. Should be quite straightforward. Or it may be more complicated.' I hear the lawyer talking. 'If he didn't have a will when he lived with you, we have to ensure he didn't make one when he moved in with Gina.'

'Gina? What's she got to do with it?'

'Perhaps nothing.' Bob finally puts down his pencil and looks at me across his desk. 'Leave it with me, Anna. Don't worry about it. Nothing you can do right now. Packing up sounds like a good plan. Keep you busy these holidays.' He rises and I get the impression he wants me to leave.

I walk out of his office into the city street. Everyone appears to be rushing off to somewhere or someone. I stand still for a few moments, bemused. Everyone has a purpose. Where is mine? I mentally shake myself. I have lots to do and two whole weeks to myself.

As I drive home, I remember I've promised to visit Heather. She's home now and sounds well on the phone. On impulse, I turn the car along Military Road towards Mosman. Pressing the doorbell I reflect, not for the first time, that Heather has done well for herself. A single career woman, she's well set-up with a waterfront home in this sought-after suburb.

'Anna! What a lovely surprise. Come on in,' Heather's familiar hoarse voice greets me and she leads me into her home. I've only been here once before, but I remember the magnificence of the furnishings. My eyes take in the large living area, and I walk over to the window overlooking the harbour.

'It's a beautiful place you have here, Heather,' I say, turning back into the room.

'Well I didn't get this on a teacher's salary.' She laughs heartily at my surprise. 'No, Anna, this house has been in my family for three generations. My parents did a lot of renovations.' She waves her arm around to take in the living area. 'This picture window was their idea, as was the outside deck. It's been a godsend, especially now.' Her face falls and I notice a touch of sadness. 'I miss everything so; the buzz, the girls, even the staff.' She chuckles. 'Let me get you something to drink and you can tell me all the goss.'

'Nothing for me,' I begin, but Heather is already on her way to what I imagine is the kitchen.

'You must try this herbal tea I've found,' her voice echoes through from the adjoining room as I sink into the soft sofa, resigned to the fact I'll be here for some time.

'Now then.' Heather is comfortably ensconced in a deep armchair opposite me. The coffee table between us holds two delicate china mugs containing an aromatic herbal concoction, and a delicately-patterned tray of sweet biscuits. 'The one vice I have left.' Heather points to the biscuits, while I eye the large ashtray at the edge of the table.

'Oh, that's just to remind me.' She laughs her throaty laugh at my look of dismay. 'I might fill it with potpourri, what do you think?' Without waiting for a reply, she continues. 'So what's been happening at the school? I do get some info as I'm still on the board, but the meetings are few and far between and there's no meat in them. I want to know what's really happening.' She picks up her tea to take a sip and looks at me greedily over the rim of the mug.

'Well…' I cast about for something to tell her. 'There's the new Head, of course.'

'Yes, we've met at board meetings. Bet he's caused a bit of a stir.'

'He certainly has. He seems to have rubbed Rhonda up the wrong way, and I'm not too sure about Fay, though she did invite him to Falls Creek these holidays, with the ski group. Apart from that, everyone loves him and can't do enough for him. It gets a bit much at times,' I confide. 'The way some of the staff seem to be bending over backwards to please him, just because he's a man.' I stop to draw breath, reflecting my remarks may sound a bit catty, and Heather takes the opportunity to speak.

'And how does he take it? He seems pretty unassuming from what I can tell at the meetings. Not one of your arrogant types.'

'You're right,' I concede. 'He's pretty laid back, embarrassed even. I don't think he's used to being the focus of so many women. It's not only the staff, there are the girls too. Drooling over him when he's not looking.' I pause to take a sip of my tea. 'This is good, Heather. What's it called?'

'Don't change the subject. And what's this rumour I hear you've been seeing him out of school?' She arches her brows and gives me the look which has quailed school girls over the years. 'Mmm?'

Her question catches me in the midst of another sip. I splutter, wiping my mouth with the back of my hand before replying, to give myself time to think.

'We've become friends, that's all. It's natural, isn't it?' I ask, while all the time a little voice inside is telling me we may have become more than friends. 'He's gone back to the States these holidays to visit his family.' That should stymie any further discussion of Marcus and me.

'Oh, has he? I thought he'd gone to a conference that was going to drag the school into the twenty-first century.' For some reason Heather seems to find this amusing.

'That too,' I say, wondering if I've said too much already. After all, the family stuff has been told me in confidence. But Heather is off on another tack now.

'You didn't go to Falls Creek this year then?'

'No. I decided to let some others have the opportunity,' I say brightly. 'Glenda has gone…'

'So I hear. Anna, it's okay to grieve.' She refills our cups. 'Do you want to talk things over? I can be a good listener, you know.'

'I do know.' I remember how Heather has taken on this role for many staff members in times of trouble. Her abrasive outer shell hides a heart of gold. 'It's been so hard, Heather. You've no idea.'

'Try me.'

'It's the waiting, and the not knowing that's so difficult. First there was the delay for the divorce to become final. Bob said I couldn't do anything till it was settled. Then Sean died. You had heard, hadn't you?' I look across at her, seeing compassion on her face as she nods. 'Well, I thought that would settle everything, and I'd be able to move on. Sell the house, buy something smaller, you know.' She nods again.

I push my fingers through my hair.

'Loving the new style by the way.'

'Oh, thanks.' I've forgotten Heather hasn't seen the new me.

'Well, Bob. He's my brother, also my lawyer.' I grimace as the two haven't always been commensurate. I run my fingers through my hair again. 'He says it may be more complicated and I still need to wait to ensure Sean didn't make a will in favour of Gina. I mean, he never made one in all the years we've been married. Why on earth would he have made one in the last six months?' My voice is gradually becoming more and more-high pitched.

'So, what are you doing about it?'

'Doing? I can't…'

'Yes, doing. The Anna I know isn't one to sit back and let life run over her.'

'I… I…' I stutter on the words. 'I've started packing up the house,' I say. 'But that's about as much as I can do. Bob has told me the sort of place I'd really like to live in Queenscliff or Fairlight will be way beyond my budget. It seems I'll need to wait till everything is finalised before I can even start looking for another place to live.'

'I don't see why. Have you thought of looking farther afield? Right here in Mosman, for instance?'

'If I can't afford Queenscliff then I could never afford Mosman!' I exclaim.

'We're not talking about water views here. For example there's a development going up at the other end of this street. Might be within your budget, if you don't want anything too big. Doesn't do any harm to have a look.'

'It's a long way from school,' I say without thinking.

'I lived here all the time I was at Grammar and I can't say the distance bothered me any. In fact,' Heather smiles, 'the trip over Spit Bridge really set me up for the day.'

'Hmm. Might be okay.' I think about the road across the bridge, over Middle Harbour, one of my favourite Sydney drives.

'Okay? It could be just the change you need. Why don't we go along and have a look while you're here?' Heather starts to hoist herself up, her hands leaning heavily on the arms of the chair.

'No, Heather!' I move forward, not sure whether I intend to help her rise or push her back down again. 'You're still not well. And I've been so remiss. I haven't even asked how your recovery is going.'

'Tosh.' She brushes off my question and my attempt at assistance. 'I told you on the phone. I'm as well as can be. I've spent too many years abusing my body to worry about taking care now.' On a more sober note she adds, 'My lung function isn't going to improve but, with a bit of care, I can maintain it at this level. I have a few good years left in me yet.' She coughs noisily as if to repudiate her words.

Half an hour or so later, we are standing on the balcony of a display unit at the end of Raglan Street. As we gaze out over the treetops a sense of relaxation steals over me.

'Is that…?' I look around as if to see where the deep rumbling sound is coming from.

'Yes it is. Taronga Zoo is around the corner and, when the wind's in the right direction, you can hear the animals. Of course if you find the noise disturbing you could always choose a unit on the other side.' Heather looks at me, her head on one side. 'What do you think?'

'It's certainly a possibility, but way out of my price range, I'm sure,' I reply guardedly, not wanting to commit myself. 'Still it's something to think about. Of course I can't make any decisions yet.' I hope this will satisfy her.

'Of course you can't. But do bear it in mind. And it gives you an idea what's out there. Now, there's something I want to show you before we go back. It's a spot I often come to – to contemplate life.'

Heather leads me to a small park which I haven't noticed on the way in. We make our way to a wooden bench, and lower ourselves onto the seat to admire the distant view through the trees of the still waters of the bay. There aren't many boats around at this time. It's restful. We sit in silence, the only sounds the wind rustling the leaves and the chattering of some birds. Then Heather begins to speak.

'Hate can destroy you, you know.' She pauses. 'I expect, right now, you believe you hate this friend of yours. Gina isn't it? You hate her for taking Sean away from you, and maybe you even blame her for his death.'

'How do you know?' I look at her in surprise, then turn away to hide my distress.

'I've been there, my dear.' Heather sighs, and gazes into the distance. 'When I was a young woman, I was in love. Yes, I know, it's hard to imagine I had tender feelings once upon a time.' She smiles deprecatingly. 'But I was intent on building a career. I'd been appointed as the youngest Head of Grammar, and I intended to make my mark. A husband and possibly children didn't figure in the equation, not for a few years anyway. I had to test myself first, see if I could do it. I thought George would wait, silly girl that I was.'

'And he didn't?'

'Oh, he hung around for a while, turning up at the house on weekends, and I spent time with him when I wasn't too busy. And you can't imagine how busy I made myself. So busy that Molly, my younger sister, took pity on George and included him in her social scene. She was a social butterfly, was Molly in those days.'

'Your sister? I didn't know you had a sister.' But Heather is intent on her story and continues to talk.

'It happened so gradually I didn't see it coming, but suddenly it wasn't me George came to see, it was Molly and, before I knew it, she was sporting an engagement ring. She was engaged to my George. That's when I realised what I'd lost, that I loved George, and my sister had ousted me in his affections.'

I smile at the outdated terminology, but I'm entranced by the story.

'How I hated her, hated them both. I felt so strongly that I couldn't be in the same room as them. I let my hate get the better of me and I let it sour my life, and my relationship with my sister and her husband, as George became.'

'So what happened?'

'After they married, George was offered a position in England, with the bank he worked for. They emigrated a year to the day after the wedding… and that's the last I saw of either of them.' There is a catch in Heather's voice as she says these final words.

'Didn't they come back to visit?'

'They didn't have the chance. They were both killed in a car accident two years later. There was no one left to hate then. It had all been such a waste.' Heather's voice becomes quieter. 'I realised you can never own another person. Everyone has free will, and Molly was George's choice. Maybe if….' She pauses. 'But I've long since stopped wondering what if. I allowed hate to spoil my relationship with my sister, and I do regret that. For that, you see, I did have control over. We can only ever control our own behaviour, our own emotions.'

We sit in silence again, watching a flotilla of yachts make their way up the harbour. The white sails billow in the light breeze, and the sun glistens on the water like sparkling diamonds. I am the first to break the silence.

'So, do you think it wrong of me to have animosity towards Gina, to blame her for everything that's gone wrong for me this year?' I say at last.

'I can't tell you what to think or feel,' Heather's voice is gentle. 'But I would urge you to consider whether this sort of thinking and feeling is doing you any good. You do need to heal, and only you can find a way to do that. Now, I've talked long enough and I can detect a chill in the air. We should be getting back.' She rises and we link arms in our walk up the street towards her house.

*

I arrive home in a strange mood. I'm buoyed up by the thought of the unit I've seen and the possibilities for change, but I'm distressed by Heather's talk about hate. However, I'm glad I gave into the impulse to drop in on her. She's given me something else to think about. I push her talk on the destructiveness of hate to the back of my mind. I can't think of it at present.

As I enter the house it closes around me like an old friend. I walk slowly through the rooms touching objects, comforted by the sight of familiar things. I end up in the living room, sitting at the piano. The evening is drawing in, but I haven't turned on any lights. I sit in the dusk and run my fingers over the piano keys. I can't remember when I last played. My fingers feel out a tune by themselves, the first one

I ever learnt. A childhood memory of painful piano lessons rears up followed by more pleasant ones of my playing for Sean in the early days of our marriage, and picking out nursery rhymes for a young Lissa. I close the piano lid and lay my head down on its hard surface. *How am I going to leave this place which holds all my memories?*

Eleven

The remainder of the holidays pass by in a blur. I want to ring Lissa, but know she must still be up north or she'd have called me. I'm disinclined to ring her there, conscious Gina will be in the background and I don't want her to be party to our conversation. So I'm waiting for Lissa to return to Sydney and call me. I've made the obligatory visit to Mum and Dad and managed to survive Mum's fussing and Dad's silent support. I've started the planned packing, but haven't made much progress, spending more time reflecting on the items and their memories than on packing them into boxes. So it's a relief when the first day of term approaches and I can see myself getting back into some sort of a routine. I'm also aware of a small voice reminding me start of term means Marcus will be back, and I can't dismiss a frisson of excitement at the thought of seeing him again.

I'm juggling eating breakfast with packing lunch and I'm at the kitchen bench my mouth full of toast, when my mobile rings. I peer down to see Lissa's happy face smiling at me. Grateful she has put her photo on my phone – I wouldn't know how to do it – I quickly swallow my toast and take a slurp of coffee before answering.

'Hi, sweetie. You're back then?'

'Duh! Wouldn't be ringing if I weren't. Does school start today?'

'Sure does.' I attempt to inject some life into my voice, reluctant to sound as miserable as I feel. 'Getting ready to leave right now.'

'Oh, I won't keep you then.' Her voice falters. 'I wanted…'

I peer at my watch and realise, for once, I'm running early.

'Hey it's okay. I have time.' I drag out a chair and plonk myself down. 'Have you been up there all this time?' I bite my lip. I don't mean to sound reproachful but it seems to come out that way.

'I have. Will had to get back last week, but I stayed.'

'So, you've been in Byron with Gina on your own?' I feel a sense of betrayal somehow, even though I know it's crazy.

'Mum, don't fuss. You know Gina and I have always got on well. She's been like an aunt to me. She *is* my godmother, after all!'

In all the fuss I've forgotten this detail. Gina, with no children of her own, has been an alternate parent to Lissa all of her life.

'Of course, I can't expect you to ignore her. It's just, oh, I don't know. I didn't expect you to stay for so long.'

'Mum!' Lissa's voice takes on an accusatory note. 'There was Dad's funeral. I had to be there for that, then there were things to sort out. Gina's devastated, you know. She can't believe Dad's gone. Gone, just like that...' Lissa's voice fades away and I can hear she's not far from tears.

'Look, I'm going to have to leave soon, but why don't you come around for dinner tonight? Bring Will too if you want. We can talk then, and you can tell me all about it. I'd like your input on a few things here too,' I add. Gina's not the only one suffering, and I'm suddenly in great need of my daughter's presence.

'I'm not sure about Will, but I'd love to come. You are all right, Mum, aren't you? I know his death must have been a shock for you too, but Gina, well, she was with Dad when it happened.' I say nothing. 'Is around six-thirty okay?'

'That'll be fine, honey. I'll see you then.' I close the phone slowly. I haven't taken Heather's advice as yet, and the thought of Gina and Sean together, even though he's no longer alive, still has the power to run me cold.

I put the thought in a box – I'm getting good at that – and concentrate on the good news. Lissa is back and I'll see her tonight. I start working out what we'll eat and settle on takeaway Indian. It's first day back and, even though it's a pupil-free day, I know I'll be exhausted at the end of it. Lissa loves Indian food, especially if I order several different dishes. With the anticipation of Lissa's visit and a glass of wine to relax us, I can look forward to the evening.

For once, I arrive at school in plenty of time and, as I'm picking up my books and briefcase from the back seat of the car, I look around to see if Marcus is anywhere in sight. I'd hoped to hear from him before today and I'm disappointed I haven't. I tell myself he's a friend, nothing more, and I just happened to be at hand when he needed someone to confide in. Nevertheless I've dressed more carefully than usual this morning. My black tailored pants are carefully pressed and my red leather jacket fits snugly over my hips and hangs open to reveal a white angora sweater. My favourite gold hoops swing from my ears.

'Good break?' Glenda greets me from behind. I turn around with a start.

'Yes, thanks. How was Falls Creek? Much snow?'

'The trip was wonderful on the whole, just a few of the girls decided to play up one evening. Fay is great with them, and they soon settled down again. Pity you weren't there. You'd have enjoyed it. Shame Marcus didn't come either.' She widens her eyes as if to imply secret liaisons.

'He went to the conference in Vegas,' I hurry to remind her, lest she start reading something into the fact neither of us made the trip.

'Yes, the conference. I'd love to have gone. Really more my scene than a ski trip. Well, catch you later.' Glenda walks off and I conclude there's no pleasing some people. No one forced Glenda on the trip. She volunteered. I shrug, and continue to gather my belongings together.

I'm doodling on my notepad waiting for the staff meeting to start, when I'm conscious of a change in the atmosphere and, looking up, I see Marcus enter the room. He's managed to develop a tan while he's been gone, and it suits him. There's a faint flutter in the pit of my stomach. To my keen eyes he looks exhausted, more than can be explained away by jetlag, but I realise I may be prejudiced. I decide to listen intently this time so as not to be caught off-guard, and I'm ready when I hear my name mentioned.

'I understand this term is when we usually have the school play. What delights are in store for us this year, Mrs Hollis?'

I'm glad I've done some preparation.

'*The Importance of Being Ernest*,' I reply. 'I have the scripts and we should be auditioning later this week. It's for Year Ten,' I explain. 'They're studying it in class too.'

'Should be some keen competition for parts then. So I can leave it in your capable hands?'

'You can, and all help is welcome,' I smile looking around the room at my colleagues. The English staff know they'll be dragooned into helping, but, in past years, others from Art, and even Maths and Science have provided their support.

A number of other matters are discussed, including the introduction of online learning which it appears is not to be restricted to Mathematics classes. Marcus sounds eager to get this started and, as he has intimated, he plans to send Rhonda and another teacher off on a course to assist in the implementation.

As I leave the meeting, I find myself side by side with Marcus. I marvel again at the bulk of the man striding along beside me. The headmaster's height and broad shoulders are testament to his rowing prowess.

'How was your trip?' I ask, looking up at him.

'Don't ask.' His voice is light but has an underlying brusqueness, which is unusual for him. I wonder what can have gone wrong, but this is not the time or place for more questions.

'Are you free tonight?' he asks quietly.

'Not tonight, no. Sorry.' We stop walking and he stares at the ground, making me add. 'It's Lissa. She's just back from Byron and is coming round for a heart to heart. Maybe tomorrow?'

'I'll get back to you.' And he walks off, leaving me staring after him wondering what has happened in the States to make him become so distant.

As I've anticipated, I'm exhausted by the end of the day. When the doorbell rings, I rush the door thinking Lissa has arrived, but it is the takeaway. I fetch my purse and I'm in the process of paying, when my daughter does arrive. As she steps out of the car, I'm pleased to see she's alone. I really didn't want to have to make polite conversation with Will tonight. My daughter envelopes me in a hug.

'Steady on, mind the dinner,' I say, but in fact I'm delighted with the comfort of her arms around me. It's been too long.

'Good to see you too, Mum. Let me take these for you.' And she grabs the two plastic bags and leads the way into the house and the kitchen.

'Now.' We're sitting at the kitchen table with a glass of wine in front of each of us, and the food containers, minus lids, open on the table between us. 'Are you ready to hear about Dad?' Lissa sips her wine, and looks at me over the rim of the glass. 'I know it's been hard for you, but I want to share it all with you.'

'All right...' I gulp my own wine down, and refill the glass. 'Go for it.'

'Well, I realise it hurts you, but really Mum, Dad and Gina were very happy up there. They had a group of friends, and he had settled into a new life. He was a different person, not the stuffy accountant he was here in Sydney. It's as if he had a new lease of life. He and Gina seemed to click. Anyway they were taking a Zumba class together – Gina is adding that to her repertoire – when he collapsed.' When I look at her blankly, she elaborates. 'You know, Zumba. It's a bit like a fitness routine to Latin music.' I roll my eyes, as she continues. 'He was rushed to hospital, but it was too late – a massive heart attack. As you can imagine, Gina was beside herself, and blames herself for encouraging him to take part.'

'As well she might,' I interject bitterly.

'No, really. He was getting into all that sort of thing.'

'The sort of thing he's rubbished for years?'

'Yes, well... Anyway it's left Gina in a sad way. She's on her own up there with a big house to maintain, and a yoga school to manage. Surely even you can feel a tad sorry for her?'

'Sorry for her? I don't think so.'

'You were friends for such a long time before... well, before all this happened.'

'True.' I remember the years of friendship, years when Gina was my first port of call in good times and bad. I shake my head to dismiss these memories. 'No, Lissa. I know what you're trying to do but it won't work. Maybe sometime in the future, but it's all too close right now.' I reach over and give my daughter a hug.

'It's okay, darling. I know, for you, she's a link with Dad. You need that and, as you reminded me, she is your godmother. I really don't mind your seeing her, but please don't try to help mend the breach in our friendship. We need to do that ourselves, and I'm not ready yet.' *If ever*, is my thinking but I keep the thought to myself.

'Look,' I say brightly – too brightly – 'the curry's going to get cold.

Eat up before it does.' But Lissa can't leave it alone.

'How long are you going to keep this up? It's eating into you and making you bitter. You never used to be that way.'

'I've never had a good friend betray me like this before,' I reply hotly. 'It may not be the same, but how would you feel if Miranda ran off with Will?' Miranda is an old school friend of Lissa's and one of her housemates.

'She wouldn't.' Lissa stares at me as if I've gone out of my mind. 'What a thing to suggest. And Will would never do that to me either,' she adds smugly.

'Do you think I ever imagined your dad would? On Christmas morning, too! The humiliation of having to lie to the whole family. It's a lot to forgive.'

'Didn't you have any warning? I mean, surely there was something?' I gaze down at the table. I've turned this over and over in my mind so many times since Christmas. I start to deny it then I remember something and reply slowly.

'Not really, but there was… he was distracted. It was as if something was worrying him. When I asked he brushed it off, said it was nothing. But that was well over a year ago. He and Gina only got together last July. Or so he said. Anyway it's water under the bridge now. Your dad's gone, and all the soul-searching in the world won't bring him back. We need to get on with our lives.'

'Mmm,' Lissa mutters through a mouthful of food. 'And what do you intend to get on to? I've got uni and Will and the others, but you're missing both Dad and Gina. Unless… what's happening with your new Headmaster? The one who took you to the dinner.'

'Nothing's happening,' I say shortly. 'But this is our busy term at school. There's the drama performance to arrange. It's *The Importance of Being Ernest* this year and…'

'Oh that old thing. I'm surprised it's still on the syllabus. I guess it'll keep you out of mischief. But, really, Mum, you need to get on with your life. I loved Dad too, but life doesn't stop and he had gone before…' Her voice tails off in embarrassment.

'I know.' I pleat the material on the edge of my shirt as I avoid her eyes. 'I will. There's a lot to settle first.' I smooth out the folds and look up. 'But what about you and Will. Is it getting serious? It's been a while, longer than your usual things.' I raise my eyebrows.

'It's not one of my usual things. Oh, Mum, I do believe he's the one!'

'Why am I not surprised? So what next?'

'Well,' Lissa smiles a secret smile, 'he wants me to move in with him!' My daughter reveals this as if the news is earth-shattering, rather than something I've been expecting to hear.

'And how do you feel about it? It's a big step.'

'I've said I'll think about it, but I don't really need to do much thinking.' She stands up and takes both, now empty, containers over to the sink, avoiding my gaze.

'So you'll be moving in. Where does he live?'

Lissa sits down again and leans her chin on her hands. 'He has this great unit by the beach at Balmoral. We'll be able to run every morning, along the beach, together. Bliss.' She sighs in delight. 'Just think, Mum. It's a dream come true.'

'You're sure it's the man and not his apartment you're drooling over?' I tease her.

'Mum! Of course it is. I'd move in with Will even if he lived, oh I don't know. Even if he lived back of Burke,' she finally states, naming the most isolated place she can think of. 'Though I'm glad he doesn't,' she adds honestly. 'Balmoral is just about perfect!'

'So when is this move going to happen?' I'm glad for Lissa, and want to take an interest, but it's hard to be excited about her new beginnings when my own life is in such limbo.

'As soon as we can get organised. Maybe next weekend. I don't want to leave the others in the lurch, but Miranda knows someone who's willing to take my spot.'

'I'm glad for you.' I walk around the table and give Lissa another hug. 'I hope it makes you happy. I'm sure it will,' I add, noting the sparkle I her eyes. I remember when I felt like that about her father, and hope she and Will are as happy as we were. It didn't last forever, but twenty-five years isn't a bad batting average.

*

The first day of classes I arrive home feeling completely knocked out. I decide to veg out and, after a long hot shower, I slick back my hair and throw on a pair track pants and a loose long sleeved tee shirt left over from one of Lissa's sporting fads. I boil an egg, make vegemite soldiers – comfort food – and curl up in front of the television with a mug of coffee. I'm flicking through the channels trying to find something worth watching when there is a ring at the door. I can't imagine who it can be at this time of night.

I open the door to be confronted by the back view of a pair of broad shoulders covered by a black leather jacket.

'What...?'

The figure turns and I immediately put my fingers up to smooth my hair, now curling wildly.

'What are you doing here?' There is an accusation in my voice.

'I thought I'd been invited,' Marcus' deep voice shudders through me. 'I've brought a bottle to share.' He holds up a brown paper bag.

'You'd better come in.' I open the door wider and stand aside to allow him to enter. He hesitates as he takes in my dishevelled appearance.

'You did say tonight, didn't you? Have I made a mistake? If it's not convenient, I'll go.' He stands awkwardly in the hallway. I sigh and lead the way into the lounge room where the remnants of my nursery style snack are lying on the coffee table.

'I'll fetch a couple of glasses,' I say, as I casually pick up the leftovers and take them out of the room with me. On my way back I detour through the cloakroom to drag a comb through my hair and add a touch of lipstick. Not that it will make much difference. I grimace to myself in the mirror. Well, too bad.

I return with the glasses to find Marcus sitting on the sofa, his head in his hands. He makes a woeful picture. I forget my embarrassment, remembering his high hopes regarding the trip to see Jonathon and his dejected appearance at school the day before.

'You seem to need this more than I do,' I hand him the glasses. 'How did it go over there? And I don't mean the conference.'

'Not good.' I note the dark circles around his eyes and the deep lines etched on both sides of his mouth. 'I didn't see Jonathon.'

'What!' I wait while he takes his time in pouring out the two glasses of wine. 'You did see Lauren, though?' I take my glass from him and sit down.

Marcus twirls his own glass, the wine threatening to spill over. 'Yes. We talked. But she was obdurate. Refuses to let me have anything to do with Jon. It's as if… as if she's afraid to let me near him.' He takes a gulp of wine and puts down the glass, running his fingers through his hair 'I don't know what to do, Anna. I can't bear to think of the little fellow pining away, thinking I've forgotten him.'

'Have you…' I begin, only to have him interrupt.

'I've thought of everything. I could reply to his letter, to the address he gave me; I could check out if he's on Facebook and contact him there. But either of these would be in direct contravention of Lauren's directive. I don't know if I should. It could rebound on Jon if she finds out. I don't want to encourage him to flout his mother's instructions.'

'I see. I can't advise you, I'm afraid. Though it is odd she's so obdurate about your seeing Jon. Have you reconsidered DNA testing?' I make the suggestion warily as, flattered though I am at his confiding in me, I'm very much aware it's really none of my business.

'I have.' Marcus takes a gulp of wine and puts his glass down with a thump. Luckily it is now half empty so none has spilled over. 'And I'm going to do it. I'm going to approach Lauren about it. It's a simple thing to ask. Surely she can't refuse?'

Twelve

I stamp my feet, and hug myself to keep warm, as I stand at the foot of the driveway awaiting my ride. When I exhale, I can see my breath rise in the cold morning air. What has possessed me to rise so early on a winter's morning? The grey car slides to a stop. The door swings open. I jump in, quickly close it, and I'm immediately enveloped in a warm fug. I smile over at the driver, fasten my seatbelt and the car moves off.

Marcus smiles back, his eyes crinkling, his mouth curling up in a now familiar grin. My stomach churns. This is what has possessed me, this man who has got under my skin and who evokes the same reaction as Sean did in the heady early days of our romance. As my thoughts turn to my late husband, I realise I haven't felt this way about him for years. Somewhere along the line, comfort and familiarity have taken the place of sensuality and excitement. Where am I going? I pull my thoughts back. Yes, I admit I'm attracted to Marcus, but sensuality? Excitement? I don't want to go there. Sean's duplicity is all too close. I need to keep a clear head.

'Penny for them?' Marcus' voice brings me back to the present.

'Not worth it.' Looking over, I notice there's something different about Marcus this morning.

'Where are your glasses?' I realise my words sound accusatory. "I mean…'

'It's okay. I'm blind as a bat without them.' He pulls up at a traffic light and looks across at me, amused. 'I can't wear them for sport though, so that's why I have my contacts in this morning.'

'Oh.'

'They're too uncomfortable to wear all the time, and I've been told the glasses give me an air of gravitas, so important in a headmaster, don't you think?'

'Sure.' The car has started up again so I steal another look out of the corner of my eye. He looks quite different without those black frames. Definitely George Clooney. I suppress a grin and pretend to be engrossed in the view, looking out at the early morning mist, rising like smoke from Middle Harbour as the dawn begins to lighten the sky. 'Do we have far to go?'

'The boatsheds are down in Pearl Bay.' Marcus points towards the water and my eyes, following the direction of his finger, can barely make out the outline of several large buildings below us.

'Looks cold out there. Why do you have to row so early?'

Marcus laughs. 'It's not the regular training time, though they do get out on the water pretty early. My old schoolmate Johnno has been a member of this club for yonks. He's arranged for me to borrow his scull. It's the best time, out on the water when the rest of the world, or in this case, Sydney, is asleep.'

I'm beginning to think asleep is where I should be. When Marcus asked me to come down to see him row, I jumped at the chance. He's promised I can run along the side of the water and the early morning start will energise me. Now I'm not so sure. I look down at the running gear I've donned while it was still dark, and remember our first meeting. I'd been running then too, running away from the disaster my life had become. Things aren't too different now. Here I am, a widow with an unsettled estate. I want to move forward with my life, but it seems every move I make I'm being held back by invisible bonds. Even the man sitting beside me is off-limits, even though the attraction grows the more I get to know him.

I mentally shrug off these concerns. I've been living in the here and now since last Christmas. I can do it for a bit longer. I pull up the collar of my jacket in preparation for the outside chill, and sink back in my seat.

'See, the sky's becoming lighter already! We'll be out there when the sun comes up. It'll be magnificent. You'll see! You're not regretting coming, are you?' I gaze up at the chiselled face beside me. Marcus' eyes are fixed on the road ahead and I'm able to examine him without his being aware of it. His new appearance takes a bit of getting used to, but I think I like it. I guess it's how he looks first thing in the morning and, despite myself, I imagine his face next to mine on a pillow, his eyes opening sleepily. He doesn't resemble Sean in the slightest. Sean's hair was wiry, bushy almost, and he'd gone grey early. His morning face was rough with a spiky beard whereas I imagine Marcus would be smoother, a little rumpled. I give myself a shake. I can't believe that I'm comparing my new headmaster to my recently deceased husband.

'Here we are!' Marcus' words interrupt my thoughts, as the car draws to a halt. He turns and puts a hand on my shoulder. I can feel the warmth of his touch through my jacket. 'It should take a couple of hours before we can leave, by the time I prepare the scull and get out on the water, then redo everything. Take the keys in case you want to come back to the car. His face takes on a rueful look. 'Maybe this wasn't such a good idea.' He hesitates.

'Of course it was. It's beautiful down here at this time in the morning.' Gazing around me I realise it's true. I rarely see Middle Harbour, unless I'm driving over Spit Bridge. It does look beautiful – sort of ethereal – at this time of day. 'Is there anything I can do to help?' I offer, wishing I was a rower too and could join him out there on the water.

'Not really. Maybe next time we'll look at getting you out on the water with me?' I flinch as if he's been reading my mind.

'Maybe.' I don't commit myself, as I'm not sure about any next time. We step out of the car and, for the first time this morning, I get a good look at Marcus in his rowing gear. I do a double take. Nothing has prepared me for the sight of his body encased in the tight rowing outfit. His shorts cling to a pair of well-muscled thighs which lead down to well-defined legs. Lifting my gaze I take in his blue lycra top, stretched across a broad set of pectorals and clinging to his muscled arms. It's as if I'm seeing him naked. I swallow and look away to hide the desire which I'm sure my face reveals.

While he makes his way to the nearest shed, I begin my stretches and seek out the running path he's mentioned. As I stretch, I take a deep breath of the chilly air which catches in my throat. I look out onto the water. It's so still, with no one and nothing in sight at the moment. Soon the entire harbour will be filled with rowers and sailboats as the weekend revellers take to the water, but right now it's a slice of pure heaven.

I see Marcus leave the shed carrying a scull and begin my run along the towpath. As always, I try to keep my mind blank, but this morning I find it impossible. Thoughts of Sean and Gina jostle with each other, as my feet pound the dirt path. I find myself trying to identify the thought which has been niggling at the back of my consciousness for months, ever since Jan first asked me if I'd noticed anything different about Sean, or our relationship.

I've just about given up hope of identifying it then, as I turn into a bend on the path, I stop dead. It's there! In my mind, I suddenly picture the scene. I walked into Sean's office and his hand reached onto the desktop as if to conceal something from me. He'd been feeling a bit more tired than usual and I'd gone in to offer him a cup of coffee. I wondered at the time what was on the paper he was trying to hide, but he'd assured me it was nothing, just some confidential client information. Surely that didn't mean anything. Could it have been from Gina? No, he told me their relationship only started when I was in New Zealand. That was July. From memory, this incident in his office took place before then, closer to March.

It still doesn't make any sense, but I can date his increasing distraction from that moment. I shake my head and continue to run, this time forcing my thoughts down pleasanter paths.

*

We're sitting in the café with brimming plates of breakfast and large mugs of steaming coffee. I've chosen my favourite Eggs Benedict while Marcus has selected the Lebanese breakfast and has a plate of roasted vegetables with humus and soft cheese. The tables are beginning to fill up and the hum of happy voices assaults our ears. It's a typical Saturday morning in Sydney. I sigh, realising how long it is since I was part of this weekend ritual.

When we were first married, Sean and I went out to breakfast every weekend, trying new spots until we found a favourite which we then made 'our place'. Our weekend breakfasts had been a time to relax, read the papers together, commenting aloud when we found an interesting titbit to share; a time to catch up with each other's weekly news and to generally veg out. When had we stopped doing that? I searched back remembering 'our café' had closed a number of years ago. Since then we'd found excuses to stay home, do other things. Perhaps that had been a mistake. But surely cutting out our weekend breakfasts together hadn't contributed to a decline in our marriage? I realise I'm now accepting something *had* gone wrong between Sean and me, even though I'd been unaware of it at the time. Otherwise, why would he have turned to someone else? To Gina? That's what rankles. Not the fact he found someone else, but the identity of the someone else. That's what I find unforgiveable. I lost my husband and my best friend in one fell swoop.

The waiter clears away our empty plates and I lean forward, elbows on the table ready to broach the subject which hasn't been far from my thoughts. But, before I can utter a word.

'I've found Jon on Facebook.' The words drop into a void. I don't know what to say, so I say nothing. 'He's a tad young but I guess all his mates are doing it. Seems to be the thing with young kids these days. I was over at Johnno's and checked the site out to see if I could find him, and there he is large as life.'

'Well all the girls at school are on it. It's their main means of communicating, Lissa too. She's been on Facebook as long as I remember. I think there's an age limit but there's no way of checking.'

'Yeah, according to his page he's sixteen.' Marcus gives a wry smile.

I smile back awkwardly, unsure what to say. I've offered all the advice I can on this subject which is really none of my business. I'm in danger of becoming like my mother, if I go any further. I break eye contact, leaning down to pick up my bag, before I realise I don't have one with me. I bob back up, embarrassed, hoping Marcus hasn't noticed.

'Shall we go now?' I start to rise but Marcus gestures me to remain seated. I look over at him wondering what's up. He picks up then replaces his cup, then carefully places his spoon in it, while I wait impatiently for him to get to the point.

'Umm,' he begins.

My attention begins to wander. I look out of the window where a family of ibis are competing for the remains of breakfast on one of the outdoor tables.

'I wanted to ask you something,' Marcus continues and my attention immediately flips back to my companion. He hesitates then seems to find the courage to continue. 'Well, it's a bit delicate, but I remember you saying you were finding it difficult to manage.' He clears his throat awkwardly. 'I just wondered how things were going.'

'It's difficult.' I pause. 'With Sean dead, I'm hoping to sell the house.' I raise my eyes which have been focussing on the tabletop and making a close study of the crumbs peppering the surface. 'But I'm at sixes and sevens at the moment. Everything's up in the air till Bob sorts things out. He says it could take months, though I'm hoping it won't come to that.' My eyes start to glisten as my words bring everything back, all the uncertainty I've tried to dismiss on my run. 'Sorry, I didn't mean to fall apart on you.' I wipe the developing moisture from my eyes, furious with myself for letting him see me go to pieces like this again. 'Maybe we'd better go.'

'Right,' he says again clearly lost for words. Tears are something most men find difficult to deal with, and Marcus has seen more of mine than I like.

We make our way back to the car in silence. The drive home seems to take forever and the silence in the car is beginning to disconcert me, when Marcus finds his voice. Clearing his throat he asks, 'What are your plans for the rest of the weekend?'

Damn the man! I don't have any plans as such, but that's the last thing I want to tell him. 'Family,' I mutter hoping that'll keep him from querying further. 'How about you?' As soon as the words leave my mouth I regret them, but I can't take them back.

'Nothing much. I thought I'd take in a movie and maybe you…' He glances over in my direction and, although I'm conscious of his eyes on me, I keep mine on the road ahead.

I mentally kick myself. A movie is just what I feel like today, and now I can't go lest I run into him there. That'd be just my luck! I guess it's going to be another quiet weekend for me. Fortunately I have a pile of marking to get on with and there's still the packing. I've made a start but have really only decided on sorting things into three piles: keep, throw out and offer to Lissa. As this is all going through my mind I realise Marcus is still speaking. I tune in to hear his last words.

'So, if you finish your family business by then maybe we can hook up.'

'Sorry, what did you say?' Now I'm feeling just a little foolish, having been caught out daydreaming.

'I was saying if your family things are finished by early afternoon tomorrow maybe we can take in a movie together after all.' We draw up at the end of my driveway and he turns to face me as the car stops.

Delighted to have this second chance even though it sounds suspiciously like a date, I open my mouth to reply, only to be stymied by Marcus continuing, 'You don't have to make a decision right now. I'll be leaving home around one-thirty so give me a call before then if you want to join me. Does that work for you?'

'Yes it does,' I say, relieved to be off the hook. 'And thanks for this morning. It was all you promised.'

'Despite your misgivings?' He smiles, eyes crinkling in the sunlight.

'Despite everything,' I agree.

As our eyes meet, he raises his hand and grazes my cheek with the back of his knuckles. I want to take hold of his wrist to maintain the contact, to keep the gentle touch of his fingers against my skin for a little longer. But I don't, and the moment is lost.

Thirteen

Gina can't seem to keep still. She paces up and down the room, twisting her hands together. I'm not sure why I've allowed her into the house. Her appearance at my front door shocked me, and I didn't want to have an argument in the street. So here we are in the living room. I eye her warily.

'I wanted to… the lawyers will have to… but I needed to talk to you first. You see…' I can't imagine what she wants to say and, as I look at her, I'm amused to realise that, if Sean had become more laid back and casual – even hippified – in their relationship, then she's gone to the other extreme. Gina, who is usually decked out in flowing garments all the colours of the rainbow, is wearing a dark grey outfit which wouldn't look out of place at a country women's luncheon. I try to hide my surprise, but find myself commenting.

'What on earth are you wearing, Gina?'

'This? It's my widow's weeds.'

I see red. I can't help myself.

'Widow! You're not a widow. I'm Sean's widow. We were still married when he died.'

'Technically. But we both miss him, Anna. We have that in common. Can't we bury the hatchet?'

'No,' I start to say when I see tears begin to flow down my old friend's cheeks destroying her inexpertly applied make-up.'

I can't help myself. Seeing my old friend standing there in tears, I sense the bitterness begin to drain away, as I remember how we have supported each other through the years. I'm swamped in an emotion

I don't recognise.

'Come here,' I step over to put my arms around her and we just stand there, tears coursing down both our faces. When we finally move away from each other I wipe my eyes and attempt a teary smile. I remember Heather's words and experience a release from the hate which has engulfed me for the past months.

'Friends again?' Gina asks though her tears.

I step back. My tears are quickly forgotten. How can she even imagine it? The bile rises in my throat and my eyes blur. It's all I can do to stop myself from scratching her eyes out. I respond to her question with one of my own.

'What are you doing down here? I thought your life was in Byron now.'

'Oh, things to do, people to see. I had a few loose ends to tidy up.' She wipes her eyes leaving mascara marks below them. 'Can I sit down?' she asks.

'Course.' I take a seat myself while she settles and fusses with her bag. I perch on the edge of my chair, unsure what will happen next. I have no blueprint for this meeting. My deceased husband's mistress is sitting opposite me and I'm being unbelievably polite.

'It's good of you to see me,' she begins. 'I wasn't sure...' Her tears begin to flow again and she dabs ineffectually at her eyes with a damp tissue.

I wait.

'I want us to be friends again. I hated that I lost your friendship.'

My anger surges to the fore and I am about to speak, say something I may regret later, when she continues.

'The divorce would have come through soon. Then it would all have been straightforward.'

'What do you mean?'

'We never meant to hurt you.' Gina is twisting her hands in her lap. I've never seen her like this, unsure of herself. 'It... it just happened. Sean was such a kind man.' She looks down at her hands and they still. She starts to speak again, but can't seem to find the words. I'm beginning to wish I'd never opened the door to her. I don't need this. I start to get up.

'I'm sorry. I think I'd better go.' She rises and we move silently to the door. 'Friends?' she asks again as she steps outside.

I say nothing and close the door. I lean against it. My cheeks are damp. I'm exhausted by the interchange and still not sure why Gina has felt it necessary to come here. I walk into the kitchen and turn on the coffee maker. It's too early in the day for a strong drink, though I could do with one. But I make do with coffee, while I ponder again on the purpose of Gina's visit. I finish two cups of coffee. I'm energised but still haven't come up with a solution. I decide to put her out of my mind.

I'm trying to figure out what to do with the rest of my day when I hear a car draw up. I'm not expecting anyone, so I peer out of the window to see my mother's silver Prius parked in the driveway. The last thing I need today is my mother offering her advice.

'Thought I'd pop round to see how you're doing.' Mum sweeps through the door in her usual takeover mode.

'I'm doing just fine.' This phrase seems to have become my mantra since Sean left. I'm getting a bit tired of repeating it. 'Well, actually...' I add, as I follow Mum into the kitchen and watch her take over filling the hot jug.

'Yes?' But she's not listening. 'What we need is a good cup of tea.' I look on helplessly while she ferrets around in my cupboards, and soon has a pot of tea sitting in front of us complete with cups and saucers – no mugs for Mum – and even a plate of Tim Tams she's unearthed from somewhere.

'Now, you were going to tell me something.' She pours the tea and settles back, finally prepared to hear what I have to say.

'It's nothing. Well it is really. I had a visitor this morning.'

'Mmm.' Mum looks at me over the edge of her teacup.

'Gina. It was Gina.' I wait for her reaction.

'Her! What was she doing here?'

'That's what I wondered at first. But it seems she came to apologise or something.'

'And well she might. I hope you sent her off with a flea in her ear.' Mum bangs her cup down rattling the saucer and threatening to break both of them. 'Never did like that girl. There was always something about her. Don't know what you ever saw in her. Well, she's certainly shown her true colours.' She stops to draw breath and is about to begin another rant when I speak.

'She's not so bad, Mum. And it takes two you know. Anyway we're both grieving for Sean and our grief gives us something in common.' Even as I say the words, I know there is something wrong with the picture of Gina and me making up. I add, in sudden realisation: 'You know, Mum, now Sean is dead it's almost as if he's come back to me. I mean, I'm able to grieve for him properly instead of feeling betrayed.' Mum is looking at me as if I've gone completely mad. I struggle on.

'It came to me when Gina was here. I'm the widow, not her. Really she has no rights over him now he's gone. It makes me more sympathetic towards her.'

'Mark my words. You haven't heard the end of her. She didn't come to sob on your shoulder. She had some other nefarious purpose. There, I've had my say, and I'll say no more.'

That'll be the day, I think, but I dutifully drink my tea in silence.

'And what about this new fella of Lissa's? Have you met him?' Mum is off on another tack.

'I have and he's lovely. He's an accountant with one of the big firms.' I know Mum'll be impressed by this. 'Has his own apartment in Balmoral,' I throw in for size and can see the approval on her face.

'Oh, not a penniless student then?' She preens as if it's all down to her. Mum can't help herself. She's a real control freak. She believes anything good that happens to any member of the family is her doing, while anything bad is up to the individual. The very idea she can take the credit for Lissa, who has been leading her own life for a number of years now, is laughable.

'You'd like him,' I state unnecessarily. Of course Mum will like him. He's exactly the partner she'd have chosen for Lissa, and my clever daughter has found him all by herself.

I surreptitiously glance at my watch. 'Will you stay for lunch?' As I say it I quickly run through the possibilities. I'd planned to have toasted cheese on the veranda by myself, but that won't do for Mum who will expect a full sit-down affair.

Mum looks at her watch, a fancy timepiece Dad gave her for her sixtieth, which she loves to flaunt at every opportunity.

'My goodness is that the time? No, darling, thanks for the offer, but

I'm meeting a friend for lunch at Manly. I think you've met her, Joan. She's on your school board, I believe.' Before I can reply, Mum is off again. 'And don't forget our anniversary weekend. I know it's in term time but it's Founder's Weekend isn't it, so you should be free. Would you like to bring anyone?' she asks archly, and I wonder if this is the real reason for her visit. 'Joan said you and the Headmaster…'

'No, I won't be bringing anyone,' I say firmly to forestall any further questions. I should have known there would be gossip about my appearance at the Board Dinner but, as I hadn't heard anything till now, thought I'd been spared this time.

I see her off with a relieved sigh. As I clear away the dishes, I reflect maybe Gina's visit has been a good thing. It has made me realise I'm allowed to grieve for Sean and I can do it with a whole heart.

As I settle down to an afternoon of weeding, I find Sean is very much in my thoughts. We had good times, I remember. In our early years we didn't have much but we always managed to make the most of what we did have. I'd always had my garden. It was where I'd do a lot of my thinking. I remember one day when I'd spent most of the afternoon doing exactly what I was doing today.

It was a glorious Sunday afternoon and Sean had planted himself in a sunlounge surrounded by the weekend papers, while I was on my knees weeding the borders. Lissa must have been about eight or nine at the time because I remember her playing on the grass with her guinea pigs. She'd received a pair for her eighth birthday, and become totally obsessed with them. They had a large cage which she insisted we move around to suit her needs. By the time she'd turned ten her interests had changed, so it must have been before then. Why that afternoon stands out, is because it was a perfect moment in time. All three of us were together, but each of us was engrossed in our own pursuits. I remember we finished the day with pizza and a video. We did that a lot those days but that particular day the movie was one which has remained in my mind. It was The Velveteen Rabbit which we'd picked up somewhere or other. I remember how, at the part in the story when the fairy tells the rabbit you become real when someone loves you, Sean reached over and squeezed my hand. It was a special time for us.

I stop and look back at the house. It's like a large empty shell now.

What happened to us? Well, Lissa grew up, and I guess Sean and I changed. We became busy and our lives went in different directions. I can see it now, but didn't at the time. I turn back to my garden, at least that hasn't changed. It is still a country garden full of my favourite flowers and plants and can still give me pleasure. I will be sad to leave it and hope its new owners will love it as much as I do.

Fourteen

'Now, how're you coping? Tell the truth.' Jan pours us another glass of wine and looks at me with eyebrows raised. I try to look away, but have never found it easy to avoid my sister when she has a bee in her bonnet. I sense I'm about to become her next project, something I'll hate like poison. I've given in to her oft-repeated invitation to Sunday lunch. Now the leisurely meal's over, Graham and the boys have vanished somewhere leaving Jan and me sitting on the back veranda by ourselves.

'Oh, you know.' I try to brush her off without success.

'That's just it, I don't. You're so damned uptight about your feelings. Keep everything bottled up. Would do you good to let it all out.' She takes a gulp of her wine, while I twirl the stem of my glass between my fingers wondering how to silence her.

'Come on, Anna, it's only us. Surely you can tell your big sister.' As she meets my eyes over her wine glass, I'm transported back to my childhood. Although she's always been what Bob and I called 'a bossy boots', Jan has always been there for me. It's only in recent years we've grown apart. Since she and Graham adopted the boys, I realise. She'd had difficulty in conceiving and, without children of their own, she and Graham had treated my Lissa as their surrogate child spoiling her silly as she was growing up. Then, ten years ago, Graham's brother and sister-in-law had been killed in a car accident and they'd taken the two boys – they'd been three and five at the time – to bring up.

Suddenly I'm back in little sister mode and there's nothing I want more than to confide in Jan, but where do I start? Sensing my changed mood, Jan reaches for the wine bottle. 'Let me top you up.'

'It's the betrayal of trust I have trouble with.' It's not till I hear myself speak the words aloud I realise what's at the heart of my despair. 'Not only Sean, but Gina, too. I think I could have borne it better if he'd left me for anyone else.'

'You lost both at once. That must have been hard.' My usually insensitive sister has whacked the nail on the head.

'It was bloody awful.' I take a gulp of wine. It goes down so quickly I barely taste it.

'And you still can't pinpoint what went wrong?' Jan can't help herself. She has to get to the bottom of everything.

'Well...' I take a small sip this time and let the wine linger on my tongue. I swallow slowly. 'I've been thinking about it. There was something, but it was back in March, so it couldn't be related, could it?' As if Jan would know, but she appears interested.

'Go on.'

'It's probably nothing but he seemed to be fixated on something... a piece of paper... in his office.' I gaze into space. 'Afterwards he was different... distracted... spent more time at the office.'

'And he didn't discuss it with you?'

'No,' I sigh. 'I guess we'd grown so used to each other, to taking each other for granted. It didn't even occur to me to ask him what was wrong. In retrospect, I should have made him sit down and talk with me, but we were both so busy. I thought I knew him. We'd been married for twenty-five years.' I laugh, a bitter laugh. 'How well do we know anyone?' I'm asking myself the question, though I'm looking at Jan.

'True,' Jan reflects, looking at her half full glass of wine. 'So you have no idea what set him off? Made him available when Gina set out to trap him?'

'Oh, come on, I'm sure she didn't...' I pause, wondering. It did all begin with Gina when I was gone, when I'd jokingly asked her to check on him while I was gone. Shit, did I push them together? Was it all my fault?

'It wasn't your fault.'

I gasp.

'I know how your mind works,' she reminds me. 'You've always taken too much on yourself. Not everything's your fault and definitely not this one. It's that damn Gina to blame. I never did trust her.'

'There was never anything not to trust, not till last July,' I remind her. 'Before then I'd have trusted her with my life.'

'With your life maybe, but clearly not your husband. Though it's just as much his fault for falling for her wiles.'

'Well, he's gone now.'

'And she's still around and getting under your skin.'

'She came to visit. It was a bit strange.' I've had time to reflect now, and I believe she did have an ulterior motive.

'What did she want?'

'That's just it. She said she wanted to be friends again, to grieve together. That sort of thing. But now I've had time to think about it…'

'Yes?'

'I think there was more to it. It was as if… as if she was apologising in advance. Oh, I'm probably imagining things. She's already taken my husband. What more can she do to me?'

'Hmm.' Jan forbears to reply, but her expression is worth a thousand words.

'Well, what?' I demand.

'Don't ask me. Just be careful, that's all.'

'Well, I'm not likely to see her again.' I pick up my wineglass and drain it.

The conversation moves to uncontroversial matters, though Gina doesn't go away. She sits at the back of my mind, like a dark cloud waiting to emerge when the time is right. Part of me is still wondering exactly why she came. I don't buy her story of us grieving together. I know Gina better than that. While I might have been briefly fooled by her attempt at reconciliation, it didn't hold for long. After she left, I remembered all the times when she'd plotted to manipulate situations to her own benefit. Of course, we had been on the same page back then, and I'd found it amusing to watch how people were swayed by her apparent concern. Not so now. She has become the enemy.

I hear my daughter's name mentioned.

'Sorry?'

'I was asking what's happening with Lissa. Has she started her Master's yet? And what's this about a new man in her life? Have you met him?'

Typical Jan. three questions at once and I have to choose which one to answer. At least there's nothing controversial in Lissa's life these days. I relax and answer, filling my sister in with Lissa's news and finishing with, 'And you have all this ahead of you when the boys are a bit older.'

'Yes, but I can wait and it's probably easier with boys,' she suggests. 'Mmm, maybe.'

Just then, Graham and the boys return, clattering onto the veranda with a plethora of cricket bats and balls.

'We're back, darl.' Graham's words are unnecessary, but make me feel like a spare chair, so much a family are they.

'Good time out there?' Jan asks as they mill around, making it seem as if there's a gang of them instead of one man and two teenagers.

'Pretty good. Anything to eat?' It's Simon, the eldest, who is even now checking out the fridge. 'Any leftovers?'

'You've just had lunch,' Jan replies, but rises to take out a couple of dishes covered in gladwrap. She's clearly used to feeding hungry teenagers.

Although Sean was far from being a hungry teenager and didn't have a huge appetite for a man, it brings home to me yet again how my life has changed. With Sean gone and Lissa now living away from home – with Will to be precise – I'm no longer part of a family. I'm a single person with no one but myself to care for. There must be a positive in it all somewhere, but I've yet to find it.

I finish my wine. 'I'd better be getting off.'

'Oh, no need to go so soon. The boys will settle down now they're back and have something to eat. We can have some adult time. Why not stay to dinner too? It won't be much but...'

'No.' I can't bear the thought of spending another few hours with them. I suddenly have a strong urge to be by myself. 'I have things to do,' I say, trying to sound as if I really do have a busy life.

Fifteen

The anniversary weekend arrives, and the family are gathered at North Stradbroke. This visit, to the island off the Brisbane coast, is a trip down memory lane for Mum and Dad. They've rented a large house for us, overlooking the beach at Point Lookout and, so far, the weekend hasn't been too bad. Not too bad, that is, if I can bear the fact my marriage has only lasted half the time of Mum and Dad's, and there is no evidence of any cracks in theirs.

I should be pleased for them. I am. But a small internal voice keeps asking me what *I* did wrong. Although I know it's not intentional, it seems this whole weekend is serving to highlight my own shortcomings in having failed to keep my husband and marriage intact. I've let the family down. Here are Mum and Dad, happy after fifty years. Jan and Graham have nearly thirty years under their belts, and their two adopted teenagers are even now out surfing the waves. The boys are a credit to them, and make the family proud to have them as part of it. My own daughter, Lissa is leading a charmed life, and has brought Will along to meet the extended family. The pair glow with their newfound love. I hope Lissa's expectations of a happy ever after will be met.

Only Bob has escaped family expectations. His decision to 'come out' as gay in his early twenties have absolved him from these and, although I know he's had a number of partners over the years, none has been invited to any family gatherings, leaving Mum and Dad to comfortably consider him a successful professional with no personal life of his own to embarrass them.

We've been enjoying a relaxing breakfast and Jan is organising the grandchildren in the clear-up when Bob draws me aside. 'We need to talk,' he murmurs under his breath. We walk out onto the veranda and I lean over enjoying the view of the ocean, a pod of dolphins splashing in the distance.

'What can't wait till this is all over?' I glance up at him, the sun in my eyes. 'Is it good news? Can I put the house on the market?' Despite my internal angst, I'm feeling more relaxed than I have done all year. The few days away from home, surrounded by my family, are having the required effect. The tension is ebbing away and I'm beginning to believe I can envision a future for myself, on my own.

'No,' Bob states. 'I've had a letter from Gina's lawyer. She's contesting.'

'What do you mean?' I gaze at him blankly. 'What is she contesting? Is there a will?'

'No will. She's claiming Sean's share of the house and business as his de facto partner.'

'But I'm still his wife, his widow,' I correct myself. 'How can she dispute that?'

'She can't, but she can make a claim to his estate on the basis they were in a relationship when he died. She can assume his intention was...'

But I don't want to listen to any more. I rush away from Bob as if, by leaving, I can deny his words. Tears blur my vision as I hurtle down the steps onto the beach. I begin to run along the edge of the sea till, out of breath, I stop, my shoulders heaving and my face wet with tears. How could she? After all we've shared. It was like we'd been two sides of the same coin. I remember times she's let me down in the past, but this is altogether too much. This is a deceit as grave as her betrayal with Sean.

'Anna!' I turn to find my brother has followed me. 'Are you all right?'

'All right? Would you be all right if you'd just learned your best friend was doing the dirty on you? I can't believe it. I saw her only a week or so ago, and she was full of what I now see was fake sympathy. "Let's both grieve together" and all that sort of thing. She fooled me, that's for sure. Lulled me into a false sense of security. Well, you'll fight it, of course.'

Bob looks down at his feet, his Birkenstocks making large

indentations on the wet sand at the water's edge. Like Mum, Bob has never had much time for Gina. But his response surprises me.

'Umm, don't you think maybe…'

'What? Do you think she has a case?'

'Maybe… maybe not. But do you really want this to drag on? A legal battle could take some time, months, years even. Whereas, if we can agree to a settlement, it could all be over soon and you could move on, sell the house and be settled in a new place before Christmas. Wouldn't that be a better plan?' As he looks at me, I can see the little brother who has always wanted to please his big sister, but who imagines he knows better. He shakes his head, and walks away, leaving me there.

I sit down on the damp sand, by the edge of the water, hands clasped around my knees, and reflect on the transience of friendship. I come to the conclusion I can only rely on myself and, once realised, I begin to have some sense of release. I rise and dust the sand from my butt. Walking back to the house, I can see my parents sitting together on the deck. Dad is reading while Mum, never one to sit idly, is intent on her latest tapestry. I don't remember what this one is supposed to be. I lost interest in them long ago, if ever I did have any. I've never been good with my hands, outside gardening, that is. My childhood has been spent lost in books or in writing my diary. My diary! I stop in my tracks. I haven't thought of it for years. I kept my entries going all the way through school and uni, right up till the time I met Sean. Then I had other things to fill my time.

That's what I'll do. It'll be a cathartic experience. I'll write everything down, exorcise it, as it were. Fuelled with a new purpose I make my way up the rest of the beach.

'Where were you, darling? We missed you. Jan's looking for someone to make up the numbers for some beach volley ball.'

Trust my sister. She can't bear to see anyone doing nothing. 'Where is she?' I sigh and enter the house.

My new resolve carries me through the remainder of the morning but, after lunch, Lissa takes me by the arm.

'Let's go for a walk, Mum. I haven't had a minute alone with you.'

'What about Will. Don't you two young things…?'

'Will's happy with the boys.' I look across the room and, sure enough, Will is engrossed in some computer game with my two nephews.

I start to head for the beach, but Lissa draws me towards the front door and we make our way to a pathway along the cliffs. At first we walk in single file with no opportunity for conversation. This suits me. But eventually we reach a lookout, and Lissa takes a seat on a wooden bench. She pats the space beside her.

'Now what's up?'

'Why should anything be up?

'You and Uncle Bob disappeared for ages after breakfast and you haven't been the same since.' Lissa taps her nose. 'I know you, and when you go all quiet – like you were at lunch – then there's something up.' She looks at me expectantly. I'm not sure how much to tell her, but I begin.

'Well, it's the house. I may not be able to sell it just yet.'

She looks surprised. 'Why not? I thought, now Dad's dead,' – her voice breaks on the word – 'I thought it was all straightforward.'

'Yes, I did too.' I break off a stalk of grass and twist it in my fingers, looking at it as if it holds the answer as to how to tell her. 'But it's Gina. That's what your uncle Bob had to tell me. She wants a share.'

Lissa is aghast. 'I know she and Dad planned to build a retreat up behind Byron. They had some investors interested, but needed to put up part of the capital themselves. Dad was going to use his share of the house and business I think. I guess I assumed, with Dad gone, Gina would have given up on the idea.'

'What?' If I've envisaged Gina and Sean together at all – and I've tried my best not to allow these images to arise – I've imagined them in some rustic seaside hideaway, lost to the world. I certainly haven't considered they'd have plans for what sounds like a pretty large-scale undertaking. This news puts a different complexion on matters altogether. I wonder if it will sway Bob, bring him around to my point of view.

'I saw her, you know,' I say, 'Gina.'

'When?'

It's my turn to surprise Lissa. 'A couple of weeks ago. She turned up out of the blue, all contrite and friendly. We even buried the hatchet,' I say ruefully. 'No mention of any of this. The bitch! She knew all along she was going to initiate this action. I expect she hoped to soften me up. Well, she was mistaken.'

'What does uncle Bob say? You *are* going to fight.' Lissa looks shocked, her eyes widening as they did as a child when she was surprised. I put my hand over hers on the hard wood of the bench, warm from the day's sun.

'Of course we are. I am. Your uncle wants to do some sort of a deal to save time. He says the whole thing could take months to sort out. I refused, though I don't know how I'm going to manage for long. Paying the mortgage and the costs of just living are eating up all of my salary and any savings I have.' I look down at my hand, tanned and hardened from gardening and my forty-odd years of living. It's in stark contrast to Lissa's firm young hand with its soft golden skin. I pat hers gently.

'Mum! I didn't realise. I can…'

'No!' I hold up my hand to silence her. 'You have your own life to live. I'll work something out. Now you go back down. I need a few minutes by myself.'

'Are you sure?' I nod and she gives me a hug. 'Don't be long, or Gran will be after your blood.' We both give a strained laugh and she dashes off.

I sit alone, contemplating the wild sea below. For a time I'm lost in my thoughts. I'm remembering Marcus and the suggestion he made just before he left me the other day.

'I met a teacher at the conference, Bonnie. She was looking for an exchange position in Sydney for six months and I suggested she come to Grammar. She's going to need somewhere to stay. Maybe….?' He'd hesitated. *'Maybe she could be a paying guest? You have a big place here and if you're short of cash…?'*

I hadn't replied immediately, thrown by the thought he met someone at the conference, a woman who is following him to Sydney. How can I ever have imagined he'd be interested in me in any way other than professionally and as a friend? And I'm not interested in anything else anyway, am I? This was a kind brush-off, a hint there's nothing between us and never could be. I'd said I'd think about it, intending to refuse later.

I realise now it might not be such a bad idea after all. How difficult can one American schoolteacher be? It will only be for the remainder of the year and, if this Bonnie and Marcus are an item, she'll be out most of the time anyway. I do need the money. I sit there talking myself into a decision, finally stretching out my hands in front of me. As I do, I notice my wedding band is still there on the third finger of my left hand. It's right there, where Sean placed it on our wedding day. I've continued to wear it all these months. I guess it's been part of the grieving process for me. A part of Sean that still belonged to me. I shake my head. It's over now, really over. I pull the ring off and, without taking time to think, I throw it out over the rocks into the sea below.

The very act gives me a final sense of release. It's as if a part of Sean which has been clinging to me has finally gone.

By the time I get back to the family, I'm feeling energised and ready to take on anything. Anything, that is, but what I find awaiting me. As soon as I enter the driveway, I know something is wrong. An uncanny silence hangs about the place, which was humming with voices when I left. My heart thuds as I climb the steps to the veranda and push open the door. I look around.

As I glance into the large living area, all I can see is my sister's back. She's talking on the telephone. There's no one else in sight. I move through the hall and into the kitchen expecting to see the rest of the family either there or out on the beach, but it too is silent. Out on the back deck there are groups of people talking in low voices. Even the teenage boys are subdued which is unheard of. I can't see Mum and Dad, or my brother. Lissa and Will are huddled together in a corner.

'What's…?'

'Thank goodness you're back.' Lissa runs into my arms. 'It's Gramps.' She bursts into tears. I hug her, helplessly trying to work out what has happened.

'Has there been an accident? Where is he? And Mum, and Bob?' I look around wildly seeking answers but am greeted with blank stares.

'Jan!' Relieved, I see my sister return. Her face is white, her cheeks damp with tears. 'What's happened?'

'Dad had a dizzy spell and is nauseous. Evidently he's had these turns before, but this one was worse. Bob drove Mum and him down to the medical centre. I've been talking with Bob and the medicos decided to take him to the mainland for a CAT scan.' Jan is sounding more subdued than usual.

'A CAT scan? What are they afraid of? A brain tumour? Dad?' I'm numb. I hear the words my voice is saying, but have no control of them. I am beyond tears. I am cried out. This is Dad, my anchor. I can't lose him too. It's not fair! I'm filled with anger. I want to yell and shout, but have no one to shout at. Everyone around me is shell-shocked. I try to sound calm.

'How will they take him there?' Only fifteen kilometres from the mainland, the usual mode of transport is a ferry, or is this serious enough for an airlift? I begin to shake as a lump rises in my throat. I'm enveloped in a sea of warmth as Jan's arms go round my shoulders. Our heads lean together, foreheads touching. 'Bob says they've arranged an ambulance. It'll take Dad to a hospital in Brisbane. Mum will go with him and Bob will follow in his car.'

'But what about us?' I want to be with Dad. I look around at the remnants of our family. No one knows what to do.

'Graham and I will have to stay with the boys. And someone needs to get this place fixed up, so we can leave it in a decent state. But I guess you're free to go with Bob, unless…' She looks over at Lissa and Will. I remember the three of us came over in the ferry with Bob. He'd hired a car to fit all of us.

'Bob has the car,' I say in horror. 'How can we…?'

'He took Mum and Dad's car. His is still here. He left the keys.'

Hearing our conversation Lissa is at our side.

'Mum, if you want to go to the hospital, Will and I will work something out. Maybe we can even get you to the ferry in time for you to travel with uncle Bob. How fast can you get your things together?'

I look down at my worn cargo pants, shirt and runners and make an instant decision.

'I can go like this if you'll pack all the rest of my stuff and bring it with you. I'll just put my toiletries into a bag and…'

Twenty minutes later I'm greeting my brother at the ferry wharf. The ambulance looks ominous as it waits to board ahead of us.

'You made it!' Bob is standing at his car door, clearly relieved to see me. 'It's going to be a big help having you with us, Mum has gone to pieces. I've never seen her like this. I can't… but you'll see for yourself when we reach the hospital. She's with Dad. The paramedics are taking them to Redland hospital. It's in Cleveland, not far from the ferry terminal.'

We wait impatiently till it's our turn to drive onto the vehicular ferry, then Bob suggests we have a coffee.

'We can't be of any use on the way over. Mum and Dad are safe in the ambulance and she won't want to leave him. A shot of caffeine would help, don't you think? It'll steady our nerves.'

I agree and find myself seated in the cafeteria looking out on an idyllic scene as the ferry makes its way across the narrow stretch of water.

'Get that down you. You're still suffering from shock.' Bob thrusts the cardboard cup of coffee into my hands. Trust my little brother to take care of me and to understand my distress.

'I hope…' I begin.

'Everything's going to be fine. Dad's got a strong constitution. It's only a precaution, given his age.'

'But you said Mum…?' The coffee is beginning to have its effect and I'm able to think more clearly.

'Yes,' Bob rubs his forehead. 'That's the odd thing. She's always telling us all what's what, and organising us out of existence, but when Dad collapsed she folded. Not like her at all.'

'Well, we'll find out when we arrive.' I sip the warm coffee gratefully, and point out the window. 'We're almost there already. Time to get back to the car.' I gulp down the last of the coffee, and we make our way downstairs again.

By the time we've located the hospital, found a parking spot, and made our way to emergency, we are just in time to see Dad being wheeled away to radiography. I go up to Mum who is wringing her hands and looking lost.

'Anna. You're here!'

'Where did you think I'd be? Of course I'm here.'

'But, the others.' She looks around, as if expecting to see the rest of the family trouping in behind me.

'They're still on Straddie. Getting packed up.' I explain. 'Now, come along and take a seat.' It feels strange to be taking charge of Mum. All my life she's always been the one in control, the one to be feared, even. Now she seems reduced to a quivering jelly.

'Fifty years,' she laments. 'Ben's been my rock for fifty years. What will I do without him?'

'No one's doing without anyone. Dad's just having some tests done. It'll be fine.' I hear myself uttering the same refrain I've uttered since Sean left, with no more confidence than I had then. But I must try to be strong for Mum. So I'm surprised at her response.

'You always were the strong one, Anna. Just like your dad.'

'But, Mum, you…'

She shakes her head. 'No. I always made a lot of noise, but it was your dad who held the reins and who made the decisions. He was the quiet one who kept his head in a crisis. You're like him, you know. Like peas in a pod.'

I take her hand and hold it tight as we sit down, while Bob goes off seeking coffee, his cure for all ills. All we can do now is wait.

Sixteen

While we're waiting for Dad to return, or the doctor to speak to us – we're not sure which to expect – I decide I needed to call Marcus. Whatever the outcome here, it doesn't seem as if we'll be able to return to Sydney on schedule. I need to ensure my classes can be covered for at least one day. My guess is that, at best, Dad won't be in a position to fly for some days, so some of the family will need to stay up here with him. Mum will certainly want to be here and, given her current performance, she won't be able to be on her own.

'Hello, Marcus here.' The familiar deep voice answers almost immediately. I've walked outside to make the call and I'm surrounded by cars, ambulances and patients sitting in wheelchairs smoking. I grimace at my surroundings, picturing Marcus sitting down somewhere nice in Sydney relaxing. So vibrant is the image, it takes me a second or two to actually respond to his greeting.

'Hi. Anna.'

'Where are you? What's all the noise? Thought you were having a quiet family celebration at Straddie this weekend?'

I remember telling him of my plans only last week. 'That's just it. Dad's had a turn. We're at Redland Hospital. I'm outside Emergency right now. I'll need… I think… If I can't get back can you arrange cover for me?'

'Redland Emergency Department? It's just up the road. What I mean to say is, I'm at my parents' place this weekend and they live in Wellington Point. I'm sorry to hear about your dad. If there's anything I can do…' his voice tails off.

I'm suddenly much calmer. I forget he's met this Bonnie person, and only remember how comforting he's been to me over the whole Sean debacle. It's as if his presence has found a way to reach me through the telephone. I clutch the phone to my ear, and start to burble on.

'We'd just had lunch… I'd gone for a walk with Lissa… she'd gone back before me… he's having a CAT scan… I'm afraid…'

'Steady on. Is there anyone with you there?'

I come back to earth. 'Yes. I'm with Mum. She's gone to pieces. And my brother's here. The rest of the family are still on Straddie. They'll be here as soon as they can get packed and cleaned up.'

'Well it sounds as if you need somewhere to stay. What say I book you all in to the local motel and meet you at the hospital?'

'Oh, I can't expect you to…'

'It's the least I can do. See you soon.'

'But…' I realise I'm talking to myself. Marcus has hung up. I walk slowly back into the cream and blue building. It's alive with people hurrying about their business. Mum looks very small and alone sitting there in the middle of a row of blue plastic seats. Bob returns with a tray of cardboard cups of coffee. I see him look around. He's probably wondering where I am. For an instant, I wish I could just disappear, that it would all go away. But that's not going to happen. I take a deep breath and join them.

'Thanks.' I accept the cup Bob is proffering and take a gulp of the hot liquid purporting to be coffee. Well, at least it's hot and wet, but that's about all I can say for it.

'Where did you get to?'

By the time I've explained my phone call, Bob is looking amused. 'So your Headmaster is coming to the rescue, then?'

'Hardly. He's only being helpful. He knows the area.'

Mum suddenly seems to come to life. 'It's kind of him,' she says. I stare at her, surprised she hasn't made some sarcastic remark about him and me and the inappropriateness of our relationship. She's certainly behaving in a manner very unlike herself. I pull myself up. Relationship? There *is* no relationship. Marcus is only behaving like any concerned boss would, if a staff member was stranded in his home town.

Who am I kidding? I'm far from stranded; I'm with my family.

His offer is above and beyond what one would expect. But that's what Marcus is like, and I shouldn't read anything into it. He has Bonnie, and when I see him, I'll tell him about my decision. There, I've salved my conscience. While I've been having this dialogue with myself, the area around us has filled up.

'I'm going to find out if there's any news.' Bob lopes over to the desk where I see him gesturing to the nurse on duty. He walks back slowly.

'Nothing yet,' he reports, sitting down beside Mum again. I take a seat on her other side and the three of us hold hands. It's as if, by holding onto each other, we can affect the outcome. We seem to have been waiting forever, when a man dressed in what looks like a blue boiler suit, comes through a plastic-curtained doorway.

'Frazer?' He peers around expectantly. Bob and I rise.

'That's us.' He walks towards us.

'We've completed the CAT scan on Mr Frazer and it seems clear, but we'd like to keep him in overnight to conduct some further tests tomorrow.'

'Oh.' I subside onto the seat again, deflated. I'm not sure what I expected, but this isn't it.

'We're taking him up to a ward and you can see him there.' The doctor continues to speak, but I've blanked him out. I hope Bob is taking it all in. I turn to Mum.

'We'll go up and see Dad now, shall we?' She stands up heavily. It's as if she's aged ten years since lunchtime, and she seems to have shrunk.

When we reach the ward, it's to find Dad propped up in bed with a raft of pillows, looking relatively cheerful.

'You old fraud,' I say going over to give him a kiss. Meanwhile, Mum walks over to the left side of the bed. She sits down with a thump.

'You had us all scared.' Bob goes to Dad's other side and takes hold of his hand. This is out of character for my brother, who usually eschews all forms of physical affection with our parents.

Mum says nothing, but is visibly brighter. She takes Dad's closest hand in both of hers holding on for grim death.

'Don't do that to me again,' she whispers, scarcely loud enough for Bob and me to hear. 'I can't go on without you, Ben.' I look away embarrassed by this show of affection. If asked, I'd have said Mum and Dad were a couple who just put up with each other. My eyes mist up.

'There, there, Susie. I'm still here to bother you for a good many more years yet.'

'Now then, Ben.' The familiarity of the nurse entering the room shocks all of us and I can see Mum bridling up in her usual fashion. Pleased though I am to see a vestige of her usual self return, I am about to say something, when I notice Dad patting her hands with the free one which Bob has released.

The nurse turns to us with a smile. 'I can give you ten more minutes then I think the patient here needs a rest. He has a busy day tomorrow with a few more tests. You can come in to see him afterwards,' she adds, seeing our dismay.

'But what tests are you going to do? What do you suspect is wrong?'

'You'll have to ask the doctor these questions.' Her tone is brisk and dismissive. She checks the chart hanging at the foot of the bed, and leaves.

We chat for a time, but it's clear Dad is tiring so we take our leave, promising to return the following day. As we reach the entrance to the hospital I see Marcus hurrying toward us. He's looking very relaxed in jeans teamed with a light blue sweater.

'Glad I caught you.' He's out of breath from running from the car park. 'I've reserved four rooms in a motel in Middle Street. It's not too far from here. I assume you have a car? You can take however many you need,' he adds, seeing only the three of us standing there.

'Our car's over there.' I point in the direction of the car park. 'And the others will be here later. Four will be good.'

Marcus coughs awkwardly. I introduce him to Mum and Bob.

'So you're the new Headmaster.' I notice Mum give him the onceover with a glint in her eye. It hasn't taken her long to revert to type, but I'm glad she's acting more like herself.

'Guilty as charged.' Marcus smiles disarmingly at us, then his expression becomes more serious. He addresses me. 'How's your dad?'

Without giving me a chance to reply Mum butts in.

'He's looking more like himself, but they're keeping him in for more tests.' Her shoulders droop again, her eyes are beginning to glisten. 'We won't know till tomorrow what they find.'

'But the CAT scan came out clear, Mum,' I remind her.

'Well that must be good.' Marcus is trying hard to make conversation, but failing miserably. 'Do you want me to come to the motel with you?'

'We'll be fine, but can I have a word?' I draw him aside, not wanting the others to hear what I have to say.

'That thing you mentioned, the exchange teacher. Can I take you up on it? Seems I may be in need of some extra cash. Sean's *friend* is suing for a share of the estate, so Lord knows how long it will take to settle.'

Marcus looks surprised, but is quick to accept my offer.

'I'll get in touch with Bonnie tonight. That'll be a load off her mind. Thanks, Anna.' His eyes crinkle up at the corners as his hand comes down gently on my shoulder. I get the feeling, under different circumstances, he would have kissed me. I brush away the thought. 'Well,' he hesitates. 'Good to meet you.' He nods to my mum and brother, turns, and walks off. I want to run after him, not sure why, but it seems he has taken some warmth away with him, warmth I desperately need.

I don't get much sleep and I hear Mum toss and turn in the bed next to mine. When dawn breaks at last, I part the curtains to peer out onto what promises to be a bright sunny day. Looking over, I see Mum has at last fallen into a deep sleep, but I can't settle and, dressing quickly, I slip out for an early walk.

Cleveland is quiet at this time on a Sunday morning, but I find a coffee shop open. Carrying a take-away cappuccino, I cross a couple of streets to reach the harbour. I lean on the barrier sipping my coffee, taking in the glistening water and the number of yachts and catamarans sitting at anchor. Some already have figures on them, making preparations for a day on the water. One of the figures looks familiar. I gaze idly at the man's back, noting the broad shoulders, lean tanned legs, the white tee shirt and shorts. My lips are curving into a smile of approval, when he turns round and waves. I take a second look and recognise Marcus. As our eyes meet, he signals me, then turns to say something to his companion.

The next thing I know, he's bounding towards me. He stands in front of me pushing back his hair. I blink. 'You're making an early start.'

'Couldn't sleep. I thought rowing was your sport of choice. Not this.' I look to the flotilla of yachts in the harbour.

'Yeah, met a mate who offered me a sail. Would be a pity to let it go on a day like this.' His waving hand encompasses the glorious view across the water. I agree and we stand looking at each other, my eyes lingering on the way the tight fabric of his tee shirt stretches over his broad chest. It reminds me of our morning on Middle Harbour. All worries about Sean's death, Gina's claims, Dad's illness recede as I contemplate the fine figure of manhood before me.

I'm brought back to earth by a loud call from the yacht. Marcus turns, acknowledges it with a wave, then turns back to me.

'I talked with Bonnie last night.' The words bring me back to earth with a thud. Of course, Bonnie, his… Well, whatever she is. 'She's good with it,' he continues. 'I gave her your email address – the school one – so you two can make arrangements. That's okay, isn't it?' he queries with a grin.

'Sure.' What else can I say? I've committed myself to hosting this bimbo of his, and arrangements need to be made.

'How are you?' He reaches out his hand, but doesn't quite make contact with me. 'Really?'

'I'm coping.' I try to raise a smile. 'At least it's given everyone something else to think about. Besides me, I mean. Sorry, I sound pretty selfish.'

'No. It's understandable. I bet you've been the main topic of conversation in the family since… since your husband left.' He coughs and shuffles his feet. I suspect he's unsure what to say next.

'Well your friends are waiting for you.'

'Yes.' He seems reluctant to leave, but he gives me a smile then turns and walks off. I turn in the other direction. It's time to return to the motel, to find out what the day has in store for us. Jan, Lissa and the others should arrive on the ferry this morning, so we can all go visit Dad together later. We just have to find some way to fill the hours till then. It won't be easy, with Dad's fate hanging over us.

Eleven o'clock arrives to find the whole family sitting in a hospital corridor. We're drinking the same awful coffee I had the previous night, thanks to Bob again. When we're finally permitted to visit Dad,

I'm pleased to see him leaning up against his pillows with a smile on his face.

'I never died a winter yet,' he greets us. This is a favourite saying of his, culled from some radio program in his dim and distant past, but the comment's a bit too close to the bone for us right now.

'What does the doctor say?' Mum is first to his bedside and grabs his hand again.

'Damage to the vestibular system,' he replies savouring the word.

'What does that mean, Gramps?' Lissa is quick to enquire for all of us.

'I'm not quite sure myself, but it's to do with my inner ear and balance. Explains why I've been feeling dizzy and nauseus. They want me to stay in for another week or so.'

Bob, Jan and I look at each other. There's no way any of us can take this amount of time away from work, but Mum has rallied and it's she who replies.

'No worries. I'll be here for you.' She sees our surprise. 'I had a shock yesterday, but now we know what's what, I'm the one who needs to be here. The motel's quite comfortable, and I can come in here to be with Ben every day. You can all go back home. Dad'll be fine here.' She smiles smugly, back in control of her family again.

Although I'm still worried about Dad, it's a relief to see Mum back to normal and to know I can be at school again on Tuesday morning. This has been some long weekend and, although part of me would like to be here for Mum and Dad, another part will be glad to return home to face what waits for me there. It's been a revelation for me, to learn Mum sees me as the strong one in the family. I hope she's right, as I have a few challenges ahead, this Bonnie person being one of them, Gina being another.

Seventeen

'Hello, you must be Anna.' The smiling face which greets me isn't at all what I had expected. It's younger for a start. I gaze at the wholesome Californian girl, her straight blonde hair falling to her shoulders from a central part, wide grin of whiter than white teeth and, most surprising of all, she can't be a day over twenty-eight. I suddenly feel old. I could be this girl's mother! She could be my daughter!

My jaw drops. So this is what Marcus likes? Why did I ever think he was interested in me? I put these foolish thoughts aside, and force a smile onto my face.

'And you must be Bonnie.' She beams, and hitches her backpack further up her shoulders, picking up her canvas holdall at the same time. As she walks past me into the hallway, I realise she tops me by at least a head. They grow them tall in America.

'Is this all you have?' I ask, as I close the door behind her.

'I travel light.' She grins and stretches out her hand. I take it without thinking, and find mine enveloped in a strong handshake. 'It's so good to meet you. Marcus has told me all about you.'

'All good, I hope,' I say automatically, wondering what on earth he can have said about me. 'Let me show you to your room.' I lead the way upstairs. 'I've put you in the spare room,' I explain, 'and you can have the use of the study next door. It used to belong to my husband.'

'Wow. That'd be great. If it's not putting you out?'

'Not at all. I have my own study downstairs and I expect you'll need somewhere to spread out. The bedroom is a bit small.' I look around the stark cream and brown room which has hardly been used.

Lissa's old room is bigger and brighter, but I can't bear the thought of putting Bonnie in there. 'I'll leave you to get settled. Come down to the kitchen when you're ready. You're probably ready for a cup of something.'

I go downstairs to the kitchen and turn on the coffee maker. I need a strong cup myself. Bonnie is so different from what I've expected. She's like a lanky puppy wagging her tail in an attempt to please. How can I not like her? What's not to like in this lovely young woman? I pick up my phone to call Marcus, but stand looking at the keypad, unsure what to say. I finally send a text. *Bonnie arrived safely*. That should do it.

An hour later we're still sitting at the table, drinking our second cup of coffee. Bonnie has filled me in on the purpose of her visit. It seems she's undertaking a Master's degree in Education at some university I've never heard of in California, and she wants to examine the relatively new Australian National Curriculum and its impact on classroom practices.

'I want to do a case study of a couple of schools over here.' She wraps both hands around her coffee mug, an intense look on her face. 'This is a great opportunity, Marcus has offered me, to really get in at grass-roots level, you know.'

I don't, but I nod anyway.

'And I'd like to observe in a few classrooms if I can. I believe they'll be very different to those back home. Marcus said you're Head of English. Maybe I can shadow you for a couple of days?'

My surprise must show on my face as she quickly adds. 'Only if you agree of course.'

'Of course,' I find myself saying. Just then, my phone rings and I excuse myself.

'Well, has she arrived? What's she like?' Lissa's voice rings over the airwaves.

'It's a bit difficult.'

'So she's arrived already and you can't talk because she's right there with you? I'll ask the questions and you can just say yes or no.'

I sigh at my daughter's simplistic grasp on life, and move my phone to the other ear indicating to Bonnie with a wave of the hand this call could take some time.

'Is she pretty?'

'Yes.'

'Young?'

'Yes.'

'Wow, a lot younger than you?'

'A bit like you.' I can't keep this yes/no response up for long.

'What!' I'm sure Lissa's shriek can be heard all through the house. I hold the phone away from my ear, and mouth: 'Sorry' to my companion, who is sipping her coffee with an amused grin on her face.

'Look, honey. This isn't a really good time. Why don't I call you back later?' Lissa reluctantly agrees and I turn off the phone. 'My daughter,' I explain as if that says it all.

'She doesn't live here?' Bonnie places her mug on the table and props her chin up with her hands. 'Pity. I'll need to find me some young company.'

I look at her askance. Surely she should be satisfied with Marcus. But then I reflect, there is quite an age difference, and that, besides Will, Lissa has always had her coterie of female friends with whom she socialises.

'She lives closer to the city. Recently moved in with her boyfriend. He's an accountant, like my husband was.' I'm not sure why I've brought Sean into this. I guess it's some sort of protection motive. I stand up in a flurry and begin to rinse my mug at the sink with my back to Bonnie. She's only been here a couple of hours and I'm already stressed by her presence. Perhaps this hasn't been such a good idea after all. I hold on to the sink with both hands, gazing at my reflection in the window. I see a middle-aged woman with blonde streaked hair and a slightly wild expression on her face. I quickly change it into a semblance of politeness, before turning back to face Bonnie.

'Your husband died recently, didn't he? I'm sorry.' Bonnie's face takes on a sympathetic mien and I realise, with something of a relief, that at least Marcus hasn't told her the full story. Though he may have had a reason for that. I chide myself silently.

'Would you like me to show you around a bit?' I offer, with a knot in my stomach which eases with her reply.

'No, but thanks for the offer. I want to get a bit of shut-eye first. I have a map. I love poking around new places on my own. I've read a bit about Sydney. I realise there's more to your city than the Harbour Bridge and the Opera House, though I want to see those too. But I'd kind of like to wander around the old area around the – what's it called – the Stones?'

'The Rocks,' I correct her with a smile, 'but I'm afraid you'll find the area's become quite a tourist trap itself. Although there is a beautiful old church and you can walk through one of the original buildings. It's a museum now.' I take her empty cup. 'Well, as you seem to be set for the day, I'll get on with mine.'

When I'm sure Bonnie is asleep I call Lissa back.

'Sorry about earlier. She was sitting right in front of me.'

'And you never were good at dissembling, were you?' My daughter chuckles. 'So give…'

'Well,' I pause trying to work out what to say. 'She's your typical Californian beach girl, blonde hair, white teeth, great smile, bubbly…'

'And full of herself,' Lissa finishes for me.

'No,' I reply slowly. 'She's actually pretty up-front and sincere. I like her,' I find myself saying and realise it's true. 'I think it's going to work out, having her here, I mean.'

'And what about your handsome Marcus?'

'Oh, that was never going to come to anything,' I reply, despite the shrinking sensation in my stomach. My fingers clench at the thought of lost opportunity. 'He's the Headmaster, for God's sake. What could anything lead to?'

'Methinks the lady doth protest too much.' Lissa knows her mother better than I've realised. I quickly change the subject.

'I had a call from Mum last night, She and Dad arrived back home a couple of days ago. Bob went up and drove them back to save Dad the plane trip. I thought I'd pop round to see them today. What are you up to? Want to come?'

'Love to, but…'

'I know. You and Will have something organised.'

'We're having a celebration lunch. Can you believe I've been living here for a whole month already? We've asked some friends around.' Lissa's voice exudes the carefree joy, with which her life is filled these days. 'I'll try to get round tomorrow. How is Gramps?'

'Mum says he seems better. Evidently the whole thing had

something to do with the fact he's a bit deaf these days. He still needs to take care, but he's home. That's the main thing. Enjoy your lunch! I'll give him your love.'

'Do that.' She pauses. 'You're okay aren't you?'

*

'Audrey King's a lovely woman, quite the lady.' We've just finished one of my mother's famous afternoon teas. I'm sitting back, feeling I never want to eat again after the lashings of tea served with scones, jam and cream followed by an apple tart to die for, when Mum makes this weird comment out of the blue.

'Who's Audrey King when she's at home?' I'm not familiar with all of Mum's friends, but I do have a passing acquaintance with most of them. I don't recall ever having heard this name before.

'Why she's your Marcus' mother of course.' Mum gives me one of her arch looks and Dad grunts.

'Thick as two thieves they've been. She didn't have much time for her old man, once that one came on the scene.'

I look from one to the other in amazement, my face turning red.

'Marcus' mother? How on earth?'

'Ask your mother.' Dad is having nothing to do with this.

'Well?'

Mum preens, but does have the grace to appear a touch shamefaced.

'It was after you all flew back. Marcus gave me a call and suggested, since we knew no one in Brisbane, his mother would be happy to provide us with any help we needed. I called her and it just went on from there.'

'They got on like a house on fire. Two peas in a pod,' Dad can't resist putting in.

'But…' My body slumps into the chair. A lump rises in my throat. 'He's my boss, Mum.'

'So…? Does that mean I can't be friends with his mother?' She bridles. 'I think I'm old enough to choose my own friends. It's a fine day when my daughter tells me who I can and can't be friends with.'

'It's not that.' I drag my fingers through my hair. 'It's just… Oh, it's all such a mess.' I begin to lose control, my hands gripping the arms of the chair as if they'll never let go.

'Steady on, girl.' It's Dad again trying to smooth things out. 'Let the girl speak,' he adds as Mum opens her mouth again. She closes it with a snap. 'What's bothering you, Anna? The fact your mother has made friends with this woman or is there something else? Something we don't know?'

'No, of course not. None of my business who Mum makes friends with, but this Audrey King, she's Marcus' mother and…'

'And…?' Mum seems to be trying to work out where I'm coming from. 'It was Marcus' idea in the first place.'

'Yes, he's like that,' I mutter, for of course it's just what he would do. I make an effort to change my attitude. 'Okay, tell me about her. I'm glad she was of help. But I thought you could manage on your own.' I can't stop my voice from sounding querulous. *What is it about my mother she can reduce me to behaving like an eight year old?*

'Yes, I did too, but I found the hospital didn't want me underfoot all day and every day so when Audrey phoned and suggested we meet for coffee, I jumped at the chance to get out of the motel room.'

'So that was it, you met for coffee?'

'The first time. We also went shopping. She knows some great little boutiques. Then she invited me to her book club meeting where I met some other ladies. They were all very charming.' Mum is beginning to sound defensive and, really, it doesn't sound too bad.

'I'm glad you had some pleasant company,' I begin with a heartfelt sigh, when she interrupts me.

'And things didn't stop there. She invited me to dinner, such a lovely home right on the water. The views…' I can sense I'm not going to like what is coming next. I'm right.

'He's such a good son – takes after his father – and they were so upset when his marriage broke up. They have a grandson on the other side of the world they don't see or hear from. Their only grandson, can you imagine? Audrey told me quite a bit about the daughter-in-law too, or ex, I should say. It seems …' I put my hands over my ears to blot out what she is going to say next.

'I don't want to hear, Mum. As I said, he's my Headmaster. His private life is none of my concern.'

'But I thought...' For once Mum looked nonplussed. 'I mean, he was so helpful at the hospital, putting me in touch with his mother and all. He may consider it your concern whether you do or not. You did mention you'd been seeing each other outside school, didn't you?'

I curse my big mouth. 'Well, yes, I did but, not that way.'

'What other way is there?' Mum looks genuinely perplexed. In her world, when a man and woman of a certain age – *my God am I really identifying as being of a certain age?* – are seeing each other, then it must be leading to something of a romantic nature. It would never occur to her our relationship might be purely professional – or purely physical. I immediately banish the unwelcome thought.

Since I don't reply, Mum continues. 'You looked so good together too, as if it was meant to be. Audrey thought so too,' she adds daring me to deny it again.

'Audrey?' My voice chokes on the name. 'She hasn't seen us together.' I cast my mind back wildly, but can't come up with any opportunity Marcus' mother has had to see me with her son.

'I showed her the photo. You know, the one you had taken at the dinner.' I suddenly remember. The professional photographer going around at the Board dinner had been snapping indiscriminately and had taken a pretty good one of me looking glam. I'd bought a copy for my parents and had forgotten Marcus was in the photo too.

'Umm.' I can't think of any response.

Pleased to have won this round, Mum gathers the tea things onto a tray and carries them into the kitchen, leaving me behind with Dad.

'She got you there, Nana,' he says using my childhood nickname. Hearing Dad say the baby term, I haven't heard for years, almost brings me to tears. Those sobs well up thinking how close I've come to losing him. I crush them down.

'Oh, Dad.' The two words say it all. They encapsulate the deep love we share, the times we've ganged up together against the rest of the family. He's always taken my side in family arguments and stood up for me against Mum. 'I'm so glad to see you well again.' I blink away the tears which threaten to engulf me.

'Someone has to be here to keep your mum under control. She'd fall apart otherwise,' he adds sagely and I realise he's fully aware of his influence, and his usual seat in the background is his way of showing strength and supporting Mum. 'You're like me, you know,' he comments, reiterating what Mum had told me in the hospital. 'Not like the others. You stand firm in a crisis. Look at how you've coped with all this Sean business.'

'Not all that well,' I say. 'It's taken a while but I think I'm through the grieving process now.' I look down at my bare finger and, automatically, the fingers of my right hand start stroking the finger which had held my wedding ring. Dad's eyes follow mine.

'I wondered when you'd get round to that,' he comments. 'What did you do with it?'

'Threw it into the ocean.'

'That's my girl. Just what it deserved.' We smile at each other with a hint of complicity. Dad and I have always seen things the same way.

He sits quietly for a few minutes then draws himself up in his chair. 'Don't take this the wrong way, Nana.'

My eyes widen as I wonder what is coming next.

'Don't be too like me. I've bottled things up all my life, haven't let my guard down. Kept control.' I open my mouth to argue, but he holds up his hand to stop me. 'Doesn't always work. That's all I'll say. Sometimes it's good to let the emotions take over. I never learnt how, but you… there's still time for you.' I open my mouth again, then swallow the words of disagreement I'd been about to utter. Dad, giving me advice like this. It's difficult to comprehend.

When Mum returns, she sits down beside Dad and begins to pleat her dress, something she does when she's not sure how her next words will be received. What now?

'When I visited Audrey and Jack,' she begins. I can't believe she's on about this again. I try to close my ears to no avail. 'They live in this retirement village at Wellington Point.' She looks across at Dad. 'Since we got back, we've been talking, your dad and I. This house,' she waves her hand around to encompass the room we are sitting in. 'It's really too big for us now. Has been for years but it's home, it's where we raised you three. It's full of memories.' Dad reaches over to pat her hand as if to provide support for what she's about to say. 'Well, we've decided it's time we found somewhere else, somewhere smaller, with less maintenance.' She takes a deep breath. 'We're going to look into retirement villages here in Sydney. It's what's called the next step in life.' She looks at me to gauge my reaction. I'm gobsmacked. I've always envisaged Mum and Dad living here till they're carried out in a box.

'If that's what you want,' I manage to say. 'Have you thought of where…?'

'We haven't had time since we got back. Your dad's not up to traipsing around just yet, but Bob's going to look into a few for us and provide us with some details. We won't be doing anything in a rush, but we wanted to prepare you.'

I'm on my way home, buoyed up with Dad's obvious recovery, though still a bit angry with Mum – the thought of her becoming bosom mates with Audrey King rankles. I'm trying to come to terms with the loss of my family home, with all of its memories when my phone rings. I glance down quickly but, conscious of the rules of the road, have no intention of answering. I do a double take when I see Marcus' name appear. I wonder what he wants. Seeing his name on my phone, coming so quickly on the revelation of his mother and mine getting together, throws me. My hands grip the steering wheel more tightly and I grit my teeth. I drive on, my mind in a turmoil.

When I reach home I sit in the car unwilling to enter the house. Despite what I've told Lissa, I'm still not too sure of how I feel about having Bonnie there. But I can't sit in my car forever. I open the front door cautiously listening for signs of my boarder. Silence.

'Bonnie,' I call, walking up the stairs. But the house remains silent and a quick peek into the spare room reveals she's not there. I let out a breath I haven't been aware I was holding, I have the place to myself. Suddenly the emptiness which had so disturbed me only a week earlier has become a solace. I sit down on my bed and slip off my shoes. My phone beeps again. A text message. I check my message bank to find a voicemail message for me. I put my phone up to my ear and press *voicemail*. I know the voice well, Marcus.

'Anna. I need to talk to you. Call me when you get this.' He sounds abrupt and again I wonder why he's calling me, not Bonnie. Ignoring the message I lie down on the bed. The late afternoon sun is making patterns on the wool carpet below the window. I can hear the birds twittering in the tree outside. My eyes close and I drift off to sleep.

It's becoming dark when I awake. I switch on the bedside lamp. Six thirty! I've slept longer than I intended. I often sneak an afternoon nap at weekends, but half an hour is usually my limit. I sit up, brush the sleep out of my eyes and smooth down my hair. I must get up. Bonnie will… Where is she? The house is still silent as the grave, the only sound the dull hum of the refrigerator coming from the kitchen down below. I make my way downstairs.

'There you are!' I jump back in shock. Bonnie is sitting at the kitchen table, looking quite at home. 'I saw you were asleep and didn't know what to do. I could have started dinner but…' Her voice tails away embarrassed.

'Sorry.' I'm not sure what I'm apologising for. 'I didn't realise you were back.' I sit down, still befuddled with sleep. 'I don't usually…' I stop. I'm apologising again. This is not like me at all.

'Shall I make coffee?' Bonnie offers tentatively. 'I know how to work your coffee maker. We have one just like it back home.' She sounds wistful and I realise she may be a touch homesick.

'That'd be great.' The delay gives me time to get my bearings. I'm going to be sharing my house with her for the next few months, so I'd better get used to it and overcome this awkwardness I have in her presence. 'Where did you go today?'

Bonnie regales me with the usual stuff which impresses the first time visitor to Sydney and finishes with: 'And I really want to climb the Harbour Bridge. I guess you've done that, Anna.'

'No, afraid I haven't.' I don't admit to my fear of heights, which makes even a walk across the bridge a bit of a feat for me. All the water so far below causes my stomach to sink. I walked across once with a group of friends and was glad to see dry land below us when we reached the other side. 'Not really my thing,' I say airily pretending to be above such activities.

'Really?' I hear the disappointment in her voice and think Marcus can take her and they can cling together at the top. The thought brings a sour taste to my mouth and reminds me I haven't returned his call. I take out my phone and press on his name.

'Hello?' His deep voice brings the now familiar shivers to my spine. I look at Bonnie across the room and suppress them.

'It's Anna,' I say needlessly. 'I'm returning your call.' I wait for the apparently urgent matter to arise. His first words surprise me.

'How's your dad?'

'Better, thanks. They're home. I dropped round earlier and he's looking good. It'll take a while, but he's definitely on the mend. There's been some permanent damage to the vestibular system which means he'll probably get some recurrence of the dizziness, so he's having therapy to help manage the symptoms. Is that why you rang?' I'm trying to get my head around this interest in Dad's welfare.

'Well, actually, it's Mum, my mum, I mean.' He coughs in the way he does when he's embarrassed. I'm surprised how quickly I've become familiar with these little habits he has.

'Your mum?' I'm bewildered.

'Yes, she… I'm not sure if you're aware I put her in touch with your parents… when they were in Cleveland… at the hospital. I thought…' I picture him dragging his fingers through his hair, as he works out how to say this.

'They told me.' My voice sounds cold, even to me.

'Right. Well, seems they got on like a house on fire, the two mums, that is. Point is, my mum forgot to ask yours for an email address. She wants to keep in touch, something about a book club and looking for a retirement village, if that makes any sense to you. I have to admit it doesn't make much to me.'

'I've just left my folks and yes, it does make a sort of sense, given what they were talking about. So you'd like *my* mum's email address?'

'That's it!' He sounds relieved to have got his request out of the way.

'I'll text you.' I'm about to put down the phone when I catch sight of Bonnie still sitting at the table. 'Bonnie's right here. Shall I put her on?'

'Uh, sure.' He doesn't sound very sure at all so I cotton on to the fact he's probably not keen to speak while I'm within hearing. Gosh, they've probably spoken today already, maybe they've even spent the afternoon together. The thought makes me uncomfortable.

'I need to catch up with something. Here she is.' I hand over the phone with a whispered 'It's Marcus,' and run quickly upstairs. I don't really have anything urgent to do, but I don't intend to eavesdrop on their conversation, much as I'd like to.

<h1 style="text-align:center">Eighteen</h1>

'I'm ready!' Bonnie's cheerful voice rings out as I shove my packed lunch into my briefcase. I've offered to give her a ride to school, even to have her shadow me for a few days this week. It's amazing what a guilt complex will do. I'm not sure what I'm feeling guilty about, maybe the unwelcoming thoughts I've been having. Anyway I'm stuck with her so intend to make the best of it.

'Lissa's so neat,' Bonnie enthuses. 'I had such a good time yesterday.' She turns and smiles at me. 'I know I'm going to just love being here.' I can't help but smile back. Lissa dropped round after seeing Mum and Dad on Sunday and the two girls soon made friends.

'She's a good kid.' I feel a glow that I've created such a warm-hearted individual. With a bit of luck, her warmth towards Bonnie will make up for my own lack of it.

'Now what's on the agenda today?' My companion is eager to begin her research, but I'm not sure exactly what she wants to see.

'It's going to be a pretty average Monday. Starts with a school assembly, a double period of Year Eleven followed by Year Twelve then Ten. Morning break and lunch come somewhere in between. I'll introduce you to some of the other teachers,' I offer, 'and I expect you'll want to spend some time with Marcus.'

'Right on. Is it true the kids all wear uniforms here?' As she speaks, she cranes out of the window to peer at a group of local schoolkids on their way to school. 'Gee they look weird, like something out of a Harry Potter movie.'

'I suppose uniforms must seem odd if you're not used to them, but they're all the go here, in both state and private schools. Wait till you see the girls at Grammar. We think they look very smart in their red blazers, white blouses and grey skirts. Along with their panama hats, of course.'

'You're joking! You'll be telling me next they wear gloves too.'

'No,' I smile, 'but they used to. Not too long ago either, though before my time. We do encourage the girls to take a pride in their appearance and believe wearing a uniform engenders that, as well as a respect for their school.'

Bonnie sits back as if contemplating this point of view. 'Well, it'll certainly be something to take back home.'

'Do you want to ride back with me after school?' We are waiting at traffic lights and I'm infused with a need to fill the silence. 'I'll be staying back for a rehearsal.'

'Rehearsal? You mean drama? I love it. Took on the main role in a play we performed at school. I'd love to come along. Can I help?'

I haven't expected her to offer assistance, so I take a few seconds before replying. I almost miss the change of lights.

'Sure. I guess so.' *Hell, I'm even beginning to sound like her.* 'I mean, if you're sure you'd like to. There are always lots of jobs going during our performance term. You're welcome to come along. We'll certainly find something for you to do.'

'What's the play?'

'*The Importance of Being Earnest.*'

'Come again?'

'*The Importance of Being Earnest* by Oscar Wilde. It's part of the curriculum. Haven't you studied it at school?'

'Not me. Oscar Wilde, isn't he that dude who…'

'Was imprisoned for his homosexual tendencies. That's right.'

'Wouldn't happen these days.' Bonnie falls silent.

We complete the remainder of the trip without further conversation. For my part, I'm wondering if she's going to take this shadowing too far. Am I going to have any time to myself? Then I remember. Surely Marcus will claim some of her time. After all, that's the underlying purpose of her visit, isn't it?

'Here we are.' We turn into the long driveway edged with Norfolk Pines, the old sandstone buildings which form the school standing imposingly in front of us.

'Wow! This really *is* like something out of a history book.' Bonnie's enthusiasm is obvious. 'We do have places like this in the States, but not the ones I attended. It's more like a university. Looks old.'

'It is, old for Australia, anyway. If you're interested, there's a ton of information in the school library. I'm sure Jenny can point you in the right direction. She's the librarian,' I explain.

As we leave the car and are making our way to the main building, I spot Marcus heading in the same direction from the opposite end of the car park. We meet at the foot of the steps.

'Dr King!' Bonnie seems to talk in exclamation marks, I've noticed. Why so formal, I wonder, but I detect an underlying mocking note. I figure they aim to keep things formal at school. Just as I have, I remember. We've been very circumspect referring to each other as Dr King and Mrs Hollis respectively when others are present.

'Ah, Bonnie.' Marcus seems distracted. 'And Mrs Hollis. All going well I trust?' He raises his eyebrows, the pile of books in his arms threatening to fall to the ground.

'Let me help you with those.' Bonnie reaches to take the top few from the pile. 'Where would you like me to take them?'

'My office.' Marcus turns a perplexed face towards me, shrugging as Bonnie leads the way into the building.

'Catch you up later,' she calls, as they disappear up the steps.

I follow more slowly, shaking my head at her youthful exuberance. No way can I compete with that.

The day passes uneventfully with Bonnie, true to her word, a mere shadow at the back of each class. She's proved a big hit in the staffroom at morning tea and lunch, with other staff members bombarding her with questions about America in general, and California in particular. She's responded enthusiastically to all their queries, never seeming to tire of repeating herself, when she hears the same questions being asked over and over again. She's certainly Miss Popularity Plus here. No wonder Marcus is besotted with her.

By the time we gather in the school hall for rehearsal, I'm beginning to flag. It's been a long day, and now I have to deal with my prima donna group of actors, with Bonnie on the sidelines watching my every move. Despite my initial ennui, the run through goes smoothly and we finish on a high note. I'm in the midst of my final comments to the girls, when Bonnie strolls over.

'What did you think?' I ask automatically.

'You're all very good,' she says to the girls, 'but the play's a bit dated, isn't it?' She looks at me. 'I mean, it's not exactly something I'd read for pleasure, would you?'

'Actually, I would.' I experience a flicker of annoyance she's chosen to criticise my choice of play. It's none of her business. She's here as an observer. However, I put on my polite face and query.

'What would you have chosen?'

'Something more in keeping with a young person's taste. I mean that story, the two men. Why not something more like *Twilight* where Bella has to choose between a vampire and a werewolf? Something more contemporary.'

'Oh, yes, Mrs H.' There is a chorus from the few girls still standing around. 'That would be so cool.'

Flustered, all I can do is reply: 'Well, too late for this one. The show is on at the end of term. We've always stuck to the plays in the syllabus,' I explain to Bonnie who is standing there, cool as a cucumber, seemingly unaware she has just stirred up a can of worms. The girls drift off, chattering among themselves, and I know I haven't heard the end of this.

'Mrs H, I like it,' Bonnie observes as we're driving home. 'Maybe I'll call you that.' She gives me a sly look out of the side of her eye and grins.

'I think not.' I'm not sure if she's serious, but I don't intend to find out. 'Anna will do fine. I get enough of the Mrs H at school. I don't need to be reminded of it outside.'

'Oh, Marcus said he'd be round tonight, if that's all right with you.' Her words come as a bit of a shock. I'd been sure they'd keep their liaison away from me. This is going to be one more challenge I'll have to face and one I can do without.

'Sure thing,' I say, without looking at her, keeping my attention focussed on the road ahead. 'Did he say what time?'

'He said he'd let us know.' Bonnie seems completely unconcerned with this lack of any definite arrangement. I can only imagine she's so sure of him, this casual sort of agreement doesn't worry her.

We've finished dinner and Bonnie is helping me stack the dishwasher – I reflect at least she's not shy about helping around the house – when my phone beeps. A quick check reveals a message from Marcus: *On my way. M*

'It's Marcus. He's en route.' I push back my dishevelled hair. A couple of weeks ago I'd have rushed to tidy up before his arrival, but now there's no point. It's not me he's coming to see.

'Isn't that a bit rude? I mean, not letting you know till he's actually on his way?' Bonnie stands up straight, her eyes wide.

I fold a tea towel and use it to wipe down the bench to give myself time to think before I reply.

'No big deal,' I say finally.

'Right. Well, we're done here. Might just freshen up.' Bonnie drifts off to the bathroom, leaving me leaning against the sink feeling flat. It's as if I've been filled with a balloon of anticipation which has suddenly deflated. No matter how often I tell myself there has been nothing between Marcus and me, that I haven't been ready for anything anyway, I still harbour a niggling thought that maybe, sometime, somehow… I shake my head to rid it of these notions and fill the coffee maker. I'll be civilised, have coffee with them, then leave the pair to their own devices.

It doesn't quite work out like that. Bonnie runs down the stairs and reaches the foot of them, when there is a ring at the door.

'I'll get it,' she trills and, from the kitchen, I hear the sounds of her excited tones interspersed with the deep sonorous note of Marcus' voice. I'm too far away to hear the actual words, for which I'm grateful. When I hear them moving from the door I come out of the kitchen, a fixed smile on my face.

Marcus takes two steps forward to greet me with a kiss on the cheek. My hand automatically goes up to touch the spot, a blush rising. I take a deep breath.

'Coffee?' I ask.

Two hours later, I still haven't been able to make my escape. The conversation has ranged from California, the conference, Bonnie's impressions of Sydney, the school and now we're dissecting today's rehearsal. I can sense Marcus is becoming restless, so I decide to make a move. I yawn and stretch, reaching my arms up in the air as far as I can. I'm surprised at how this delivers me a burst of energy.

'I think I'll call it a day.' I rise, and am surprised to see Marcus rise to his feet too.

'I'm sorry if I've kept you two ladies up.'

I signal him to be seated again.

'No, it's just me. You don't have to leave yet. I'm sure you two have things to say to each other.' I intercept an unidentifiable glance between them, then Marcus subsides into the chair as Bonnie begins to speak again.

'Yes, I'm eager to hear how you're going to implement the ideas you brought back from the conference. Maybe I can help.' It doesn't sound very romantic to me, but perhaps they're just waiting for me to leave, before they get it together seriously. I leave with my eyes clearly focussed on the stairway, as I climb up.

I lie awake, trying to forget what might be going on downstairs, and I'm surprised to hear the front door close after only half an hour. There are the usual night sounds of Bonnie preparing for bed, then I hear the light go out and silence. But still I can't fall asleep. Everything is going round in circles in my head. Sean, Gina, Dad and Mum, Marcus, his parents, the school, the play, Bonnie.

After tossing and turning for what seems like hours but, when I check my bedside clock, has been less than one, I give up. I struggle into my robe and feel my way downstairs. When I reach the kitchen, I breathe a sigh of relief and turn on the light, blinded for a moment by the brightness. I fix myself a mug of hot chocolate – surely that will make me sleepy – and plonk myself down at the kitchen table.

Strangely, it's the conversation with Bonnie at the end of the rehearsal which is repeating itself in my head. *Twilight*. What possessed her? But the more I think about it, the more I like the idea. Surely it makes sense to meet the students where they're at. Use the books they enjoy reading, as a focus for study. I seem to recall Lissa reading the *Twilight* series when she was home. I wonder if there's still a copy lying around somewhere.

I gather my robe around me with one hand and, clutching the

warm mug in the other, make my way into the living room where the bookcases hold a plethora of books gathered over the years. I turn on the lamp to browse the shelves with no luck, then… here it is. I grasp the slim volume with a grunt of satisfaction. It's still warm in here so I curl up in the large armchair below the lamp. I open to the first page.

When I hear the clock chime three I realise I've been lost in this book for several hours. I'm beginning to feel sleepy. I close the book reluctantly. If I don't get some sleep, I'll be useless tomorrow. As I climb the stairs again I reflect that Bonnie's idea has some potential. I need to work out how to structure the program. Time enough for that another day.

*

Next morning, Bonnie and I arrive at school early. I've arranged for her to shadow Glenda today, so I'll have a bit of a break. She's good company, but her unstilted enthusiasm can become wearing.

As she leaves me she calls, 'No need to wait for me today. Dr King's promised to introduce me to a car dealer. I need my own set of wheels.'

'Right.' I'm wondering why she still feels the need to keep the formality while talking with me, when a tall shadow appears in front of me. Marcus takes me by the arm.

'You don't have a class first period, do you?'

'I…'

'I've checked.'

I allow myself to be led across the courtyard into Marcus' office. He closes the door. I look at the closed door, then back at him. Whatever he has to say, he means business. His office door is one which stays open, regardless how serious the misdemeanour.

'I didn't get the chance to speak last night,' he begins.

'But…' He cuts me off before I can say more.

'I needed to speak with you. I contacted Lauren about the DNA testing. Remember we spoke about it?'

I nod.

'Well, it's taken all this time, but I finally received a reply.'

'From Lauren?'

'From her solicitor, telling me politely to get lost.' He sighs. 'She has no intention of giving me the proof I need.'

'But can't you go through the courts here? I mean, isn't your son an Australian citizen? Surely she can't deny you the right to confirm her story?'

Marcus takes off his glasses and rubs them with a rag from his desk, making them dirtier than they had been to start with. He replaces them, then, realising his mistake removes them again and examines them in bewilderment. I pass him a tissue.

'Thanks.' His voiced is distracted. 'It's Jon, don't you see? If I take this further, go through a court and all it entails, what'll it do to him?'

'So what do you intend to do?'

Marcus looks down and twiddles his fingers. 'I'm not sure I'll do anything.' He falls silent.

'But why not?' I'm at a loss to understand why he has delayed this process which will give him the information he wants. 'Is it a complicated process?'

'No, not really. In fact there's a company who will do it for under $300 and give results in around three days.' My mouth must have fallen open, as he quickly continues. 'That's if there are swabs for both parties. I have an old hair brush of his – a relic from when he was a baby, so I could use strands from that. However, with hair the matter can be a bit more complex. But that's not the problem. I'm…' he hesitates. 'I'm not really sure I want to know. What if the test really proves Jon's not mine? What have I left to hope for?'

I become impatient. 'But isn't that what you want to know?'

'Ye… es.' But he doesn't seem sure. I decide there's no point in pursuing the matter. It's really none of my business.

'I hoped you might have some ideas. You've been pretty helpful so far.' He looks at me pleadingly. I yawn. My lack of sleep is beginning to catch up with me.

'Sorry, didn't get much sleep last night,' I apologise, lest he think he's boring me. 'I can't come up with anything off the top of my head. Let me think on it and get back to you.' I feel sorry for the man, but can't help thinking Bonnie is the one he should be sharing this with. She's the one who's involved with him, not me. He looks so despondent, I have an urge to hug him. I quash it down. That would be completely out of character for me and unwelcome from his point of view.

'How is Bonnie settling in?' he asks.

'It's early days, but she seems pretty easy to get along with. She has a lot of enthusiasm.'

'She does that.' He gazes off into the distance, his eyes crinkling up at the corners. 'At the conference dinner, I think she was on the dance floor all night. Such energy!' I try to imagine him keeping up with her, but can't quite picture it. He doesn't seem the type to dance all night.

'And how about you?' Marcus takes a step closer. I find myself backing away. His nearness is somehow unsettling. I can smell his aftershave. It reminds me of the reassurance of his presence when I heard the news of Sean's death. But that was before Bonnie came on the scene.

'Oh, you know.'

'That's it. I don't. You said this erstwhile friend, Gina, wasn't that her name? You told me she's making a claim on your former husband's estate. Where is that going for you?'

His words bring me back to earth with a bump. I've been trying to put it out of my mind.

'I'm meeting with my brother on Thursday after school. These things evidently take time. He's received information from her lawyer now, and I'm to go in to see the letter. Bob doesn't want me to fight it.'

'You should.'

'I guess. It's not so easy.' Suddenly my cheeks are damp with tears. I wipe them away with the back of my hand. 'Sorry. It's just…' Before I know it, Marcus has taken two steps forward. I find myself clutched against his blue striped business shirt. I note its crisply ironed surface under my fingers. I imagine him sending his shirts out to a laundry, unable or unwilling to launder them himself at home. I relax against him, the scent of his body and aftershave in my nostrils. It feels good to have a man's strong body against mine again. I enjoy the sensation for a few minutes, then reason prevails and I lurch away.

He's looking as if he's as surprised as I am at his movements.

'It's okay,' I say with a tremble in my voice. 'I won't tell anyone if you don't.'

'I'm sorry, Anna. I didn't mean to…' He steps away and starts shuffling through a pile of papers on his desk. I'm sorry if…'

'I said it's okay,' I repeat. 'Well if that's all, I'd better get back.'

'Right, yes. You'll let me know how the meeting with your brother goes, won't you?'

'Will do. And I'll let you know if I think of anything that would help… you know.'

'Please do.' He has become the Headmaster again, and I can't leave soon enough. I walk out and close the door behind me. Let him open it again if he wants. All I want to do at the moment is to find a quiet corner in which to hide. The bell signalling the end of first period puts paid to that idea, so I front up to my Year Ten class the consummate professional, giving no indication of my inner turmoil.

The class has almost finished, when one of my more exuberant students puts up her hand.

'Mrs H have you thought any more about us doing the *Twilight* books in class?' Her question is greeted by a low murmur of approbation from the rest of the class, leading me to believe she's been selected as their spokesperson.

I remember how engrossed I became in the book I found, so smile into their expectant faces. 'It might be a possibility.' They begin to cheer silently. 'But, and it's a big but, if we do, we'll be treating it like any other English text, examining plot structure, characterisation and all the rest.'

'Oh, yes, we understand.' It's one of the quieter students this time. I'm surprised to realise how these books have struck a chord right across the group.

'Well, we'll see,' I concede, as the bell goes and they file out.

Morning break in the staffroom is the usual melee of chattering females, interspersed with the two male teachers, music and art, who somehow don't seem out of place in this predominately feminine environment. Marcus rarely joins us. His morning tea – or coffee, I don't know which – is served up by the stalwart Betty. Heather never used to join us either. My guess is they provide us with this time free from intrusion, where we can let go and discuss anything under the sun. Not surprisingly, the topic of conversation usually centres around school and the students, coming examinations, and the end of term performance.

Today, I'm relieved Marcus won't be joining us. I still haven't recovered from my lapse of control in his office. I don't want any reminder of how comforting his arms felt. It's paradoxical, just as I'm beginning to be able to feel something again, for another man, the man in my sights has found someone else. And someone so young and vibrant too. Someone with whom I can't possibly compete. I think back to my younger days, when I first met Sean. The magic was there, no doubt about it. I search my mind. Can I find that magic again? Probably not. But now I'm capable of different emotions, a more mature love. I shake myself, who am I kidding? This feeling I have for Marcus isn't love, at least not yet. It's lust pure and simple. I've been without a man for over six months now, and my body is beginning to notice the lack of human touch. To answer my sister's earlier question, Sean and I did have an adequate sex life though, I have to admit, it had become a little lacklustre of recent times. However this isn't the sort of conversation I'd ever have with my sister, or my mother for that matter. It's always been Gina who's received these confidences. Shit, did I actually confide this to her? And was that why she'd zeroed in on Sean as soon as I was off the scene? How long had she been lusting after my husband? She'd always said sex was only a physical act and she could take it or leave it. Well, she'd certainly taken it where Sean was concerned. How could he have been so weak? And how could I have been so blind? There's no answer to any of these questions.

I put my hand up to my face, as I remember its contact with Marcus' firm chest inside the crisp shirt. Then I let it drop. This is not the time or the place. I gather my books together and pick up my coffee mug.

'How's your morning going?' I go over to where Bonnie is sitting with Glenda.

'Just great.' Bonnie turns to greet me. 'Glenda is doing *To Kill a Mocking Bird*. It's one of my all-time favourites. It's interesting to see the different reaction kids here have to it.'

'Really?' I sit down and cup my hands round my mug taking a sip, while I wait for her answer.

'They're not so aware of the race issues that have beset the US, still do really. Glenda had to explain it a lot more than I'd have expected.'

'Maybe you'd like to give them your perspective next time I have that class,' Glenda puts in.

'Can I? Would it be permitted?' Bonnie gives me a doubtful look.

'Well, I know you're only meant to be an observer, but I can't see any harm in your presenting your point of view. America is very different from Australia in lots of ways. We do seem to be somewhat insular here.'

As I gather my books together, ready to return to class, I think back to my conversation with Marcus. While I'm flattered he's sharing his personal problems with me, I really mustn't allow myself to become involved. Maybe I should bring it up with Bonnie? I sigh. Why does everything connected with Marcus have to be so difficult? I have enough to worry about without shouldering his problems too.

Nineteen

'What's this? Is it something important?'

Bonnie and I have been having a quiet evening. She's been working in what was Sean's study, while I've been marking papers in the lounge room. I look up from the year ten essay which is causing me grief. *How can Alice have reached this stage of her education without having a better understanding of the basic rules of grammar?* Bonnie is waving a piece of paper at me.

I put my pen down. 'What have you there?'

'Found it behind the desk. I wasn't prying,' she assures me. 'I dropped some papers and they went all over the place.' Bonnie pulls back her hair which has managed to escape from its band. Now that we've been sharing a house for some time, I've come to realise she's not the picture perfect girl I first imagined. She's like any other young person I've known; a bit of a klutz when there's no one else around and now, I count as no one. 'Looks like some kind of medical thing,' she adds.

'Let me see.' I take the paper from her. 'It's a letter…' I read the page in amazement, 'from…' I realise it's not from a doctor I know. The heading looks as if it's from a specialist of some sort. It's addressed to Sean and dated in March of the previous year.

I read on in growing amazement. It refers to a series of tests which aren't identified, and asks Sean to make another appointment to discuss his results. I turn the letter over, then back and re-read it as if by doing so will reveal more information. I'm so lost in contemplation of this missive, I forget Bonnie is still standing there.

'Everything's okay, isn't it?' She looks awkward.

'Yes. Fine,' I reply, distracted. 'Thanks. Glad you found it. I fold the letter carefully and place it on the coffee table beside me, determined to chase the matter up next day. *What else has Sean been keeping from me? Is this one more betrayal?*

When I go upstairs to bed, I take the letter with me. I sit on the bed and re-read the words over and over as if my doing so, will reveal the letter's secrets. Finally I realise there's nothing more to be discovered. When I close my eyes, my mind wanders back in time. Suddenly, I sit up as if propelled by some unseen force. March! It was in March I surprised Sean in his office hiding a piece of paper from me. *Can it have been this letter?*

I dream of letters flying around above my head just out of reach, and waken exhausted. After a piece of toast and a banana for breakfast, I take the letter and my phone out into the courtyard. I check my watch. But it's still too early to make the call. By the time I've finished my second coffee, I'm wound up as tight as a watch spring. I dial the number and nasal voice answers.

'Can I speak with Dr Denholm, please?'

'May I ask your business; are you a patient?'

'No, my husband was a patient: Sean Hollis.'

'Then your husband must call. Does he want to make an appointment?'

'He's dead.' How blunt the stark words sound said aloud.

'I'm sorry.' There is no empathy in the voice on the other end of the line.

'Can I make an appointment?' I ask, frustrated.

'Do you have a referral?'

'No.' I haven't expected this runaround.

'I'm sorry, I can only make an appointment with the doctor if you have a referral from your GP. Dr Denholm is a specialist, you must realise.'

'What sort of specialist?' But she has already hung up. I debate calling back but realise it will do no good. Well, if Sean needed a referral, surely his GP can help me. We have both attended the same medical practice but see different doctors. I decide to make an appointment with Dr Farley, Sean's GP. No sooner thought than done and, a quick call later I have a three-thirty appointment fixed.

I'm glad it's a school day, so I don't have too much time to think about what I might discover at three-thirty. The day seems to drag, but at last school is over and I'm sitting in the doctor's waiting room. My foot taps impatiently on the floor and I hold my hands together tightly to stop them trembling. As usual, the medicos are running late. It's after four before Paul Farley walks out with my file.

'Anna Hollis?' He looks round and I follow him into his room.

'You usually see my colleague, don't you?' He raises his eyes from my file which he has been studying. 'What seems to be the matter?'

'I'm fine.' I twist my hands together. 'It's Sean, I mean, you were seeing him before he died?'

'Your husband was my patient, yes.' He frowns and takes off his glasses.

'Was he sick?' As soon as the words are out of my mouth I realise how silly that sounds. Of course Sean was sick when he came here. That's why one visits a doctor. 'What I mean is, really sick?' I rush on. 'I found this letter from a specialist. It mentioned some tests and results. The specialist won't talk to me so I've come to you for information.'

'Mrs Hollis, Anna, I don't really see…'

'He's dead, Paul. Surely that changes everything? There's no point in keeping secrets anymore. I'm his widow."

'Yes… well…' he prevaricates. 'He didn't want to worry you unduly until… I had no idea he…' My God, was the man ever going to get to the point.

'What was wrong with him? I have a right to know.' For a moment I wonder if he had some communicable disease. Maybe I should be the one having tests now. Then I relax. If that was the case, someone would have contacted me. I place my hands firmly on the arms of the chair. I don't intend to move till I receive an answer.

With a sigh, the doctor speaks into his intercom. 'Therese, can you find the file on Sean Hollis for me? Should be in the archive.' He sits back and we wait.

The file arrives and Paul Farley studies it, while I impatiently tap my foot and glare at him. Eventually he looks up. He clears his throat. 'Sean came to see me last February. He was suffering from chest pains. I referred him to a cardiologist.' He refers to the file again. 'Dr

Denholm.' He looks up. 'I'm afraid that's all I can tell you.'

'He didn't come back to you?' I ask weakly.

'No.' He closes the file. 'If that's all…?' I rise and take my leave. I walk past the reception desk in a daze and, once in my car, tears trickle down my face. Sean had been sick, really sick. He had kept it to himself.

I start to drive, my eyes blurring and my hands trembling on the steering wheel. I don't know where I'm headed, till I stop the car outside Jan's door. By this time my tears have been replaced by anger. How dare Sean keep his visits to a specialist from me? His reasoning is beyond me. We've always shared everything. *Except this*, a little voice is telling me.

I erupt into Jan's kitchen like a tornado.

'The bugger was sick. He had heart problems. He kept it secret. He didn't tell me. How could he, the bastard. I'll kill him!' The words tumble over each other till I run out of steam, realising how ridiculous my last statement is.

'What's got into you, Anna? What are you talking about?' Jan grabs me in a hug.

'I'll leave you two girls to it.' Graham departs, shooing the boys in front of him and Jan and I are left alone.

Jan slowly releases her hold on me. 'Are you all right?' she asks helplessly.

'Sorry. I just… I think I need to sit down.' I plop down at the table and bury my face in my hands. Jan leaves me alone for a few minutes, then takes my hands in hers and draws them away from my face. When I open my eyes, she's sitting beside me still holding my hands tightly.

'Tell me!' she orders, and I blurt out the full sorry story.

'So now I know why…' I begin.

'Why what?'

'Why he seemed distracted. I've been thinking back and he became distracted around last March. That was the date on the letter from the specialist. Do you think he received bad news?'

'No doubt.' Jan's dry tone surprises me. 'And is that why he went off with Gina too? Seems to me he has a lot to answer for, or would have, if he were still with us.' She loosens her grip and my hands move back to cover my face.

'Do you think…' I begin cautiously, 'do you think he knew he was going to die? That he wanted one last fling before he did? Why couldn't he have told me? We could have done all the things we had left to do; the trip to Europe, the round Australia venture, the island-hopping in Hawaii…' My voice is becoming higher and higher as I recount our retirement plans.

'Oh, my darling,' Jan's voice takes on a plaintive note. 'He wanted you to see him as he had been, not as a sick man.'

'But Gina. Do you think she knew?' But I already know the answer. Gina knew.

'So,' my sister pauses as if unsure as to my reaction. 'Will you contact her? Ask her about it?'

'Contact her? Absolutely not. I never want to see or speak to that woman ever again!'

Twenty

We're watching a television program about inland Australia, when Bonnie points to the screen, which is showing one of the islands in the Whitsundays. The presenter is expounding the glories of the resort, while commenting many visitors prefer to stay in small cabins on the beach.

'That's where I want to go in the Christmas break.' The words bubble out of Bonnie in her usual exuberant fashion. 'After the Red Centre. We're travelling across the Nullabor, then back round the top end. We'll take a few days there to relax and recover from the trip.'

'That'll be some trip.' This is the first time I've heard her speak of it. 'How do you intend to travel?' I'm only mildly curious, but realise something is required of me.

'Trail bikes, of course.' My active imagination sees her clinging to Marcus' waist, as they ride off into the sunset, like a scene from one of the romantic movies Lissa and I used to watch on wet Sunday afternoons, while Sean worked away in his office. The couple would ride off – though often in a car or on horseback – while the credits slowly rolled up the screen.

'Hank's always had a bike, and we rode together through the National Parks last year.'

I barely hear her, I'm so caught up in my imagined scenario. Hank, I think, are there really guys called Hank outside of bad movies and comic strips. I come to earth with a jolt.

'Hank. Who's Hank?'

'My fella. I haven't mentioned him before because, well, with you having recently lost your husband and all, I didn't…' her voice tails off at the stunned look on my face.

'Hank? Your fella? But I thought Marcus…'

She laughs.

'Marcus? But he's old!'

If Marcus is old, what does that make me? But I keep this thought to myself. This new piece of information is such a surprise, I can't think of anything to say.

'He's actually a bit more than my fella.' Bonnie fingers the silver chain which she always wears, and pulls out the end from which hangs an antique emerald ring. 'It belonged to his grandmother. It's far too small for my big fingers.' She holds out her hands in despair. 'We're going to have it resized, but I wanted to wear it right away. He gave it to me right before I left.' She smiles tenderly, as if remembering. 'We plan to marry next year.' She smiles again, coyly this time. 'I'd rather you didn't say anything at school. I want to be taken seriously, not as someone who is filling in time till I marry.'

'I… I'm sure they wouldn't…' I'm lost for words. It's difficult to take it all in. It contravenes all I've been imagining, since I first heard Marcus mention Bonnie.

'Another glass?' Bonnie is waving her empty wine glass in front of me. I realise the program ads have come on and yes, I do need another drink in order to digest her words. I hand her my empty glass.

'Yes please.' While she's gone I remember the strange look on Marcus' face several times recently, when I've tactfully left the two of them alone. Now it's beginning to make sense. What a fool I've been. I just assumed, and I was wrong. Then another thought occurs. What on earth must Marcus think of me? I must… no, I can't apologise. That would just make it worse. Damn! As I'm trying to muddle through these thoughts, Bonnie returns holding aloft two glasses of red wine.

'Here you go.' She hands me one, and settles down again on the floor, legs curled up beneath her.

'Now, about you and Dr King,' she begins.

This is all too close to my recent thoughts.

'What about him?' My voice sounds abrupt even to me.

'Well, I've noticed the chemistry when you're together. I mean, I'm good at detecting these things. It's not my imagination, is it?'

I don't want to have this conversation, but this is my home and I can't leave. I can't easily leave the room either, having just accepted a glass of wine. I think carefully before replying.

'We're friends, friends and colleagues, that's all.' I turn my attention to the television again, but my eyes are a blur. I'm hoping she'll leave it alone. Not a chance.

'But you're both… I mean… available, aren't you? He hasn't got a wife tucked away and you're a widow…' her voice tails off, perhaps realising my widowed state is pretty recent.

'I'm sorry. I didn't mean to intrude. I do that. Mom's always on at me for it. I don't know when to keep my big mouth shut. Subject closed. Promise.' And she turns her big baby blue eyes on me, and makes a moue with her mouth. 'Forgive me?'

'Of course.' I'm just glad she's decided to leave well alone. I can only hope she doesn't bring it up with Marcus too. I consider asking her not to, but realise it's making too much of what was probably a stray remark on her part.

We watch the remainder of the program in silence, apart from Bonnie's enthusiastic comments on the Australian scenery. When it finishes, she turns to me.

'I'm done. Think I'll turn in for the night. What about you?'

'Yeah, me too.' I rise and stretch my arms above my head. 'I'm ready for bed.' And ready to do a lot of thinking. I need to be alone to process the news she and Marcus are not an item, and to consider where it leaves me.

Once in bed I toss and turn. I can't decide whether to be pleased or not, at Bonnie's revelations. While I thought Marcus was off-limits, I could easily – well maybe not easily – subdue any feelings I felt for him. But now he is, in Bonnie's words, available, it puts a different perspective on things. Or does it? He's still my Headmaster and therefore definitely off-limits to a mere staff member. And I have to remember I'm only recently widowed, although my life with Sean now seems to be in a different time altogether. I feel poles apart from the person who was Sean's wife only a year ago.

Unable to sleep I pull my dressing gown around me and go to the window where the full moon is throwing its light on the back garden, illuminating the angel trumpet tree. I reflect that, when we discovered all its parts were poisonous, we'd been tempted to get rid of it, but I'm glad common sense prevailed. I love its long white pendulous blossoms and its heady scent.

I picture my younger self out there, laughing with Sean over some joke he's made. He was a serious man, but I could always make him laugh and he did have a weird sense of humour which always struck a chord with me. He was so gentle with Lissa, when she was a baby. She was always the light of his eye. These were good times. We were so happy. I never thought it would end. But it had to end sometime, and now I'm forced to acknowledge I'd have lost him to death now anyway. I've no reason to believe he'd still be alive, if we'd stayed together.

*

When I see Marcus at assembly next morning, I'm somewhat self-conscious. Although I try to tell myself nothing has changed, for me it has. I need to get my head around the fact that Bonnie is not his new squeeze, and I'm trying to decide how this affects me, if it changes anything. He smiles across the room to me, as if nothing has happened. Of course, for him nothing has. I smile back. I turn round to see Bonnie standing behind me with a wide grin on her face. I reflect that only yesterday, I would have read all sorts of things into her grinning like this at Marcus, but now I know better. It is just Bonnie being her usual self. I turn back and listen intently to the weekly announcements, gazing in front of me as if my life depends on it.

'What's up with you today?' Glenda whispers into my ear as we leave the assembly hall. 'You look like the cat that's swallowed the cream.'

'Nothing.' I whisper back. 'Just feeling good today.'

'About time. You've been in the doldrums for too long.' My eyes widen as I look at my friend in surprise. Have my feelings really been so obvious to everyone, or is Glenda super sensitive to my moods?

'How about a coffee after work? We haven't done that in an age.'

'Okay.' Now Bonnie has her own car I've become more independent. 'Catch you then.'

*

The day passes quickly, and before I know it, I'm sitting opposite Glenda in the local coffee shop, with a large cappuccino in front of me.

'Now, spill.' Glenda picks up her cup with both hands, and leans her elbows on the table. 'What have you been up to?'

'Oh, you know, this and that,' I prevaricate, unsure how much to reveal. Glenda is a friend, but she's a colleague too, so I certainly can't confide in her about Marcus, and Bonnie has sworn me to secrecy about her engagement. That only leaves Gina or my parents. I decide on the latter.

'We've been worried about Dad,' I begin. 'After his bad turn on Straddie, he has to slow down.'

'Not easy, I imagine with their big house in West Pymble. They have a huge garden there, don't they?'

'Yes,' I say ruefully, taking a sip of my coffee. 'And a slew of steps down through it. It's become too much for them both. Mum took a beating with Dad's turn and she's lost a bit of confidence too.'

'So what are they going to do?'

'They're planning to move. They're looking at retirement villages. I didn't ever imagine it'd come to this.' I place my cup carefully on the table, and lean on it mirroring Glenda's posture.

'Sounds like a good idea, but you don't agree?'

'I do, I guess. But the house, it's where I grew up. It's full of memories. I suppose I thought…' I consider what had I thought. I continue. 'I thought it would always be there and they would too. It's hard to think of them getting older and being unable to cope.'

'But you have to think of it from their point of view.' Glenda is always pragmatic and I know she's right.

I sigh. 'Everything's changing.' I run my fingers through my hair. 'Sean's death, Dad's illness, and Lissa moving in with her Will. I'm the only one who is staying the same.'

'But you're going to be moving too, aren't you?' I remember I've confided in Glenda I would be selling the house and looking for something else.

'That's the thing. I can't sell yet. Gina, the one Sean ran off with, she's making a claim on the estate.'

'What?' Glenda's eyes reflect her shock. 'Can she do that?'

'Mmm. I spoke with Bob only yesterday. It seems the bitch has a legitimate claim.'

Twenty-one

The next few days pass in a blur. I manage to muddle through my teaching and playground supervision without having to meet Marcus. After Bonnie's revelations, I feel rather shy where he is concerned. I need time to come to grips with my new insights. It's not till Friday afternoon that I turn away from closing my classroom door, to find myself face to face with the cause of several sleepless nights.

'Been avoiding me?'

This is so close to the truth that I look down, a blush colouring my cheeks. There is silence. I realise he's waiting for an answer, and isn't going to leave until he gets one. I raise my eyes to meet his quizzical gaze.

'No. Why would I do that?' I essay a smile, which fails dismally.

His brow furrows. 'Is it something I've done… said…? The other night… did Bonnie…?' The poor man is clearly perplexed and his confusion puts me at ease. I hasten to reassure him.

'No, nothing you've done… or said. I've been busy.' My voice dries up and I look away again. I give myself a mental shake. *This is your boss, Anna. For God's sake can't you at least be polite and make some sensible conversation?*

I turn to walk away, and Marcus turns to walk with me, taking the heavy satchel out of my hands. 'Let me take that for you,' he mutters, as we walk down the now deserted corridor. 'Seems we're the only two left.'

He's right. I've been delaying my departure each day, to avoid just such a confrontation. It's close to four o'clock, and all the other staff and students have departed, leaving Marcus and me. We walk through the school, our footsteps echoing in the empty corridors and I reflect, not for the first time, how a school only comes to life when the students are there, rushing hither and thither and chattering madly.

'Bit like a ghost town, isn't it?' His words echo my thoughts and, for a moment, I forget my awkwardness to smile up at him. My breath catches in my throat seeing he is smiling down at me, his hair flopping over his forehead. He raises a hand to push it back, then nudges his glasses up the bridge of his nose. It's all so familiar and endearing. We stop at the entrance.

'Where's your car?'

Speechlessly I point to the solitary vehicle in the staff car park. He moves awkwardly from one foot to the other. 'I wondered… that is… if you're not…' His awkwardness has the effect of putting me at ease. A genuine smile forms on my lips, as I wait to hear what he is trying to say.

'Dinner?' he finally utters. 'Tonight? Or is tonight too short notice? Would tomorrow be better?'

Knowing the whole weekend stretches emptily before me, I pause before replying, then anxious to put him at his ease, 'Tomorrow would be good,' I say.

He sighs with relief. 'I'll see you to your car.' And he begins to walk briskly towards my *VW*, while I try manfully to keep up with his long strides.

I drive home in a daze. Regardless of what I've believed about our past meetings, this time I can't argue with the fact I've agreed to a date; a date with the boss. Not a good idea. Never mind the fact that it's only a few months since my husband died. I think of Sean. The two men are very different types, but I think Sean would have liked Marcus. I stop myself. Thinking in this vein is not going to be helpful to anyone. I turn my mind to more mundane topics. I begin to plan dinner; dinner for one, as Bonnie has now found herself a social life and her weekend starts on Thursdays. I think she and Lissa have become good mates, but haven't enquired too much. What I don't know can't hurt me.

I walk in the door to find the phone ringing. I drop my bags to answer it.

'Good, you're home!' Jan's tone irritates me. It's been a hectic Friday at school, then there was Marcus with his dinner invitation, now my big sister seems to be accusing me of God knows what. I sink into the armchair, strategically placed beside the hall table which holds the telephone.

'What do you want?' I try to keep the irritation out of my voice, but clearly don't succeed.

'What's up with you?' But, in typical fashion, without waiting for a response, Jan goes straight to the point. 'Have you spoken to Mum and Dad? Heard what they intend to do?'

'Well. Yes…'

'Don't go anywhere. I'll be right over. Graham's fixing the boys' dinner, then taking them to a movie.'

I stare at the now dead phone and, hoisting myself up, collect my bags and slowly make my way upstairs. I need a shower and a glass of something alcoholic before I can face my sister. It'll take Jan at least half an hour in Friday traffic to reach here. That should give me time to freshen up and prepare myself for the onslaught her visit is sure to bring.

Thirty-five minutes later, Jan has arrived and I'm in the kitchen dressed in my casual gear of white cargo pants teamed with a sky blue tee shirt, pouring out two glasses of red.

'Now!' We're seated at the kitchen table wineglass in front of each. 'What do you think? We can't let the house go. It's our family home.'

'But Mum and Dad…' I begin weakly, not sure where this is going.

'Yes, yes, I know they need to move. That became patently obvious when Dad was in hospital. They can't go on rattling around in that big place. All those steps too. But this idea of a retirement village. It makes them sound so old.'

'They *are* getting old,' I interject when she takes a breath. 'We'll all be there one of these days. They're working out a solution for themselves. I don't think it's any of our business.'

'It's these people Mum met up in Brisbane, who've put them up to it.' Jan fixes me with a glare. 'You introduced them, didn't you? This Audrey and Jack they're always on about now. Why on earth…'

'Steady on.' I can't let this pass. It's time I set the record straight. 'It's nothing to do with me. What I mean is that they are nothing to do with me. I don't even know them.'

'Then who…?'

'This Audrey and Jack they speak about. They're…' I gulp. 'They're Marcus' parents.' There is silence while my words sink in.

'Marcus? Your headmaster? Where does he…? Oh, that's right, he helped with the rooms and stuff when we were up there.'

'Right, when Dad was in hospital and Mum fell to pieces.'

'But how?' Jan looks astonished.

'It seems that Marcus gave Mum his mother's number and somehow the two of them…' I open my arms to display my own amazement at this turn of events.

Jan looks bewildered. 'But I thought you said that you and he weren't…' Her right hand makes circles in the air as she tries to describe the relationship which I've already denied.

'We weren't, we're not…' I cross my fingers as I utter this little white lie, and tell myself there's still nothing between us. Our date isn't till tomorrow night.

'So they just got together by themselves? And now they're acting like long lost buddies. Well!' Jan sits back and takes a gulp of wine, emptying the glass, then holding it out towards me. 'I think I need another.' She ferrets around in her bag while I pour a refill. 'Have you seen these?' She proffers a handful of colourful brochures depicting older couples purportedly having fun playing bowls, frolicking in a pool, chatting around a barbecue. 'I was round there earlier today and this is all they can talk about. You mean you haven't seen them?'

'No.' I wearily take the material from her outstretched hands, placing them on the table. 'Why are you so against this move?' I ask.

'I'm not, not really. But… it's all so sudden.' My stoic big sister's voice breaks and I see the glimmer of a tear begin to emerge from the corner of her eye.

'I know. It's hard to think of them getting old, isn't it? But if this last year has taught me anything, it's that nothing is forever. Look how my life has changed since last Christmas and it's not even a year ago.' I'm about to go on, but Jan interrupts.

'Sorry, sis. I should have realised.' She wipes the back of her hand over her face. 'Don't mind me. I suppose you think I'm overreacting?'

'No. I think you're doing what any concerned daughter would do.

You want to be part of their decision, don't you? You see, that's the difference between us, well, one of them.' I attempt a laugh which doesn't quite work. 'You like to be the one in charge, organising things, in this case Mum and Dad's future. I think you're more upset that they've taken advice from Marcus' parents and not you, than that they're planning to move.' I raise my eyebrows, and see a flush come to her cheeks. I'm right!

'And you're the little goody two shoes happy with anything they decide.' Jan's words hit me with a shock. I'm still trying to fashion a reply, when she speaks again.

'Sorry. My big mouth getting away from me once more. So, there's nothing going on between you and the Headmaster, mmm?'

'No. That is… shit!' I know that my face is giving me away so decide to come clean. 'Well, he's asked me to dinner.'

'A date then, a real one, this time.' I recall with embarrassment, how I've denied that my earlier encounters with Marcus were actual dates. I take a sip of wine before replying.

'Guess so,' I mumble. 'But,' I qualify my words, 'it still doesn't mean anything. 'He's just being kind.' I realise how lame that sounds. I don't even believe it myself.

'Kind! Have you looked in the mirror recently? I know I shouldn't be saying this, but you seem to have blossomed since Sean left.' She puts her hand up to cover her mouth. 'Sorry sis, that didn't come out right. I mean no disrespect but it's true. You look different and you seem to be coping pretty well, considering.'

'Considering my husband left me for my best friend, then was careless enough to die, leaving her claiming his share of my home, you mean?' I slam my glass down on the table. Fortunately it's empty, and the glass is strong enough not to smash. 'I think you've said enough.'

Jan gets up to leave. 'Call me when you've calmed down. You know I always state it like it is, and that's like it is. Also, we need to talk about Mum and Dad. We at least need to check out these places they're looking at. Don't you agree? And we need to talk about what's going to happen to the house.'

'Yes, yes.' I'd agree to anything to see her leave. In the short time she's been here, she's managed to stir me up. I need some time alone to recharge my batteries and find some calm. I show Jan out and sit down on the bottom step of the stair. *How have I allowed myself to get into this situation? Surely I have enough happening in my life without Marcus and the possibility of a new relationship?* I catch myself mid-thought. *Steady on! Where did this idea of a relationship come from? But I can't kid myself. I do find him incredibly attractive. Attractive, yes, but a relationship? That's something else entirely. I'm definitely not going there!*

A quick sandwich and too many biscuits. later, I'm watching an unmemorable sitcom on television when I hear a key in the front door.

'Look who I found skulking outside the pub' Bonnie breezes into the room, with an embarrassed Marcus lagging behind her.

'Sorry, sorry.' He raises his hands in a defensive gesture. 'I was out walking. I told Bonnie you'd be busy tonight but…' His hands spread. 'She's a difficult girl to argue with. Wouldn't take no for an answer.'

'She is!' I push my fingers through my dishevelled hair, looking around at the detritus left by my evening's snacking. Clearly, I've not had a busy evening. 'My sister came round,' I say in my defence, knowing perfectly well that I sound belligerent. 'She's not long gone,' I add, in an attempt to explain the plates and empty wine bottle on the floor beside the sofa. I stand up. 'So!'

'So!' Marcus repeats.

'I'm off to bed. See you in the morning.' And with those parting words, Bonnie sails up the stairs, leaving Marcus and me standing looking at each other in silence.

'Can I offer you something?' I ask at last. 'A drink?'

'That would be good,' is his reply, 'maybe a mug of that hot chocolate of yours?'

'Hot chocolate it is.' I move to the kitchen thinking I'll have time to recover from his unexpected appearance but, when I turn round, I see he's followed me in.

'Cosier in here.' Marcus seems to have recovered his equilibrium, and lost his initial embarrassment.

'Yes,' is all I can say, as I busy myself with the makings of the hot drinks. I'm wondering why he has come, while trying to figure out what to say. I'm not usually tongue-tied, but there's something about this man, which can reduce me to either a babbling mess or a dumb idiot. The latter is the case tonight.

Marcus sits at the table, stretching his legs out under it. He leans his elbows on the surface, propping his chin up on his hands. I glance over then away quickly. He looks so at ease there, as if he belongs. A vision of Sean sitting at that same place comes into my mind. He had belonged here too. But Sean usually had his head buried in a paper, I think resentfully, whereas Marcus is regarding me as if I am something special. There is a look in his eye, which I can't quite identify, but which makes my hands shake so much the chocolate powder spills. It's as if he's undressing me with his eyes. I've never seen Marcus in this mood before. It's unsettling. I'm so flustered I can't think straight.

'Skulking. I wasn't skulking. I don't skulk.' As he harks back to Bonnie's comments I suddenly realise my esteemed headmaster is a trifle under the weather.

'Of course you don't.' A sound which is remarkably like a giggle escapes me, and I immediately regain control of my actions. The man's been drinking! That's why Bonnie found him outside the pub. No wonder he turned down the offer of another drink. He's had quite enough.

It amuses me that this pillar of the community, the model of rectitude, hero to the school, staff and students, can occasionally let himself go. He's not as stiff a character as I've imagined. It makes him more human. I feel myself relaxing.

Two hours later, we are still sitting here and my eyes are beginning to close. With two cups of hot chocolate inside him, Marcus has begun to sober up. He rises to his feet.

'I'd better go and get out of your hair.' He drags his fingers through his own. 'It's not been quite the sort of evening I envisaged spending with you. I'll be better tomorrow. Promise.'

I follow him to the door and, somehow, in the process of my opening it and his going through it, I am caught up in what, in earlier years, would have been called a clinch. Given our differences in height, my face is pressed against his firm chest and I can hear his heart thumping. Mine is matching it. I can move neither forward nor back. We seem to jostle for a few seconds then his face leans down to meet mine and our lips touch. It's a gentle touch, but more than a graze. I stop trying to analyse it, and give in to the sensation. His lips are soft and gentle as they nibble on mine. Then his arms reach around me and crush me to him. I'm caught up in the ecstasy of the moment, then, as suddenly as it started, he draws away.

'Sorry, sorry. I keep saying that, don't I?' Marcus rubs his chin ruefully. 'Let's wait till tomorrow. We can be more private then. Pick you up at seven.' And, without waiting for my response, he's off.

Twenty-two

I spend the whole of the next day preparing myself. Well, I justify, I may not be ready for a relationship, but sex is something else and I certainly am ready for that. As I wash my hair in a fragrant shampoo, shave my legs silky smooth, luxuriate in a foamy sweet-smelling bath and manicure my nails in Number One Red, my thoughts veer in one direction after another.

On the one hand he is my headmaster and, as such, I should steer clear. *What will the school – staff and students alike – think if they find out?* On the other hand there is this strong attraction, chemistry even – Bonnie was right – between us, and I've been missing the physical side of marriage. It's been almost a year since… I don't allow my thoughts to go there as *there* includes Sean who is no go territory.

What the hell, I decide, putting the final touches to my make-up – a tad more than usual – and slip into the red dress I wore to the cocktail party, the party where I first met him as Headmaster. I slide my hands down my hips, turning this way and that to admire myself in the mirror. Not bad for my age. I give a last pat to my hair. I sweep downstairs, just as the doorbell rings. I'm ready for anything. Bring it on!

'Wow!' Marcus' admiration is obvious. He twirls me around, the skirt of my dress billowing out around my knees. He's taken both of my hands in his, so I'm standing on my tiptoes trying not to lose my balance.

'I remember this dress. Didn't you…?'

'Yes. I've worn it before, the night we first met' I wonder now if it's been a mistake. I don't want any reminder of my embarrassment on that night. But I have no need to worry.

'Yes.' He puts me down gently and his eyes glaze over. 'It was hot then, and it's hotter now.'

Not as hot as my cheeks. I put both hands up to touch them. Is it the effect this man has on me or is it a hot flush? Whatever, I'm feeling a lot warmer than I did coming down the stairs.

'Shall we go?' I ask, reaching to the hall table for my bag.

'What? No offer of a pre-dinner drink?'

'Oh.' I'm taken aback. 'Sorry, did you…?'

'I'm only teasing.' His familiar grim appears, his eyes crinkling up. He pushes his glasses further up his nose – I've noticed he does this when he's nervous. So I'm not the only one apprehensive about this evening and what it might bring. 'Let's go.'

'Where are we going?' He's handed me into the car and we're moving down the road towards Manly Beach.

Marcus gives me a quick glance out of the side of his eye. 'I thought seafood with a view. Does that work for you?'

'Perfect.' I snuggle down in the soft leather seat, prepared to be spoiled. Seafood is my favourite, but Sean wasn't too keen, something about having seen his mother with a fishbone stuck in her throat as a child. I'd never understood, but it meant that we rarely, if ever, went to seafood restaurants. *Stop it. Sean is gone. Leave him alone. Enjoy the now.* I close my eyes in an attempt to bring a shutter down on the past.

'Not falling asleep on me already are you?' The jocular note in Marcus' voice leads me to open my eyes with a snap.

'Just thinking,' I mumble and determine to focus on enjoying the evening ahead.

The evening passes without incident. Marcus is particularly attentive, and I enjoy the unexpected treat of sparkling wine to accompany an entrée of salt and pepper calamari followed by a shared lobster dish. We finish with a dessert wine to accompany my favourite crème brûlée. Replete, I sit back and fold my napkin.

'That was delicious, thanks.' I meet Marcus' eyes across the table and smile warmly. 'It's been a perfect evening.' I stretch my hand across the table to meet his.

'I'm glad. I sensed that you needed some TLC.'

'Oh!' *Have I misread his intentions? Is he only intent on providing some compassion to a fragile staff member.* I draw myself up and quickly take my hand back, stroking the tablecloth as I do so, in an attempt to pretend it has strayed to his side of the table by accident. But it appears that I'm wrong again, as his hand immediately snakes over to cover mine.

'So how about it? Some tender loving, I mean?' I nearly choke. What does one say to such a question? Is it too blatant to accept unreservedly, or should I play coy – difficult for someone of my age and experience – and pretend to misunderstand. I'm still grappling with finding a reply when the waiter hands him the bill and Marcus takes my hand in his.

'Shall we go?' We rise together.

'I must go to…' I point to the Ladies room and, pulling my hand from his, walk off as elegantly as I can manage.

Fortunately the room is empty. I stand at the sink with a sensation of 'here I am again'. I've been here before, wearing this very dress too. The difference being, last time I was hiding from Marcus while this time… I'm not quite sure what I'm doing here. I'm tempted to splash cold water on my face but, just in time, I realise that to do so would ruin my careful make-up. I take a deep breath. This is it, if he means what I think he means. I've fantasised about it often enough, but fantasy and reality are two different things. I haven't had sex with anyone but Sean. He was my first and only. How can I? Should I? The door behind me opens and a couple of chattering women walk in. I can't stay here forever. Marcus will be wondering where I've got to. I renew my lipstick – Number One Red to match my nails – drag a comb through my hair, lift my head up high and walk out. I can do this.

'There you are!' Marcus is waiting for me in the foyer. He takes my arm and steers me through the door. My body reacts to the warmth of his hand. I'm suffused with a longing which convinces me I'm doing the right thing, though, I remind myself, I'm not doing anything as yet. I'm still not sure if I've correctly interpreted Marcus' intentions. We make our way to the car, with his hand still firmly holding my arm.

'Afraid I'll run away?' *My God, did I really say that?* 'I mean…'

'I thought you had. You were gone so long.'

'Yeah, I considered climbing out the bathroom window but it was too high.' *Where am I finding this less than witty repartee?* But Marcus plays right along.

'And now I have you captive and I'm taking you off to my lair.' He laughs. 'A nightcap at my place?' He takes my silence as assent and we drive in the opposite direction to home. It's not too late. I can still chicken out, but I've read somewhere that agreeing to go back to a man's apartment is tantamount to agreeing to have sex with him. I can't use the euphemism 'sleep with', even to myself. I slept with Sean every night of our marriage, but towards the end sleep was all we did. I have no intention of *sleeping* with Marcus. That's not part of the plan.

Despite the air conditioning, I open a window letting the breeze cool my now feverish cheeks. Fortunately the traffic noise precludes any further conversation, and we drive on in silence. We slow down outside an apartment block right on the water's edge. With a flick of his wrist, Marcus sets a garage door open. We drive in and park.

'We're here,' Marcus says unnecessarily. I sit, frozen in place, unable to move. This doesn't seem to faze him and, as if he does so every day of the week, Marcus walks around to my side of the vehicle and opens the door. Realising I can't sit here forever, I swing my legs out, my dress riding up over my knees as I do so. *Damn, what if he thinks I've done this deliberately?* I surreptitiously pull it down as I rise. His hand on my back, Marcus guides me towards the elevator which smoothly takes us up and up. It seems his confidence grows as we ascend and, now he is on his home ground, the awkward Marcus I'm familiar with, has vanished to be replaced by a confident man-about-town.

Suddenly the elevator stops. My companion leads me out into the hallway of an enormous apartment. At the other end of the long corridor I can see the lights of Sydney though a window as tall as the wall.

'Gosh!' I'm struck dumb. This place must cost the earth. Surely he can't afford it, on even a headmaster's salary.

'It is a bit like that, isn't it?' As we walk through to the lounge room, my feet sink into the deep carpet. Three white leather lounges are strategically placed facing the window, while the walls sport huge works of art which wouldn't look out of place in the Sydney Art

Gallery. I gaze fascinated at the window which takes up the whole wall and I'm drawn towards it.

'Gets everyone that way.' Marcus follows me over, casually swinging an arm around my shoulders. 'Look, you can see the bridge and the Opera House. He points with his free hand. 'And, over there, is Australia Square where we had lunch.'

'But, how…?' I pause realising it will sound rude if I ask how he can afford a place like this, but that is the question foremost in my mind.

He must guess as he quickly says, 'Oh, it's not mine. My mate, Bryan, lent it to me. He's overseas right now. Bit of luck, really, his going off around the time I arrived. He's a sort of entrepreneur. Not quite sure what all he's into, a bit of property development and a bit of this and that. All legal, I'm sure,' he adds, seeing my doubtful expression. Anyway, it has meant I can have this place till he gets back. Pretty nice, isn't it?'

'Nice? It's fantastic!' My eyes can't leave the vista of Sydney stretching out before us. This is a place to die for. If I am going to give in to my baser instincts, what better spot than this?

'A drink?' He turns me to face him and lifts my chin with his finger. 'But first.' He bends his head down. His lips touch mine. I am drowning in him. My knees turn to water. I am about to fall when his arms encircle me and draw me to him. I feel his firm body press against mine. I am lost in a sea of emotion, unable to think of anything other than the sensation of his lips on mine. Any doubt has been eradicated. This is what I want.

He draws back, releases me and my feet sink back into the carpet. My whole body is shaking. 'I've been wanting to do that all night. Now, how about that drink?' His voice seems to be echoing from the distance.

Slowly I return to the present. 'A drink? Yes.' I topple into the deep sofa and slip off my shoes, while Marcus produces a bottle of champagne – French, I note – and two glasses. He pours us both a glass, before joining me on the sofa. It sinks beneath his weight. I notice that, although it is a wide sofa, there is very little space between us.

Marcus raises his glass. 'To us.'

'To us,' I repeat and take a sip. Conscious of the amount of wine

I've already drunk at dinner I'm wary of drinking too much. I put my glass down. Marcus' arm goes around me again. It feels good, safe. He's altogether more muscular than Sean, I note with one part of my brain, while another part is enjoying his proximity. I dismiss all thought of my former husband as my body responds to the immediate situation. Marcus' hand begins to stroke my upper arm causing tiny shivers of excitement to run up and down my skin. I'm vaguely conscious of Marcus depositing his glass on the table beside mine.

'You're beautiful.' He strokes my cheek with the back of his hand, his fingers making my whole body tremble. My breathing quickens. I quiver in expectation. 'I think we should retire to the bedroom,' he says thickly. By this time I'm willing to go anywhere with him, but the bedroom sounds good. He picks me up. My arms encircle his neck and he carries me off, like a caveman carrying his prize to his lair.

Marcus lays me gently on a bed which seems to be enormous. I sink into its depths and feel as if waves are lapping up around me. I'm not sure how it happens, but suddenly we're both naked and reaching for each other hungrily. Lips meet, tongues meet and our hands reach for each other's bodies as we attempt to assuage our hunger. I sigh with satisfaction when I feel Marcus' practised hands on my nipples, which have hardened to meet them. I push myself against his bare flesh. I've forgotten how hard and comforting a man's body can be. I ache to feel him inside me. Recognising my need of him, but in an attempt to prolong my pleasure, Marcus delays the vital moment, choosing instead to provide me with as much anticipatory ecstasy as his tumescent body will permit. His mouth travels down my body bringing me to a writhing state of desire. Finally, when neither of us can bear it any longer, he thrusts into me causing me to emit moans of delight and for a while we are lost in each other, the pleasure so heady, the moment sublime. We lie together, spent and damp with perspiration, our bodies still entwined.

'My love.' Marcus strokes my shoulder, his hand travelling down my arm causing me to quiver once again. His lips touch the sensitive spot below my collar bone and travel up, parting my moist lips and teasing his tongue into my waiting mouth. I want to swallow him whole, to become part of him again. His firm body feels so wonderful against my own soft flesh, the hairs on his chest touching against my breasts with an exquisite torture.

'Everything is all right. We are together. All is as it should be.'

I lie in a trance enjoying his soft voice and the sensation of closeness before I fall into a deep sleep, completely spent.

*

I awaken slowly and stretch my arms wide. They encounter something, another body, and I open my eyes in shock, sit bolt upright and peer around me. Of course, Marcus. The room comes into focus as I recall our night of passion. Realising I'm naked, I quickly flop back down, pulling the doona up to my chin and peer at the bedside clock. My God, it's almost five. I've fallen asleep. I look around the room seeing the garments discarded in haste. A sigh escapes me. Staying overnight was not in my plan. If I had a plan, it had not included sleeping together.

I move to slide out of the bed, but I'm halted by an arm and a leg encircling me like an octopus.

'Where do you think you're going?' Marcus' voice is sleepy, but his arm has the strength of a chain as it restrains me. I look down on his morning face, the overnight growth of beard, the tousled hair, and a small groan of satisfaction escapes me.

'Home,' I reply. 'I can't… I shouldn't… I need to be home before Bonnie emerges.' My voice squeaks, and I suppress a giggle as a hand tickles me under the covers. 'I must go,' I reiterate pulling away, much as I'm tempted to remain here in this comfortable bed with its sexy occupant. I lean down to place a kiss on his lips, his warm arms coming around me again.

'Well, if you're sure…?' I'm not at all sure, but I know that I must.

'Yes.' I force my voice to sound deliberate, but realise it won't take much to change my mind. Marcus's lips are firm beneath mine and, as his tongue enters my mouth, all thought of leaving disappears in the wonder of his touch. Last night I'd been befuddled with champagne, but now, I experience the full sensation of the length of Marcus' strong body against mine. My hands reach around his wide shoulders as his legs encircle me.

'Not yet,' his voice is thick with desire, and somehow I'm on top of him, my eyes close and I'm transported into another world again, a world where time and space have no meaning and I move with the gentle rhythm of him, of us.

As I slowly return to the present I hear a murmur in my ear: 'Coffee?'

'Wha…' I croak.

'I asked if you'd like coffee… before you go,' Marcus is smiling down at me. At this distance I can see every line and wrinkle on his familiar face. 'Maybe a shower too?'

I push my hair out of my face. 'Coffee would be good.'

With a kiss on my forehead, Marcus leaps out of bed, and I barely have time to admire his rugged physique before he dons a blue striped towelling robe which barely covers him, and is tying the belt as he looks around to find his glasses. 'Where did I leave them?'

I pick them up from the table on what has been my side of the bed and wordlessly hand them to him.

'Thanks.' He peers at me. 'There you are. Blind as a bat without them. I'll get the coffee   going while you…' he points to the ensuite.

Holding the doona to my chest, I wait till he leaves before I swing my legs over the side of the bed, my feet sinking into the thick carpet. I shiver. I've just made love to the man, but feel nervous at the thought of him seeing me naked. I ignore the fact that we've been together, naked, for the whole night. Somehow, everything appears different in the stark morning light.

The bedroom, which I haven't noticed the previous night, is decked out in much the same style as the living area. The large king-sized water bed takes pride of place and is flanked by wide bedside tables each holding a pile of books alongside a bedside lamp. The entire length of the wall opposite the bed is taken up with a mirrored wardrobe while one of the other walls is another ceiling-length window. It appears that we have failed to close blinds or curtains the night before and, in the rising dawn, the sun is beginning to glow behind the city buildings in the distance.

I shower and collect my clothes from the floor, make what reparations I can to my hair and face, and leave the bedroom, following the welcome aroma of percolating coffee to the large airy kitchen.

'Morning,' I say nervously. *How does one behave after a night of passion?* It's unfamiliar territory for me, but maybe not for Marcus?

As if sensing my uncertainty, Marcus immediately wraps me in his arms and kisses me on the top of my head. 'No regrets?' he asks gently.

'No,' I say quietly. 'You?' I wait apprehensively for his reply, but I needn't have worried.

'How can you ask? It was indescribable. *You* are indescribable. I've waited for this moment since… since I first recognised you across the room, at that dreadful cocktail party.'

I'm glad my face is still buried against his chest to hide my blushes. He pulls apart and tips up my chin with his finger. 'You were wearing this same dress and I'd never seen anything so beautiful.' His lips meet mine in the gentlest of caresses. He moves away slightly. 'Now, coffee, if we're to get you home.'

'No need for you to do anything, I can…' I begin only to have Marcus remind me that my car is sitting in the garage at home.

'What sort of man would I be to let you find your own way home?' he asks, shock in his voice and I realise, not for the first time, what a gentleman he is.

We drink our coffee sitting close together by the high kitchen bench. It's as if he can't bear to be apart from me. I feel incredibly cherished and wish I could stay here like this forever. But this is not to be. I need to go home and face Bonne's inevitable questions about my *date*.

As we drive back to Seaforth, I see I'm not the only person in Sydney to be returning home in my evening attire this Sunday morning. I only hope I can reach my bedroom undetected. It will never do for my house guest to see me skulking – one of her favourite words – in at this time of the morning.

Fortunately the house is quiet. I creep upstairs past Bonnie's tightly shut door, breathing a sigh of relief when I reach my room. I undress and throw myself on the bed, my body glowing as I relive the ecstasy of the previous night and again this morning. Making love with Marcus has been all I have imagined, all I could have hope for. I wrap my arms around my body in delight, but remind myself not to become carried away. This is not a relationship, it's a… I can't put a name to it. Affair sounds too quaint, episode, too damning. Well, whatever it is, I aim to enjoy it.

I must have fallen asleep again, because the next thing I know there is a rattling at my door and Bonnie's voice is calling me. 'Hey there, sleepy head. I'm planning on brunch at the marina. Want to join me?'

Brunch? What time is it? My mobile phone is lying on the bedside table and I see that it's already past eleven, closer to midday. I prop myself up on one elbow. 'Sure thing,' I yell. 'Give me time to shower and I'll be right with you.'

'No hurry. I'll do some coffee. Need a caffeine hit after last night.'

When I finally make it downstairs, Bonnie is sitting in the kitchen with a large coffee mug in front of her. 'I'm sorry I didn't… didn't let you know…' I listen, waiting for her to elaborate. 'Went out with Lissa and her crowd last night and didn't make it home.' She blushes. 'Bunked down on her floor, a bit hard, have to admit. She rubs her hindquarters and I bless the endurance of the young, realising I needn't have gone to such trouble when I returned.

'No worries,' I say.

'And how was it with Marcus? I'm all ears.'

'It was good.' I'm not one to kiss and tell and certainly not in this instance. 'We had a nice meal, seafood, and a good chat.' I leave it at that though I see a gleam in her eyes suggesting she knows there is more to it than what I've said, but she lets it go without further comment.

Twenty-three

The next few weeks pass in blissful togetherness. Marcus and I manage to maintain our professional relationship at school, while afterwards we fall into each other's arms, usually at his apartment. After the first occasion I am careful to leave before midnight, preserving my belief that the actual nature of our relationship can remain secret. I imagine we are being very clever and that no one guesses until, one day, after a particularly gruelling morning with Year Eight, Glenda nudges me in the staffroom.

'What's with you and the Headmaster?' she whispers.

'What do you mean?' I open my eyes wide, feigning surprise. 'What's with me and Dr King?'

'You know,' she winks.

'I don't. There's nothing going on.' I bite my lip, hoping I sound believable.

'Come on, you can tell me. I've heard your car's been seen in his neighbourhood.

I breathe a sigh of relief. Is that all?

'My car's been in a lot of places this year. Since Sean left I've been out and about more than before. So who's this super sleuth who's been stalking me?' I try to laugh it off. Glenda looks sheepish.

'It's just something that's going around. But if you swear, then I'll quash it. That's what friends are for, after all, and we are friends, aren't we?'

'Of course we are,' I reassure her.

'And you would tell me, wouldn't you? If there was anything, I mean.'

'Of course I would,' I lie. 'Now let's fix ourselves some coffee or the bell will be going. I need my caffeine to keep me going today.' I move across to the coffee maker, conscious of Glenda's suspicious look. Maybe she believes me, maybe she doesn't, but we'll need to be careful after this. I'm not exactly sure why, but we've both felt the need for secrecy at this stage in our relationship. There I've said it, even if it's only to myself. Marcus and I are in a relationship. I can no longer fool myself that it's only sex. This stuff between us has gone way beyond that.

I ponder. I guess it's so new for both of us that we'd like to keep our relationship secret for a bit longer. Though it won't be long before Bonnie guesses, and my family. I'm not such a closed book to them. Lissa, in particular can read me really well and if Jan sees me… I'm conscious I'm smiling more and, when I look in the mirror, I see a glow which wasn't there before.

I make it through the rest of the day without incident. I'm not seeing Marcus tonight. It's time I saw my family so I'm off to Lissa's after school, then to Mum and Dad's for dinner. But these arrangements don't mean we won't be in touch. I'm still bemused by the difference technology has made to relationships such as ours. Phone, email and, most of all, texts, mean that we're never out of touch for long.

As I leave the building at three-thirty, I send Marcus a quick text warning him of Glenda's suspicions. He texts back he'll call me later this evening, and I set off on my duty calls. No, that's putting it too strong. I do enjoy seeing my family, but Lissa is fast growing away from me as her relationship with Will deepens, and Mum and Dad… They are in change mode and seem to have forgotten that there is another world out there beside their own.

*

This will be the first time I've visited Lissa in her new abode. Driving over Spit bridge I turn left to Balmoral Beach, remembering the many times Sean and I have taken our daughter there as a young child. Balmoral became a favourite birthday venue till she felt too grown up for a family affair and chose more sophisticated events. It's like driving down memory lane. I park in front of a tall, white apartment block and gaze across the road at the beach. No wonder Lissa has raved about this spot. It's idyllic! I lock the car and walk to the entrance.

'Wow, Mum. You're looking good!' In her usual fashion, Lissa starts talking as soon as she opens the door

I look down at my workaday pink striped shirt teamed with navy pants, which don't usually receive such approbation from my fashion conscious daughter. Seeing the direction of my glance she laughs.

'Not those old duds. Your face. It's… I don't know. You seem… younger or something. If I didn't know you better I'd be asking if you'd had a facelift.'

I think quickly. How can I carry this off? 'Must be my new makeup. You like it?'

She peers at my face intently, her own face close to mine. 'Mmm, not sure. Seems to be coming from inside you.' She chuckles. 'What's my old mum been up to?'

I quickly change the subject.

'This is a great place. How can Will…?'

'Don't ask!' Lissa trills and, now distracted from my appearance, leads me to the window. 'Isn't this fab?' Her waving arm encapsulates the 180 degree view. Standing, as we are, on the eighth floor, it certainly is a view to die for. I'm not aware of voicing these thoughts so Lissa must be a mind reader.

'Will received an inheritance from his grandfather,' she says on a more serious note. 'No, he hasn't bought this place,' she anticipates my next question, 'but the interest pays the rent. Let me show you around.'

Fifteen minutes or so later we are ensconced in a deep leather sofa. Unlike those at Marcus' apartment, this one is a deep sea blue, in keeping with the seaside theme of the whole apartment which is decked out in different hues of blue and yellow.

'It's very…' I begin.

'I know. I love it!'

'And Will too, I hope.'

'Course,' she replies dreamily.

'Now, how's uni going?' I pick up my cup of chai tea and take a cautious sip. It's not my usual tipple, but I enjoy the tingle of the spices on my tongue. 'Mmm this is good,' I say in surprise.

'Ha, thought you'd like it. Aunt Gina bought it for me in Byron.' I replace the cup hastily, as if the liquid is poison.

'Uni?' I repeat.

'Oh, good. I'm enjoying the research side of it, spending hours in the library.'

'And the tutoring?'

'That hasn't happened yet, so I'm still doing a bit of waitressing, though Will says I don't need to. Still, it's nice to have my own money. Stops me feeling like a kept woman.' She hesitates, biting her lip. 'Thing is, Will's in for a promotion. They might want him to move interstate.'

'And how would you feel about that?' I take another sip of the tea which I am enjoying, despite its connections to my avowed enemy.

'I'm not sure.' Lissa looks down at her hands. My eyes follow hers and I note she is twisting her fingers, a sure sign of distress. 'I mean… we… it's only been a few months.'

'What about Will? Does he want to go?'

'Oh, he's too caught up in the idea of a promotion. I don't think he's even considered the consequences of being posted somewhere other than Sydney. Anyway,' she looks up with a smile, 'may never happen. Meanwhile, everything's going great.'

I reach over to tuck a stray hair behind my daughter's ear. I've forgotten how resilient the young are. They live for the moment. Maybe I can learn something here. While I'm musing on this, Lissa begins to speak again.

'How about you? What about this hunk of a headmaster. Is he the reason you're glowing all over?'

A rush of warmth rises to my face. I feel my cheeks redden. I rise and turn my back to Lissa, pretending to take in the view. Definitely not a hot flush this time. I should have known she'd guess something was up.

'Marcus?' I ask, trying to sound unconcerned.

'That's him. Bonnie has told me all about him,' she adds. 'Sounds like he's quite a dish.'

Hunk, dish, where does she find these words?

'Bonnie…?' I stutter at last, turning back to face her.

'Bonnie, your house guest. Remember?' Lissa looks at me fondly and, for a moment, it's as if she's the adult and I'm the child. 'She's been full of it, says she can feel the chemistry when the two of you are in the same room. Well?'

'Maybe.' I allow a small smile to escape. 'We are… we have been…'

'You're an item. I knew it! Oh, Mum, I'm happy for you. You need someone in your life, someone your own age who shares things you like. He does, doesn't he?' She bounces up and down in her seat.

I wave my hands in the air as if to dismiss her words, but I needn't have worried because Lissa has already moved on.

'Bring your tea into the kitchen. I need to take care of a few things.'

I dutifully pick up my cup and follow her into the designer kitchen with its view across the dining area to the ocean. Will must be paying a packet for this place.

Two large cakes are sitting on a wire rack. While I perch on a high stool, Lissa busies herself with the cream cheese, sugar, butter and vanilla, already sitting in wait. Turning on her mixer – a gift from Sean and I, which I'm pleased to see being put to good use – she proceeds to beat the cream cheese and butter before adding the remaining ingredients and beginning to assemble the cake. I watch the beaters moving, then her deft fingers as she spreads the icing and let my mind wander.

'Have you looked at any units yet, Mum?' Lissa finishes icing the cake and, running her finger along the blade of the knife she removes the excess icing and licks it off.

'Mind you don't cut yourself.' The warning comes out automatically. It's been a habit of hers since she was old enough to reach up to the kitchen bench. 'Sorry,' I add.

'I'm not a child anymore.' Lissa continues to lick the knife, then returns to her earlier question. 'Units, have you seen any?'

'No.' I twirl a strand of hair around my finger and prop up my elbow with my other hand. 'I'm going to wait till the house is sold. Once I know what's left after the mortgage is paid out, I'll have some idea what I can afford. Something small, I think.'

'What happened to the ocean views? The apartment on the beach?' Lissa is in the process of filling the empty mixer bowl with water. The noise drowns out any need for me to reply which is fortunate, as her words immediately conjure up an apartment with ocean views; one which I am at pains to forget.

'Well?' She turns round waiting for my response.

'Probably a bad idea,' I say flippantly. 'Might be best to buy something without a mortgage, a garden unit perhaps with a small courtyard.'

'Mmm, then you can still keep your plants, I suppose. But won't you feel claustrophobic after our Seaforth house?'

'There'll still be room for you when you choose to descend on me. Will too.'

'Hmm. How do you think this looks?' Lissa indicates the cake which now sits in the middle of the bench-top and I can tell my future is not a priority for her. 'It's Will's birthday cake,' she continues. 'Red velvet, his favourite.'

'I'm sure he'll love it,' I say rising to my feet. 'You won't want me around when he gets back. Where is he, by the way?'

'Job interview.' She hesitates. 'I hope…' She bites her lip and I pause, waiting for her to continue but she doesn't. I recognise my daughter's concern.

'Right. Well, I'm off. Shall I give your love to Gran and Gramps?'

'Yes please.' She comes over to give me a hug. 'It's not that I want to get rid of you, but I have a special evening planned; just for the two of us, you know…' I know only too well. I return her hug, hoping the evening will go according to plan and everything will turn out as she would like.

As I drive away, I reflect how difficult it is to let go. I want the best for my little girl and if Will is what she wants then I want him for her too. But I don't want to see her being hurt. When she was little it was easy to protect her from hurt, and a hug and kiss on the sore spot often sufficed. That won't work any longer. She's grown up now and will have to take the knocks and tumbles of being a woman in a mature relationship. All I can do is look on and be there when she needs me. I sigh.

*

'And you're even allowed to keep a small dog,' Mum says smugly. I gaze at her, mystified. Mum and Dad don't have any animals and I've never heard her mention a desire to have one.

'Right.' I can't think of anything else to say, but Mum doesn't seem to notice as she continues.

'You must come with us at the weekend. Dad and I are quite sold on this village, aren't we?' She glances towards Dad, who is looking blankly at us both.

'Are you sure?' I ask. 'Sure you're doing the right thing?' I also glance towards Dad as I speak. I'm not clear if this is another of Mum's wild notions and he's being carried along in its tide, but it's Mum who answers again for both of them.

'Of course we are. We can't stay here forever.' Her widespread arms take in the expanse of the family room in which we are all sitting. Suddenly she drops her arms and her face begins to crumble.

'There, there…' Dad pats her hands which are now lying limply in her lap. 'It'll be alright.' He looks at me. 'No sense in upsetting her, you know. She's been through a lot with me these past weeks. And your mum's right. We do need to move. We can't keep this place up any more. If I…' His voice breaks.

Shit, now I've upset both of them.

'Tell me about this place again,' I say. 'Located close to the train station, you said. It won't be too noisy for you?'

'That's the beauty of it.' Mum is back in her stride again. She rises. 'Let me show you the brochure.'

She's back in a moment carrying a glossy booklet declaiming the advantages of this particular retirement village. I flick through it, feigning interest. I can't really imagine my parents living anywhere other than the house where we all grew up.

'Audrey says…' Mum begins, then stops short at my exclamation.

'You mean you're still in touch with Marcus' parents?'

'Of course. They're our friends and they've been most helpful in our search. In fact this village is a sister one to their village up in Queensland. It was Audrey who put me onto it. She'd heard they were building a new one down here and suggested we get in quickly before they were all sold.'

'Right.' I wonder if now's the time to tell them about Marcus and me but hesitate. If Mum has become so close to Audrey King, she'll be on the phone to her before I've reached home. I don't want Marcus' parents finding out about us from my mum. God, why is it all so difficult? Why can't I have everything out in the open like everyone else? Because I make things complicated for myself, I answer my own question. I'm worried about what people will think. It's less than a year since Sean left and even less since his death. I don't want… I guess I don't want people to imagine I've rushed into this with Marcus. Then there is the added complication of his being my boss; the esteemed Headmaster of Grammar. Not that his position should make any difference. We're both free and over forty. A couple of intelligent human beings who have a lot in common. Why shouldn't we pair up? No reason at all. Then why…? My head starts to ache with all this thinking. I consciously close my mind to Marcus and any thoughts of us.

'What's that you said, Mum?' I realise all the while I've been having this inner conversation, Mum has been talking too and I've missed all of it.

'Do you want anything?'

Seeing my blank look, Dad leans forward. 'Your mum was asking you if there was anything here you wanted. We're going to have to downsize quite a bit. Can't take all this with us.' He looks longingly at his well-stocked bookcase, many of the tomes lovingly collected over the years, and strokes the well-worn arm of his favourite chair. 'We wanted to ask you, and Jan and Bob too, of course, if there is anything you particularly want from the wreck before we toss everything overboard.'

'Now, Dad,' Mum remonstrates. 'It's not quite that bad. 'Though it would be nice,' she adds, 'to take the opportunity to buy some new bits and pieces, things more suitable for a smaller place.' She, too, looks around sorrowfully. 'These pieces have been with us for so long. They fit here. They might be out of place in a smaller house.' She sighs. 'Well, I'd better see to dinner.'

When she's left the room Dad leans over and says quietly. 'She's not as excited about the move as she makes out. It's all my fault, of course. If it hadn't been for this silly ear stuff, we could have stayed on here.' He looks around again. It's been their home for so long.

I sense Dad's reluctance to leave and try to jolly him along. 'Don't be silly, Dad. The two of you couldn't have stayed here for much longer anyway. It's far too big and look at the garden. There are lots of reasons for you to move.'

'You've changed your tune. Who was upset at our selling in the first place?'

'I've had time to get used to it. Besides I'm going to be selling too. I know what a wrench it is but sometimes it has to be done.'

'You're right there, Anna. And how's that girl of yours? Saw her today, did you?'

'Lissa's great, Dad.' I relax at the change of topic. 'Yes, I dropped over to see her earlier. Awesome place they have. She was in the midst of cooking – a red velvet cake. Remember how she used to do that in her teens?'

'When she was bored? I remember. She wasn't even all that interested in the eating, it was the cooking she enjoyed.'

'Well this one is specially for Will. It's his birthday and evidently he had some interview today...'

'That'll be the one she was worried about.' Dad interrupts me.

'You seem to know more about it than I do.'

'Your mum spoke with her on the phone the other day and she might have mentioned it.'

'Do you know why she's worried?'

'Not rightly sure. No doubt you'll hear all about it in due course.'

'Dinner's ready! Stop chatting you two and come through before it gets cold.' Mum bustles in and leads the way into the dining room. No kitchen table for her, though Dad and I would have been more comfortable with its informality. The delicious aroma of roast pork is rising from a casserole dish as we take our seats. Mum's been busy.

I decide to redress my earlier boorish behaviour.

'About the Retirement Village, Mum. This weekend you said? I think I can make it.'

'You can? Oh, that would be so good, Wouldn't it, Ben? I do value your opinion, you know.' I'm flattered to hear my mother's words. This move has hit her hard and I want to try to make it easier for her if I can. 'What about Jan and Bob?'

'Oh, Jan! She can't understand why we're moving. Has some silly notion about it being her inheritance or something.'

'Has she said as much?'

'She doesn't need to.' It's Dad answering for Mum again. 'Your mum can see right through her. It's not what she says. It's what she doesn't say. But we'll carry on regardless. Eh, honey?' He stretches over to pat Mum's hand and I smile at this unexpected show of affection. These are my parents, still in love after all these years.

'And what about you? Have you been seeing Marcus? He's such a nice boy.' I'm tempted yet again to spill the beans but decide against it.

'At school, yes. We work together, remember.'

'How could I forget? Audrey and Jack are so proud of him. But they seem to think he won't stay there?'

'It's a temporary appointment,' I explain. 'Gives the Board time to recruit a new Head. They'll be advertising soon. I thought they'd have done so already,' I add thoughtfully.

'And what about you? Isn't it time you stepped up? You've held your position for a few years now. Time for a change?' Dad puts down his knife and fork to favour me with one of his long looks.

'Me? You sound like Heather.' But he's given me food for thought. Maybe it is time. This year has taught me to stand on my own two feet. Perhaps what I need is a bit more responsibility. 'Maybe,' I allow. 'Heather would agree with you.' And I suddenly realise Marcus would probably agree too. I know he's hoping for a university position in the New Year so I wouldn't be in competition with him, but I have no idea who else will be in the running. 'It's certainly worth thinking about.'

'My girl; Headmistress at Northern Beaches Grammar. Wouldn't that be grand?' He rubs his hands. 'What do you think, Susie? That would be one in the eye for your tennis buddies, wouldn't it?'

'Do you think you'd have a chance, dear?' Mum is gathering the plates together. She stands up. 'Don't you be giving her any false hopes, Ben.'

Dad winks at me as she carries the dishes into the kitchen. 'Don't you worry about what she says. She'd be as proud a punch.'

'Well, we'll see. I haven't decided to apply yet.'

Twenty-four

Marcus and I are enjoying the unexpected bonus. Bonnie has gone off walking in the Blue Mountains, providing us with the opportunity to spend a whole weekend here together at my place.

'You *are* going to apply, aren't you?' Marcus and I are sitting in my courtyard late Friday afternoon, a tray of coffee and biscuits between us. I've been enjoying the silence of just being with my special person when his voice interrupts the peace of the afternoon. The school board have advertised the position of Head in the last few days.

'You're sure you won't stay?' I look up at him with a smile. 'You know everyone loves you.'

'As long as you do, I don't need the others. But to answer your question, no, I don't intend to stay. Grammar was only ever a temporary stop for me. I've high hopes of a uni position either here in Sydney, or back in Brisbane. I have those two applications in, remember?'

I do remember, and I'm not sure where it leaves me if he gets the position in Brisbane, but I've decided to put that to the back of my mind.

'So?'

I realise he's still waiting for an answer. 'Do you really think I should? I mean…'

'You're the obvious person. And Heather thinks so too,' he reminds me. I recall an earlier conversation with my long-time friend and mentor and know he's right.

'Maybe,' I say slowly, and I'm about to qualify it, when Marcus takes my hand and squeezes it hard.

'Great. I can help with your application if you want. God knows, I've had plenty of practice in writing them.'

'Thanks. I think I can manage, but I might ask you to look it over before I send it off.'

'Happy to. Now, how are we going to spend the rest of the weekend?' And we proceed to discuss our plans for the next two days.

*

We're having a leisurely late breakfast next morning, when there's an urgent ringing at the door. We look at each other in surprise and dismay.

'I'd better answer that.' I put down my coffee and wipe the toast crumbs from my mouth as I go through the hallway. Still in my night-time attire, I'm really in no position to entertain visitors.

'I've barely opened the door, when my mother brushes past me, her arms full of what looks like sheets. 'I've brought these over for you,' she begins, when she catches sight of Marcus. He is clearly very much at home, lounging at the kitchen table drinking coffee in shorts and tee shirt with his bare feet stretched out on the wooden floor.

'Well! Dr Marcus King!'

'Guilty as charged.' Marcus holds up his hands in surrender, managing to look like a little boy caught in the act.

'I'm surprised to see you. Lovely to meet you again,' Mum gushes. She looks daggers at me over his head. I interpret this as her desire to talk to me later.

'Would you like some coffee?' Marcus asks sweetly, leading Mum to preen and join him at the table.

'Love some,' Mum favours him with a smile, completely ignoring me.

'I'll fix it.' I'm already standing and don't want to disturb this mutual admiration society which is taking place under my nose.

'Thanks, hon.' Marcus is making no secret of the fact we're a couple, though I have to admit, given the way Mum has found us, it will be difficult to deny. I take my lead from him.

'Okay, sweetie,' I reply giving him a smile which is almost a grimace.

'Now, tell me all.' Mum leans towards Marcus like an old friend. 'When did you two get together. We've been hoping for this, you know.'

We have? Who's we? I don't have long to wait for the answer.

'Audrey and I were talking about how we could get you two together. And here you have managed it for yourselves.' She smiles at us both as if, indeed, she has managed it for us.

I shake my head. Mum has really gone too far this time. She's taking credit for the fact that Marcus and I have… Well what have we? I'm not sure, but one thing I do know, I'm going to let her take the credit for it. That way, she'll go along with whatever we decide.

'What's this you've brought me?' I ask to change the subject, pointing to the pile Mum has dumped on a chair.

'Bed linen. I'm clearing out and thought you could maybe make use of these.' Her voice falters when she sees my look of astonishment. 'No? Well, maybe Jan… They're going to be no use to us when we move and I can't bear to throw them away.'

'How about St Vinnie's?' I ask, mentioning the charity shop to which Mum has often donated in the past.

She purses her lips. 'Maybe.'

Marcus is watching this interaction with amusement. 'No wonder you and Mum get on so well,' he says. 'You're like two peas in a pod. What's this about a move?'

Delighted to be invited, Mum goes into a long explanation of Dad's condition, the size and high maintenance requirements of their present home and concludes with, 'If it hadn't been for Audrey – your mum – I don't know how we'd have managed. She's been such a help, and Anna's promised to come to the village with us this afternoon to check the place out.'

Shit, I'd forgotten my promise. I can't renege now. I can see our special weekend going down the gurgler, when I hear Marcus offer, 'Why don't we both come?'

'That would be wonderful.' Mum beams and gives me a look as if to say that at least Marcus knows how to behave.

'Okay, that's a plan.' I try my best to sound gracious, shooting Marcus a glare as I do so. This is not the plan I had in mind. 'Shall we meet you there?'

'No need for that.' It's Marcus again, being gallant. 'How about we pick you both up after lunch? About two, say?' While I'm wondering how we are all going to fit into his tiny sports car, he looks over at me. 'We'll be in Anna's car. Right?' This last is directed at me with such a winsome look I can't refuse.

Mum seems relieved.

'Two it is. We'll see you then.' Marcus takes control and ushers her out.

'What on earth did you do that for?' I start to berate him as soon as he returns to the kitchen.

'They're your parents. We have all the time in the world, but they won't be around forever. They remind me of mine,' he adds. 'And this visit is obviously important to them. They want your approval.'

'But…' I begin, then think better of it. I know he's right.

'Come here!' He holds out his arms and I move into his embrace, laying my head on his shoulder. 'It'll be all right, you'll see. It might even be fun. Have you been to one of these retirement villages before?'

'No,' I mumble, my voice muffled in his embrace. I'm envisaging a place full of old people, depressing and dull. I don't want to think of my parents living in a place like that. They've always been full of life and, until this setback of Dad's, they've been healthy too.

Marcus holds me away from him and looks at my face. It's as if he can see what I'm thinking. 'The place probably won't be as bad as you imagine. That's why you need to go with them. My folks live in an over-fifties village and it's a very lively community. If this one is run by the same group, I expect it will be too. You'll be surprised.'

'Over fifties?' My voice registers surprise. 'But I'm nearly fifty. Do you mean to say…?'

Marcus laughs and plants a gentle kiss on my cheek. 'I'm not suggesting it as a solution for you, though…' He ducks, as I pick up a tea towel and aim in his direction. I miss, and it lands on the floor.

'Well, we've still got some time before we need to be off so let's make the most of it.' And with that he leads me back to the bedroom for the remainder of the morning.

*

As Marcus has predicted, the over-fifties community Mum and Dad are proposing to move into is nothing like my worst imaginings. It's beautifully set out and landscaped. Each house is free-standing with a small courtyard and walking paths wind throughout the cleverly designed grounds. The location is close to a National Park so the area abounds with wildlife, ducks making their way across the paths and water dragons sunning themselves at the edges of the gardens. There's even a lake complete with moorhens and water lilies.

'I think we can be happy here.' Mum sighs, looking towards me for agreement.

'I think you can,' I agree, surprised I mean it. If Mum and Dad have to move – and I've accepted that they must – then this is a good next step for them. 'What about you, Dad?' I turn to my father who has been very quiet during the tour of the house and grounds.

'It'll do me fine, I can still have my garden and your mum and I can get back into bridge and a few other things. The croquet looks interesting.' I gaze at him, surprised. This is a side of Dad with which I'm not familiar. Seeing my surprise he adds. 'We used to be real pros, before we had you kids.' He rubs his forehead with his hand. 'It was a long time ago, but it'll be fun to get back into the swing of things. What do you think, Susie?' He nudges Mum who, to my amazement, blushes and nods.

'It was in another lifetime. And this will be a fresh start too. So you approve, Anna?'

'I do.' This time I smile with genuine pleasure. It's good to see my parents re-energised and excited about the future after the worry we've been through.

'Now, how about some afternoon tea?' Marcus has taken charge again. I agree, amused at how my parents are eager to fall in with his suggestion.

Tea, served with scones and cream in the village café, is a pleasant affair. As expected, Mum dominates the conversation, eager to show Marcus how well acquainted she is with his parents. The conversation is dotted with references to what Audrey suggested and how Audrey finds village life but, instead of being annoyed with her blatant name-dropping, I'm amused to hear Marcus pick up on her comments and add some of his own. It's a game of verbal sparring and I'm not sure who's coming out in front.

I sit back and close my eyes letting the conversation flow past me. Suddenly I hear my name mentioned and my eyes fly open.

'What was that?' I sit forward. My father lays his hand on mine.

'Steady on girl. Your mum was only asking if Marcus thought you have a chance at the Head's job when he moves on.'

'But I haven't even decided to apply.' I object.

'You will,' Marcus replies in a very definite voice, then turning to my parents adds: 'She's a shoo-in. Don't you worry, I'll make sure she gets her application in. After all of her work on the play every year, there's not a member of the Board who doesn't know and admire Mrs Anna Hollis.' He smiles across at me and reaches his hand in my direction, but I fold mine under the table. My parents knowing we are a couple is one thing, but to be outwardly demonstrative in front of them is taking things too far.

*

Next day I receive the anticipated call from Mum. 'What a nice young man, though he's exactly what I expected having met his parents. I spoke to Audrey this morning and…' I tune out holding the phone away from my ear, much to Marcus' amusement. We've been sitting outside reading the Sunday papers and it's as well Mum can't see us as we're in our night attire again.

I've only this minute put the phone to my ear once more, preparatory to bringing the call to a conclusion, when my mother surprises me.

'I know it's been a difficult year for you, Anna. Losing Sean was a big upset and you're probably finding it hard to accept Marcus' friendship after all of that, and so quickly too.' She hesitates as if wondering whether to go on, and I hear her take a deep breath. 'But you have a life to live and Dad and I want to see you happy; as happy as we are. And if Marcus is the right one, who can bring that glow back to you, then we're right behind you.'

I remain holding the silent phone in my hand. I can't believe my autocratic mother has been so sensitive to my feelings.

After a wonderful weekend together, Marcus leaves early on Sunday evening. I reluctantly wave him off, then sit down at the computer to search out the position description for Head of Northern Beaches Grammar. I read the document carefully, mentally matching my skills and experience with the essential and desirable criteria for the position. On the face of it, I'm a good fit. I drag my chair closer to my desk and set about writing my application. It's not an easy task. It's years since I had to apply for a job and it's well after midnight before I press **Save** and shut down the computer.

I push my chair back, reach my hands above my head and stretch my whole body. It's done! At least the first draft's done. I'll re-read it again tomorrow evening, then – maybe – I'll put it in front of Marcus. I'm somewhat reluctant to do this. It seems to be laying myself bare. But, I remind myself, the whole of the Board and interview panel will see it, so surely I can allow Marcus to have first look.

Twenty-five

There is a hush in the auditorium and a couple of the girls peering through the curtain whisper to each other before scampering backstage to await their entrance.

'This is exciting!' Bonnie is by my side having volunteered to act as prompt. I give the thumbs-up signal and the curtain rises on the first scene.

Despite my trepidation, everything goes to plan and the final curtain comes down to tumultuous applause. Parents and friends are delighted yet again and I let out a breath of relief. No one has forgotten her lines, everyone has made her entrance on time and Grammar has celebrated yet another successful production.

I'm so caught up in the moment, I'm unaware of Marcus moving outside the curtain to give a vote of thanks until I hear my name and Bonnie pushes me onstage.

'Here she is!' Marcus intones, 'The lady who has made this happen, our Head of English, Mrs Anna Hollis.' He holds out his hand and I take it, knees trembling.

I accept the beautiful bouquet of lilies and roses proffered by one of the mothers, and somehow find the words to thank her, Marcus, and all the girls for their contributions and dedication which have contributed to the success of the evening. The curtain opens again to final applause then closes leaving Marcus and I standing together in the middle of the stage. Regardless of who might be watching, he places his hands on my waist and lifts me up in the air twirling me around and around till I plead for mercy.

'The performance was wonderful!' he exclaims. 'I didn't… I've attended some of the rehearsals but nothing prepared me for such a magnificent event.'

'Congratulations!' Bonnie steps out of the wings followed by those teachers who have assisted in the production. I stretch out my hands to them.

'We couldn't have done it without all of you.' My thanks are sincere and I quickly move out of Marcus' orbit.

As the party gets underway, it's difficult to keep out of Marcus' way and I finally give up. We leave together, holding hands as we walk slowly to our cars.

'Guess the cat's out of the bag here too, now. Do you mind too much?' Marcus swings me around to face him.

'I guess not.' I find I'm picking up his American phrases. 'It's just…'

'I know. You'd hoped to keep it secret till the end of the year. Once my stint here is over, our conflict of interest, as you term it, is no more.'

I nod, embarrassed he's read me so well.

I arrive home on a high. The play has gone well, and Marcus and I are out in the open. Although I've been at pains to maintain the secrecy of our growing relationship, it's a relief to be open about it. It's likely that most of the staff may have guessed, but I think we've been fairly circumspect. I sing to myself as I make my way upstairs. I know I'll sleep well tonight.

Next morning I rise late and wander downstairs to be greeted by a jubilant Bonnie. *How can she manage to appear so fresh after the late night we've had?* The staff, Marcus included, partied on into the wee hours, high on the success of yet another school production. Thank goodness today's Saturday, and I have the weekend to recover. I slump down in a chair and blink at Bonnie's bright young face.

'How do you do it?' I ask, propping my head up on my hands. 'Did you have any sleep at all?'

'I left just after you did,' she retorts. 'And I was up early checking my emails. You'll never guess?'

'You'd better tell me then.' I struggle up and make it over to the fridge where I find a fresh container of orange juice. Opening a cupboard, I draw out a glass and fill it with the life-saving liquid. It slides down my parched throat like nectar. That's better. I sit down again. 'Well, then?' I turn to Bonnie who, although seemingly bursting with her news, hasn't said a word during all this.

'It's Hank! He's coming to Sydney!'

'Yes?' I'm puzzled. 'That's the plan, isn't it? You do your research, then he'll come over to join you for your trip round Australia?'

Bonnie sits down opposite me. 'Yeah, that's what we planned. But Hank's swung some early leave and he's arriving next week. Imagine! Only five more days and…' She's grinning from ear to ear.

'Right.' I'm being particularly dense this morning as I try to work out how this will affect me. 'So what does this mean? You'll still complete your research, I assume.'

'Yes, but…' She looks across at me. 'It's about time for me to move on anyway, visit another school, that is. And,' she pauses. 'Marcus has helped me get in touch with one up in Brisbane – where he used to live,' she adds, as if I didn't know. 'So I'll be off up there at the end of next week. I'll be out of your hair.' She must notice my stunned gaze as she quickly adds, 'I'll be sorry to leave. It's been cool… but…'

'I know. Fresh fields beckon. I'll miss you.' As I say the words, I realise it's true. Although initially only a financial arrangement, I've come to enjoy her company and her departure will leave an empty space in more ways than one. 'So Hank arrives…?'

'Thursday. I wondered…' she purses her lips. 'Would you mind…'

I anticipate her question. 'Of course Hank can stay here for a couple of nights. Where will you stay in Brisbane?'

'Oh, it'll be a Backpackers Hostel for us. Might as well get used to roughing it a bit before we hit the road. You're sure you don't mind? Thanks a heap.' She bounces around the table to envelop me in a hug. 'Give you and the boss more private time too, eh?'

I extricate myself from her youthful exuberance. 'So, what have you planned for today?' She's already dressed in her weekend uniform of jeans teamed with a tailored shirt, her hair tied up in an immaculate ponytail.

'I need to book for us up there. Check out with people here. Lots to do,' she bubbles.

She's gone before I can rouse myself to fix breakfast. After I shower and dress I wander around the house unable to settle. In addition to missing Bonnie's lively company around the place, I'll miss her contribution to the coffers. I rub my arms as a shiver of despair runs up them, then I reason with myself. This business with Gina is bound to be settled soon, then I'll be able to sell the house and all will be well. Also, the money Bonnie has paid in rent over the past couple of months has made a hole in my bills – that should enable me to soldier on for a bit longer without too much trouble.

My wanderings take me into my study where I spy the red cover of my diary peeking out from underneath a pile of school papers. It's a plastic-covered notebook this time, quite unlike the leather bound one of my youth but, since the anniversary weekend, I've been diligently recording my innermost thoughts. It's been a therapeutic process, taking a few minutes each day to empty my mind onto the lined page. I slip it out of its hiding place and begin my record for the day.

I'm interrupted by a phone call from Marcus, eager to relive the previous evening. We agree to meet for lunch – he'll join me here, so I now have something to focus on as I ferret in the fridge to find ham, cheese, olives and a couple of baguettes. By the time I've arranged them on a tray and taken them out into the courtyard along with a pitcher of orange juice to slake my ongoing thirst, I hear his car draw up.

'We'll miss her,' he sighs, as I recount Bonnie's latest news. 'I know I put her onto the Brisbane place, but I'd hoped we might keep her down here a bit longer.'

'Yes, she's proved useful – not only as an observer,' I note, remembering the times she's stepped in when a teacher has been absent or needed to rush home on an emergency.

'I hope the time has been just as useful to her,' Marcus observes.

'Oh, I'm sure it has.'

'You'll miss her here too.'

'Yes,' I respond. 'However…' I smile.

'There is that.' Marcus reaches over to stroke my hand, his foot grazing mine under the table. 'No chaperone.' Changing the subject, he pushes himself away from the table with both hands. 'Christmas, do you have any plans?'

My brow furrows. 'It was last Christmas …'

'Sorry, I can be a clot sometimes. Of course, you don't want to be reminded. But Mum and Dad are thinking of coming down here. Evidently your folks mentioned something about a family do – a chance for everyone to get acquainted? And for my guys to check out the new pad,' he adds seeing me frown.

'I don't know,' I say slowly. 'I haven't made any plans. I've always had Christmas here, but not this year. I've been trying not to think about it.' As I speak, I realise that, of course, the rest of my family are going to want some celebration, but I don't think I can be part of it, not this year, anyway. 'I don't want to make any plans,' I state more definitely. 'But if your folks are down…'

'Understood.' Marcus smiles holding up his hands in mock surrender. 'Now, how about we make the most of today? How does an afternoon on the harbour sound?'

I brighten and begin to clear away the remains of our lunch.

*

'Look, you can see Heather's place from here.' I point to the shore where her home is one of many on the edge of the water. We're on what's called a Captain Cook Coffee Cruise and are enjoying pretending to be tourists.

'How is Heather these days?' Marcus' hair is blowing awry in the stiff breeze, making him appear even less like a Headmaster than usual. He pushes his glasses further up his nose as if fearing they're going to blow off.

'Much better. I saw her briefly before the play last night. She said she couldn't miss it, though I guess she missed being the centre of attention. She always loved that, schmoozing all the parents at school functions. That was one of her charms.'

'And I don't have that talent?' Marcus pretends to be upset. I punch him in the arm.

'You're charm itself,' I dig him in the ribs as he makes a funny face, pretending to twirl an imaginary moustache. 'But seriously, She's missing the daily hurly-burly of school life. There's always something going on. Won't you miss it too?' I gaze up at his handsome face which is taking on a more serious guise.

'No,' he sighs. 'Actually, part of me will be glad when the term ends. Young women in large numbers are not my usual fare. Not that this year hasn't been a blast – and I did meet you.' He ducks as I make as if to punch him again. 'But I'm much more at ease in a university setting. A girls' school is not the most comfortable for me. Whereas you…' He gives me an admiring glance. 'It'll suit you down to the ground. You did get your application in, didn't you?'

'I did.' I smile smugly.

'If I had any say in it, the position would be yours. They need their heads looked at if they choose anyone else.'

I'm not so sure, but I do feel ready to take on this added responsibility. It's been a hell of a year. However, the worst is behind me now and I can look forward to a fresh start next year.

'What about you? Any word from the universities?' I'm aware Marcus has attended two interviews in the past couple of weeks, one in Brisbane and one here in Sydney. I look down into the water as I await his reply.

'I won't hear for ages yet. Universities are notably slow in reaching a decision – so many committees to go through. But I'm optimistic. Sydney would be good. It's such an old, established seat of learning.' I can almost hear him rubbing his hands together at the thought. I raise my eyes to meet his.

'And would you accept it, in preference to Brisbane, I mean. If you were offered both, that is?' I hold my breath as I await his reply.

'What do you think?' He grabs hold of my hand and swings it. It's not the answer I was hoping for, but one which I'll have to make do with. I hope fervently he means "yes".

*

The next week is a flurry of activity in my house as Bonnie makes ready both for Hank's arrival and her own departure. With Marcus' agreement she's decided to finish up at school on Wednesday so as to be able to meet Hank's plane and show him the sights before they head off up north. Her popularity with both staff and students, despite the short time she's been with us, has ensured a number of farewell teas and lunches, so there hasn't been an opportunity for us to spend much time together. Her evenings have been taken up with farewells to her Sydney friends. It's not till late Wednesday that we have time alone. Bonnie arrives home exhausted at ten o'clock and, slipping her shoes off, subsides into an armchair, 'I'm bushed,' she says, dropping her high heels onto the carpet. 'Wow, it's tomorrow. He'll really be here tomorrow. In the air right now,' she gloats. Then, realising I'm still up, though already dressed for bed, she adds, 'You didn't need to stop up for me.'

'As if…' I laugh. 'No, but I may not see you in the morning, and you'll be tied up with Hank for the next few days before you leave. I wanted some time to talk, to say how much I've enjoyed your visit. More than I anticipated,' I admit.

'I bet,' she laughs. 'You *were* a bit uptight when I arrived.'

'Just a bit,' I laugh too. 'You weren't quite what I expected.'

'Better, I hope.'

'Oh, much better. And I can't wait to meet Hank.'

'About that. The next two days are going to be full-on, but I wondered… on Friday… I'd like for us to take you and Marcus, Lissa and Will too, out to dinner. To say thanks to you all for making me so welcome.' Her last words come out in a rush, as if she's been preparing them.

'Sure, we'd like that,' I respond answering for the others as well. 'I know Marcus will be up for it, but I'll need to check with Lissa and Will.'

Bonnie looks a trifle shamefaced. 'Umm, I've already mentioned it to them,' she admits. 'You don't mind, do you? We were all out drinking the other night and I managed to have a quick word with them both. They're good.'

I realise I should have expected something like this, reminding myself that they're of a different generation. 'No, not at all. Well, guess we should both be getting to bed. Tomorrow's a big day.' We rise, Bonnie hugging herself in delight in anticipation of her reunion with her Hank, while I conjecture how easily I can accept an invitation on Marcus' behalf. We've certainly come a long way.

Twenty-six

'What?' I can't believe my ears. I'm leaving my car ready to start another week of teaching, when I hear Marcus' voice. There are only four weeks of the term left. The senior students have completed their final exams, Christmas is around the corner and the girls are moving into holiday mode.

'The States? You mean you're going back there now?'

'I didn't want to tell you like this.' Marcus drags his fingers through his hair and pushes his glasses up his nose in the gesture with which I've become familiar and grown to love. 'I had this call from Rick last night. I don't know what's going on, but Jon needs me and I have to go to him. I have to put him first. You *do* understand?' He ruffles his hair again and looks so much like a little boy himself, that I long to take him in my arms and tell him everything will be alright.

'When do you leave?' I heave my pile of books higher, wishing he'd get on with it. I have a class first period and my Year Eight will need my full attention. Surely we can discuss this after classes finish this afternoon?

'That's the thing. I'm off to the airport now. I was able to arrange a flight. I called as soon as I hung up on Rick. It was a lucky chance.' He stops perhaps realising that, as far as I'm concerned, luck has nothing to do with it. It's a disaster.

'But what about…?' My voice tails off as I think of all the things we've planned to do in the lead-up to Christmas, culminating in his parents' visit. My stomach churns and I begin to tremble. I feel sick. There's a lump in my throat. *Will I ever see him again?* My nails dig into my palms and my books threaten to slip from my grasp.

I pull myself together. 'Right, so this is it? Of course you must go if Jonathon needs you. I guess I should wish you a good trip and all that. I do hope you find everything okay with Jon.' As I speak I wonder if, by encouraging Marcus to leave, I'm sabotaging my own future. There's a question mark in my voice as I know that Marcus still hasn't resolved Jon's paternity.

'Morning Mrs Hollis, Dr King.' A trio of senior girls, taking liberties with their school uniforms by wearing their hats at a jaunty angle and turning up their skirt bands to bring their skirts well above the regulation length, walk by giggling. Under normal circumstances, I'd have been right on them. But this isn't turning out to be a normal morning. However, their young voices break into our conversation and I realise I must move on. I begin to step away, only to feel Marcus lay a restraining hand on my arm. I raise my eyes to meet his.

'I didn't want it to be like this,' he repeats, a frown appearing between his eyes. 'I wanted…' But what he wanted is drowned out by the school bell calling us all to class.

'I must go.'

'I'll be in touch.'

We both speak at the same time and I rush off to where twenty-odd lively girls are waiting for me.

*

I go through the day in a blur. Thank goodness I have a full day of teaching, so I have no time to ponder Marcus' precipitate departure. I am about to leave for the day when I receive a call on my mobile. After a brief conversation I hang up bemused. Today has certainly been one of surprises and, like Marcus' departure, this one has come out of the blue. The Chair of the Board has invited me to act as Head for the remainder of the term. I'm flattered, of course, and wonder if this portends a favourable result for my application. He has warmed me against making any assumptions, of course, but I can't help my thoughts.

I drive home, my mind in a turmoil. Once home, I can't settle. Now

Bonnie has gone, I'm finding the house empty again and can't wait to have it sold and turn it over to the new owners, whoever they might turn out to be. I consider calling someone, but can't decide who. Mum and Dad will be pleased as punch at my appointment, regardless of how temporary, but I'll have to explain about Marcus too, and I'm not sure how to do that. His sudden departure to the States without any warning has shaken me. I know how important his son is to him but… Then, I consider. If Lissa was on the other side of the world and needed me, I would be on the next plane without thinking twice.

I make myself a cup of camomile tea to relax me, and I'm sitting in the kitchen going over the events of the day when the phone rings. I grasp it eagerly even though I know it can't possibly be Marcus as he'll still be in the air.

My sister's voice echoes in my ear as I wonder what she wants this time.

'What are you doing this weekend? We need to talk.' Without waiting for my reply, Jan continues. 'How about lunch on Sunday? It'll just be salad but you'll come, won't you?' In my weakened state, I agree and, unwilling to chat, I manage to finish the call without divulging my distress.

I wander around the house picking things up, then putting them down again. I can't settle. Marcus has gone. What isn't clear to me is why he's left so suddenly, nor when he intends to return. What if…? But it's foolish to even consider he won't return. It's only four weeks till the end of term and Christmas is rapidly approaching. Surely he'll be back by then?

Then it hits me. I'm to be acting Head for the remainder of the term. Marcus' defection has had the result of elevating me to the position for which I've applied. But any pleasure I might have had from this accolade has been tempered by his sudden and partially unexplained departure.

Now I take time to think about it, I realise it's an opportunity to demonstrate to the powers that be how well I can do the job. Sure, it's only a few weeks, and it *is* end of term, so there will be no major decisions to be made but I will be Queen Bee. I smile as I recall Heather's nickname. No one can surpass her. I decide to ask her advice and, checking my watch, lift the phone to call.

'So, be sure to keep in touch. You can do this and remember, you have a good chance of being offered the position on a permanent basis, so treat it as if you are really the Headmistress, not only acting in the role. Promise.'

I promise and hang up the phone. The talk with Heather has buoyed my spirits and given me a renewed sense of purpose. All thoughts of Marcus are on the back burner as I realise my wardrobe may leave much to be desired if I'm to take on my new role next day. I go upstairs and a search of my work clothes reveal them to be fairly okay for a head of department, but sadly lacking in the executive department. I'll need to rope in Lissa for another shopping spree.

I shake out a short-sleeved blue suit which has been hanging at the back of the robe, pushed there after I wore it to a wedding a number of years ago. I look at it critically. Yes, it'll do for starters and I can find some other garments to add to it on the weekend.

*

'You, Headmistress!' Lissa's peal of laughter bubbles over the phone.

'Don't you think your old mum is up to the job?' I ask, chagrined.

'Of course you are,' Lissa's voice takes on a more serious tone. 'It's just… well, you're no Heather. But, on reflection, that's probably a good thing. You're no Marcus either.' And she bursts into laughter again.

'Get serious, Lissa!' I'm beginning to lose patience with her. 'I need your help. My current wardrobe isn't up to it and I don't have much to spend. I need your advice.' I wait while my daughter digests this. I really am at my wits' end as to how I can look upmarket without it costing me the earth.

'Sorry, Mum. Of course I'll help. It's cool. Gran and Gramps will be real chuffed. Have you told them yet?'

'No.' I've kept the news to myself as I know that by telling the rest of my family about my acting position, I'll also have to come clean about Marcus leaving. I don't want to do that just yet. Maybe once I've heard from him. He should have arrived in California by now so I'm expecting a call or email any time.

'So, I'll see you on Saturday morning then?' I want to get this locked in before I face Jan on Sunday.

'Will do. Meet me here and we'll check out Paddington. I know a few good spots where we might be able to pick up some used pieces…'

'Used?' I cringe at the thought of wearing secondhand clothes. I have a vision of looking like a charity case.

'Pre-loved is the term and I'm talking about designer labels. They may only have been worn once or even bought and never worn at all.'

'Really?' This is new territory for me, but I trust Lissa whose fashion sense has always been superior to mine, even when she was a little girl. 'Okay, I'll be there at nine.'

As I leave the phone my eyes stray to my laptop lying on the table. I check my emails one more time. Still nothing from Marcus. Should I begin to worry? Should I email him? I give myself a shake and rub my eyes. Goodness knows what awaited him when he arrived. I need to give the man time to adjust, time to deal with whatever it is he's been summoned there for. Patience is not my strong suit and I'm both anxious to hear from him and keen to tell him my own news. My first few days as Headmistress have gone well. Girls and staff alike have accepted me and I feel that the role fits me like a glove. I've had to continue my teaching responsibilities which has no doubt helped dispel any concerns they night have had. Marcus has been missed, of course, and I don't have his sort of charisma, but I've managed, by being myself, to gain their respect and approval.

Twenty-seven

'About Christmas.' Jan interrupts her chopping and gives me a look, one which I know does not bode well, as far as I'm concerned anyway. 'You won't want to do it this year, will you?' It's not really a question as, before I can frame a reply, she continues. 'We can have Christmas here, all of us, just like…' She pauses, realising it won't be 'just like' anything. She's never done Christmas. We always celebrated at Mum and Dad's till Sean and I took it over around ten years ago.

'Whatever. I may not be here.' My words go down like a lead balloon.

'Not here? Of course you will. It won't be like Christmas without you. We'll all be there, Mum and Dad, Bob, us, Lissa and her fellow, what's his name?'

'Will,' I answer weakly. Of course I'll be there. Christmas has always been a family affair. It'll bring it all back, the betrayal of last Christmas, but at least I can escape immediately afterwards. If Marcus isn't back, I'll go off somewhere on my own, somewhere quiet, up north, maybe.

'And Marcus?' Jan raises her eyebrows. 'Will he be in Sydney? I know his folks are in Brisbane, so I guess he could be going up there. But now that you two are…'

I'm wondering how to reply, and have my mouth open when she starts up again.

'I know you haven't been together for long but Mum says…'

I interrupt her this time. 'Mum doesn't know yet.' I clear my throat. 'Marcus has gone back to the States.'

Jan puts down her knife and stands arms akimbo. I've clearly astonished my usually unflappable sister.

'What on earth?'

'Some family crisis. To do with Jonathon, his son. I don't know any more than that,' I add to forestall any further questions. 'And, guess what?' I quickly change the subject. 'Guess who's the acting Head till the end of the year? Yours truly, that's who.' I pause to let the news sink in.

'You are?' As I thought, this distracts Jan and she comes over to give me a hug. 'Well done, sis. So it's in the bag, then? The job for next year?'

'I wouldn't go that far, but…' I preen myself. 'You never know. Heather is confident I'll get it and this is a trial period for me. I'm coping so far.'

'Course you are.' Jan returns to her chopping board. 'Just wait till Mum and Dad hear. Mum'll go ape. Her daughter; Headmistress at Grammar. She'll dine out on it for weeks.'

'Steady on. I haven't got the job yet. This is only an acting position.'

'But you'll get it. Have faith in yourself, Anna. You always put yourself down. You're more capable than you think. You can do this. You're proving it.'

Wow. This, coming from my closed-up sister. It's the first time I can remember her praising me. I mentally pat myself on the back. At last I seem to have done something she values. But I'm congratulating myself too soon.

'Just don't mess it up,' she admonishes, as she slides the remaining salad ingredients into a bowl. 'Would you take this into the dining room?' she adds, as if she hadn't just burst my bubble of self-satisfaction. Oh, well, that's family for you. They can build you up one minute and pull you down the next.

'Sure.' I take the bowl and carry it through to the next room.

We enjoy a pleasant meal. Fortunately the boys take up most of the conversation and it's difficult for the three adults to get word in. I enjoy their mad banter, so different to that of Lissa and her friends when they were growing up. Boys are different I reflect, thinking about another little boy and wondering, not for the first time today, what's happening with Marcus and what it is about Jonathon that has demanded such a sudden trip.

It's not till I'm leaving and she is hugging me goodbye that Jan returns to our earlier topic of conversation. 'Christmas. You will be here, won't you? I know it'll be difficult for you, but it is a family time and…'

'Yes, yes, I'll be there.' I know that I'll be subject to continual nagging until I agree, so it's easier to agree now.

'And Marcus? If he's back?'

'Maybe, I can't answer for him,' I shrug and give her a peck on the cheek. 'Talk soon.'

'Let me know…' Her words follow me out to the car and I enter it quickly and drive off, cursing.

*

In the hustle and bustle of my role as Headmistress, albeit *acting*, Jan's comments are relegated to their rightful place at the back of my consciousness. I'm enjoying the unfamiliar sense of responsibility the position brings. Although I'm accustomed to being a Department Head, I'm finding that being Queen Bee – to use the girls' term – is quite a different kettle of fish.

To my amazement, in my first week in the role, I enter my Year Ten class to a rousing applause. As I indicate to the girls that they should be seated, I can't hide my delight.

'So, are you still going to be our English teacher, Mrs H?' one of the bolder girls asks, while the rest of the class murmurs in assent.

'Yes,' I reply, gathering my papers together. 'And, now your exams are over…' I smile as I anticipate their reaction, 'I've decided to accede to the request you made earlier in the year.' For a moment, they look mystified, then one of the brighter girls raises her hand.

'You mean…? You don't really mean?'

I hold up the copy of *Twilight* which I've brought in to class. 'This novel will fill the literature section of our study for the next four weeks.' I pause to allow the subdued muttering to die down. 'We'll read aloud in class, discuss characterisation and plot, and I've outlined a major assignment on this sheet.' I proceed to hand out the assigned work, aware that, for once, I've surprised them.

Although still teaching Year Ten, I've passed on my younger classes to others, and assigned my Year Eleven some individualised reading in preparation for their Year Twelve studies, so I'm able to spend most of my days in the large office which once housed Heather, then Marcus. It's the size of an average lounge room. The Tasmanian oak desk, a relic from older times, stands side on to a wide bay window which reaches from floor to ceiling providing an excellent view over the courtyard and playing fields. I now know how Heather was awesomely aware of everything going on in the school. It's easy to sit here and watch staff and students pass by, and to note who mingles with whom. The positioning of the desk also enables me to look across the entire room, taking in the ornate fireplace no longer used these days, but serving as a reminder of grander times, as does the portrait above the mantle of Dame Hilary Brenton, the school founder. The rest of the room is fairly bare. A sofa and two armchairs flank a low intricately carved coffee table all designed to put new parents and students at ease. The only other furniture comprises a couple of round-backed chairs, which I recall Heather purchasing several years ago to replace the hard straight-backed ones of her predecessors. These are set opposite the desk and are reserved for more formal meetings with staff or students.

'How are you finding things?' Glenda is at my elbow as I leave class. 'Not too important to mix with us lesser mortals?' She laughs, but I detect a note of something which I can't quite identify in her voice.

I sigh. 'More administration than I expected, given exams are over for the seniors, but other than that, everything's fine. Are you going to the staffroom? I'll join you for a cuppa.'

She looks surprised, but I've determined not to follow in Heather and Marcus' footsteps. I'm only *acting* after all, and I want to maintain my easy relationship with the rest of the staff. I might well be back to being one of them in the new school year. Although I'm optimistic, I can't take anything for granted.

As I walk into the staffroom, there's a pause in the conversation, then a cheer echoes around the room.

'Anna,' a voice which sounds like Fay's, says: 'Come to take tea with the plebs?' But I detect a note of approbation in her words. I bow mockingly as I make my way across the room. The conversations resume and I breathe a sigh of relief. The staff are going to accept me as Headmistress. That's one hurdle over.

The next few weeks pass in a blur. Exams are sat and report cards written, classrooms are packed up, holiday plans discussed, and still no word from Marcus. I'm almost – but not quite – too busy to notice. It's in the evenings, alone at home, when I feel his absence most keenly. I'm trying to keep myself occupied and have almost finished packing up the impedimenta of twenty-five years. Unlike Mum, I haven't offered my cast-offs to Lissa, but we've spent an evening together going through old photographs and stirring up old memories. The evening has brought us closer if anything.

On the last day of term, I pack up my desk. As I leave I draw my fingers slowly across the polished surface and gaze longingly out of the window. I wonder if I will be the one to take my place back here again in the New Year. Next year is to be a momentous one for Grammar – its diamond jubilee. What an honour it would be to lead the school through these celebrations. I sigh, pick up my bag and head for the staffroom.

'Here she is!' Glenda comes forward to lead me to the centre of the room. Tradition dictates that Grammar staff celebrates the end of the school year with a staff party the day classes finish. I'm last to arrive having spent the day ensuring I've left all the paperwork in order and have removed all evidence of my presence in the office – in the event that I'm unsuccessful. Everything that has happened during the past four weeks has led me to believe the post is mine, but I am conscious of becoming too complacent. I don't want to tempt fate.

As I walk in to the room, I'm surrounded by a smiling bunch of my colleagues.

'Welcome, Headmistress!' they chant in unison, but there is a mocking note in their voices.

'Okay, okay.' I hold up my hands to silence them. 'As of now I'm back to being one of you.'

'Still no word from the Board?' Glenda asks, placing a glass of champagne in my hand.

'Not yet,' I begin, only to be interrupted by Fay calling out.

'Now that Anna's here, we can start. No questions about the Head's role. We're all on holiday as of now. Let's forget about this place and talk about anything and everything else. We're done with this for another two months.' With that, everyone migrates toward the food, and the conversation becomes more general. I'm caught up in the combined festive spirit and it's not until I'm driving home that I come back to earth. Only a couple more weeks of this year to go. I aim to ensure next year will be a better one for me. I'll be in control of my destiny. I press my lips together and grip the steering wheel firmly as I make my way home.

Twenty-eight

Christmas is the nightmare I've expected. My only communication from Marcus has been a brief email wishing me a Merry Christmas and promising to write in more detail soon. I've hesitated before deciding to reply in kind, but I can't dismiss my disappointment. We've been so close. At least, I thought we were close, but perhaps was wrong. I head off to Jan's with an armful of gaily wrapped gifts and a heavy heart.

I pretend to participate in the jollity, all the while wishing the whole catastrophe to be over. For Lissa's sake, I've dressed up – the red dress again – and wrapped everyone's present in the usual way. The decorated boxes sit under the tree throughout Christmas lunch keeping me hostage to the party – I'm not permitted to leave till all of them are opened. Jan has done us proud. For her first family Christmas she's pulled out all the stops and, even in my fragile state, I appreciate the results.

At last, just as my fixed smile is beginning to turn to rigour, we all leave the table and, fortified with yet another glass of champagne, retire to the lounge room to open the presents. Bob fiddles with the CD player to find some Christmas music and Jan's boys eagerly descend on the pile of gifts, taking turns to distribute them. Amid the resulting cacophony, I turn to Lissa and whisper in her ear. 'I plan to go soon. Think I can slip away easily?'

'No whispering!' Bob is quick to descend on us. 'What about a game of charades?' This is too much for me.

'No, I need to go.' I begin to gather the books, scarf and chocolates I've received, avoiding Mum's steely glare. I think I've managed escape and am placing them all into a plastic bag when she begins.

'You're not leaving already, Anna! After all the trouble Jan's gone to. It smacks of ingratitude.' I flinch. Even at my age, Mum still has the power to make me feel like a child.

'I…' I begin, but Dad interrupts.

'Leave the girl alone, Susie. Can't you see she's done in? It's taken it out of her, being here with us all. Reminds her of last year, I'll be bound.'

'Leave it, Dad.' I can't take their talking about me as if I'm not here. 'Jan, it's been great. You've put on a fantastic feast. You may have set a precedent here. Who's going to be able to compete with all this?' I spread my arms to encompass the Christmas tree stretching to the ceiling, the miniature train making its way around the tree's base and the mass of wrappings covering the floor. 'But I really must go. I'll get a cab,' I add, as I see Graham open his mouth to offer me a lift. 'I don't think any of us is fit to drive right now.' I must get out of this room before the tears which threaten to fall down my cheeks actually begin.

I sit back in the cab with a sigh. I've finally managed to extricate myself from the family and tomorrow I'm off. I've given my apologies to Jan and I have to admit she was pretty okay about everything. I'm fed up to the teeth with family. I need to be by myself. Everyone except Bob is part of a couple – and I wouldn't be surprised if he has someone tucked away, someone he wants to keep to himself, away from the family.

Next day, bright and early, I hit the road, the road north. I've booked myself into a mid-range hotel at Peregian Beach, north of Brisbane and I intend to veg out there for the next few weeks. It's been a hectic year and I need time to recharge.

I enter my hotel room, drop my bags on the floor and throw myself on the bed with a sigh of relief. It's been a long drive, with a brief overnight stop at Coffs Harbour in the only accommodation I could find. I'd forgotten the annual mad rush to leave Sydney every Boxing Day. Although I'd set off at the crack of dawn, the roads were already full of other holiday makers. Every second car seemed to have piles of luggage and surfboards tied to the roof and several had bikes attached to the tailbar. When I stopped for lunch it had been difficult to find an empty table so I'd resorted to McDonald's, not my favourite fare. On the second day of my trip I've been more organised, stopping at a bakers on the way and taking my food with me. Now I can relax!

I enjoy the next few days. It's a long time since I spent time by myself, on myself. Not since I met Sean, not even before then. This may be the first time I've been able to be truly alone with no chance of interruptions. I relish it. I spend my days poking around the small village-like beach suburb with occasional forays into Noosa for the buzz and high-end shopping. I become a regular for breakfast at the Baked Poets Café enjoying its exquisite version of latté which entails pouring a small jug of coffee into a tall glass of hot milk, and its "egg in a glass" – a peeled boiled egg served in a small glass, delicious. I discover Annie's Bookshop where I browse for hours, coming out with an armful of books and a promise to return. I'm disappointed I've missed one of her regular author talks on the sidewalk with drinks and nibbles. I check out a new restaurant every night. I feel as if I've entered a different world, one where all my cares are swept away and I'm at peace. Even my annoyance with Marcus and his lack of communication disappears as I walk along the almost deserted beach, listening to the crash of the surf and watch the brave young men kite surfing in the wild surf. I vow to return.

It's on one of these days when I've spent two hours walking along the beach and return energised to my room, that I find Bob waiting for me.

'What the…' I say, knocking the sand off my feet. 'What are you doing here? Dad…?' My immediate thought is Dad has suffered a relapse, but that doesn't explain Bob's presence. Surely he would have called in an emergency.

'No, everyone's well,' he assures me. 'It's the other thing. I've something to discuss with you. I had a few days leave. so thought…'

'Why not interrupt your sister's holiday,' I finish for him.

'You're looking good.' Now he's here, Bob doesn't seem anxious to share the reason for his visit. I decide to go along with him.

'It's a gorgeous spot. Don't know why I haven't been here before. I can show you around. How long have you got?'

'Only a couple of days. Look, is there somewhere we can have a meal? My shout.' He moves from one foot to the other waiting for my response.

'Sure. Let me shower first. Can't offer you a drink, I'm afraid.'

Half an hour later we're sitting out on the deck at the surf club, watching the sunset over the distant ocean, and waiting for our meal, with a couple of drinks in front of us.

'Okay, spill! I know it's something serious to bring you all this way.'

Bob looks down into his beer and moves the glass around the table, making wet marks where it touches the table top. 'It's not easy,' he begins. 'You won't like it.'

'Well, it won't get any better by waiting. What have you come all this way to tell me?'

'It's this Gina business. None of us wants this to go to court, so her solicitor has come up with an offer to settle.'

'Settle?' I ask, bewildered. I'm not used to his legal jargon, but I have the impression we're talking money.

'Yes, they'll settle for five hundred thousand.'

'Five hundred?' My mouth gapes and my glass thumps down on the table spilling wine onto the wood. 'I don't have that sort of money, Bob. You can't be serious suggesting…'

'Hear me out. They're willing to settle for five hundred thousand and forego the court case. If it goes to court, Anna, she could win. She could get half of everything. Seems to me five hundred's a pretty good deal from your point of view.'

'But…' I look around wildly. *Where am I going to find five hundred thousand dollars? I can barely meet the mortgage now that Bonnie's left.*

'Sell the house. With this settled, we can get probate pretty much immediately and the place should sell well. We can build a delay into the agreement with Gina. You can pay her off when you sell.'

'You have everything all cut and dried don't you?' My voice cracks. My peaceful holiday is ruined. I'm back in the morass of debt and jealousy I've come here to forget.

'But,' I object, 'the house, the business, Sean's super, it's all worth a lot more. If Gina's willing to accept five hundred thousand, surely that means she – or her solicitor – thinks they'll lose if it goes to court? So shouldn't we…?'

'It doesn't work that way, sis. Taking a matter like this to court is expensive and it can stretch out for years. My guess is Gina's anxious for some money now. Didn't you say she had some project going up there?'

'Yes, Lissa talked about it. Some yoga thing. She and Sean were…' My voice tails off as once gain I picture the pair of them together. Damn, I've been doing so well, too.

I'm about to question Bob more when the waiter brings our meal. 'I'm not done with you,' I assure him. 'But we should eat this while it's hot. We tuck into our steaks and salads as the sun finally drops below the horizon. It's a pity Bob's news had spoiled the beauty of this idyllic spot.

I spend the next day showing Bob around and stewing about the money. With reluctance, I finally agree to the terms. At least this means I can put the house on the market.

'I can talk to the realtor now, can I?' I check with Bob to make sure.

'Give it a few days. We need to get the legal stuff sorted out first. Wait till I give you the go-ahead.'

'I've waited this long. What's a few more days, weeks, months…?'

'Won't be months. Weeks, maybe.'

'Well, I'm up here for the next week, so maybe when I get back you'll have some news for me.'

'We'll see.' Bob has become the lawyer again, wary of committing himself to anything. 'But enjoy the rest of your stay here.' He looks out on the ocean. 'Wish I could stay.'

I say nothing. Although, despite the news he's brought, it has been good to see Bob. Now I can't wait for him to leave. I'm keen to regain my solitary composure.

I say farewell to Bob, driving him down to the Sunshine Coast airport which seems to belong more in Hawaii than South East Queensland, with its tropical vegetation and casually dressed passengers. The only things missing are the flowered leis.

'It'll be right, you'll see,' Bob whispers as he hugs me goodbye. 'I'll be in touch soon.'

I wave him off with mixed emotions and slowly drive back up the highway to my refuge.

At last, I'm on my own again. But my peace has been shattered and, having agreed to it, I'm now worrying about this settlement. What if the "legal stuff", to quote Bob, falls down? What if Gina decides five hundred thousand isn't enough and wants more? What if the house doesn't sell and Gina wants her money? After tossing and turning for most of the night, I drift into a troubled sleep and wake at the crack of dawn. Seeing the bright sunlight creeping round the curtains, I rise and make my way to the beach, hoping a run will blow away my confused thoughts.

I have the beach to myself. The tide is out so I walk down to the wet sand and, taking off my sandals, begin to pound along the edge of the water. The sea looks magnificent in the early morning light. It seems to go on forever, the waves breaking strongly on the shore. I run and run till, out of breath, I stop and bend over, hands on knees to take some deep breaths. I turn and look out to sea, marvelling at the immensity of the ocean and how small and insignificant I feel compared to its vastness. I walk back slowly, swinging my sandals and, this time, take time to look at the sand beneath my feet.

I'm amazed at the evidence of sea creatures. The odd white blob of jellyfish, the deep holes surrounded by hills of freshly dug sand, presumably the night work of sand crabs and the remnants of shell and cuttlefish lying on the surface. I sit down on the wet sand, close my eyes and raise my face to the sun. It feels good. The warming rays banish the worries of the night. Sydney, and everything it represents, fades away. I'm left with a sense of peace. I wish I could stay here forever. In this very spot. I don't know how long I sit like this but I'm jolted out of my reverie by the sound of voices coming closer, and the panting of a small animal. This panting reveals itself to be a small white terrier whose tongue begins licking my hand. I open my eyes and smile at the little creature. Rising, I stretch, then pick up my sandals and walk back to my now favourite café for breakfast.

My time on the beach has resulted in a calmer me, one who is prepared to accept whatever might happen with the house and Gina's claims. My only cause for worry now is Marcus. As I sip my long latté and gaze around at the singles and couples enjoying breakfast at neighbouring tables, the children playing on the large fig tree nearby, I reflect what will be will be. This trip has been good for me. I've come to realise I'm not dependent on any other person for my happiness and wellbeing. It's a revelation to me. All of my life there's been someone to depend on – or dependent on me in the case of Lissa. First my parents, then Sean, then – a period I don't want to remember when I almost lost it, followed by my meeting Marcus and our burgeoning relationship. Now it's just me. Lissa has her own life. My parents are moving on with theirs. And Marcus, well he may or may not return. While I'd like it if he did, I know I'll cope if he doesn't. It's as if I've found myself, here on a deserted beach.

Buoyed up by this feeling of faith in the future, when I return to my room I turn to my diary and drop to the floor on my knees. Before I enter today's epistle, I flick back through the earlier pages. In my new frame of mind, I'm aghast at the negativity and distress which has poured out of me in previous months. It seems to my jaundiced eyes I've written more when I've been depressed, making only a few brief notes when Marcus and I were together.

I sit back on my heels and survey these pages, covered in my hurried scrawl. I feel a strong need to rid myself of them. Like a flash of lightning I remember a ceremony I attended with Gina a number of years back – a Burning Bowl ceremony. Sean had derided it at the time as being a load of mumbo jumbo, but I remember coming away from it feeling calm, cleansed and renewed.

I hold my diary with both hands remembering the evening. It began with a short mediation, then, silently, all of us – a group of around a dozen women – wrote down all the things we wanted to rid ourselves of. Then, one by one – still in silence – we moved slowly outside to place our writings into a bowl where they were burnt. Once back inside we then wrote down all the things we wanted for our lives in the coming year. We then sealed this in a stamped addressed envelope which was to be mailed to us some time later. I don't recall much about the future bit, but I do recall the therapeutic nature of the burning.

Suddenly I know what I'll do. I tear out the pages and, carrying them in one hand go outside. I sit down at a small table on the veranda and systematically shred the sheets into tiny pieces. I look around wondering how to destroy them. To light a fire in the Queensland summer is unthinkable, even in a bowl, if I had one suitable. I cast around for a solution, finally deciding to bury them in the sand. I wait till almost dark, then – thankful for the low tide – go out and dig a hole in the wet sand. I place the pieces in the hole and cover them up as the tide begins to turn. I stand watching the incoming tide wash over them, taking them out of my life.

Maybe my new feeling of independence has worked its magic. Next morning, after an early morning run and breakfast, I return to my room, shower, dress then boot up my computer. Checking through my emails, there it is; the one I've been looking for over the past weeks. Marcus has made good his promise to send me a longer missive. I curl up in the armchair, laptop on my knee and begin to read.

My Darling Anna,

Sorry, sorry, sorry! I'm ashamed I haven't sent this to you before now and I hope you're still speaking to me and will read this email and not consign it to the deleted file, unread.

When I took off so suddenly I had no idea what awaited me in California. In his rushed call, Rick had only said Jonathon needed me. As a parent yourself I hope you'll understand my desire to reach him as soon as possible. Even though Lauren had told me Jonathon wasn't my son, in my heart he is and always will be.

I arrived at San Francisco airport fearing the worst. Rick met me and took me to their palatial home in Nob Hill. You wouldn't believe these homes, the Eastern suburbs of Sydney have nothing on them, believe me. He didn't say much in the car, apart from the fact that both Lauren and Jon were well, so I couldn't imagine what had prompted the emergency call and why I was there.

When I arrived there was no sign of anyone but the maid who answered the door and stood awkwardly while Rick introduced me. When he asked where Jon was, she pointed to the stairs and sniffed.

'His room,' Rick muttered, 'That's where he spends all his time these days.' I looked at him dumbfounded. The Jon I know is an open loud sociable little guy, a proper boy, if you know what I mean, not a recluse who hides in his room. I asked if Jon knew I was arriving and Rick didn't deign to answer. At this point I felt like punching him but instead, I took the stairs two steps at a time yelling Jon's name. I didn't have any idea where to go when I reached the top so I went along the corridor yelling and opening doors till I came to one which was locked. When I kept yelling and tried to turn the handle, I heard a small voice from within saying, 'Dad, is that you? Is it really you?' The door opened a crack and there was Jon's little face peering at me. The face was thin and pale and looked nothing like the eager lively boy who I'd last seen leaving our home in Oregon with his mum.

I stop at this point and put my hands up to my face, my eyes filled with unshed tears. I can imagine Marcus' distress at the change he's found in Jonathon and can't imagine what can have caused it. I rub my eyes and continue to read, scrolling down the page.

The door gradually opened wider and I could see his whole body which flung itself against me and hugged me as if he'd never let me go. 'I knew it wasn't true. I knew it!' he sobbed still holding on to me like grim death. I gradually released his grip and sat down on the floor at his level determined to find out what had happened.

Well the long and short of it is that, in what they thought were Jon's best interests, Rick and Lauren told him I wanted nothing to do with him and Rick was his father now. God, I wish I hadn't been so circumspect on my last trip. I thought I was staying away for his own good, to appease Lauren and make life easier for him. Nothing could have been further from the truth.

Well the result is that Lauren admitted she lied when she told me Jon wasn't mine. Seems she wanted to punish me or something. As a result she punished Jon too and he's now a shadow of his former self. But getting better every day, now that I'm here.

I'm reading this through tears. How can a mother be so intentionally cruel to her own son? I shake my head in disbelief. But does this mean Marcus has decided to remain in the States to be with his son? I stiffen my back and read on.

We've been through a lot of legal stuff and the end result is I now have custody of Jon. Lauren will have him for some holidays, of course. I'd never deprive her of that but, most of the time, he'll be with me, us, if I haven't lost your trust completely.

I gasp when I read these words. We haven't reached that stage in our relationship. I stand up and walk around trying to come to grips with the implication of this. Taking a deep breath I return to my spot and continue with the email.

I'm bringing him back with me to Sydney. I still have the keys to my mate's apartment. He's not due back till after Easter, so Jon and I can doss down there for the time being. I want to have him settled in before schools starts.

I know it's a lot to ask after my cone of silence, but I wondered if you could meet us at the airport.

I read on to the end in a daze. This is the last thing I expected. I'm not sure how I feel. I'm glad Marcus is coming back. I have a flutter in my stomach of what I recognise as excitement at the thought of seeing him again. But with his son! What difference will that make? I'm used to being around girls at school, not boys. I recall my reaction to Jan's two at Christmas. I enjoyed their company, but they're more of a rough house than the girls I'm used to. And Jon has been through the mill. Can I cope with a disturbed young boy who may resent me and hate having to share his dad with me? Before I lose my courage I quickly reply that I'll be at the airport and press *Send*.

I remain sitting there hugging myself for a few minutes then rise and run my fingers down my body. Marcus is coming back. This is the news I've been waiting for and I can't keep the smile from my face. Even the new independent me is delighted. I notice a spring in my step as I make my way out to have lunch. As I chew on the thick *Volkhorn* bread served with a variety of dips, which has now become a favourite with me, I begin to plan. My holiday will be cut short if I'm to be back in Sydney for Marcus' return. I take my planner out of my bag and spend the next half hour making plans. My sojourn here is over. It's time for me to return to whatever Sydney has in store for me.

Twenty-nine

'Is she your honey?' Jonathon stares at me with the same deep brown eyes as his dad and hunches his shoulders.

'She has a name. This is Anna and she's…' Marcus cocks his head to one side as if considering his next words. 'She's a friend of mine, a good friend and I hope she'll be yours too.'

'Mmm,' Jonathon shrugs, and shifts his bag higher up his shoulder. 'Can we buy ice cream on the way, Dad?' I've already been relegated to the grownups who don't matter file and don't know whether to be pleased or upset.

I've come to meet Marcus and his son at the airport, not without some trepidation. Marcus, yes, I know I'll be pleased to see him and he me, judging by his comments at the end of his long email and subsequent one, received after I'd agreed to meet them. But Jon is the unknown quantity in the equation. I have to expect things to be different with a young boy around. But if he's going to become part of my future – wow, how amazing that sounds – I need to become accustomed to his presence and even build a relationship with him.

'Good to see you.' Marcus gives me a casual hug combined with a peck on the cheek, which is not the sort of welcome I'd expected. I console myself with the thought that, after all, Jon is right here, and to him I'm a complete stranger. Still, I had expected something more of Marcus given his references to our "being together". It's good to see him. Over Christmas I'd given up hope of this day ever happening. So what if it's not quite what I expected? Perhaps he's waiting till we're alone.

'Where are you parked?' Marcus looks around as we stand outside the terminal and I realise I've been lost in my ruminations.

'Miles away,' I laugh. 'This is Sydney Airport, remember?' And we trudge through the multilevel car park to find my little *VW*.

'This yours? Cool,' is Jonathon's first comment since we left the terminal and he utters not another word as Marcus loads their luggage into the boot.

As we drive through the city Marcus points out the famous landmarks to a still silent Jonathon; the Harbour Bridge, the Opera House, Australia Square, Circular Key. Finally he leans back, sighs and reaches over to place a hand on my thigh.

'It's going to take time,' he says. 'Bear with us.' I steal a quick glance across at my passenger and note the creases by his eyes are more pronounced than before. His manner as he pushes his glasses up the bridge of his nose, demonstrates a weariness caused by more than the transatlantic flight. The trip has aged him. I can see he's still worried about his son. Jonathon may be here with us now, but he is still the damaged little boy whose father is worried about him.

'I'll just drop you off.' I turn to Marcus as we pull up outside his apartment building. 'You'll want time to…' I'm not sure what I mean. I only know the two of them need space; time to adjust both to being together again and, for Jonathon, to being here in Australia. 'Call me,' I add, 'when you're ready.' Ready for what I'm not sure, but Marcus seems to understand what I mean. He clasps my hand, and gives me a warmer hug than before followed by a kiss on the lips.

'Thanks!' His tone is heartfelt. 'I'll be in touch. It may take time…' his voice tails off and his eyes follow Jonathon who has run over to look at the ocean.

'Right. I'll be off. Bye!' I call to Jonathon who is unaware of my words, so caught up is he in the scene in front of him. 'Didn't he see the ocean back in California?' I ask as I prepare to drive away.

'No,' Marcus says shortly. 'He lived in a palatial prison away from the sea. This is all new to him. Hey buddy!' he calls, and I realise Marcus, too, has begun to relegate me to the past. I drive off.

The next few days are difficult as I try to come to grips with the fact that, although Marcus is back in town, he's otherwise occupied. I know he has to spend time with his son, and don't begrudge Jonathon his father's attention, but I do wish Marcus could make more time for me. He texts and calls me every day and I have to be satisfied with these inanimate communications for now.

I'm therefore surprised to find the pair of them standing at my door one morning, just as I've decided to do more sorting and packing.

'Hi,' Jonathon says shyly.

'Hi to you too.' I look up at his father towering above both of us, his wide shoulders evident in the tight white tee shirt he's wearing with equally tight worn blue jeans. I hear my own intake of breath at the overt masculinity of the man.

'Jon wanted to see where "my honey" lives, so here we are.'

'You'd better come in.' I stand aside to let them pass.

The kitchen is redolent with the chocolate chip cookies I've made, in anticipation of a visit from Lissa. They've always been her favourite.

'Wow.' Jonathon looks hopefully up at his dad.

'Help yourself,' I laugh. Maybe boys aren't too different after all. Jonathon helps himself to a cookie and looks around the room with interest.

'Do you have any children?'

'No, only a daughter and she doesn't live here anymore.' I wish I could eat my words when I see his little face droop.

'You mean she's…?'

'She's old enough to have her own home,' I quickly explain. 'She comes to visit a lot, but she lives nearby with her boyfriend. She's coming to visit today which is why I made those cookies.'

'Oh.' His hand which has been snaking up to take another cookie, jumps back.

'It's okay. There are plenty for everyone. Have another.' I hold the plate out towards him

This earns me a timid smile.

'I'm afraid I don't have any games here anymore, but would you like to explore my garden?' I offer, while realising that a garden might hold little attraction for someone of his age. But it seems I've said the right thing. Jonathon's face lights up and he looks around as if the garden is going to magically appear in the kitchen.

'Out here.' I lead him through the French windows into the courtyard and he immediately runs off into the far corner.

'You pressed the right button.' Marcus has followed up and he throws an arm round my shoulders as we watch Jonathon run from one spot to another. 'He loves plants; anything growing, actually. Prefers them to people these days. He'll be right for some time now.' Marcus draws me back into the kitchen and into his arms. His kiss is long and lingering, his mouth taking little nibbles from mine and his arms stroking my back till my knees go weak and only his firm grasp is keeping me upright.

'Oh, God, how I've missed you! I wanted to do that at the airport but…'

I move back while remaining inside the circle of his arms. 'Me too,' I murmur lazily. I've forgotten the effect his nearness has on me. How can I have imagined I'd be able to live without this?

Marcus drags his fingers through his hair. 'It's going to be difficult for a time,' he says ruefully. 'Being together, I mean. Jon hasn't let me out of his sight since we returned. I can't leave him and…' I place my finger on his lips, thrilling with the feel of their softness under my fingertip.

'It's okay. I understand. He's just got you back again and it's difficult to ask him to share you with anyone, never mind a scheming woman.'

'There's only one woman I'm interested in and I'd hardly call her scheming.'

We're still standing in the circle of each other's arms, when a voice calls from inside the house.

'Cooee, anyone home?' Jonathon comes running back and Marcus and I jump apart as if stung.

'Hi Lissa. Through here.'

'Hello, stranger,' Lissa addresses Marcus and smiles secretly at me: 'You're back! And who is this?' Lisa's gaze holds Jon's and he reddens slightly. He's clearly not too young to be susceptible to Lissa's charm.

'I'm Lissa and this is my mum's house. What's your name?'

'Jonathon King.' It's a small voice, but combined with an outstretched hand which takes Lissa's in his.

'Well, Jonathon King. I smell some chocolate chip cookies my mum has made for me. Would you like one?' Jonathon looks guilty, as if afraid of censure. Lissa catches on right away. 'Have you already tried them? Are they as good as they look?' He nods silently. 'Well, how about you and I finish them off. And what say I make a chocolate shake to wash them down?'

Jonathon's eyes open wide at this invitation and he follows Lissa into the kitchen. When Marcus and I join them some time later, they're both seated on high stools by the kitchen bench, chocolate around their mouths. I hide a smile. Lissa is still a kid at heart, regardless of her apparent grown up status.

'Looks like you two are having fun.' Marcus has been holding my hand and squeezes my fingers tightly at the sight of the grin on Jonathon's face. 'Have you left any for us?' Jonathon's grin fades and he glances sideways. 'Just kidding, old fellow.' Marcus says hurriedly. 'Bit too sweet for me, I shouldn't wonder.' He squeezes my fingers again and I understand his unspoken message.

'Now,' Marcus addresses Jonathon again. 'Perhaps we'd better leave these two good people. Wipe your face, mate. Time to go.'

'You can't go yet.' Lissa surprises us. 'I haven't shown Jon my room.'

'But I thought you didn't live here anymore.' Jonathon looks mystified.

'I don't, but I still have my room here, for when I want to come back,' she explains.

Jonathon gives her a serious look. 'Like I have at Mom's?' he asks.

'Exactly like that. Bet you left a few of your favourite things there too.' It seems she's said exactly the right thing as he nods furiously while trying to appear nonchalant. 'Come on upstairs with me. Bet we can find you something I don't need anymore. Even though I'm a girl, you might be surprised what's there.'

Jonathon stomps upstairs after Lissa with a brief a backward glance at his father to ascertain his approval which Marcus gives with a smile.

'Well!' I turn to Marcus smiling. 'Lissa seems to be working wonders. Who'd have thought it?'

When they come back downstairs, Jonathon has his arms full of books and a couple of boxes, with a well-used skateboard balanced precariously on top of the pile.

'Wow!' Marcus eyes the skateboard. 'We had to leave Jon's back in California. It's top of our list to replace. Good, one, eh, Jon?'

Jon grins at this. 'Super, Dad,' he enthuses. 'Practically an antique.'

Our eyes meet over the boy's head.

'Do you have something to put these in?' Lissa flashes me a smile. 'Thought we'd help with your clearing-out. All stuff I've outgrown. It was like a treasure trove for Jon. What happened to the For Sale sign anyway? I was expecting to see it as I drove in.'

'Realtor's putting it up next week,' I say in astonishment. 'And there are some spare boxes in the garage.' Lissa and Jonathon go happily in that direction while Marcus and I look at each other in amazement. Lissa has wrought a miracle with his troubled son.

'So?' Lissa and I are alone and I'm anxious to hear why she's dropped over. Her voice on the phone had sounded urgent when she rang about her need to speak with me but, since her arrival, she has been so chatty with Jonathon. I wonder what all the fuss was about.

'I need coffee.' Lissa takes her time in fixing it, then sits down opposite me. But instead of drinking her much vaunted caffeine hit, she twists her hands and drops her eyes.

'It's Will,' she says at last. 'Remember he had an interview?' I cast my mind back.

'But that was ages ago. Before Christmas wasn't it?' So much has happened since then that I've completely forgotten about Will's interview and Lissa's excitement.

'Yes, they've taken their time.' She looks up. 'It's his firm. The interview was for a promotion, one he deserves and has been working towards.' I see her bite her lip.

'And he didn't get it? He must be disappointed.' I can't understand why this has led her to being in such a state.

'He got it.' Lissa takes out her handkerchief and wipes her eyes. 'He's been offered the promotion but… but it's in New York.' She begins to sob uncontrollably.

I pass her a box of tissues.

'He's… They want him there before Easter, Mum, what am I going to do?'

'Liss.' I wrap my arms around my baby girl. 'It's not the end of the world,' knowing as I say the words, that, for Lissa, it certainly seems like it. 'Maybe…' I try to find the right words to say to comfort my distraught daughter.

'He wants me to go with him.' She looks up at me, her eyes huge and full of tears. 'How can I? And how can he even think of going and leaving me?'

I hug her tightly. My daughter is beginning to learn a few hard truths. Sean and I spoiled her as a child. She's always managed to get her own way and, to our amusement, devised ways of manipulating us to ensure she did. We've done her no favours.

'And you can't go because?'

'My Master's,' she wails. 'He knows how important it is to me. But…'

'But this job's important to him?' I hazard.

'Mmm,' her voice is muffled. Then she looks up. 'And it's not fair to you either, or Gran and Gramps.' She begins to sob again.

'Hey,' I say gently, putting my finger under her chin and looking her straight in the eye. 'Don't bring us into this. It's between you and Will. Consider this. How will you feel if you let him go on his own and he finds someone else over there, or decides to stay? How important to you is he? And remember, this is his career we're talking about. He's no longer a rolling stone, a student like you. He's a grown man with a future to consider.' I stroke her hair to show I'm on her side, but I want her to try to see Will's point of view. 'How long is this stint in New York to last?'

'A year, he says.' Lissa wipes her eyes and glares at me. 'I can't believe you're taking his side.'

'I'm not taking any side,' I remonstrate. 'But let's think about this sensibly.' I rack my brains to find a way to get through to my daughter. 'Your Master's, tell me about it. There are classes?'

'Yes.' Lissa wipes her eyes and itemises her words on her fingers. 'Four seminars with weekly tutorials – I'm planning two per year – then there's my thesis. I can do it alongside the seminars. Then there's the tutoring. I've only just managed to have that set up and I'm to tutor first year students. It's all planned.'

'I know you like to have everything planned out, but sometimes life isn't like that and throws you some curly ones.' I reflect how I'm very much aware of this, given the events of the past year. 'Let's look at the positive side of all this.'

'Positive? There's no positive. My life is falling apart.'

'Stop it, Lissa!' My voice is angry. 'This is nothing like what happened to me last year. Your life isn't falling apart. It's just beginning. Can you look at Will's appointment as an opportunity? Consider him instead of always thinking of yourself? Do you love him?' I ask abruptly.

'Of course I do! That's why…'

'If you really do, then you'll think of him and work out a way.'

'I want to be with him, I do. But I want it to be here. Everything has been going so well. I thought… I thought, if he got his promotion… maybe we'd be engaged and…'

'Has he asked you to marry him?' I'm a bit taken aback by her words as I haven't realised things were so serious between them.

'No-oo, but…'

'But you lost it when he told you about New York and haven't given him the chance?' I know my daughter too well. She nods.

'Where is he now?'

'He's having a game of squash with a mate. They play every week at this time. That's why…'

'That's why you came around here, hoping I would agree he's being unfair. I can't do that, honey.'

'But if Dad had wanted to take another job and go off somewhere, away from everything…'

'I'd have gone with him,' I say softly, almost to myself. 'I loved him. We loved each other. We were a unit. We did things together. That's what being in love is all about.' My voice drops.

'And he let you down.' Lissa's voice changes. It's as if she's suddenly realised how I must have felt last Christmas. 'I do really love Will and I want what's best for him. It's just…'

'I know, sweetie, sometimes life can be hard. Now,' I take her hands in mine. 'Let's think. Is there a way you can continue with your studies at a distance? With all the technology at our fingertips these days, surely you don't have to be actually there in person to complete all the requirements?'

'Maybe…' I can see her considering this. 'Maybe not. But what about you? And Gran and Gramps? If I'm not around? With the house and everything.'

'I hope everything will be settled long before Easter. And you don't need to worry about us. You have your own life to lead. That's why we brought you up to be independent; to make your own way in life; to fly off with Will if that's what you want. We're all very proud of you and will continue to be, whatever you decide. But it's your decision. No one can make it for you. Not me, not Will. You must decide. It's your life.' We sit in silence while she appears to digest my words. 'Now, what about some lunch?'

'No Mum, thanks.' I can see Lissa straighten up, her head high again. She rubs her, now reddened eyes with her fist and stands. 'I should go home, be there when Will gets back. I… we…'

'You had a fight?'

'Yes, sort of. But you've made me think. Perhaps I can… I'll check with the uni to see… New York might be fun.' She manages a smile. The young are so resilient. I'm feeling like a wet rag which has been through the wringer, and here she is looking forward to New York!

'Thanks, Mum,' Lissa hugs me goodbye. 'By the way,' she surprises me. 'If you and Marcus want a babysitter for Jon any time, you've only to ask.' And, with a wicked grin, she's off to mend bridges in her own life.

Thirty

'I think he's fallen in love with your daughter.'

'Sorry,' I laugh. 'I believe she's taken.'

On a more serious note Marcus adds. 'It's the first time he's come out of himself since we left the US. He's been talking about Lissa since we got back here. I can't believe it. And these books and games she gave him, he's been in his room with them for ages. Plus the skateboard. That's been a real winner. We had to leave a lot of his stuff back there,' he adds ruefully. 'I guess we need to stock up again.'

'If he's really taken with Lissa,' I say slowly. He raises his eyebrows and pauses, beer glass halfway to his mouth. 'When I spoke to her last she offered…' I look away and blush as I know my next words will make me sound like a forward hussy, but I needn't worry because Marcus reads my mind and beats me to it.

'Don't tell me. She didn't offer to mind Jon while we…'

'She offered to mind Jon. She wasn't specific as to what we might get up to.' I favour him with what I hope is a lascivious smile as I down my drink in one, nearly choking in the process.

Marcus thumps me on the back. 'Don't pass out on me now. You mean it? She really did?'

We're sitting on the balcony at Marcus' apartment, having spent the day with Jon on the beach. He has disappeared into his room leaving us alone, but conscious of his presence close by. This has been the case in our few encounters since the pair returned and, while we've become closer, we've both been experiencing the frustrations of having a young boy always either present or within earshot.

'She did. It may have been out of gratitude.'

'What did you do for her to earn such a show of gratitude?' Marcus lazily strokes my bare arm, sending shivers all through me. I reach over and kiss his cheek, feeling his day's growth of beard against my lips. How I love the feel of the man. I inhale his scent.

'I offered some good motherly advice, which wasn't too welcome at the time.'

'And she took it, I presume.'

'She did, and now she's working out with the uni how she can take some of her Master's seminars over there, at Columbia, I think. Will is delighted so all is well in Lissa's world, and some of the bounty is about to fall on her mother.'

'Beauty!' The very Australian expression sounds strange coming from Marcus' lips but it describes both of our feelings more precisely than any other.

'Exactly!'

'And when is this to take place?'

'What would you say to tonight? Might as well strike when the iron is hot.' Seeing Marcus' delight, I rise. 'I'll call her now. They can come over here, can't they? Will too?'

'Course. Then we can adjourn to your place.'

'I believe I have a bottle of something on ice.'

'Dinner?'

'Salad?'

'Done.'

It's easy to arrange for Lissa and Will to come over. They agree to spend the night, and Jonathon is over the moon. He's dying to show Lissa his room, though a bit anxious about meeting Will. His apprehension quickly disappears when the young couple arrive bearing pizza, ice cream and a Harry Potter DVD. Jonathon can't get rid of us fast enough.

'Be good, children,' Lissa admonishes, tongue in cheek, as Marcus and I slip out the door. Since I've arrived at Marcus' in my car, we drive back separately. Marcus follows me up to the house and I drive into the garage then meet him at the door.

An hour later we're sitting on the floor of the lounge room surrounded by the remains of a picnic dinner. We've elected to eat right here with the gentle evening breeze filtering in through the open French window and the dying rays of the setting sun adding a glow to the sky. We've barely eaten any of the barbecued chicken, salad, crackers and cheese and made few inroads into the bottle of champagne I've been saving for just such an occasion. The conversation has been desultory as we both anticipate how the evening will progress. I'm about to reach for a piece of cheese, when Marcus' hand encircles my ankle.

'Oh!' The sound explodes from my mouth, already open to accept the cheese. My lips widen in a smile as Marcus' fingers begin to stroke my leg. My head falls back, my eyes closing as I give myself up to sensation.

'I've missed this… and this… and this,' Marcus murmurs, as he rains kisses on my neck, shoulder and breasts, which have somehow become freed from their coverings. His lips find my nipples and I groan in ecstasy as the heat from his tongue sends ripples of arousal through my body. I'm lying on the carpet unaware of the hard floor beneath me as the weight of his body bears down on mine. He lifts his head. 'Are you all right down there?' His voice is thick with desire.

'Mmm, don't stop now.' My arms clasp him to me and I'm lost in a sea of passion.

Thirty-one

I return from a morning's shopping, feet sore, but satisfied to have found everything on my lengthy list. I unpack and brew some coffee, settling down on a stool at the kitchen bench to check my phone messages. There are a couple from Lissa asking me to call back but, checking my watch, I work out she'll most likely be out around now. I make a mental note to call her later. The next message takes me by surprise. The voice is Heather's.

'Anna. A quick call, no need to call back. Don't be alarmed, but I've just returned from a board meeting. It was an emergency meeting to discuss the year's staffing. I know you have an interview today and I want you to prepare yourself for a shock. Can't say any more now, but call me afterwards. I'm going to be out of town till then and won't be contactable. Take care.'

I put the phone down, a crease forming on my forehead. What can she be talking about? Well, it seems I can't do anything about it now. I finish my coffee and go upstairs singing to myself. This is it; my interview. Perhaps by this time tomorrow I will really be Head at Grammar, not merely acting in the position. I've bought a new outfit especially for today and I smile to myself in the mirror as I admire how well the cream suit of raw silk fits my new slim figure. A pair of high sandals set off the outfit and, satisfied with the image I present, I set off.

I enter the room with some trepidation, the sight of the group of board members spread along both sides of the long table doing nothing to still my shaking legs. I take the seat indicated at the end of the table and, crossing my ankles, clasp hands together on the table on top of the folder containing my resume and references. I take a deep breath, reminding myself of the positive affirmations I've been practicing all weekend.

'Mrs Hollis, thank you for coming in today.' It's the Chairman of the Board who introduces the other members of the interview panel, most of whom require no introduction as I've met them in the school on various formal occasions. I'm surprised to see there are no outside representatives involved. I lean back in my chair, lulled into a sense of relaxation by the familiarity of the group. I'm prepared to put forward my philosophy for the position and my plan for the future development and growth of the school, when the Chairman's next words surprise me.

'Before we go any further I want to hand over to Canon Jenkins who has some important issues to raise with you.' I turn to my right where the prim character, the uncle of the man who was my neighbour at the dinner, is shuffling some papers. He and I have never seen eye to eye, but I can't imagine what he can possibly want to raise at the start of this interview.

'Er... umm...' He peers over his half-moon glasses, seeming to be having difficulty in finding the words. My mouth dries up as I try to smile. 'It has come to our notice, the Board's, that is, there have been some changes in the reading lists for Year Ten.' I look at him in amazement, then move my glance around the room. Since when have board members taken notice of the actual curriculum? Their concerns are funding, staffing, capital works, but details of the curriculum? Never.

'I believe you have added a text called...' He refers to a paper in front of him and looks up again. '*Twilight*. Would that be correct?'

'That's right,' I say lightly, then deciding he might require further information, I add: 'We were studying *The Importance of Being Earnest* last term.' I look around the table and see a few nods. Emboldened, I continue. 'You will remember we produced the play towards the end of the year.' I notice a few smiles and begin to relax. 'Well, the girls,' I decide to keep Bonnie's name out of my explanation. 'The girls had all been reading the *Twilight* series and asked why we couldn't study the books in class. There are similarities, you see, both have two men…' my voice falters as I feel the temperature in the room drop. I plough on. 'So, after the exams we did, study them that is.'

Canon Jenkins removes his half-moons and places his papers neatly before him, tidying up the edges as he does so. 'I also understand these books refer to vampires and werewolves?' This time I don't imagine it, a chill fills the room.

He stands up straight. 'Vampires and werewolves,' he repeats, 'in a Church school. It won't do. It won't do at all.'

'We're not living in the dark ages. For Christ's sake!' The anger I've been suppressing all year boils up and threatens to choke me. 'I'm not suggesting the girls engage in witchcraft.' There's a deathly hush and I realise I may have gone too far.

'It's popular literature,' I try, 'written by a respected author. Surely it makes sense for the school to capitalise on the students' tastes and use it to…' My voice fades away as I realise that most of the others in the room are looking at me as if *I* am going to turn into a vampire or werewolf before their very eyes. I make another attempt, 'My intention was to use the novel as a base from which to analyse plot and characterisation. The girls completed a thorough analysis of the material and wrote both reviews and critiques of style and content.'

'Enough! I think we have heard enough.' He subsides into his chair, rustling his papers again.

The Board Chair clears his throat and I eagerly turn to face him. Surely now we're going to hear the voice of reason.

'I'm sorry, Mrs Hollis, but your choice of text is not the only matter before us this morning. I'm afraid we have a more delicate matter to bring up. It has come to my – our – ears that you and the previous Headmaster, Dr King. That you and he are…' He pauses and his nose wrinkles as if to something distasteful, 'are co-habiting.' He brings out the word with such venom I have to hide a smile. Wait till I tell Marcus. Co-habiting! My God, this interview is going mad.

'We're not living together!' The words burst out involuntarily into the hushed room.

He holds up a hand as if to stifle any further comments from me. 'Regardless. You are not providing the role model we wish for the young women under your care. It is therefore my sad task to inform you…'

I start to shake. This is not what I expected from the interview. My mind is going round in circles. What… I force myself to concentrate on what he is saying. 'While we have valued your contribution to the school over the years, we feel we can no longer accept your presence within these halls.'

'You mean…?' I'm aghast. He can't really be saying what I think he's saying.

'Your services will not be required in the coming year.' He pulls the papers lying on the table in front of him into a semblance of order. I sit, unable to move. My fingers are trembling so much I can't pick up my own papers. The Board secretary, an elderly man who I only know by sight, takes pity on me and steps over to help me from the chair. I totter out and, as the door closes behind me, I thump the wall with my fist. How dare they! The sanctimonious prigs! As if their lives are squeaky clean. Marcus and I are unattached mature adults, Surely what we do in the privacy of our homes is our business? Just as everything is beginning to work out for me, this happens. What will I do now?

From somewhere I find the strength to walk out of the building and down the front flight of stairs to where my little car is waiting for me. As soon as I close the car door, my eyes fill with tears, tears of anger. Those little men have tried to sully this beautiful thing between Marcus and me, but I won't let them. My phone beeps and I look to see a missed call from the object of my thoughts. Marcus has been trying to reach me. No doubt he's keen to hear how my interview has gone. Interview! Bah! More like a wake. I don't want to talk to him right now. I wipe my eyes. I send a text. *Can't talk. On my way.*

As I drive over to his apartment I try to work out what to say. Knowing Marcus he'll want to take responsibility for my sacking, when it's nothing to do with him. It's those narrow minded clergymen who're still living in the dark ages. I fume.

I erupt from the elevator. I've recovered from any distress and I'm a heaving mess of anger ready to explode. 'You'll never guess,' I begin, only to see Marcus point over to the coffee table where Jon is engrossed in a game of solitaire.

'Kitchen,' he mouths and we move into the shiny white galley. Marcus motions me to sit and, once I'm perched on a high stool, legs swinging, I begin again.

'You'll never guess?'

'They gave you the job?'

'I wish. It wasn't a job interview.'

'Not…?'

'More of a disciplinary interview.' I realise I'm not far from tears again. Only my anger is keeping them at bay.

'You're joking!'

'Wish I was. You're now looking at Mrs Anna Hollis, former Head of English at Northern Beaches Grammar.'

'What!' Marcus is astounded. He comes over to wrap his arms around me. I lean into the hug my eyes filling with tears again. My body is limp against his. 'My poor baby,' his voice soothes me. Then he holds me away from him. 'What on earth happened?'

'Heather was right,' I sniffle. 'She left me a message. Told me to prepare for a shock. She knew this was going to happen.'

'But why?'

I sniff up the tears and, as best I can, I recount the meeting to Marcus. 'And they've terminated my employment at the school as of now. They don't want me back.'

'But that's preposterous!'

'It is what it is,' I repeat an old saying my grandmother used to use when things went awry. 'I should ring Heather, I expect. She'll be waiting for my call.'

'Wait till you've calmed down. You came in here like one of the furies from Hell. Take your time. There's no rush.'

'Dad,' Jonathon's voice calls through the dining hatch. 'Is there anything to eat? I'm hungry.'

'Kids! He's a bottomless pit. Don't know where he puts it all. We had lunch just before you arrived.' Marcus looks abashed. 'Oh, are you hungry? You won't have had lunch.'

'Couldn't eat a thing.' In fact I feel as if there's a stone stuck in my throat.

'How about a peanut butter sandwich?' Marcus yells back to his son.

'Cool, with jelly?'

Marcus manages a grin. 'It's the American influence. It'll be some time before he takes to vegemite like a true Aussie, but I live in hope. Sure I can't fix you anything?'

'Maybe a coffee,' I relent. 'I'll just fix myself up.' I slide off the stool and make my way to the bathroom where I repair the ravages the tears have made in my make-up. The day started off so well, I think, as I reapply my lipstick and press my lips together.

'Feeling better now?' Marcus' voice is solicitous and I reflect that, unlike many of the men I've known – and I have to include Sean in this list – Marcus is not fazed by a woman's tears.

'Much.' I give him a watery smile. 'Now will you excuse me while I return Heather's call?'

'Make it on the balcony. You'll have more privacy there.'

Nodding my appreciation at his thoughtfulness, I walk outside and, gazing down on the Pacific Ocean, make my call.

'Well?' Marcus puts down the paper he's been reading. 'Come over here. He pats the seat beside him and I subside into the soft cushions with a sigh of relief.

'Heather doesn't understand it either, but someone complained to the Board about my… about my choice of texts for last year, and about us. Evidently my car has been seen here "at a late hour",' I quote.

'But you've never stayed over here!' Marcus explodes. 'We've been quite circumspect in that regard.'

'I know, I know. Because of Jonathon. But I guess whoever this complainant is, she – and I bet it's a she – didn't know that. Probably a mother who fancies you herself. Who have you scorned?' I try to turn it into a joke, but it falls flat when I see Marcus' hurt expression. 'I didn't mean that,' I reassure him. 'Anyway, evidently I was the only appointable candidate so…'

'They're not going to ask *me* back, I hope.'

'No.' I essay a laugh. 'They've asked Heather to fill in for a short time and she's agreed.'

'But what about her health?'

'I know. I'm worried about her, but she assures me she's been better lately and has given them a deadline of Easter.'

'What now, Anna?' A warm glow encases me. I don't know what the future is going to bring, but it seems that this man is going to be by my side and I know I can get through.

'I honestly don't know. Today has knocked me for six. Ask me tomorrow.' Then I remember Lissa's messages. 'Hell, I need to call Lissa. She's been leaving messages for me all day. I hope nothing's wrong there. I couldn't bear it if…'

'Stop right there.' Marcus' finger points at me accusingly. 'Don't assume, because your day has gone off-course, then hers will have too. Call her now.'

I take my mobile out to the balcony again and make the call. Lissa's voice bubbles in my ear.

'We're getting married!'

I have to sit down. My baby girl married! I haven't expected this.

'Can we come round to celebrate?' She's on top of the world. I can't burden her with my news.

'You must. We're at Marcus' apartment. You know where it is?'

'We sure do. We stayed there with Jon, remember?' How can I have forgotten? This afternoon's debacle has made my brain go soft.

'Of course you have. We'll see you soon, then?'

'We're on our way!'

I return to Marcus bemused. 'They're on their way over. They're getting married; Lissa and Will.'

'Not tonight, I hope,' Marcus laughs and rises from the sofa. 'Better see if we have any bubbly left.' He goes into the kitchen, while I stand in the middle of the room taking a step first in one direction then another.

'You need a seat and a drink in that order. Doctor's orders,' Marcus laughs, handing me a glass of something which looks suspiciously like scotch.

'But I don't drink…'

'Get that down you. Purely medicinal. You've had two shocks, one after the other today and it'll settle you for Lissa and Will. I take it you didn't tell her?'

'No. You won't, will you? This is her moment, hers and Will's. Nothing must spoil it for them.'

Lissa and Will arrive beaming and, over a glass of champagne, we celebrate their news.

'So you'll be going to New York together?' Marcus' question is unnecessary.

Will throws his arm around Lissa, who looks up at him in delight. She's glowing. I suddenly see the woman she is to become and I know this is right for her.

'So when's the big day?' Marcus poses the question casually. The pair look at each other.

'Finally it's Will who speaks for both of them. 'I… we have to be in New York by Easter so we thought… before then.' They look at us to gauge our reaction.

'Easter? That's…'

'Two months away. It's ages,' Lissa pipes up.

'Two months to organise a wedding.' I know my voice is going up in decibels. Since Lissa was a little girl I've envisaged her marriage; a big church wedding with all the trimmings, big white dress, retinue of bridesmaids, the works. 'It takes time, you know.'

'Oh we don't want a big wedding. Save your money. Just the close family, and you, of course Marcus. Well, you're almost family, aren't you?'

Shocked by her words, I glance at Marcus out of the corner of my eye to see how he is taking this blatant statement, but he looks amused if anything.

'Why the rush?' I ask, trying to keep my voice level. Surely…' I peer at Lissa in an attempt to see if she might be pregnant.

Will opens his mouth to speak, but Lissa throws him a look.

'It's the best plan. Mum. I checked with the uni, after we spoke. Remember you suggested I contact them?' she asks, as if somehow this rush to the altar is all my fault. I nod. 'Well, seems I can do some courses over at Columbia, and Sydney will give me credit towards my degree here.' She risks a look at Will. 'But they're going to cost the earth.' She pauses and takes a deep breath. Then Will…' I see him take her hand tightly in his. 'Will discovered his firm will pay for my tuition if we're married.'

'But that's no reason to rush into marriage,' I object, shocked at the apparent callousness of the young.

'Oh, that's not why we're getting married, Anna,' Will hurries to assure me. He tightens his hold on my daughter's hand. 'We love each other and it was only a matter of time. Lissa had already agreed to come with me. Thanks to you.' He raises his glass as if to toast me and I almost regret my "good motherly advice". 'The firm's policy only brought the wedding forward. It seemed crazy not to take advantage of it.'

'You *are* happy for us, aren't you?' It's my little girl again, seeking her mother's approval.

'Of course I am. Come here, both of you,' I give them a big hug. 'We must tell Gran and Gramps. We'll have an engagement celebration.'

The remainder of their visit is taken up with making plans. When the happy couple finally leave, I drop into a deep armchair, exhausted.

'Quite a day!' Marcus sits down opposite me.

'Not what I expected, on any front,' I agree. 'But I'm glad to see Lissa settled. Will'll be good for her, keep her on an even keel. Oh my God, I'm sounding just like my mother!'

'You're sounding like any concerned mother would when her chick is ready to fly the nest.'

'But she's been gone from home for… Oh, I see what you mean.' We sit in silence and I reflect how comfortable this man makes me feel. I can be myself. I have no need to pretend. In the short time we've known each other, he's come to know me very well. I give a loud sigh. 'I must go,' I say, but make no move to go anywhere. We look at each other. I feel my desire for him rise and see evidence of a similar desire in his face.

'Jon,' he says.

'I know. Not tonight.' I rise and gather my belongings together. 'I'll call Mum when I get home. She'll go straight into planning mode. At least it'll take her mind off the move.'

'Have they sold yet?'

'No. It's taking longer than they thought. The market isn't good at the moment and it's a big old house. Needs a lot of work. Buyers seem to be looking for a place they can move into and live in as is. I haven't sold either, but I've only recently started seriously looking for somewhere else to live, so I can wait. Their hearts are set on this villa they've seen; the one we went to look at with them.'

'Mmm.' Marcus has lost interest. He comes toward me and his embrace gives me the strength I need to keep going.

Thirty-two

When we arrive at my parents' home, Marcus is surprised.

'I can't see the house,' he exclaims. 'Is this it?'

'Down there.' I point to the winding stone steps leading down from the side of the road.

'Wow!' It's Jonathon who bounds out of the car and down the steps, then comes running back up again. 'Dad! You have to see this. The garden is awesome!'

Marcus raises his eyebrows at me.

'It's just a regular Pymble house,' I say. 'A bit tired and difficult to maintain. The garden was Dad's pride and joy but, of recent years, he's let it get a bit away from him. More like a jungle these days, I'm afraid.'

As we carefully make our way down the cracked stone steps, for the first time, I see the place with the eyes of a stranger. 'I'm beginning to understand why they're having difficulty in selling,' I remark as I negotiate a particularly awkward corner. 'I'm only surprised they've lasted here as long as they have.'

'It's certainly different.' Marcus looks around with interest.

'Look, Dad, there's been a pond here. And look at that tree! Perfect for a tree house.' He turns towards me. 'Did you ever…?'

'No, not me, but my brother Bob climbed it lots of times. Fell out of it too,' I laugh, as I remember Bob tumbling down from the topmost branches and managing to land with no more than a few scratches. 'Come on in and meet the folks.'

'You must be Marcus.' As we reach the door my dad comes forward to shake his hand and Jonathon slides out from behind Marcus where he's hidden. 'And you must be Jonathon. You don't want to be with all us old folk. I think my two grandsons have a game of cricket going out back. Why don't we go out there and see what they're up to?'

To my surprise, Jonathon, normally extremely shy with strangers, heartily agrees. As they walk off Marcus looks at me.

'That's a first. I've never seen him go off with a stranger like that before.'

'It's Dad,' I say easily. 'He's always had the magic touch where kids are concerned. They love him. When Lissa was little, it was as if we disappeared when Dad came on the scene.' At this point Mum realises our arrival and bustles over to kiss me and shake Marcus' hand.

'Don't I get a kiss too?' Marcus teases and Mum primps and reaches up to plant a kiss on his cheek.

'Now, come right in. Lissa and Will are here, and Jan with Graham and the boys. Bob's late, as usual,' she complains.

'Is he bringing anyone?' I ask in pretended innocence.

'Bob? I don't think so,' Mum frowns, and I regret teasing her.

'No, probably not,' I agree, and see her face clear.

'Champagne anyone?' Jan is in her usual hostess mode, walking around with a bottle in one hand and two glasses held by their necks in the other. She pours one, hands it to Marcus and nods in the direction of the back yard. 'The men are all out there. Something about getting the barbecue started, but I don't smell any steaks as yet,' she laughs. 'So it's just us girls in here, right Lissa?' This last is directed at my daughter, who is walking into the room.

'I do hate this Australian habit of the segregation of the sexes. I vote we go out and join them.' Lissa is about to usher us out when Mum stops her.

'Not yet. We, Gramps and I, wanted to talk about the wedding.' I can see my daughter becoming wound-up, afraid that her grandmother is going to insist on a big church do. 'We thought,' she continues, if you and Will agree. We'd like you to have the wedding here.'

The three of us gasp. Lissa is the first to recover.

'Do you mean it? Really? I've always loved this place. That would be too perfect. Oh, Gran.' Careless of the glass in Mum's hand she grabs her and whirls her around.

'That's very good of you, Mum, but…'

'It'll be our last opportunity to hold a family event here and,' she looks at Lissa fondly, 'what better ending could we have than our granddaughter's wedding. You did say you didn't want a big do, didn't you?' she turns, but Lissa is already running outside and we hear her yells from the safety of the kitchen.

'Will, you'll never guess. We can be married here, right here. Won't that be cool? A garden wedding.' We follow Lissa out to see her embrace her grandfather, then bounce over to Will and include him in her delight.

'A toast to the happy couple.' Dad raises his glass and we follow his lead.

'Lissa and Will,' we chorus as they beam, a glowing couple so obviously in love.

'So,' Mum takes charge. 'When's it going to be?'

'We thought…' Lissa glances sideways at Will. 'We have to be in New York before the end of March, so we thought the wedding should be early March or… Valentine's Day would be nice.' She looks around wistfully.

'So soon!' Jan can't contain herself. 'Two weeks, we'll never…'

'Tush.' It's my mother again. 'Valentine's Day would be so romantic. If we all help, I'm sure we can do it. How about it?' She looks around the group.

'Anything for my favourite granddaughter.' My dad gives Lissa a hug. 'Well, guys, we'd better get this show on the road. The barbie should be hot enough by now.' The male members of the party move over to the barbecue and we women are left in a huddle again.

'What can we do to help?' I look at Mum and Jan who've been the movers and shakers behind today's celebration.

'Might be time to bring out the salads, and there are a few nibbles to keep the boys from starving.'

'I take it you mean the small boys,' I laugh as I follow her back into the house. 'I think the big ones are quite well occupied. I look back and I'm amused to see Marcus fitting right in with my family.

'What have I missed?' Bob's voice comes booming through the hallway.

'We're in here,' I yell, only to find he's already found his way through.

'No need to yell. Hi, big sis.' He gives me a hug. 'And bigger sis.' He hugs Jan too.

Bob looks around. 'Guess the menfolk are outside. Better take out reinforcements.' He hoists up the carton of beer under his arm and saunters outside.

As we put the finishing touches to the selection of salads Mum has prepared, we discuss the logistics of a February wedding. Jan and I insist on bringing in a caterer and Lissa knows just the person. An old school friend of hers is starting up her own catering business and will be glad of the work.

'She's great, too, Mum, really. It won't be a stop gap and I know she'll be available.' She and Mum go into a huddle, so it's not till we are beginning to carry the bowls of salad out into the garden that Mum corners me.

'How did your interview go? Have you heard anything yet? It's getting awfully close to the start of term.' Behind Mum's back I see Jan mouthing, 'Haven't you told her yet?' and I shrug my shoulders.

'I didn't get the job, Mum. Tell you all about it later.'

Mum's face falls. 'You… but…'

'Tell you later,' I repeat, and keep walking out into the courtyard.

'And what about your folks, Will? They couldn't make it?' Bob hands Will yet another beer. The steaks have been duly eaten and the boys have gone off on some mysterious errand led by Dad. He's acting as if he's in his second childhood and he and the three young ones are loving it.

'They'd love to be here.' Will takes the can from Bob and opens it, beer spouting up. 'Whoops! Fact is, they're overseas right now. So I told them they could wait till the wedding. They'll be back by then. They've already met Lissa and we talked with them on Skype yesterday. They're delighted. They've always wanted a daughter.' He makes a face at Lissa who pouts back.

'Will…?' But Mum pre-empts me. 'Anna and I'll get in touch with your mum. We'll have it all arranged in no time.'

Lissa looks around the group. 'But it's our wedding. I want to…'

'Don't worry, there'll be lots for you to do. We grownups will just take care of the boring bits. How many do you think?' Mum looks at Jan and me.

'Just family and a few friends, say twenty to twenty-five?' She queries looking at her grandmother. 'And…' she looks at me. 'I know it may be difficult, Mum but…' she pauses then speaks in a rush. 'I'd like Gina to be there.'

You could hear a pin drop. I feel as if someone has stabbed me with it and I've deflated like a balloon. It's been such a happy day till now.

'Lissa…' It's Mum trying to smooth things over, but what's been said has been said and there's no denying it.

'It's my wedding!' Lissa is becoming petulant. 'Surely for that one day, you can forget your differences? Be nice to each other, make it up and mean it? She's my godmother and she has a right to be at my wedding.' Lissa flounces off with Will in hot pursuit.

I sit down with a thump. I'm dizzy. I hear the buzz of voices. I hear Jan's voice coming from far away.

'Would you like…?'

'Water, a glass of water,' I whisper through parched lips.

I drink it down in one gulp.

'Are you all right?' Marcus hovers, unsure what to do.

'How could she?' The words burst out.

'Gina, wasn't she the one who…'

'My nemesis, formerly best friend.' My voice is bitter.

'And your daughter's godmother?' Marcus' voice is gentle.

'Yes,' I admit.

'Well that seems to have killed the party.' Bob is first to recover. 'Let's help you clear up, Mum, then we'll leave you and Dad to it.'

'Talking of Dad, where is he?' Jan looks around to see him returning from the far end of the garden with three happy boys in tow.

'Here he is! Come on boys. Help clear up then we'll be off home.'

'Can I help too?' Jonathon is at my elbow. 'Gramps Ben is real cool,' he says.

'He's not your gramps,' Marcus adjures, only to hear Dad butt in.

'I said he can call me that. He doesn't have a gramps in Sydney and the other two are happy to share. Isn't that right, boys?' The other two agree and the three boys start to stack the dirty plates ready to carry them into the house.

'That's an awesome house.' We're driving home, first to drop me off, then Marcus and Jonathon will go back to their apartment. 'It'd be cool to live in a place like that.'

'Yes, it's a nice place. Your parents will be sad to leave. No interested buyers yet?'

'No nibbles at all, Mum said. I think they've become resigned to having a long wait. It's an old place, needs a bit done and these steep winding steps at the front will put off a lot of people. It's hard to shift in this current market.'

'Pity. It's a real home.' No more is said. Marcus opens the car door for me and walks me to the front door. 'It's a shame the day ended the way it did.'

'Yes, I'm sorry. Maybe I over-reacted but… I'll talk with Lissa later, when we've both calmed down. I put my face up for Marcus' kiss, reflecting how lucky I've been to meet him. But I'm troubled as I turn my key in the lock. Gina! I thought we were all done with her.

Thirty-three

We're sitting on the beach eating ice cream cones when Marcus raises the subject again. He's waited till Jonathon has gone to play in the shallows and we're lazily watching him jump the waves as they splash onto the shore – white horses I called them as a child.

'Yesterday,' he starts, 'when Lissa mentioned Gina. I was surprised at the strength of your reaction.' He waits while I gather my thoughts.

'Mmm,' I murmur, hoping he might change the subject, but Marcus is determined to have this discussion. He picks up a handful of sand and lets the grains trickle through his fingers.

'Do you... could you... would it really be so bad if she came to the wedding?'

I sigh. I've had a feeling this was coming. 'I understand why Lissa wants her there. I do, really. If the wedding was a big affair it wouldn't be so bad. We could politely ignore each other. But a small family wedding. We'd be in each other's face all day. I don't think I could bear it.'

'What would make it easier?'

Damn the man! I love him, but sometimes... sometimes he acts like my conscience. I consider his words seriously, taking my turn to sift the sand through my fingers while I work out how to reply.

'If... if... oh, I don't know! Do we need to talk about it now?' I turn my face up to the sun to discourage Marcus from continuing this line of questioning. It works. His next words surprise me.

'I put in an offer on a house today.' I turn round with a snap.

'You what? But the apartment?'

'It's not a proper home for a growing boy. He needs space to run around, somewhere he can lose himself. Seeing him with your dad and the other two yesterday. He was a different person. And Bryan will be back soon, so we'd need to find another place anyway. I'm ready to put down roots. Aren't you going to ask me where it is?' He seems to be having some sort of joke with me. I shake my head.

'What if I tell you it's an older house, one with a large garden and it's in Pymble?'

The penny drops.

'It isn't? You haven't? You can't mean…?'

Jonathon runs up to us and sprays us with sea water. 'Have you told her? We're going to live in that house we went to yesterday. Gramps Ben's house. Where you grew up. Only it won't be Gramps Ben's house any more. It'll be ours. Dad's and mine.'

'If our offer's accepted, that is. Don't count your chickens, buddy.'

'Chickens? Maybe we could keep some chickens.'

We both laugh.

'Come here, buddy!' Jonathon falls laughing into Marcus' arms and they roll over together in the sand. I lie, propped up on one elbow watching the byplay and wonder if I can ever be part of this happy family. *With them* as Marcus put it when they returned.

'Do Mum and Dad know yet?'

'Yep. I sounded out your dad before we left yesterday. He thinks it's great idea.'

'He would. They're anxious to move, now they've settled on buying into this over-fifties place. Your parents are happy in theirs, aren't they?' I can't dismiss a tinge of disquiet at the idea of my parents surrounded by old people like themselves. It seems the ultimate cul de sac.

'Happy as Larry,' he re-joins. 'Really. The move gave them a new lease of life and their social life has improved in leaps and bounds.'

I digest this as we pack up to leave the beach. Perhaps it is for the best, after all.

'What's happening with the sale of your place?' We're having lunch at the local *McDonald's* as a special treat for Jonathon, who is happily wrapping his mouth around a Big Mac.

I finish chewing, then wipe my mouth with a paper napkin.

'Nothing so far. The For Sale sign went up last week and there's to be an open house next Saturday.'

'It's a good place. Shouldn't have too much trouble in selling.'

So why didn't you offer to buy it instead of Mum and Dad's place? The words are on the tip of my tongue, but I realise it would be unfair to utter them. And do I really want Marcus buying the house I've lived in with Sean for all those years? The answer is a resounding "no". But the deal with Gina is hanging over me. I want to get it over with; have her out of my hair for good. I haven't told Marcus about the deal, as part of me is ashamed at giving in so easily, even though Bob told me it was the wisest way to go.

'Mmm. I need to do a big clean-up before the open house, and I guess I should start looking around seriously for a smaller place.' I risk a glance at Marcus from the corner of my eye, but his attention is now focussed on his son.

'Would you like another, Jon?' he jokes, as the boy finishes his meal.

'Awesome!' This seems to be the favourite word of the moment. 'Can we go now?'

'Steady on! Anna and I may want coffee.' He raises his eyebrows in enquiry. I shake my head.

The next two weeks pass in a flash of wedding arrangements and realtors. It seems like hordes tramp through my home on the open house and, to my surprise, I receive what I consider to be a reasonable offer early the next week. I pass on the good news to Bob who, cagey lawyer that he is, counsels me to wait a bit. Sure enough another, much higher offer is made later in the week which, taking my brother's advice, I accept.

I know, now my house had sold, I must look for alternative accommodation and, somehow, in the madness of the next week, I manage to allocate time to view a few townhouses in the Manly area but nothing I can bear to live in. Everything looks so tiny. I remember, with a pang, the apartment I viewed with Heather many months ago, but know I can't afford anything like that what with the payout to Gina and no job in sight. I need to scale down.

Now that I will no longer be working in the vicinity, I realise there's no need to remain in this locality, but it's the one I'm used to. My doctor, dentist, hairdresser – they're all here, as well as my favourite shops. It's home.

I haven't done anything about finding another job yet either. Everything has fallen in on me since that dismal interview and, when I have taken time to consider my future, I'm not sure another teaching position is the answer. Trouble is, I'm not sure what the answer is. I'm not getting any younger and, from what I've read, most employers consider forty too old. I'm closer to fifty!

I debate these issues while packing up. Now there is a buyer I can pack in earnest, despite the fact I have nowhere to go. It'll be some months before settlement takes place. Surely long enough for me to find somewhere? Heather has offered her spare room as a temporary solution and we have had a laugh over the possibility I may be jobless *and* homeless in a few months. But it's no laughing matter and I know I must start job hunting. I'm just not sure where to start.

I'm leaning over one box trying to affix the masking tape which seems to have a life of its own, when I'm rescued from my thankless task by phone ringing.

'I hope I haven't interrupted you in anything important,' Marcus' deep brown voice floats over the airways. I sit back on my heels in delight. Since he has started his new position as Professor of Education at Sydney University our time together has been somewhat limited. His new responsibilities coupled with settling Jonathon into his new school with its resultant traumas, have taken up most of his time and energy, leaving little for me. Much of his energy is expended in driving around Sydney. He and Jonathon are still living in the Manly apartment but, given his anticipated move to West Pymble, he has enrolled his son in Knox Grammar. The school is close to their new home but, in the short-term, it entails an early start as the pair drive across Middle Harbour and up the Pacific Highway to Jon's school. Then Marcus has to face the traffic back down the highway and across the Harbour Bridge to his office at Sydney University. Doing this every day in both directions means we've only been able to meet briefly a couple of evenings each week. We still have weekends together, but I miss seeing him every day.

'You're in close competition with an unruly end of masking tape,' I joke. 'It's good to hear from you. How's things? Anything exciting on the horizon?'

'That's why I've called,' he seems to hesitate, then continues. 'I've received some additional funding for a tutor's position. The way the funding is worded I have carte blanche in who I appoint. It's a temporary thing. One year. Supervising students in schools and helping them plan their work. What do you think?'

I push a stray curl out of my eyes, making a mental note to book a hair appointment before the wedding. My new style isn't so new any longer and sorely needs attention. I'm bemused Marcus has rung me to discuss his new funding and to ask my opinion.

'Think? Why should I think anything?' I blow at the curl which is proving intransigent.

'For you, I mean.' I can hear Marcus smiling on the other end of the phone and inconsequentially realise that it's true, you *can* hear a smile. 'I know it's not what you're used to but, I thought, while you're looking. You'd be very good at it,' he finishes lamely.

'For me?' My voice rises and ends in a squeak. Teaching in university; it's something I'd never considered. 'I don't think so.'

'Come on, with your experience you're a natural. The students will love you.'

'But they're grown up,' I object. 'I'm used to schoolgirls.'

'First years are only a year older than you're used to. Tell you what, why not come in to chat about it. I can show you the program and…'

'Now?' I look around at the mess of boxes and packing paper which has turned my house into a tip. 'I can't…'

'Well if not now, how about tomorrow? I have a free hour between ten and eleven. We   might even manage to squeeze in coffee.' With the temptation of coffee and time alone with Marcus, I reluctantly agree and hang up. He's certainly given me food for thought.

*

By the time I'm driving into the city next morning I've almost convinced myself this is a good idea. How difficult can it be to help young would-be teachers and supervise them in schools? After speaking with Marcus, I recall the various teacher education students who've passed through Grammar in recent years. They've all been interested, idealistic young people dedicated to making a difference in the lives of the youngsters they taught. It could be rewarding to play a part in the careers of these students. And it could mean I'd be seeing Marcus on a more regular basis too.

As I enter the university grounds it dawns on me that the last time I entered these hallowed halls was for Lissa's graduation. Before then, it would have been during my own university days. I've allowed plenty of time so, when I've found a parking spot, I walk around my old alma mater soaking up memories. The older buildings don't seem to have changed much, the sandstone still dark with time and use, but lots of newer ones have sprung up giving a piebald effect, and I find myself dodging around workmen and builder's vehicles. It seems every spare space is being built on.

Checking my watch, I make my way to Marcus' building. When I locate his office, the door is open and Marcus sitting at his desk poring over a large document. He looks up when he hears my steps, a large smile wreathing his face.

'Welcome. You've found my hideout, then.' He jumps up and wraps his arms round me. I glance around guiltily worried lest we are seen. I don't want to start off here with everyone knowing I have a relationship with the professor.

'Now,' I say, sitting down opposite Marcus who is again seated behind his desk, 'tell me about this position you have.'

As Marcus outlines the duties and responsibilities of the position, I consider how I would like working here. Marcus' office space is cramped, and he is a professor. What would mine, as a mere tutor, be like? But I like the ambiance of the university. The place has good vibes and fond memories for me, memories of a time when I had no worries; memories of my early days with Sean and the heady sense that anything was possible. Perhaps I can regain that sentiment. I have a sense of euphoria and, in that moment, I know I'm going to accept the position.

'Yes,' I blurt out.

'Yes?' Marcus peers over his glasses with a smile. 'But I haven't finished yet. Don't you want to know the salary we're offering?'

'Oh, of course.' I look down at my hands. *Have I sounded too eager?*

'It's a bit less than you were being paid at Grammar…'

'I'll manage. Now I've sold the house. I'll find a smaller place so I won't have a huge mortgage hanging over me. It'll be a completely fresh start. I think I'll enjoy it.'

'I'm sure you will. Now, there's just someone I need to have you meet.'

'Meet? I thought you were making the decision.' I'm beginning to regret my eagerness and wonder if I've put too much faith in Marcus' discretion to appoint.

'I am, and the job's yours. But you'll need to work with the Dean too, so I mentioned to him you'd be dropping in. His office is up the corridor. It's nothing to worry about,' he assures me. 'He's a regular guy. He's responsible for the overall running of the department, has more to do with staff and less with students.'

'Right.' I'm not prepared for this. I smooth down the skirt of the suit I've deemed appropriate for a university staff member, though everyone I've seen so far, staff and students alike, have been dressed in jeans. Marcus is his usual casual self, his shoulders stretching the fabric of his chambray shirt and his cream linen pants tight round his butt as he walks ahead of me down the corridor. Stopping before a partially closed door, he puts up a hand to smooth down his unruly hair before knocking and pushing the door open.

'Ah, Marcus,' says a voice from inside, and I reach the doorway to see a small round bald man swing round in his chair. 'So this is the little lady you told me about?' I cringe and put a false smile on my face. I don't need to like the man.

'There, that wasn't too bad, was it?' Marcus is sitting opposite me in the cafeteria. He leans back in his chair. 'What do you think?'

'I love all this.' I wave my arms around to encompass the historic buildings and the grassy courtyard where, even before the start of the university year, students are lying in groups on the grass and playing desultory games of tennis on the courts. 'But Tony...'

'He's not so bad really. Likes to come across as the stereotypical chauvinist, but he's a pretty decent guy at heart.'

'Hmm.' I'm not so sure. 'However, he hasn't put me off, if that's what you mean.'

'Good.' Marcus reaches over and his thumb caresses the back of my hand, sending shivers down my spine.

'When would I need to start?' I determine to keep the conversation unemotional.

'Semester doesn't begin till March, but it would be best for you to come on board before then. How about the middle of February some time? Gives you time to get over the wedding and you can be here for Orientation week.'

'I'd like that.'

'And you realise you'll be eligible for a staff scholarship?'

'Staff scholarship?' I repeat stupefied. 'What do you mean?'

'As a junior member of staff, even in a temporary position, you can be offered a place in our Master's program without incurring the usual fees. Is that something you'd consider?'

The thought of further study has been something I've toyed with over the years, but I've always found some reason to dump in the "too hard" basket. First, Lissa was too young, then my teaching became a big commitment, and when I was made Head of English, the required preparation made anything else completely no go.

'A Master's? I just might. Let me think on it.'

'Don't think too long. If you do decide to take it up, we'll need to get you organised with reading lists etc.'

This is all too much for me. I take a sip from my coffee and place the cup down slowly, avoiding Marcus' eye.

'You have a bit of foam just…' Marcus leans across the table to wipe the foam from my top lip. My tongue pops out to do the same and encounters his rough fingertip. 'There!' he finishes. He breathes heavily. 'We need to make some arrangement. We don't seem to be able to rely on Lissa these days.'

'She does have a wedding to arrange,' I reply lightly, knowing he is referring to more than Lissa's occasional forays across the bridge to mind Jonathon.

'Thought your mum had the wedding in hand,' Marcus laughs, and takes both of my hands in his. 'Now, when the big day's over I want…' But I don't find out what it is he wants because, at that moment, his mobile rings and, after a brief conversation I hear him say, 'I'll be right there.'

'Sorry, Anna.' He gives a grimace. 'Duty calls. My presence in required at a planning meeting. Can you…?'

'Sure. I can find where I left the car. I might stroll around a bit first, to remind myself.'

'Great!' His mind is already elsewhere. I watch him walk across the quadrangle; a tall broad-shouldered hunk of a man with a determined stride. It's difficult to believe he's mine. I qualify that. He doesn't belong to anyone but himself. But he does seem to want to spend time with me. I smile and mentally hug myself in delight. Life is good and getting better.

I spend the next hour revisiting the memories of my youth – the youth containing memories of Sean – and I leave the university grounds feeling cleansed. It's as if, by stirring up these old memories, I've been able to put the past where it belongs; in the past. The memory of Sean no longer conjures up feelings of bitterness, but rather one of acceptance and, yes, sorrow. Sorrow that my loving and loved husband didn't have the courage to share his innermost fears with me, sorrow that, in his time of need and insecurity, he turned to my best friend. Sorrow that the good man I married with such love and trust and hope for the future is no longer with us.

I wipe a tear from my eye and meander back to where I parked my car. I'm ready to start anew. Anna Hollis, university tutor. This will be the new me.

Thirty-four

Valentine's Day dawns at last. I open the curtains to a glorious Sydney summer's day and breathe a sigh of relief. The weather hasn't let us down. I go downstairs to make an early morning pot of tea and take it, along with a plate of toast, up to Lissa's room. Although she and Will stayed up late last night talking, he obeyed tradition to leave before midnight and my daughter has spent the last night of her single state in the old bedroom she grew up in.

'Are you awake?' I whisper, as I use my hip to nudge open the bedroom door.

'Almost.' Lissa stretches her arms. 'It's really arrived, my wedding day!'

I place the tray on the bedside table and reach over to hug and kiss her. 'It truly has, and it's a beautiful day, too. Look!' I go over to open her curtains and let the sunlight shine in.

'Ooh, too bright.' Lissa shades her eyes. 'I can't believe it's really here. By tonight I'll be Mrs Will Cartwright; Lissa Cartwright. She shivers in delight. 'Thanks for the tea, Mum. Sit down here.' She pats the bed and I curl my legs under me at the bottom of her bed.

'I just wish…' Lissa has finished her tea and toast and is gazing wistfully out of the window. I know what she's thinking.

'Dad would have been so proud of you, and Will,' I say leaning up to stroke her forehead. 'He'd like to have been here too. But it wasn't to be.'

'No.' I detect a touch of a sniff in her voice.

'Don't be sad, darling. This is a day to be happy. Be happy for yourself and Will, for us, for your dad too. Imagine he's right there watching you exchange your vows.'

We're both silent as we envisage Sean and how he'd have loved to see his little girl married.

'Now,' I rise and gather up the tray. 'Time for your shower. Your hair appointment is in an hour.

The morning passes in a flash, and in no time Bob arrives to whisk Lissa and me off to the wedding venue. Shunning tradition, Lissa has chosen a dusky pink skirt and top in a cheesecloth type of material which swirls around her legs as she walks. My eyes are misty as I hand her the single red rose she has elected to carry. I can't help remembering my own wedding day with a pang of regret. I was happy then too.

'Is…?' She leans over Bob's shoulder.

'Groom, best man and bridesmaid all present and correct,' he assures her. 'I delivered them myself and the whole crew are awaiting your arrival with bated breath and not a few strawberry daiquiris. Where did you find these caterers?'

'I have connections.' Lissa taps her nose and laughs in delight. 'Wait till you taste their food.' I'm amazed she's so calm. Remembering my own wedding day, I have expected at least a few last minute jitters, but she is serenity personified.

We arrive at my parents' house and as Bob helps Lissa out of the car, she gasps. I follow her gaze to the white and pink streamers lining the steps down into the garden, where a noticeable crowd is gathered on the path, glasses in hands and looking up at us expectantly. It looks to me as if the twenty or so has grown to closer to thirty. Mum and Jan *have* been busy.

A glass is put into my hand and Mum ushers everyone to the back of the house where rows of chairs face a table I haven't seen before. It's covered by a white lace cloth, and standing beside the table is a well-dressed lady with short dark hair who, I presume, is the marriage celebrant, and right in front of it is an arch covered in the same streamers as were on the steps,. I was disappointed neither Lissa nor Will chose a religious service, but I'm impressed how formal this all appears.

As the service progresses I resort to my handkerchief to wipe away incipient tears several times, then the pair surprise me. After they say their vows and exchange rings, Lissa, still holding Will's hand, recites a Shakespearean sonnet.

Let me not to the marriage of true minds
Admit impediments. Love is not love
Which alters when it alteration finds
Or bends with the remover to remove
O, no! It is an ever-fixed mark
That looks on tempests and is never shaken;
It is the star to every wandering bark,
Whose worth's unknown, although his height be taken.
Love's not Time's fool, though rosy lips and cheeks
Within his bending sickle's compass come;
Love alters not with his brief hours and weeks,
But bears it out even to the edge of doom.

If this be error and upon me proved,
I never writ, nor no man ever loved.

The tears trickle down my cheeks as she speaks these words with such confidence and love. One of my favourite sonnets and so appropriate for a wedding. But, as I wipe away the tears, I see Lissa smile into Will's eyes as he begins to speak.

Shall I compare thee to a Summer's day?
Thou are more lovely and more temperate:
Rough winds do shake the darling buds of May,
And Summer's lease hath all too short a date:
Sometime too hot the eye of heaven shines,
And oft' is his gold complexion dimm'd:
And every fair from fair sometime declines,
By chance or nature's changing course untrimm'd
But thy eternal summer shall not fade
Nor lose possession of that fair thou owest;
Not shall Death brag thou wanderest in his shade,
When in eternal lines to time thou growest.

So long as men can breathe, or eyes can see,
So long lives this and this gives life to thee.

The tears really begin to flow now and I can tell from the sounds behind me that I'm not alone. My favourite Shakespearean sonnets. My Lissa and her Will have chosen well. The ceremony concludes with the pair toasting each other, arms entwined. This is such a joyful day!

I kiss the happy pair and, as I follow them down the aisle between the two rows of chairs, I catch sight of a face sitting at the back. It isn't… it can't be, but it is. Gina! My heart pounds, my face burns. I never did have the conversation with Lissa about her wish for her godmother to attend the wedding. So much has happened in the past two weeks, this one important issue slipped my mind. If I've thought about the matter at all, I've assumed Lissa will have taken my feelings into account.

I hold my head up and walk past, declining to make eye contact. I'm not going to allow Gina's presence to spoil the day for me. As we mingle with even more strawberry daiquiris, the rosy liquid giving a festive appearance to the triangular shaped glasses, and the fruity flavour lulling us into a false sense of security, the bubble of conversation grows in volume. I move from one group to another accepting the congratulations due to the mother of the bride on such a day, finally finding myself alone with Marcus under my parents' large poinciana tree.

'Even the tree is showing its festive dress.' Marcus waxes lyrical at the red blossoms above us. 'What a happy day for you, Anna. And everything is going so smoothly. You must be very pleased and proud.' He draws me into his arms and I feel his lips, soft on mine. I am lost in his embrace, oblivious of time and place. I'm brought back to the present by the sound of a gong in the distance.

We turn and, hands entwined, arms swinging, as if we haven't a care in the world, we are making our way back towards the house when a figure looms up in front of us. The sun is in my eyes and, for a second, all I see is a shape with a wide-brimmed hat. My vision clears and standing right in front of me is Gina.

'Anna!'

'Gina!'

I stop as if struck by lightning. She's here, in my parents' garden, at my daughter's wedding. We stand opposite each other like two dogs ready for a fight. My stomach churns again and my knees threaten to buckle. My arm stills and my hand tightens in Marcus'.

Marcus defuses the situation. 'So you're Gina? Marcus.' He holds out his hand and falteringly, Gina takes it.

'You're?' she enquires.

'I'm with Anna.' He tightens his hand protectively in mine. 'And you're…' Gina and I both stiffen. 'I understand you're Lissa's godmother.'

My body begins to relax, my anger curbed by the calming influence of his voice.

'Thanks for inviting me today, Anna,' Gina's voice is subdued, belying the vivid colours of her long, halter necked dress. I note she's reverted to her usual taste in clothes; no sign of her widow's weeds today. I catch myself up short. She isn't the widow; I am. I glance down at my carefully chosen turquoise outfit, the three quarter length skirt swirling around my legs and the tunic top barely touching my hips – not very widow-like either. I realise we've both moved on.

'I heard you'd met someone. I'm glad. You seem like a good man,' she addresses Marcus. 'Anna deserves that.' She turns to me with a glisten in her eyes. 'I'm sorry, Anna, sorry for the hurt I caused you. I… I don't know… well, I'm sorry.' She turns and walks away.

I'm tempted to run after her. We're not finished, she and I. I still have lots to say to her, none of it pleasant. Only Marcus' firm hold on my hand stops me and we walk sedately on.

As mother of the bride, I'm seated with Lissa, Will and Will's parents at one table while Marcus and Jonathon have joined Jan, Graham and the boys at another so there's no time to discuss our encounter. It isn't until the speeches are over and guests are moving between tables, that I find myself sitting next to Marcus again.

'So that's the famous Gina! How do you feel about her being here?' Before I can answer he adds. 'She seems a bit bereft. Has she always been like that?'

'No. She was always the life and soul of the party. Led me into a lot of scrapes back then.'

'Seems she's on her own now.' I look across to where Gina is sitting alone at a table with a drink in front of her. I see Mum go over to speak to her and begin to rise, before dropping down into my chair again. For the first time I realise I no longer harbour any bitterness toward her. Marcus is right. She's a lonely woman. I look up at him with thankfulness. I've found someone special. I wonder whether my subconscious has led her to be here, by ignoring my overt desire to discuss her attendance with Lissa, but this is too deep, even for me.

I squeeze Marcus' hand then, with deliberation, rise and walk over to the pair. I reach out and touch Gina on the arm. 'Thanks.' We both know to what I'm referring. 'I'm glad you came.' My mum favours me with a smile and I know what I've done is right. I turn abruptly and find my face bumping against Marcus' chest. I inhale the inherently male scent of his aftershave mixed with good healthy sweat and my arms automatically circle around his waist.

'Let's get out of here,' Marcus leads me outside and across the yard to a wooden seat in the far corner of the garden. We sit silently for a time, drinking in the ambiance of this special place.

'I love it here,' Marcus sighs. 'I'm glad Jon fell in love with this house.'

'Where *is* Jonathon?' I look around as if expecting him to leap out of the bushes.

'With the other kids. He's made friends with your two nephews. They've been busy with their own little world all afternoon, apart from when they were stuffing their faces.'

I relax. 'Well, this'll soon be your home.'

Marcus clears his throat and does the little thing he does with his glasses when he's unsure of himself.

'I'm hoping it will be ours,' he says. It takes me a minute to realise what he means. He puts out his finger and tilts up my chin gazing straight into my eyes. 'You *will* share it with me, with me and Jon, won't you?'

I'm shocked into silence, which Marcus takes for uncertainty. A bubble of excitement builds up inside me, starting at my toes and rippling up through my body. I try to find my words.

'Oh hell, have I been too precipitate? I waited… I waited till now, because I wasn't sure you were ready to commit. But now Lissa and

Will are… Now you seem to have settled everything with Gina… I'd hoped. Was I wrong?'

I reach over to kiss his lips and find myself being thoroughly kissed in return. 'No,' I say, when I can draw breath again. 'I mean yes. I mean you weren't wrong.'

'So you'll do me the honour of becoming Mrs King? You will marry me?'

'Yes, yes, yes.' Marcus lifts me up and twirls me around and around and, at that moment, Jonathon appears, running toward us.

'Did she say yes, Dad? Is Anna going to live with us?'

I give Marcus a look of pretended annoyance. 'Do you mean I haven't been the first to know about this plan of yours?'

'I told Dad he should ask you,' Jonathon shouts with glee. Marcus ruefully looks down at the boy and messes up his son's hair.

'Don't let too many cats out of the bag, buddy. Some of it was my idea.'

'Cats as well as chickens!' Jonathon yells. We gaze at him in amazement, then shrug and laugh.

'Can we tell everyone now?' Jonathon is beaming with an excitement I'm beginning to share. I don't want to detract from Lissa and Will's big day, but reckon their part in the day is almost over.

When we reach the house Jon runs in ahead of us.

'We're going to have another wedding!' he announces to the group who have gathered to see off the happy pair.

Lissa whirls round. 'Mum! I'm so glad. I didn't want to think of you alone somewhere when I was at the other end of the world.'

'Good for you, Marcus!' Dad comes up to shake his hand. 'You do realise you're taking on a parcel of trouble with this one?'

Marcus smiles at me fondly. 'I think I can handle her.'

We bid farewell to the newly married pair and everyone begins to drift off. Soon only Marcus, Jonathon and I are left, along with the caterers who are going about the business of clearing up unobtrusively.

'And when are you thinking of having this wedding?' It's Mum with a worried look on her face.

'We'll wait till we're settled into the house. It'll be a winter wedding,' Marcus replies. 'You won't have to do a thing.'

'And it'll be even smaller than this one,' I put in, knowing Mum will want to be in control of everything again. 'Family only, no friends. That is…' I glance over at Marcus. Here I am organising the wedding which we haven't had time to discuss.

'Okay by me.'

'Oh, Audrey and Jack will be delighted.' I can tell Mum is dying to call her friend.

'You'd better call your folks before Mum pre-empts you,' I urge Marcus.

'Sure thing.'

*

It's not till we're back at my Seaforth house, that Marcus and I have time to ourselves. A delighted Jonathon has been taken off for a sleepover with Jan and Graham's boys in a tactful move to give Marcus and me some space.

'Have you had a surfeit of alcohol or can I tempt you?' Marcus holds up a bottle of champagne.

'Where on earth did that come from?' I know I haven't bought any recently.

'A little secret between Lissa and me.'

'Did everyone know about this except me?' I ask, pretending to be annoyed, but secretly flattered Marcus has gone to so much trouble. 'You must have been very sure of my answer.'

Marcus doesn't reply immediately, instead he fills two champagne flutes to the brim and hands me one. 'To us, to our future together.'

We take a sip together, then Marcus pulls me down on the sofa beside him. He throws an arm round my shoulder and squeezes me tightly.

'I wasn't sure at all. There's been so much happening in your life this past year. I was terrified you would think it too soon and I'd scare you off for good.'

'Mmm,' I murmur nuzzling into his neck, soft and warm beneath my lips. The champagne forgotten, we kiss more deeply before I raise my head and take his hand to lead him to the bedroom.

Tonight we're in no hurry. Once in the bedroom, we stand

immobile, bodies pressed together, the moonlight streaming through the uncovered window across the deep pile of the carpet. I'm on tiptoe as Marcus' fingers caress my shoulders and back, his hands following the line of my body until they cup my hips and lift me off the ground. His lips searching, his tongue seeking mine as I'm lost in the ecstasy of the moment. Time stands still. My body aches for him. Slowly, he peels off my dress and lays me on the bed. I lie there, quivering with desire. Somehow Marcus manages to continue stroking me while he divests himself of his own clothes. Then we are naked together, lying face-to-face. Gently, he takes my face in his hands, and rains kisses over it. Our bodies are close, but not touching. The tension is almost unbearable. I want him to take me, but he's in no hurry.

'I want this to be special for you,' he murmurs, his voice thick with desire, as his fingers reach to pleasure me. My body arches in ecstasy as he brings me to heights of delight which I have only ever imagined. I twist my fingers through the tousled hair I have come to love. I feel the day's growth of his beard rubbing against my face. My hands slide across his shoulders, stroke his strong back and reach down his body. It's not till I cry out in anguish that I feel him bear down on me and I experience release. As Marcus towers above me, his wide shoulders blotting out the moonlight, his firm torso rubbing against my breasts, and his lips pressing on my eyelids, I know that I've come home. This is what I've been waiting for. This sense of belonging, of complete assurance that everything is right. The anguish of the previous year fades away to nothing in the knowledge that, in Marcus, I have found a soulmate, someone who will always be there for me, a tower of strength, but also a gentle man, one who cares deeply for me and who I love to distraction and can trust never to hurt me.

*

After a night of unadulterated bliss I'm awakened by a kiss as Marcus holds me closely. 'Now I have you I'm never going to let you go,' he jokes. 'Do we really need to have a winter wedding? I can't wait to waken every morning like this.'

His body feels good against mine. We lie, legs entwined, touching and stroking, still sated from our night's lovemaking, but unwilling to leave this cosy nest we have made our own. I smile as Marcus' finger tips my chin.

'I love you so much, my darling,' he whispers in my ear. 'I never thought…'

'Me too,' I touch his face with my finger, tracing the familiar features from his forehead, across his eyebrows, down his nose to rest on his lips. His mouth opens to nibble my finger gently. We remain, wrapped in each other's arms, lost to the world until the raucous laugh of a kookaburra outside the window brings us back to the present.

'Suppose we should rise,' I begin.

'Not yet,' Marcus pulls me closer and plants another kiss on my bruised mouth. 'We still have time…'

Our morning lovemaking is slow and gentle, an echo of the night before. When we eventually surface again, the sun is high in the sky and we both realise that we must rise to meet the day.

Relishing the fact that we are alone in the house and have the day to ourselves, we shower together, Marcus making me laugh as he soaps and tickles me under the cascading stream of water. We are still laughing as we head downstairs.

Seeing the still unfinished bottle sitting on the coffee table, Marcus picks it up. 'Probably a bit flat by now but do you have one of those cap things?'

'Sure. Kitchen drawer, second one down. You may have to rummage around a bit.' I rub my eyes, gather up the empty glasses and follow him into the kitchen.

'Can't see… oh, got it! But what's this?' Marcus holds up a gold wedding band with a strange expression on his face. 'Your wedding ring, I presume?' His lips twist into a smile.

'No, I threw it away.' I gaze in horror at the gold band as if it has returned to haunt my newfound happiness. 'No, it's not mine. It must be… it can't…'

Marcus hands the ring to me and I drop the gold band onto the kitchen surface where it lies, much as it had lain in the centre of the table on that fateful Christmas day. I find my voice. 'It must have belonged to Sean,' I force the words out. 'I have no recollection. I must have put the ring there after he left and it's lain there, in that drawer, among all the odds and ends ever since.'

As we eat breakfast, I am very conscious of the ring lying there. I know what I must do.

'Shall we go ring shopping?' asks Marcus. 'Now you've agreed to marry me, I want to make my mark on you. Stamp you as mine. Jonathon can stay with Jan's crew a bit longer. What do you say?'

'I say yes.' I go over to stand on tiptoe, link my arms around his neck and nuzzle him from behind. 'Can we make it this afternoon? There's something I need to do first.'

I persuade Marcus I'll meet him later and see him off. The ring sits there, a reminder of the year I'm trying to forget. I dress quickly and slip it into my pocket where it burns a hole. Not for long. I drive down to the ferry wharf, radio blaring.

I sneak my car into the last parking spot, put on the handbrake and contemplate what I'm about to do. I close my eyes in silent prayer, jump out, and join the queue of people waiting to board the ferry. I buy a round ticket. When the boat arrives, unlike my usual habit, I make my way to the side and take up a position away from others. Fortunately for my plan, the ferry is less busy than usual so I'm able to enjoy the first part of the trip in solitude.

When I judge we are about half way to Circular Quay, I look around. I raise my face to the sky and feel the warmth of the sun on my skin. I put my hand into my pocket and curl my fingers around the ring, all that remains of Sean; all except the memories. Pulling it out, I hang my hand over the side and drop the band of gold into the water. It sinks without a trace.

THE END

Thank you for purchasing this book.
If you enjoyed it, please leave a review at:

http://www.amazon.com/
http://www.goodreads.com/

About the Author

Born and brought up in Scotland, Maggie Christensen emigrated to Australia in her twenties and now lives with her husband near Peregian Beach on the Sunshine Coast of Queensland. The café and bookshop in Peregian Village in this book are actual places which she often visits and enjoys. After spending many years in teaching, lecturing and education management, where she wrote course materials and reports, Maggie began writing the sort of books she enjoys reading. Band of Gold is her first novel.

Look out for The Sand Dollar which will be coming soon.

You can find Maggie at:
http://maggiechristensenauthor.com/
https://www.facebook.com/maggiechristensenauthor